The army of Peter the Great was a wild savage horde of men, quick to pillage and destroy. Cossacks, Dneiper horsemen and Samoyede tribesmen united uneasily behind the towering figure of the Soldier Czar.

It was an army where tribal warfare was quick to explode—where Cossack would fight Cossack to the death with a hide whip—where blood was sufficient reward for victory.

And against this background Katrina fought to survive the intrigue and violence of the Czarist dynasty . . .

Mervyn Lane

KATRINA

CORGI BOOKS
A DIVISION OF TRANSWORLD PUBLISHERS LTD
A NATIONAL GENERAL COMPANY

KATRINA

A CORGI BOOK 0 552 09091 3

Originally published in Great Britain
by Robert Hale Ltd.

PRINTING HISTORY
Robert Hale edition published 1956
Corgi edition published 1967
Corgi edition re-issued 1972

This book is set in Intertype Times

Corgi Books are published by Transworld Publishers Ltd.,
Cavendish House, 57-59 Uxbridge Road,
Ealing, London, W.5.
Made and printed in Great Britain by
Hunt Barnard Printing Ltd., Aylesbury, Bucks.

KATRINA

BOOK ONE

Chapter One

AT THE SHELTERED side of her mother's hut, where the earth was clear of snow, young Katrina crouched over a she-goat. She had caught the tattered animal unawares and was trying to milk it.

Her fingers coaxed a dribble of yellow milk into the wooden bowl. The goat was old. Warts were painful upon its dugs. It bleated and cried to be free. Katrina had to clench her firm, white teeth in the old nanny's grey ear, to make her stand and be milked.

The goat's ear tasted prickly, but Katrina hummed in contentment and wriggled her slender shoulders at the tickle of sunshine upon her back through the rough cloth of her Borodin blouse.

Behind her, the forest trees of Sweden's outpost city of Marienburg in Livonia, on the dark Russian frontier, were whispering under their thawing snow. Silvery trickles like snail tracks ran down the black branches. The brief spring of Russia was stirring and the deep winter's snow had begun to soften.

Distantly eastwards, the guns thundered. Not even Katrina's six-year-old brother, Michael, any longer took much heed of the guns. The siege of Marienburg had been going on for two years now. All that winter of 1702 the Russians had held off, half a dozen miles beyond the forest.

"Katrina!" called little Michael suddenly, "when will Mama finish! I want to go in!"

Katrina flipped the dug against her wooden bowl's edge to rescue the final drop of milk.

"If you go in now," she said patiently, "you can be sure that Mama will beat you. Also, Dakov will probably beat you, too. And if Dakov beats you, it will be with his whip. So you had better wait, you see." She smiled at him softly with her generous mouth. Her eyes were the colour of dark green olives.

Michael stood on his small, uncertain legs, considering this. "But I'm hungry," he said.

Katrina held out the bowl. "Drink, then!" The child put his face to the bowl, watching her as he drank. The goat had bounded away, stiff-legged with indignation, but after four hops, halted and nuzzled into the bare black earth at a cabbage root.

"That is Dakov's goat!" said Michael accusingly, when Katrina at last took the half-emptied bowl away.

"Ssh!" she laid a finger across her smiling mouth, and shook her fair hair. The pale sunshine lit gold sparkles in it.

"But why does Dakov come here—and Chudov, and Gorshkovin, and all the others?" he said shrilly. "They fight with Mama and hurt her. I have heard her crying out in pain."

Katrina spoke with authoritative finality. "Mama was not crying in pain. They are friends of Mama and they do not hurt her. Also these men bring Mama food and wine and sometimes a little money."

Michael persisted. "If they are friends, why can we not go in the hut when they come? And they do hurt her, too, for I have seen . . ."

Katrina squeezed his small hand tightly and began to run towards the trees. "Come," she said, dragging him along, "we shall climb our tree and ride horses in the sky upon its branches."

The Swedish cavalry dragoon who had been the father of the sixteen-year-old Katrina and little Michael, had died in an early sortie of the siege. He had galloped his fine horse into one of the exploding fire-pots of the Russians—an invention of the giant devil, Tsar Peter, whom legend said was more than ten feet tall!

Since then, Anna, their mother, had brought many men to the hut that was their home, among the black trees of Goreki wood. Always, at these times, she sent her two children out into the snow to play, and turned the holy ikon to the wall.

The bland Holy Face that was painted crudely upon the ikon, disturbed Anna. She knew it disapproved of the sins of the flesh. Sometimes she burned a fish candle to please the ikon. This—a dried, oily fish—worth one-tenth of a kopek, and so frightening an extravagance that Anna's face always went white as she lit it, would burn, spluttering greasily, half the night, as children sat up in awe to watch this wonder.

But the ikon did not seem to relent. Anna resigned herself, therefore, to damnation and the fires of hell, but she did not wish Katrina and Michael to catch the taint. So when the men came, her children were bundled outside. In winter they stood tight against the black logs of the hut, warming themselves at wisps of steamy smoke that crept through gaps and jewelled itself like warm sweat upon the wrinkled wood.

But in spring they could play among the trees, and it was here that Dakov found them as he came away from the hut.

Dakov was important. He was a sturdy-shouldered man, butler to the Manse household of Pastor Gluck, and fond of using upon the subordinate servants the greasy brown whip that hung at his belt.

He came upon Katrina and Michael, as they bobbed up and down in play, astride a low, springy tree branch, riding their imaginary horse.

"Hey, there!" he bellowed up at them. "Your mother wants you, m'girl!" He grinned, displaying teeth brown and putrid as old plums. Katrina's slender white ankles dangled on each side of the broad branch. She had kicked off her heavy winter boots of linden bark to climb the tree.

Dakov grabbed, and seized her ankles brutally. Katrina's skirt went to the top of her thighs, and she gave a short cry of alarm. The branch rocked. Her arms were around little Michael, steadying him. Michael's chin quivered, as the tears came. He was afraid, feeling his sister's fear.

"Stop—Dakov—you hurt—me!"

His grin broadened as he pulled. "I know it!" He see-sawed her, enjoying her discomfort. Then she kicked free from him and scrambled high on the limb of the tree, perched like a squirrel, with Michael in her arms, out of Dakov's reach.

Dakov's grin became sly. He regarded her slowly. "I could reach you with this!" He patted his whip. "And tomorrow we shall meet again—on the ground, m'girl. Your mother wants you—she will tell you!"

He nodded to Michael in a not unkindly way. "Ha, boy!" Katrina watched Dakov lumber back to the hut. The goat trailed anxiously after him.

"Pig!" said Katrina, straightening herself. The fun had gone from the rocking-horse game now. They descended slowly, and dawdled toward the house. Katrina filled her skirt with big fir cones for the stove as she went.

Anna was lolling, contented. Her hair, that had once been as fair as Katrina's, was now graying and in disorder. She smiled as the children entered, and scratched vigorously inside her open bodice, then inspected her fingers absently.

"Come in, come in! See—four kopeks, Katrina—four! And a bottle of wine and two lard loaves! Generous Dakov!"

Dakov stood, grinning self-consciously, by the stove. He had lifted up his tunic to warm and rub his buttocks. He was indulging his favourite comfort of sucking his bad teeth in little clucks such as one might use to coax a hen.

Little Michael danced around the loaves and the skin of wine, Katrina smiled, too, at the sight of such splendour. Then she came, as always, straight to the point.

"What did Dakov mean—about tomorrow?"

Anna's eyes narrowed with quick cunning. "Tomorrow?" she echoed. "Ah, yes—tomorrow." She threw a glance of appeal at Dakov who answered it with a slow nod.

"We could use you up at the house, m'girl." He prodded with his blunt thumb at a back tooth, and spat.

"It's a good chance for you, Katrina," said Anna urgently. "Good food—and warm stoves in winter—and Dakov—he'll be generous to you, dearie. Taken a fancy to you, he says." She giggled. She was a little drunk. Dakov smirked and rocked himself self-consciously before the stove.

"I'm an important man at the house, m'girl, a word from me'll go a long way to making you happy—or not."

"How much shall I get?" asked Katrina. Even when her pulses thudded and her heart seemed to weigh like a stone in her stomach, Katrina could manage to be practical.

"We'd have to see," said Dakov significantly. "Yes, we'd have to see."

That night Katrina was wakeful. She lay with her eyes wide and dark staring into the chilly blackness of the hut. Her little brother slept warmly beside her, his white face mirroring a peaceful dream. Any other night she would have been happy and sleeping, too, her stomach contented and filled with the food Dakov had brought, but now she was troubled. A great fear seemed to nag at her mind, like a light which would not go out. She tried again and again to snuff the flame, but it persisted till her unhappy thoughts were bright and brittle with it.

She felt afraid of the huge, gaunt house; of Dakov; and the ready whip at his belt.

She gazed around the hut in the uncertain glow from the dying fire. It was a small dingy place, and barely shelter against the biting cold. But it was home, all she had known in her brief childhood. She cried. Tears rolled down her face leaving clean channels in the grime, uncovering the weather-blown red of her cheeks. Eventually, just before dawn she slept. . . .

Grey mist was still swirling over the broad river next morning as Katrina walked toward Pastor Gluck's house. Michael went with her as far as the bridge. Anna still slept.

"Goodbye, Michael," she said and kissed him. "Be good to Mama."

She watched him go, and gripped the lumpy rail of the wooden footbridge as she waited until he was out of sight. She had to fight the tears and the urge to run back with him.

The Glucks' house lay behind the church, under the walls of Marienburg. It was a rambling wooden house, painted red and white. The sun and winter frost had peeled thick strips of paint from the tall, onion-shaped towers. Katrina had often envied this splendid place. She opened the iron gates, and looked down the long, tree-lined carriageway. There was no watchman in sight and the dark windows of the house stared back at her silently. From the forest that lay beyond the town walls came another rumble of cannons. In the still air it sounded very near.

Katrina wondered how her mother and Michael would manage without her. But it was no use arriving gloomily into a new life. She brought a smile to her nervous lips—then from behind some distant bushes came the quick, terrified scream of an animal. She ran across the dew-wet grass towards the sound.

A girl, smaller than Katrina, held a brown puppy by its tail and was beating it angrily with a broad stick. The dog, quivering and yelping, hugged the earth for protection.

"Hey, now!" said Katrina. "What has he done to deserve this?"

The girl had looked up with fear in her pale blue eyes. She was beautifully dressed, in white frock and silk-embroidered shawl. Her hair, in thick yellow ringlets like a bunch of fat bananas, was tied behind her ears with purple ribbons.

Katrina knew her. She was Pastor Gluck's younger daughter, Miss Veda. And it took Miss Veda only an instant to recognize from Katrina's clothing that she was no person of authority.

"Get out!" she screamed. "Get out! How dare you speak to me! How dare you!" She whizzed a blow at Katrina with the thick stick and caught her across the shoulder. "Get out! Get out."

Katrina backed away. There could have been only a year or two between their ages, and the girl was hitting out recklessly with the violence of a demon.

"Peasants and scum—servants and slaves—go round to the——back—of the—house!"

Katrina ran. Her shoulders and arms were welted where some of the blows had caught her.

The puppy tried to wriggle away, but its back was broken. After a moment, Katrina heard its thin, despairing shrieks again from the bushes, and the repeated thud of the stick.

In the outhouse behind the Manse was a small door that creaked as she pushed it open. The narrow passage beyond was almost utterly dark, its stone floor puddled from water that streaked the green walls, soft and damp like soaked chalk.

Light came from another door ahead of her. She lifted the heavy bar and entered a kitchen that was misted with steam and charcoal smoke. Fat, black flies crawled and circled dozily.

Two legs stuck out from the flat top of the stove, where old fur pelts were spread. Rags, frayed and filthy, bound the broken bark boots. At the sound of Katrina's own boots upon the hard-packed floor the legs were slowly drawn inwards.

"Well, and what can you be wanting?"

The owner of the rumbling voice showed his face from over the top of the stove. A yellow striped cat fell to the floor.

"I've come to work here," said Katrina. "Dakov knows."

"Dakov knows, eh?" The man climbed down from the stove and shuffled towards her. He was big, but shapeless as a potato. His face was red with stove warmth and pitted with pox craters full of dirt. He rubbed sleepily at watery sores in the roots of his straggly beard.

"Dakov knows, all right, eh?" He reached out his hand towards her, drunkenly shaky, yet certain of where to touch.

Katrina backed away and stepped on the cat. As she recoiled from its high, scalding screech, the man grabbed her.

His breath smelt like bad stew. She wriggled her face from him and saw that a woman had appeared silently upon the top of the stairs that led down into the kitchen, and she was watching, solemn, hands dug into the bulk of her hips.

She caught Katrina's eye and came slowly down the stairs as though each new step was a careful ritual. Just as methodically, and without a word, she doubled her big red fists and thumped at the man, who let Katrina go at once and stood grinning stupidly while the woman hit him.

He began to chuckle, his belly shaking with rumbles of laughter. Her red fists pounded him.

She stopped at last for breath. "Where did you find her, eh? Who is she?" She turned on Katrina ferociously.

"She's there, Denka. Ask her!" He chuckled again, walked back to the stove, heaved himself up on it, and settled his fat buttocks contentedly.

"Well?" The woman Denka glared at Katrina. The word was a command.

"Dakov sent me," said Katrina, "and he—" she jerked a glance at the man on the stove, who was grinning like a thirsty dog— "he grabbed me as soon as I came in."

"Him!" The woman spat at the stove. "He hasn't enough for me! He's none to waste on you!" Suddenly she threw back her head and yelled: "Gerda-a-a-a!" It was so unexpected and so loud that Katrina was startled.

The shout was answered from beyond the room. A girl came in, pushing the heavy door with her back. She carried a big wooden bucket that slopped dirty water as she moved. She was about the same age as Katrina, but thin and gnarled with work. She wiped sweat from her face onto the shoulder of her dress.

"Is this the new one?" Her voice thin and shrill. "Another for it, eh?"

Katrina smiled at her, hoping to have found a friend. The smile was not answered, except by a long, sharp glance.

"Come on," Gerda said bitterly, "I'll show you!" She went to the other door, opened it and threw the contents of the bucket into the dark, wet corridor, then led Katrina up the stairs from the kitchen.

"Has she got to do all that Esme did?" she demanded from the top stair. "That's going to be funny." She darted a malevolent glance at Katrina. "But not for you!" She moved unhurriedly to dodge a murderous chunk of firewood the woman Denka threw. It thumped into the half-shut door behind them.

They were in the main hall now, a wide pillared place that shone with bright colours—red, blue, gold and purple draperies, and tessellated tiles. The stairway was marble, Katrina touched it curiously as they ascended. She had never seen marble before, not even in church.

The pale blue doors that led to the bedrooms were all shut. Gerda paused outside one of them and stopped to listen before she pressed the gilded handle and turned it noiselessly.

The room was big and airless, with two tall beds, frilled by white lace and covered with blue silk, under a single, foamy canopy. The hanging draperies were striped blue and white, and similar material covered couches and chairs. Mirrors glittered from every vacant wall space.

Gerda shut the door after a careful stare down the corridor, and flung herself onto the nearest bed, wriggling sensuously on its yielding comfort. This was obviously her secret pleasure.

Katrina was fascinated by the mirrors. She approached the nearest in awe. A strange face stared back at her. Her own hands, feet and body, Katrina knew. But her face she had never seen. She stared at her own clear green eyes, and moved her mouth to watch the resultant smile. She was enchanted by herself.

Gerda rustled off the bed, and plucked the coverlet straight. "They'll kill us if they catch us in here!" she said, and went to the door for another peep down the corridor before opening one of the ornamented closets. She ran her hands down the row of richly coloured gowns and furred cloaks. Katrina could smell the scent of faded flowers and oily perfumes that came from the big cupboard.

Gerda pulled out the billowing skirt of a blue and white velvet gown and spread it across her thin shanks. Katrina came near, fascinated.

"Oh, it's lovely," she said, and touched the soft cloth.

Gerda's fingers immediately pinched her wrist viciously. "Nosey!" she hissed. "You leave 'em alone, see. You common bitch!"

There was a noise in the corridor. Gerda, quick as a ferret, dropped the dress from its hook onto the thick carpet of the floor and darted through the far door. Katrina stumbled over the sprawled velvet on the floor and ran after her.

Gerda was pressed against the wall of the further room, her shoulders quivering with laughter.

"I thought they'd got you. Miss Veda would have killed you if she'd caught you touching her dresses." She giggled. "You got to be quick when Miss Veda's about!"

This new room was much bigger, and had huge crystal chandeliers filled with yellow, plump candles. Heavy draperies festooned all sides of the room. There was thick luxury everywhere, cloying as cream.

Alongside the great white cavern of a bed stood a gilt cage. In it sat a dwarf on a stool, his broad and misshapen back towards them. He wore a gaudy uniform of red velvet, decorated lavishly with gilt brocade. On his shoulders, draped in flowing curls, was the most beautiful red hair that shone silkily as he turned at the noise of their approach.

His face was big, and puffy with lack of sunshine. He got off his stool, stepped over his little gilt chamberpot, and stuck his bulbous, hairy nose between the bars of the cage.

"Gerda!" he whispered eagerly. "Have you come to let me out?"

"I might have, Mister Grog, and I might not have."

"Please!" the dwarf pleaded, his face comically ugly. His brown eyes were sad and pouchy as a bloodhound's.

"Why is he locked in there?" asked Katrina, regarding the dwarf compassionately.

"Ignorant little bitch, ain't you!" Gerda said. "Every lady keeps a dwarf beside her bed to do her hair."

"But why in a cage?"

"So he'll be there when she wants him, of course!"

"Each time you come in, Gerda, you promise. Are you trying to break my heart?" The dwarf's voice was deep, resonant, and did not seem natural to his tiny stature, for he was barely three feet tall.

"Freaks and monkeys don't have hearts."

"Let me out," pleaded the dwarf. His stubby fingers clutched at the bars.

"Perhaps next time," Gerda said as she went laughing from the room.

Katrina stayed behind, fascinated. The dwarf turned his dark eyes towards her, with a new hope. His shoulders, under their gay colouring, heaved with a deep sigh.

"The key," he said. "Mistress keeps it in that gold box. At least, let me see it!"

The gold box was on the dressing table, its reflection tripled in the tall mirrors. As Katrina reached her hand towards it, she knocked over a blue glass bottle that shattered at her feet, spilling oily, rich perfume.

"Never mind," boomed the dwarf eagerly, "never mind—give me the box!"

Katrina had never seen a key, nor knew what one was. The huts of peasants were latched by wooden bars. She held out the box to the dwarf, but her eyes and thoughts were upon the costly ruin that was spreading over the carpet.

As she stooped and began to pick up the splinters of glass, the deep, musical voice of the dwarf came again—from just above the level of her ear. He was out of his cage. The little gilt door hung open. Trinkets and jewels were scattered around where he had spilled them from the box in his hasty search for the key to his prison.

He danced a few comical steps, reached his little leg into his cage through the narrow bars, and maliciously kicked over the chamberpot. Then he filled his pockets with jewels.

"Whatever are you doing?" asked Katrina. The dwarf made no answer, but bounded onto the dressing table, kicked over more of the fragile blue glassware, and reached a slow burning taper down from its bracket.

"Watch!" he said, and touched the taper to a candle, took the beautiful red wig off his large, bald head, and calmly held it over the candle.

"I'm sorry for you if they catch you. Mistress Gluck will have you whipped. I shall be far away and she won't be able to reach me with her knout. Listen!" He cocked his ear to the window. In every movement he was like a spry little tropical bird.

"They're getting nearer," he said with satisfaction. "The guns—the Russians are coming!"

Katrina shuddered. "They'll kill us all!"

"Not them!" He sang a deep tuneful trill of music. "Tra-la-li-lee! They'll not kill me!" His thick sensitive mouth puckered into a beatific smile. "I'm a dwarf, a singing dwarf. The great Tsar Peter collects dwarfs, jesters, freaks—" he glanced at Katrina—"and beautiful young girls! See—grab some jewels and come with me. We'll find the Russians. Why stay here to be knouted?" There came a sound of voices in the corridor. Quick as a squirrel the dwarf jumped to the window and climbed out onto the narrow verandah.

"They'll beat you," he said, "if they catch you, girl! You must run! Run!" He sprang for the overhanging wooden drain trough and swung himself up out of Katrina's view. "Run!" she heard him shout again. Then he was gone.

She looked wildly around her at the havoc he had left behind him. Around the dressing table, splinters of precious glass lay among puddles of yet more precious fluids, their scents mixing with the acrid stench of the burnt wig. Jewellery winked from the stained carpet. The floor of the little gilt cage was now indescribable. With a whimper of terror, Katrina ran from the bedroom.

In the corridor outside, Denka had the girl Gerda by the ear and was pulling her along with her peaked, pallid little face twisted in pain.

"There you are!" grunted Denka, as she saw Katrina. "Wasting time tormenting that damned dwarf, eh?" From the open doorway she glimpsed the empty cage. Her mouth opened. Her expression darkened into malignant horror. She even released Gerda's ear. "You'll both be beaten," she whispered. "Wait until Madame and the Master return home tonight. You'll be knouted for this, as you've never been knouted in your lives!"

Gerda was crying. Her hands shook with fear. "It wasn't me," she gasped. "It wasn't—it wasn't."

"No," Katrina swallowed slowly. "It was me."

All that long day, hardly any of the servants spoke to Katrina. They watched her silently, as if she was a ghost already dead. They indicated, in silence, the work she was to perform. By nightfall her back ached. She knew why Gerda's back was twisted; it made the ache easier to endure. It had been a nightmare of work.

The Glucks had not returned. Gerda went to bed, and after

a while Katrina followed her, into a tiny wooden loft over one of the outhouses. Gerda was already asleep, looking like a bundle of rags in the uncertain flicker of the lard candle that dripped its grease over a broken stool, propped against the wall.

Katrina lay down without undressing. There was a ragged old fur pelt to cover her. It had been faultily cured, and was stiff and rancid. Insects dropped dismally from the low roof. She could see a patch of frost-clear night sky through a window hole in the wall.

She lay stiff and apprehensive, unable to sleep. After a long while she heard horses' hooves and the rattle of a carriage, jingle of harness and bells. The Glucks had returned.

Soon there were heavy footsteps upon the ladder. Light streaked through warped planks of the wall. Katrina looked around frantically for some way to escape. Gerda, too, was sitting stiffly upright, staring with pale eyes that seemed to gloat.

"Won't be long now," she whispered, "and when they're done with you, Mistress Katrina, you'll be lucky if you ever walk again!"

The door wobbled inwards. A rat scurried away as orange light gushed into the room.

"Where is she?" It was Dakov's harsh voice.

Katrina watched him heave his body off the ladder and into the loft. The torch hollowed ghoulish shadows into his face. As he tramped heavily upon the uncertain floor, there came a shrill howl that sounded at first like the wind, but grew nearer and louder, in eerie haste. It passed overhead with a thunderous crack, and shrieked away into the frosty night. The Russian cannon had penetrated to within range of Marienburg's walls.

Dakov dropped his flaming torch with an oath. It rolled, spluttering, upon the dirt-caked floor. A thick grey spider, caught asleep, shrivelled and perished.

Dakov stooped to retrieve his pine-knot torch, coughed at the sting of its scented fumes and shook his head when he saw the fate of the insect.

"Ah, pity," he said. "Unlucky, that!"

He peered around the room, and saw the terrified eyes of

Katrina. She gazed at him over the rancid fur pelt that covered her.

"Come on, m'girl. Up ye get. Mistress Gluck wants a word wi' ye." He reached for her shoulder. Katrina shrank from him, slithering along the floor with the fur pelt clutched in front of her like a shield, until she was pressed against the farthest wall.

Gerda sat up and sniggered, her pale mouth twisted with unwholesome wisdom.

Dakov, losing patience, gripped Katrina and pushed her towards the door. She almost stumbled down the uncertain wooden rungs that led from the loft into the yard. Her legs were numbed to clumsiness by fear. Below the ladder, the dark ground seemed to pulse, toward and then away from her.

Beyond the fortified walls of Marienburg the night sky glowed red. Distant guns were muttering like marsh frogs below the horizon. A nearer gun belched suddenly orange to send yet another incandescent ball searing across the sky in an arc like a falling star.

Dakov had Katrina firmly by the shoulder, his fingers twined among the rough cloth of her dress.

"Devils, those Russians," said Dakov. He sniffed the sharp air. "Ah, smell it, m'girl—you can smell the gunpowder!" He grinned down at her. "You've chosen a noisy night for your beating," he said. "I shall have to cock a sharp ear for your yells."

Katrina shivered. She knew from the sound of gunfire that the advancing Russians must now be among the black trees of Goreki Wood, where her mother's hut stood in its clearing. In sudden terror she wriggled to free herself. "Dakov! Please—my mother, and little Michael—I must go to them!"

"Hey, steady there, you nearly twisted my fingers off!" He pushed her before him, into the house.

They went along the wide marble hall where shadows lurked behind pillars and folds of coloured draperies and seemed to dance as Dakov swung his torch.

Katrina blinked in the bright lamplight that waited for her beyond the double doors of the salon. The red tiles chilled her bare feet. The door was half open but Dakov did not enter, though voices could be heard. He fixed his torch in a link bracket and knocked. Katrina watched his scaly, chapped fist rap upon the innocent rotundity of a carved, flying cherub.

"Come in!"

Both Katrina and Dakov winced at the high-pitched wrathness of the command. It was Madame Gluck's voice.

Madame sat enthroned in a high-backed chair, dominating the big room and all its stuffy, overdecorated furnishings. She sat tall and stiff. Her low-cut silk gown hung flat upon her limp bosom.

A red wig towered above Madame Gluck's white powdered face. Her skin was pitted, and crumbs of powder, clinging to her moustache, stirred as her mouth twitched angrily.

"The girl, m'lady," said Dakov, uncomfortable.

Madame Gluck came straight to the point.

"Where is my dwarf?" She screamed the words. Only a narrow table separated Katrina from the anger of Madame Gluck, whose wrathful face was mirrored and distorted upon its highly polished surface.

The face in the tabletop seemed to melt like warming butter, and Madame Gluck was speaking again.

"Look, wretch," she said, "look at what the dwarf did!" With hopeless eyes, Katrina followed the direction of the outstretched arm of Madame Gluck, and saw the black pyramid that was all Grog had left of his mistress's other red wig.

Madame Gluck gathered it up. She held it out vindictively at Katrina's face until the girl backed away from the fumes of scorched hair.

"My best one!" Madame Gluck flung the ruined wig across the room. It smacked into the wall, to smudge the white surface before it fell to the carpet, charred and shrivelled like the spider.

All this scene had been watched silently by Pastor Gluck, the master of the house. He was shifting diffidently on thin, black-garbed legs, as far from his roaring wife as the big room would allow. He played with the silk tassels of the window curtain, which he had pulled out so that the curtain half hid him. His wrinkled, timid face blinked out from behind it like a rebuked monkey's.

"Haven't you got a tongue in your head, girl?" Madame Gluck raised her gaunt body from the tall chair, towards Katrina. "I asked you where is the dwarf?"

"He—he's gone," whispered Katrina.

Madame snorted impatiently.

From the wide stairway, a delicately scented white ermine cloak around her shoulders to keep out the cold of the stonework, little Veda Gluck crouched, listening with a smile of tense excitement. She heard her mother's high, ranting voice: "...and beat her, Dakov, d'you hear, man? Beat the girl until she learns..." Veda nestled into the warmth of her furs and watched the shadows grow big upon the white door as Dakov and Katrina came towards the hallway.

She crouched, quiet as a mouse, watched Dakov push the shaking but silent Katrina down the corridor towards the kitchen, saw Katrina's green eyes wide with fear in the gleam of the lantern that Dakov had picked up in the hallway.

Then, stealthily on her embroidered satin slippers, Veda crept after them, followed the dancing light and the leaping shadows of the slender girl and Dakov's huge shoulders, as they went down the winding stone stairs into the cellars.

"Please, Dakov," Katrina whispered, after they had descended the cellar stairs in silence. "You aren't going to really beat me? I want to go home—to mother and little Michael, please. Dakov, the Russian soldiers—"

Dakov sucked his teeth, and held her with one slender wrist twisted painfully by the grip of his big, calloused hand. "M'girl, it's this way. It's you who gets whipped—or it's me, see?" He laughed deep in his chest at his own joke and repeated it. "It's you or me, d'you see? I shall have to beat you since Madame orders it, even if the Russians were to come and watch!"

Little Veda, half a dozen steps behind in the shadows heard his laugh go echoing down under the low rafters of the cellars. As they passed the kitchen another cannon shot went wailing past the house. Dakov kicked upon the kitchen door. A waft of hot, greasy air smote them. Denka and her husband were asleep on top of the stove.

"Hey, you two! Stir yourselves!" Dakov took pride in his deep-voiced bellow. "D'you want the Russians to waken you with cold steel at your useless throats?" Denka and fat Shuvaroff stirred. The man's jowled face appeared over the edge of the stove. "Eh?"

"Up there!" boomed Dakov. "This is no time for snoring like pigs! Upstairs with you, both—help the Madame and the others. We're to leave the house at dawn!"

As Shuvaroff's large red feet, wrinkled with frostbite sores, fumbled for the ladder, Dakov pushed Katrina on down the damp corridor towards the meat cellar. Behind them, Veda gathered her cloak closer around her frilled nightdress and slipped unseen past the open kitchen door.

There were several steps down into the meat cellar. It was the lowest room in the house, damp and colder than the winter's night outside. There was no window. Barrels of salted meats lay piled upon the hard-packed earthen floor. From low rafters hung the carcasses of pigs and recently slaughtered sheep, with frozen red stalactites of blood upon their snouts.

Dakov put his lamp upon the nearest barrel. Katrina stumbled away from him as he let go of her wrist. A pulse in her neck seemed to beat louder than her heart. Fear had wearied her. She felt small and frail, suddenly too tired to fight. She did not try to hold back her tears that spilled down her face onto her rough, home-woven blouse.

Dakov stood between her and the narrow doorway, and searched in his pockets for a piece of cord. "Crying, eh?" he said conversationally. "If ye'd been a good girl, I'd not have had this pleasure!" Veda crept into the shaft of deeper darkness just outside the door, where she could watch. Her small pink tongue edged across her lips.

Dakov sorted out a length of cord to his satisfaction, pulled Katrina towards him, and twisted her to the floor. He put his bulky knee upon her, and wrapped the cord around her wrists, pulling it tight until her skin puckered and blenched.

"Can you feel that, m'girl?" he asked, grinning, and put his face very near to hers. Katrina sobbed hopelessly and Dakov hoisted her to her feet with the cord, her wrists bound in front of her. He reached up to the nearest unoccupied meat hook and tugged the cord over it until Katrina hung, her toes barely on the ground. Pain seared through her wrists like circles of heat as the cord took almost her entire weight.

Her body pivoted half round, swinging against the stone-hard carcass of the frozen, salt-caked pig nearby. The rows of carcasses hung like bizarre tree trunks.

Dakov seized her blouse at the shoulders, and ripped it down. Veda, with a little whimper of eagerness, took a step forward into the cellar. A rat rustled across her gleaming slippers and she did not notice.

Dakov fumbled at the greasy brown whip, his badge of authority, that hung at his belt. His small eyes shone as he watched Katrina's chill-pointed breasts. He reached out a hand and as Katrina tried to shrink away, the cord bit deeper into her wrists. She revolved slowly, and Dakov's frost-chapped fingers dragged roughly over her skin. She threw back her head, and screamed. It rang hollowly through the crowded tunnels of the cellar, and in the darkness there was a multiplied scurrying.

"The whip's a selfish playmate," said Dakov.

He walked around one of the pigs. The flame in the lamp was guttering, and shadows danced around the cellar like tethered ghosts. Veda slid into the cellar and leaned behind the shelter of a tall brine barrel.

Katrina screamed as the first stroke painted a red ribbon, sudden as magic, from her shoulder to the sloping indent of her waist. It was a scream that almost strangled her, harsh in her throat. It reverberated among the gloomy stone archways until it spent itself about the rambling house.

Dakov walked to and fro, measuring his strokes with tilted head, appraisingly.

A booming shudder reverberated from somewhere overhead. Roof and earthen floor quivered. Each carcass clinked and shook upon its suspending hook. The rats in the dark corners gave thin, frail screams like tearing calico, and Veda fell against the barrel. A cannon shot had struck the Manse. Dakov's lunge had been unbalanced, and the end of the whip coiled entangled around Katrina's neck. Dakov tried to snatch it back, and Katrina coughed, hoarsely and desperately.

With an oath, Dakov came nearer to free the knotted lash. The lamp guttered again and dimmed suddenly into a faint orange glow that carried its light no further than the edges of the barrel. Dakov shook the lamp angrily, and at once it went out. The guns seemed now to be almost inside the house, and in sudden terror of the darkness and the oncoming danger, Dakov plunged for the doorway, blundering.

He passed within inches of Veda but did not see her.

Miss Veda stood completely still and listened to his footsteps departing upon the winding stone steps beyond the corridor. Then she crept forward. Katrina, hanging in total darkness, did not hear the tread of her satin slippers. Katrina's back was not hurting her. It was numb. But a throbbing cramp had begun in her muscles, and she could feel soft warm trickles from her wrists and down her shoulders, into her dress at the waist.

She felt another touch at her throat. It was just as gentle, and as silent, as the running blood. It took Katrina several long seconds to realize that it was the touch of fingers, fumbling to disentangle the lash of the snarled whip.

"Who's that?" Her whisper was dry and tense. She detected a whiff of perfume, and remembered the smell of the gowns in the closet of Miss Veda's bedchamber.

"Is that you, Miss Veda?"

There was no answer. The persistent, sensitive fingers had untwined the thong and Katrina felt the whip being withdrawn from her neck.

"Thank you," she murmured. There was still no answer. Miss Veda had stepped back. Suddenly, out of the darkness, the whip cracked, and a quick hot pain came to Katrina. It was a poor blow, a clumsy blow, compared with Dakov's practiced strokes. It stung, rather than numbed her. Several more strokes fell. Some spent their force upon the carcasses that swung alongside.

At the sound of footsteps, the distant gleam of a lamp, Miss Veda dropped the whip and shrank against the shelter of the big barrels.

Shuvaroff entered the cellar, blinking and peering. Veda slipped past him still unseen and scurried away up the stairs towards the bright-lit chambers of the upper house.

Shuvaroff held in his plump arms a roughly made bundle of his own possessions. He put these down carefully and hacked a generous side of salted bacon from the pig carcass that hung nearest to him.

Shuvaroff had tucked the bacon under his arm, and was turning to pick up his bundle when he noticed Katrina. She hung with head drooping, eyes shut.

He slowly put down the bundle and the bacon, waddled over to her, and cleared his throat.

"Hello, Katrina," he said. When she did not answer, he touched her. His finger encountered blood. Shuvaroff regarded it, and licked it off. His little, fat-creased eyes wandered up and down her motionless body and dwelt upon her. He reached up with his kitchen knife and cut the cord.

Katrina crumpled to the floor like a discarded coat. Shuvaroff was for an instant surprised at this. Katrina's fair hair spread like a fan around her white face. One of her arms lay across Shuvaroff's ragbound foot. The wrist was ridged with purple weals where the cord had bruised her.

Shuvaroff's slow brain debated a problem of time.

Faintly now, thin as gnats' cries among the distant thunder of the battle for Marienburg's outer ditches, could be heard bugle calls. The sharp splutter of musketry was nearer, and the thud of exploding fire-pots was beginning to shake the solid earth.

Denka, his wife, waited upstairs. Shuvaroff considered all this and gazed at the unconscious girl sprawled in front of him. With one unsightly, clothbound foot he pushed back Katrina's skirt. Her limbs shone in the lantern light. Shuvaroff gazed, sighed resignedly, shook his head, picked up the hunk of bacon, his bundle of other belongings, and lumbered off with them, out of the cellar.

Chapter Two

For a long time Katrina lay without stirring, her half-unconscious body as chilled as the hard floor beneath her. Dawn had begun to streak the sky, increasingly paled by the fires which began to spread and burn along the narrow streets until all the houses of the little town seemed to be aflame.

She was finally aroused by the urgent trilling of a panic-stricken grey column of rats scurrying through the unlit cellar. She clambered stiffly to her feet, groping with pain-swollen hands towards the faint light of the exit.

Smoke was billowing down the stairway. She could hear the roar and crash of flames, like a strong wind among tree branches. There was gunfire and shouting all around the house, and in the town beyond.

Katrina did not know it, but the Cossack armies, under the terrible command: "Let loose the Red Cockerel!" were storming through the houses, with free license to rob, pillage, rape and destroy. It was the reward that had kept the temperamental cavalry of the Don waiting for two years, camped upon the windy hillsides around the besieged town.

In his tent, the Russian Infantry Commander, Marshal Sheremetiev, strutted anxiously. He could see the glare in the sky over Marienburg.

"Those filthy Cossack hooligans," he said softly, and his aide-de-camp nodded soberly. "There will not be a handful of loot in the city, nor a wench for the slave markets, sir," he agreed, "unless—"

"Unless what?" demanded Sheremetiev.

"Unless we send rounding-up parties, sir—on their heels—to bring back to camp here what possible slave stuff they can find, and get the valuables from the houses before those lustful Cossacks fire the entire town!"

Sheremetiev gestured with his hand, upon which diamonds sparkled. "Get it done, man!" The aide-de-camp saluted triumphantly and hurried from the Marshal's tent.

When Katrina reached the garden of the Manse, the whole building was already billowing with red sparks and yellow tongues of fire. She could see dark figures among the lawns and fountains. Torches showed glimpses of bearded faces, glitter of swords and lances, and gleams of cuirasses.

Columns of fire were rushing heavenwards from a hundred points in the town. Shouts, shrieks and shots rose like discordant bubbles of terrible sound bursting from a seething pot.

The frosty air salted pain into the welts upon Katrina's back. She wanted to go home, and draw such comfort as she could from her mother and little Michael. She moved between the bushes and trod on something warmer to her naked feet than the cold soil. It was the white ermine wrap that Veda had worn over her nightdress.

Katrina put it over her shoulders and was soothed as she ran for the bridge.

She passed corpses, grotesque in sudden attitudes of death. Some were citizens, some were Swedish soldiers in their familiar blue uniform. And others wore a red uniform she had never seen before.

The thud of her bare feet sounded to her like hammer blows as she ran over the frail bridge.

From the dark trees came a new scent of burning. Katrina ran on until she reached the old, familiar clearing. Then her legs dissolved, and she sank slowly to the icy grass. The cabin was gone! Its jagged, crusty outline glowed in a dozen places. The little hut had been burnt out. Memories of home crowded into Katrina's mind, and she felt a stirring dread of what else she might find among the splotches of debris around the gutted hut.

A low white mist had swirled in from the river and above it the sky lightened, bringing an eerie filminess to the woods. Crisp pine needles dropped on her from the low branches above. Their perfume was everywhere around her. A large cone with its wooden shelves wide open, lay by her clenched hand. A few hours before it would have seemed a treasure, not only as fuel, but as a message of coming warm days. Now she ignored it, and tried to look into the dim half light. At first, she could see nothing of her mother and Michael. She listened, but the forest was silent except for the crackle and hiss of the embers.

She got up and walked towards the remains of the hut. On the other side of a clump of burnt trees she saw them. They lay together.

They must have been ablaze as they ran from the hut. Their clothing was flaked away in layers like the pages of a charred book. The two skulls, big and small, were hairless and bare, baked cinder-grey. Little Michael had flung up his arms to protect his face. The arms were burnt to stumps.

Katrina found soft earth among the warm cinders, where the fire had lately been. She dug with bare hands at first, then with a split piece of stovelid. When the shallow grave was finished she pulled the two bodies into it. They felt surprisingly heavy, and hard as charred logs.

Not until they were covered with earth and she had made a rough cross for headstone, did she feel for them, that they who lay in this grave were really mother and baby Michael.

Then she knelt and wept, her face striped with dirt and tears. She did not hear the soldier who came upon her from behind, yet when his two thick arms imprisoned her, and she felt the buckles and buttons of his tunic press against the sore welts of her shoulders, she gave no more than a breathless, muted gasp, and looked down almost calmly at the arms that held her.

The sleeves of the tunic were red—strange, unfamiliar red

cloth. The breath that came upon her bent neck, had the tang of foreign spices.

Katrina did not begin to struggle until the soldier tried to pull her towards the little path that led deeper into the woods.

When she did protest, kicking and clawing with her nails against the grip, it was unavailing. The soldier seemed insensible to such slight pain as she could inflict upon him. He laughed into her hair, and Katrina felt a stir of revulsion at the alien odour of his breath.

He had pressed his short, stubby black beard into her bare shoulder, and only one side of his face was visible to her. Katrina saw a broad face, yellowish and pulpy as though sculptured from pumpkin flesh. His eye was unwavering and unemotional as a stoat's.

"Did you—did you kill my mother and baby Michael?" asked Katrina, and her voice was so low that it was almost without tone at all.

"Nah!" Speaking slow Slav tongue, the Russian shook his head in denial. "Not me—not old Romanov! He never—nothing cruel." He released her, and there came neither smile nor frown to his face as, with a heavy chop of his hand, he knocked Katrina to the earth.

She fell between the soldier's feet, and he was standing over her, fumbling with the thick rope that held his baggy dark red breeches, when there came sounds of crashing through the nearby bushes. For the first time, the soldier's dark eyes showed expression—a beady gleam of fear.

But it faded at once as he saw that the men who came into the clearing were Russians of similar uniform to his own. They were led by a Russian infantry corporal, who grunted with no apparent surprise at what confronted him, and struck the soldier Romanov across the mouth.

Romanov stood firm and unflinching as a statue to this buffet, neither blinking nor seeming to be in any manner dismayed.

"Pick her up," said the corporal, "and if she cannot walk you must carry her. You knocked her down. You be her legs." The other soldiers chuckled and gathered around Katrina to stare with the simple curiosity of children at her fair hair.

"Our only bit of luck," said one. "And that spoiled, if old Romanov had taken his way." He spat at Romanov's beard. With no hint that this had offended him, Romanov wiped the insult off on his sleeve. "Aye," he said slowly, "those Cossacks —cleared all town—of women."

"Like locusts over a field of crops," agreed the soldier who had spat. They nodded at each other dully, without further enmity. The angers of these big, slow Russians seemed to drift and depart with no more trace than that of wind over tall grasses. Romanov stooped, slung Katrina across his shoulders.

"Let's be getting back," grunted the corporal, abruptly. "We don't want to meet any of our damned Cossack comrades in this wood, now we have a girl!"

The soldiers turned towards the path, and trudged deeper into Goreki wood, away from the burnt-out hull of the hut that Katrina had known as home. Head downward, her fair hair spilled over the bobbing shoulders of the Russian soldier, Katrina was carried from all she knew.

The Russian army encampment was an untidy throng of tents made from animal skins, of holes dug into the hard ground, and covered for roofing with brushwood, earth and skins. There were a number of breast-high earthworked hovels among them. Small fires burned in a hundred places. Soldiers, bearded, hairy men in fur helmets or floppy sheepskin caps, stood or sprawled around the fires. Some of the nearer ones shambled over to Katrina, as Romanov dumped her onto her feet, near an earth embankment that was lined with huge black iron cannons, their muzzles facing towards Marienburg and streaked grey with spent powder.

"Fetch her near the fire, lad!" called a soldier. "Let's all see!"

The corporal did not interfere as Katrina was thrust towards the fire by a dozen hands that plucked and pawed at her. She looked around the closely pressed circle of unkempt and bewhiskered faces. They were staring hungrily, without smile or gesture, and suddenly Katrina felt a strange compassion for them, and for the urgency in them that made them probe and nuzzle at her. They discussed her and fell back as the corporal pushed Katrina through the throng, to where other captives were bound to trees around a small copse that protected a large skin tent from which a banner flew.

The corporal picked up a heavy rope, put Katrina against a tree, and tethered her to it with a couple of turns of rope. He made a methodical, unhurried knot, out of her reach, and jerked it securely tight. Her arms were left free.

Katrina saw several hundred other Marienburg citizens, similarly captive, around her. Young girls and lads had been sorted out, and were tied in ones, twos and threes, to the trees. Huddled groups of older captives were squatting on the ground among the trees, roped roughly together. They all looked morose, weary and unfriendly. Some wept, but none of them spoke to her.

Among the young girls, Katrina saw Miss Veda Gluck, whose silken nightgown, although torn and smudged with dirt, was still a startlingly clear splash of colour against the drab, muddied and rougly-handled prisoners, who were the poor of Marienburg. Most of the rich citizens had escaped to the south, but the Gluck household must have been overrun by the first party of invaders to breach the city's walls. Miss Veda leaned against her tree, with head tilted arrogantly, as if the ropes that held her were there by her own proud choice. Most of her yellow curls were still tied in ribbons. Miss Veda had obviously not demeaned herself by struggling with her captors. After a long while she saw Katrina but did not answer her glance with any sign of recognition.

The prisoners remained thus until dusk. With the darkness, the wolves crept nearer, and the youngest children among the captives began to cry and huddled closer to their mothers.

Katrina had wriggled and twisted, trying to ease the heavy ropes across her body. They were tight above and below her breasts, and rasped her skin when she breathed.

From the group of elderly folk who were pinioned almost at Katrina's feet, a derelict scarecrow of a woman lunged towards Katrina as far as the communal bonds would allow. The old woman's skin sagged and drooped from her bones. She stared up at Katrina.

"Pity's sake, dearie!" Her voice rasped like that of a frog. "Where'd they find you?"

Katrina sighed. "In the woods, old mother." The old woman strained closer. "Soldiers, dearie?" Katrina nodded.

"Then they wouldn't hurry, bringing you in, I shouldn't expect," Her reddened eyes glinted hopefully, and in the best she could do with her voice for a whisper, she said urgently: "Got any food left, dearie? D'they give you any bits of bread?"

Katrina shook her head. Her torn skirt hardly hid her thighs. It could not have concealed much bread. But the mention of food made Katrina realize that she, too, was hungry. It had been a long time since her last bit of food.

"Here comes some officers! Comin' to pick a few girls, I expect. That'll mean you, dearie!" She shouted at Katrina, her voice raucous—a typical market-hawker. Several eyes among the prisoners now regarded Katrina interestedly for the first time, and Katrina's cheeks grew hot. The old women squatted to watch the show.

Torches were coming through the tent lines, held carefully to illuminate the uneven ground for two officers who picked their way fastidiously.

All the unkempt little bivouacs seemed suddenly to become silent. The soldiers stopped their grumbling and occasional snatches of song. The few balalaikas that had been plucking nasal music, were hushed. One of the two approaching officers was Marshal Sheremetiev, stomping awkwardly on bowed legs. His jewelled sword glittered as it clanked against his polished thigh boots. Gold braid winked upon his purple jacket, and a broad silk ribbon of even deeper purple was stretched across his chest. He wore a blue shoulder cape, trimmed with white ermine.

The officer who came with him was tall, gaunt and clumsy. A patch covered one eye. He walked with an obsequious stoop, leaning down absurdly toward the little Marshal.

Marshal Sheremetiev made his unhurried choice among the young girls.

"This!" He pointed sharply toward Katrina with his gold-studded cane. The tall officer, whose badges showed him to be the senior camp doctor, stooped to examine Katrina, with his lumpy red hands.

Katrina's mouth tightened back from her lips. The ropes creaked against the tree bark as she tried to wince away. The doctor straightened himself, and reported. "Untouched, your excellency."

Sheremetiev nodded. "Feed her then." He passed on among the trees.

Katrina, turning her head away from the sight of the old woman's toothless, prurient face, watched the Marshal and his companion continue their search by torchlight. The Marshal was about to pass the tree where Veda was hobbled, when, with quick fingers she undid several of the blue ribbons that fastened her hair, and shook them loose, at the same time straightening herself as far as her bonds would allow, so that her breasts became clearly outlined under the thin silk of her nightgown.

Sheremetiev halted with an amused sneer upon his petulant lips. "That one, also!" he said, and turned abruptly to his tent beneath the flag.

A soldier came immediately and gave Katrina a crust of rough grey bread and a quick mouthful of water from a bulging skin. When the old woman reached up for bread, the soldier kicked her dispassionately. Then he passed on towards Veda, who was combing her hair with her fingers as she waited for the ropes to be untied from her body.

The two girls were thrust into the Marshal's tent, which was ablaze with lights in sharp contrast with the night's darkness outside. There was a carved and polished table covered with maps, dishes and bottles. Ornamental serving stools were loaded with sweetmeats and dried fruits. There were several gilt chairs, very thick in their bases like miniature thrones, and a big bed with a towering feather mattress painstakingly fluffed up, a dozen fine furs laid upon it for night covering.

Marshal Sheremetiev yawned and flung his uniform cap upon the table, where it scattered the maps. At once a servant stooped to retrieve them. The Marshal's uncovered head, Katrina observed, was completely bald, shaped like an egg, and narrowing at the peak. While his servants undressed him, he continued to yawn. The sturdy gilt chair creaked under his weight as the attendants tugged at his long, tight boots.

"Pour me some wine," said Sheremetiev, when satin slippers had been put on his feet. He was bare to the waist now and his body displayed folds of soft, unhealthy flesh that even two years of campaigning had not diminished.

After he had supped two deep draughts of a rich, dark and almost purplish wine, Sheremetiev twisted in his chair and for the first time paid any attention to the two silent girls who stood with a tall, spade-bearded Caspian Infantry soldier behind each.

He surveyed both girls and rasped his chin with plump, jewelled hands thoughtfully.

After a moment, he stumped over towards Katrina and Veda.

"Last night I had no choice," he said, his small alert eyes intent on their bodies, "and tonight I seem to have two toys. But that, of course, is the fortune of war!" He breathed heavily. "Now which is it to be?"

Veda giggled at this, unlike Katrina, who stood watchful and apprehensive. Veda sensed excitement in the night. She felt that she knew, from some guileful wisdom inside herself, how to play this unexpected part. Her regret was that she had been forced to share the moment with a kitchen slut like Katrina.

Too quickly for her guard to stop her, Veda darted towards the startled Marshal. His hand jumped towards his heavy sword, but before he could grasp it, Veda—with a mincing little smile—had reached for his wineglass, and was pouring another drink of wine for the Marshal. She did this very coolly and neatly, without spilling a drop, and proffered the goblet to him with both hands.

"So?" said Sheremetiev interestedly. "A touch of civilization among you barbarians?" He took the wine, then motioned to his servants to finish undressing him. A soft, silk and lace nightgown was slid over his yellow flesh, and a tasselled nightcap put upon his head. He waddled towards the bed, scratching at his hips where the tightness of his uniform breeches had left a welt of irritation.

He lolled and luxuriated for a few moments upon the puffed mattress that sighed with each of his ponderous movements, then raised his hand towards Veda. A servant reached for her but she knocked the man's grasp contemptuously aside and, fluffing out her hair with a haughty little gesture, mounted into the bed and was engulfed among its yielding feathers beside the bulk of Sheremetiev.

"And the other one, your Excellency?" said the senior servant, hesitantly.

Sheremetiev raised himself upon his plump elbow, and grinned thoughtfully. His glance had fallen upon a heavy bullion trunk that stood near his bed. "Open it," he said. The servant carefully undid the big lock and heaved up the trunk's studded lid.

"Put her hair in, and shut the lid down," said Sheremetiev. "Leave the key here on my bed table. Good—now you may extinguish the torches."

Katrina, on hands and knees beside the heavy box, with most of her thick, fair hair imprisoned within its tight-shut lid, tried in the darkness to free herself. The pain made her gasp. After a while, she rested her forehead against the chill metal studs of the box and cried silently in the darkness.

There was a wood stove burning in the tent but in spite of its warmth, as the night went on, Katrina's legs became cold and numb. She could not properly lie down. She heard the servants grunt as they settled down for the night, close to the tent flaps. But Katrina had to crouch, painfully awake. She listened to heavy breathing and subdued, fluttering whimpers from the bed. Veda emitted a little animal moan, and for a while afterwards there was silence. Then the soft scufflings began again, and this time Veda's murmurs and cooings seemed to blend with Sheremetiev's stertorous breathing.

Weariness finally brought an instant of sleep to Katrina—a sleep in which she seemed to be falling nightmarishly, to be halted by her hair, caught in a tree branch! She woke with a little scream at the sharp broken-glass pain of it, and straightened her cramped arms to take the weight from her hair.

She watched the daylight come gradually into the tent. The noises of the camp began faintly outside. Bugles blew distantly, then more closely, and soldiers shouted with hoarse voices that rang in the cold dawn air. From his bed, Marshal Sheremetiev stirred, and cleared his throat. Two servants leapt up alertly from the mats upon which they had lain, and hastened to tend their master.

There was a soft gurgle of wine, and Katrina could smell the maddening warm perfume of new-baked loaves and hot meats. She could hear Veda's voice and Sheremetiev's growl. There was a burst of laughter, and the bed creaked. Katrina saw Sheremetiev's purple silk slippers within the restricted orbit of her vision.

"So!" he said amiably, down at her. "It is morning and you have done no work—yet you wish to be free, hey—" There was a scraping swish, as Marshal Sheremetiev drew his sword from its twinkling scabbard. Veda sat up, tousled in the bed, and craned over exultantly to watch.

"It is my little playmate's idea," said Sheremetiev, "that you shall be freed without any further delay, by my sword." With a swift slash, he whisked the sharply honed blade through Katrina's bunched hair. But sharp as the sword was, the blow jerked her forward, bumped her forehead hard against the metal studs of the box, and tugged viciously at the roots of her hair. The blade thudded into the ground. Katrina fell back. She did not fully realize what he had done, until she put a hand slowly to her head and felt at the cropped tufts. At the sight of her shocked surprise, Veda gave a high peal of mirth, and Sheremetiev laughed thinly.

Katrina sat on her haunches and stared at the mass of fair hair imprisoned in the jamb of the trunk. Her father, when he was alive, had loved her hair, enjoyed to stroke it and cherish the golden growth of it through the years of her childhood.

Now it was gone at the whim of a fat, arrogant old man.

She sprang at him. The expectant servants grabbed her before she could touch him. Sheremetiev backed away, his sword upraised.

"Spread some of the furs," he said. "We'll see if she can be subdued."

Early sunlight slanted through a gap among the tent's skins as Katrina was spreadeagled upon the warm rugs. She threshed, tossing from thigh to thigh. Marshal Sheremetiev, his bulky arms over her, pressed his face to hers—then recoiled with a shrill oath as Katrina ripped open both his fleshy cheeks with her nails.

The two servants, in terror for their own punishment that they had allowed this to occur, pulled Katrina the full width of the tent away from Sheremetiev, and by doing this undoubtedly saved her life, else he would have killed her.

He knelt upon the furs, panting, with blood dark in the grooved scratches upon his cheeks.

With the suddenness typical of his race, his anger passed. "Throw her out," he said. "No use to waste saleable slaves. Put her back with the others."

Some passing soldiers guffawed as Katrina was flung bodily from the Marshal's tent, and sprawled on the frosty earth outside.

All the other prisoners had been grouped into bunches of ten, and shackled by the neck in the standard collar sets used by the Russians for their slave markets. When he saw Katrina, a commissar colonel narrowed his eyes crossly. "What the devil," he said, "am I to do with her?"

Sheremetiev solved the problem by appearing at the flap of his tent, unabashed in his bloodstreaked crumpled nightgown.

"Put her with the freaks, Colonel Kuban," he called. "We have an idea for that one."

The freak pen was an enclosure, ringed by stout, freshly hacked palings, and reserved for the human oddments captured in the sack of Marienburg. It held about eighty inmates. These were the oddities, who commanded the highest prices in the Russian slave sales, where a healthy youth or girl was valued less than two kopeks, but a deformed or demented creature might command five or twenty times this price.

Near to Katrina was a poor creature whom she had often seen in the cobbled streets of Marienburg. He was a hunchback, his face overgrown with hair and his eyes blank with idiocy. There was a delicate little girl with a clubfoot, who sobbed vainly for her mother; and a tall thin lad with wildly staring eyes, whose only vocal sound was a shrill chirrup like a grasshopper. There were a couple of lepers, whose ears and limbs seemed like wax half melting. The Russians had no fear of lepers, and treasured them for their quaintness. All the lame and distorted of Marienburg who had survived the massacre were gathered in the pen. Among them Katrina saw the warty old crone who had spoken the evening previously. She hobbled over and leered up at Katrina, who now saw for the first time that the woman was deformed with a hunched spine.

"So you didn't please him, dearie?" she sniffed, and chuckled. "We'll have to give you lessons, I can see! You've the body for it, dearie." Her crinkled, lascivious little eyes surveyed Katrina. "When you meet a man who interests you, you'll not leave him alone."

A soldier came into the pen, his lips moving slowly as he counted the prisoners. He handed out hunks of the grey, harsh bread, one to each. When he came to Katrina, he halted in front of her and gave a not unfriendly grin. "What are you doing among these?" He did not wait for her answer, but handed her a large hunk of bread.

"Rations for two, girl," he said. He was young, tall and with alert brown eyes. He was a city Russian—a Muscovite.

As soon as the soldier had gone, the old woman snatched at

Katrina's bread, and tugged a large piece of it away. She wolfed part of it, spluttering crumbs angrily. A crust fell on the ground, and as Katrina stooped to pick it up, a large, black and hairy paw covered the bread. The paw had long claws, that clinked upon the icy ground. It was a big black bear, and it scooped up the bread awkwardly.

The old woman backed away, chattering in fear. But the bear made no sudden movement. It stood and regarded Katrina with brown, amber-ringed eyes, and then came slowly nearer to her. She could smell the odour of stale musk about it. The bear squatted in front of her, and held out the piece of bread to Katrina in his scaly, padded paws. She took it, hesitantly, and the bear grunted. She realized that it was tame —a dancing bear, the property of some hapless troubador who had been caught in the siege.

Katrina shared the bread with the bear, pushing small pieces at its expectant, damp snout.

A dwarf came over to watch, with a grin upon his comical face. His broad, rounded back was garbed in bright red velvet, with gilt brocade flapping loose from it, and Katrina at once recognized him.

"Grog!" she said. The dwarf, puzzled, came nearer.

"Ah! You're the little servant girl who unlocked my cage!" His deep voice, booming from his tiny body, was still as surprising to Katrina as the first time she had heard it.

Grog grinned broadly. "I told you—you see—run to the Russians. Everybody gets slaughtered in Marienburg—but not us. We're on our way to the greatest city in the world—Moscow—and the tallest King in the world. . . ." He jigged on stumpy legs, then said: "Oh, saints!" and darted behind the bulk of the bear for hiding place. Marshal Sheremetiev was approaching the freak pen, resplendent in his day's new uniform. And with him, combed, washed, fed and sparklingly fresh, was Veda, haughtily wrapped in one of the Marshal's furred army cloaks.

"Oh, ikons!" muttered Grog, from behind the bear. "Look at her! There's bad luck for us!"

Sheremetiev searched among the creatures in the pen, until he saw Katrina. He minced over to her fastidiously and bent his head to her with ironical courtesy.

"My little playmate has thought of an amusing idea," he

said, and patted Veda's plump legs. "Haven't you, my love?"

Veda smiled brightly back at him. She was cuddled as close to the Marshal as his own bulk would permit.

Two burly soldiers came into the pen, carrying a brazier on metal poles. They set it down, and the elder of the two, a greying-haired and fatherly looking man, looked expectantly at Marshal Sheremetiev.

"That's the girl," said Sheremetiev, his jewelled fingers twinkling in a gesture towards Katrina.

The soldier regarded Katrina, and nodded. "Yes, your Excellency," he said. The soldier reminded Katrina of her dead father. She stared at the brazier, as the soldier thrust a long, thin poker into its red embers.

The heat from the brazier reddened Katrina's face and neck. The soldier took hold of her wrist. Upon his other hand was a thick, padded glove. Veda was grinning, her small white teeth bared intently.

"It's the devil-mark," she chanted excitedly. "The devil-mark, the devil-mark, you're going to be branded!"

Grog dashed suddenly from behind the bear, which had drawn slightly away from the fire. Grog threw himself upon the nearest armourer, and grappled with him, winding his short arms about the man's sturdy legs. The second armourer picked Grog off effortlessly by his red velvet collar.

"Look at Mister Big Ears trying to be a hero," he said. And, pleased with his joke, at which the Marshal laughed, the chief armourer chuckled and tossed Grog onto the ground.

He had not released his grip upon Katrina's wrist. Now he took the poker from the glowing fire, and she could see that it was pale red and almost transparent with heat. Katrina stared fixedly at it.

Sheremetiev pulled out a scented handkerchief, and gave it to Veda.

"Here, my little lovie," he said. "Put this to your nose. The branding iron at work makes a wretched smell!"

Veda took the handkerchief, but her eyes were unblinkingly upon Katrina and the armourer.

"Go on," she whispered, "go on! What are you waiting for?"

The armourer blew upon the branding iron, and studied with a craftsman's satisfaction the tiny yellow stars that sparkled upon its incandescent tip.

"If you will only hold still, girl," he said to Katrina, "we shall do this job without smudging it." He turned her wrist until he had the soft white underflesh of her forearm uppermost and positioned to his liking. Katrina could feel the glowing iron's heat. It stung like frost although it was still several inches from her skin.

"Good craftsman, that fellow," murmured Sheremetiev, almost to himself. Miss Veda's pale blue eyes shone, rigid and entranced, from the furred fringe of his cloak.

The chief armourer stiffened with pleasure at the Marshal's praise, and glanced across the brazier at his assistant with a curt self-satisfied nod.

"Do it!" commanded Veda, urgently, her voice breathless with uncontainable excitement. The elderly armourer smiled at her impatience.

"We must do it right, Missy," he said. "Sharp, clean and sudden, like—so!"

The adroit, hissing jab of the branding iron took barely a second, but Katrina's eyes came almost out of her head at the frozen pain of it. When the armourer steadily withdrew the iron, it seemed to pull with a desperate suction of its own, as though the skin were curling off with it.

"There, Your Excellency," said the chief armourer, stolidly pleased with his work. He showed Katrina's arm, and the puckered, blistered red indent upon it. "Clean as a bit of carved wood that will be, sir—when it's cooled down."

Veda's tiny white teeth were bared, and her small nose quivered appreciatively.

"Poof!" said Sheremetiev, perfumed kerchief to his nose. "Never can endure the tang of it, somehow. Yes—a good job, my man. Now get to the devil back to your guns!"

The instant that the armourer let go her wrist, Katrina pressed the burned part of her forearm tightly to herself, and clutched it for comfort. Grog the dwarf had picked himself up, shaking his head dazedly. He had been flung with full force to the ground. The bear, which had shambled away as soon as it saw the glowing brazier, came loping back now, and stood near to Katrina.

"See, it's the devil-mark, you slut!" said Veda gleefully. "Make her show it to us again!" Sheremetiev, already growing bored, gave a disinterested wave of command, and one of his attendant soldiers pulled Katrina's hand away from her body.

The twin Satanic hooves, the brand mark used by both Russian and Swedish border folk as the universal danger sign—the devil-possessed mark for rogue horses and fever-maddened breeding cattle—was inflamed but clear, printed upon Katrina's arm.

Suddenly Marshal Sheremetiev chuckled. "I say, what an amusing trio—a dwarf, a dancing bear, and a she-devil! Get them shackled together, the three of 'em. They'll make a pretty novelty for the market!"

He watched this joke accomplished. The iron collar that was put around Katrina's neck was still warm from the field smithy. A short and heavy chain linked her to Grog and the bear.

Sheremetiev yawned and turned away. "Good," he said and strangled another yawn. "Slept badly last night thanks to you, my lovie!" His pouting mouth twisted into an almost tender smile for Veda, and she snuggled against him as they walked off together towards the Marshal's coach-sleigh, whose five polished black horses pawed impatiently, their snorts sending white plumes of breath upon the morning air.

When they had gone, Grog rubbed his bruises and looked up doubtfully at the bear. "By the Lord's Supper," he grunted, "we've got a testy travelling companion here, Katrina!"

The bear, being the tallest of the trio, was in the middle.

"He's—I think he'll be all right," Katrina whispered through clenched teeth, pressing the brand blister with her free hand.

Grog turned sympathetic eyes upon it. "Here," he said, "let me bandage it." He tore some of the ragged linen from his little shirt, and bound Katrina's arm. "Keeps the air out, and it'll soon stop stinging," he said.

"You were very brave," said Katrina suddenly.

The dwarf was embarrassed. "I saw the whip bruises upon your shoulders," he said, "and I guessed they were for me." They stood, the three of them, in awkward silence. Without warning, the bear dropped to its haunches. Katrina was tugged down, and Grog with her, as the chains clanked and tightened.

The Russian guards who were coming to herd the prisoners into waiting cattle carts, roared with mirth at this sight.

"Easy to see who's going to be head man of that lot," said one, as tears streamed happily down his eyes. "It'll be the bear, every time!"

"Come on, you three," said the corporal. "You're in luck. You ride with the animals and cripples, now you're a part of the bear." He nodded, happy with his joke. "Now you're part of the bear," he repeated, savouring it, and added: "The others all walk to Pskov!"

"To where?" whispered Katrina, as they were shoved unceremoniously but with surprising good humour by the amused soldiers into the nearest cart, after Grog had prodded the unwilling bear from behind, and Katrina had coaxed him by the heavy chain, in front.

"To Pskov," said Grog, his big voice shaky with the dismay that he strove to conceal. "It's a cattle market town just over the border. We're not to go to Moscow, after all!"

"What difference does that make?"

"It means," said Grog, "that unless there's a miracle, we'll both end up as the slaves of some poverty-stricken boyar, out in the wastelands!"

Chapter Three

THE MORNING AIR was chill, and the mist swirled like grey smoke. The sun had not penetrated through the belt of coniferous trees that encircled the encampment of Sheremetiev's army. Katrina shivered, the pain in her arm still disturbing her.

The triumphant Russian infantry had already moved off and was half a mile ahead, with bugles shrieking and drums thundering. The Cossack cavalry remained in Marienburg among the broken towers and tumbled defences of the surrendered Swedish city.

The Cossacks were delaying themselves to play their favourite sport with several hundred of the surviving women prisoners. They had them pegged prostrate in rows like vegetables in a planted field, across Marienburg's wide and picturesque main square in front of the Cathedral. The cries of the women, many already delirious from thirst and abuses, which were now entering their second day, came faintly upon the wind like the shrill and distant calling of hundreds of marsh birds, as the drums and bugles faded.

Grog eased the heavy chain collar that gripped his neck, and regarded Katrina soberly. "Perhaps we are lucky," he said. "The end of that little game, as the Cossack plays it, is to stage a mass mounted cavalry charge across the bodies, when they have tired of other sports."

"Yes," said Katrina. She bent her shorn blonde head slowly to watch the progress of a brown beetle that was clambering laboriously down the bear's furred flank. "At least we are alive."

"Push back there!" shouted a Russian supply column guard, and lifted his musket to press the cramped occupants of the wooden cart yet more tightly. When he saw the bear, he did not use his musket butt, but said almost mildly: "Shove back there! We need more room on this cart."

"By the Holy Sepulchre," grunted Grog, "have a heart, soldier! There's a dozen souls crammed in this cart already, not counting the bear!"

"Souls!" The soldier grinned, and surveyed the freaks. "Shove back, dwarf, before I make a jam pulp of the lot of you." He made a threatening gesture with his gun butt, but it was the apprehensive, backward lurch of the bear that made the extra space. The bear crushed against Katrina with all the weight of his three hundred pounds.

"Steady, old fellow," she gasped, with difficulty. "Steady, bear!"

The bear turned his solemn amber eyes towards the sound of her voice, and slumped obediently in a great brown mound at her feet, his weight warm against her thighs.

The Russian soldier, having then succeeded in making enough space for two more chained slaves, thrust them in. One was the young clubfoot girl with the white face and wide violet eyes. She was tethered by a short, thick chain to an older woman. The soldier watched thoughtfully as the woman tried to clamber painfully into the cart. He laid a detaining hand upon her. "Old woman," he said curtly, "you bleed!" He pulled the woman's hand away from her body, disclosing the bayonet wound she had been trying to conceal.

"Nah!" said the soldier firmly. With mallet and cold chisel from his belt, he knocked out the shackle pin of the old woman's neck chain

"Off the cart, woman!" he said. "We bring no corpses to Pskov market!"

The long column of heavy carts had begun to move forward. The seemingly endless files of chained, sluggish slaves, trudged beside the carts. The driver cracked his big whip, and his horses lurched, with the others.

The little lame girl began to scream.

"Let me stay! Let me stay with my mother!" she pleaded. The older woman, who had fallen to the ground, watched the carts go. Her face was parchment yellow, and her eyes inscrutable as she crouched upon the ground, watching the cart until it disappeared. Then she walked slowly towards the grey and chilling embers of the night's dead fire.

Most of the vultures who had been circling the encampment since first light, flapped off with the departing column. But several of the birds stayed behind and circled, staring long-necked and hopeful below them at the old woman huddled by the grey ashes.

The little girl did not stop screaming until long after the battered towers of Marienburg had dropped beyond the horizon.

The tall trees of a great forest hung over the mud road now as the carts and trudging column passed. Katrina saw the trees through a mist of hunger that made them waver like shadows under dark water. She did not notice the stench in the cart, nor the groans and sighs that arose as ceaselessly as the creakings of the wooden cartwheels upon their cumbersome axles. She fell forward in a sleep that was more than half a faint, and it was many hours later when she began to awaken. The carts had stopped to give food and water to the horses and prisoners.

They were on an open plain where the snow lay white and uncrimped for rolling miles.

Before she opened her eyes, Katrina remembered where she was, and prepared herself for the nightmare she knew would confront her. The wind was cold around the cart, but she felt strangely warmed and comforted. The whip welts upon her neck and body had ceased to feel aflame. Something was pressing down upon her with a weight that made her shoulder numb. She had been sleeping against the bear, and his big brown paw now claimed her. She opened her eyes. The bear returned her stare liquidly, and watched her with downcast little black mouth agape, its red tongue lolling.

Katrina disentangled herself gently and with care from the bear, and found Grog's pouched eyes staring at her.

"Hungry?" he said. "They came with bread and you were asleep. I saved some for you."

Katrina took the bread gratefully, and rubbed her numb shoulder as she ate. "I feel better," she said. "Nothing hurts quite so much." She touched herself gingerly.

"It's the bear," said Grog. "He's been licking you, as you slept. I tried to stop him, but he went on, as if it comforted him. It might have done you good." He touched her whip bruises.

"I was correct, wasn't I?" he said, hesitantly. "You did get those for me?"

Katrina nodded, and the dwarf's bloodhound-like eyes filled with tears. He rummaged in his velvet pockets. "I didn't eat all my bread," he said. "Please take it."

The carts rumbled on. The sky darkened with impending storm and the wind gathered, stirring the dry snow. Katrina felt comforted by the nearness of Grog and the bear. Big splashes of icy rain drummed upon the open cart and drenched their half-clothed bodies. Katrina held her face to the rain, and gathered precious drops, honey-sweet, upon her tongue. The rain swept down the grey, ragged column like a bead curtain. After the rain, the warmth of the bear was good and Katrina and Grog clung closely to him, though his fur now stank mustily and was spiked with dampness.

It was early nighttime of the next day when the prisoners reached Pskov. Katrina had slept again, and woke with the cart trundling more smoothly upon a trodden road between log huts, from which pale yellow lights shone. The market place was thronged with citizens and soldiers. Tar barrels had been made into great roaring torches, whose flames flared against the night sky.

Soldiers swarmed everywhere like shaggy red bees, around the wine casks and the raucous vendors of meat pasties, honey cakes, and strings of dried, spiced meats. There were dozens of girls among the soldiers, flaunting themselves and chattering, whirling gaily coloured frocks, grinning with flat-nosed, almost square faces, beneath coloured head scarves. Their cheeks were daubed red with beetroot juice and white with clay dust. Soldiers and girls rolled together without diffidence upon the warm ground beside the spluttering tar barrels, bodies pressed urgently into each other. Some were dancing, whirling and stamping and shrieking hilariously, in celebration of the capture of Marienburg.

The ordinary slaves, in groups of ten, had been shackled to the long rows of stone selling posts to wait for daylight. The comparatively valuable freaks, to save them from injury and from being mauled by the drunken mob, were kept chained in their carts. Katrina and Grog climbed as high up the wooden sides of the cart as their thick chains would permit, to glimpse the wild scenes in the square.

"I can smell those meat pasties and honey cakes from here!" growled Grog hungrily. Katrina's eyes were fixed upon the ceaseless rivulet of wine that sparkled out of the nearest barrel, to be caught in dozens of ready, outstretched mugs. The light of flame from the tar barrels flickered through the liquid, and lit it into an amber cascade.

After awhile the bear curled up to sleep, and pulled Katrina and Grog down with it. They lay, listening to the wild shouts and music. The frosty stars had begun to grow pale before the hubbub subsided.

At daylight, they were wakened roughly, and unchained from the cart. Food was given to them, and a little water.

"It's not because they love us. It's so we won't look too hungry when they come to sell us," mumbled the warty old crone, and leered mockingly at Katrina.

"You're a fine one, ain't ye? Wine and soldiers—pretty pasties and kisses—you might have had it hot and strong, last night—but where are you?" she chuckled. "Parcelled up with a dwarf and a bear, guzzling water and a crust!"

"Shut up!" bellowed a soldier suddenly, and stiffened himself like a man about to be seized with an epileptic fit. Muskets banged to the frosty ground, and clumsy, broad-bladed infantry swords rattled against iron cuirasses as the guards scrambled up to their feet, wineskins rolling and gurgling away from them, tousled sleepy girls fleeing beneath the carts.

"My crown in heaven!" said Grog huskily. "It's Marshal Sheremetiev—and Veda!"

Katrina pulled herself up as far as she could, and her movement was so urgent that the bear, alarmed, scrambled to its feet and almost choked Grog as it tugged him up by the chain.

Katrina could see the familiar swaggering figure of Marshal Sheremetiev approaching the cart. Veda was with him, dressed in a pink gown, her thick curls tied with multi-coloured ribbons, and her cheeks stained red like the Russian girls.

But this time, Sheremetiev did not walk with his arm around her, nor was his own gait so pompous as previously. He was struggling alongside a tall officer whose uniform was even more richly resplendent than Sheremetiev's. Katrina caught the furtive, awed mutter of the nearest soldier:

"It's the great Prince Menshikov himself!"

Grog turned his crumpled, excited face up to Katrina. "I've heard of him," he whispered quickly. "He's the great friend of the giant Tsar Peter—used to be a simple pie-boy on the streets of Moscow when he was a lad. He and the Tsar Peter built an army together out of stableboys and gutter brats that won the Tsardom back for Peter! What a man, eh? And what luck for us! He could take us straight to the Palace of the Tsar!"

"But I don't want to go to the Palace of the Tsar," said Katrina, with a little shiver. She had no time to say more, for the three of them—Katrina, Grog, and the bear—were pulled out of the cart, and found themselves being examined quizzically by the tall officer, through a diamond-studded fop's glass, while Sheremetiev beamed proudly, and Veda, preening her curls, fixed her pale blue eyes upon Prince Menshikov.

The bear lurched nervously away from its captors, and swung Grog and Katrina by the chains. Their weights made the bear stumble, and the trio fell to the ground. Katrina sprawled almost at Prince Menshikov's feet, and saw herself, mud-caked and dishevelled, reflected for an instant in the rich gloss of his tall black boots.

It was like the mirrors at the Gluck Manse. She saw her shorn blonde hair, tufted and soiled, her face daubed with mud smears. Soldiers dragged her to her feet.

"There it is, Your Highness!" said Sheremetiev, in high, affected tones. "My little joke, what! A dwarf, a she-devil, and a dancing bear!"

"She-devil?" echoed Prince Menshikov. His voice was rich, warm and half laughing. "Why she-devil?"

Sheremetiev gave an exasperated little squeak. "The bandage," he cried, "the bandage—who permitted her to put a bandage on her arm? Take it off at once!"

Katrina's bandage was removed, and Prince Menshikov surveyed the devil-mark through his quizzing glass. He put it away, and lit an enormous pipe from a jewelled flint-box. Sheremetiev, regarding the pipe as if it were something that might explode, watched in silence for a moment, while Prince Menshikov continued to survey the trio. What the Prince saw was a soiled, half-naked girl, standing proud as a young queen, with green eyes like great foreign jewels, her fair, dirt-caked hair shorn roughly short like a lad's, her fragment of Borodin blouse held almost haughtily across as much of her firm young breasts as it would cover. Her waist was nipped and slender, curving to thighs that were as long as a colt's.

She was shackled by the neck to an untidy bear whose fur was patchy and unkempt, with sores beneath its iron collar, its long black claws curled back guardedly; and a dwarf, garbed in vivid velvet suit, streaked and dirtied, yet whose eyes shone with such a burning eagerness that it caused Prince Menshikov to turn and say:

"But what do they do? Do they dance comically? Or is there merely some bawdy performance among the three?"

Sheremetiev cleared his throat nervously. "It's a—a novelty trio, Your Highness—just like I told you—a dwarf, a she-devil, and a bear!" His laughter was nervous and artificial. He sniffed his scented handkerchief. "It was my little joke, Your Highness—a gift for my little Veda, my little lovie. . . ."

He turned his glance to Miss Veda for support, but she tossed her curls disdainfully and continued to regard Prince Menshikov with yearning intensity.

"I see," said Menshikov, and laughed. "Yes, a good joke, true! Pity they do no little comic act. You must train 'em, Sheremetiev, then they'd fetch you a decent price in Moscow." He turned away, and Sheremetiev turned with him, explaining in a high, ingratiating voice that was clearly audible to Katrina and Grog: ". . . good idea, Highness. But my little Veda pleads with me to give them to her as a plaything. She has many amusing devices for them. . . ."

Katrina and Grog exchanged quick, agonized glances. Suddenly, Grog's deep voice boomed out, with all its surprising power:

"Your Highness—Prince Menshikov, sir!"

The three, Menshikov, Sheremetiev and Veda, whirled round in amazement. A soldier jumped forward and buffeted the dwarf viciously across the mouth. A trickle of blood gushed from Grog's lips, and he spun the length of his chain, then recovered himself unabashed.

"Your Highness—" he began again, and Menshikov gestured that he should be permitted to continue.

"We do a little act, Your Highness!" said Grog, his eyes blazing with desperate eagerness. "It is an act that we want to perform before the great Tsar Peter—but not as three poor, tormented creatures, chained together. We have each an act of our own, Your Highness!"

"You have, eh?" Menshikov took a pull at his pipe. His mouth curled in quiet amusement. "And what is yours, then?"

Grog's answer was to throw back his disproportionately big head and sing with all the power of his huge, miraculous voice. It was a Russian battle song, and its rich music filled the square. Citizens turned, surprised, and stopped their bartering at the slave stalls. Windows opened and faces peered out. People walking nearby began to move nearer to the sound, surprised at the depth of voice and volume of sound that poured so richly from such a tiny and misshapen creature.

When Grog had done, there was a bellow of excitement from the crowd, and through it rose Grog's voice again, with an ancient Russian river chant that hushed his audience to listening silence that lay like snow for long moments after the song finished.

"Please—Your Highness," pleaded Grog, boldly. "I want to sing for the great Tsar! And she—Your Highness, she is not a devil, but a cruelly branded angel, whom even a wild bear loves. Take us to the Tsar, great Prince! Take us to your friend the Tsar!"

"But—" began Sheremetiev, and Veda's blue eyes went cold with contempt at his uncertainty.

Prince Menshikov considered the trio and puffed at his pipe. The dwarf, he decided, could certainly sing, and might amuse the Tsar. Menshikov knew only too well that it was shrewd policy to keep the Tsar amused, for when the Tsar was driven to seeking his own amusements, the sport could be rough indeed!

"Very interesting," he said finally. "You sing well, little fellow. And the bear, no doubt, dances, as bears do. But what of the girl?" He surveyed Katrina with sympathetic amusement. "This fallen, wild-eyed young angel—tell me, what can she do, to amuse the Tsar—or me?"

And suddenly, under his cool, smiling scrutiny, Katrina put both hands across her breasts, and blushed for her lack of covering.

She felt his glance—tangible, almost, and wondered at the strange feeling which overwhelmed her. She turned her eyes down and concentrated her gaze on her cold and muddy feet, yet she did not see them.

Prince Menshikov sucked at his pipe. "Have them conveyed to my palace," he ordered.

"To—to Nyenskans?" asked Sheremetiev, and Menshikov permitted himself a faint smile. "If the Tsar heard you call it anything but Petersburg, my little Marshal, he would sweat the fat off you over a torture brazier. Use my coach for them. I shall be riding with my soldiers." He blew a cloud of smoke thoughtfully over Veda's blonde curls. "Work hard at your bed-making duties, my little one," he murmured. "I am sure my friend the Marshal needs the exercise more than I do!" He turned upon his polished heel and strolled away. Grog watched Veda and the Marshal departing with as much dignity as they could muster, and a grin played around his mouth.

"Phew!" he said. "We're well out of that pickle!" His jubilation grew inside him, and he began to jig, rattling the chains rhythmically, so that the bear remembered its training and shuffled clumsily in tempo.

"Stop, stop!" said Katrina. "This iron collar is sawing my neck off with your antics!"

Still chained together, the bear, dwarf and girl were pushed into a glossy black coach, its doors embossed with fierce crimson two-headed eagles, and drawn by black, satiny horses that shook glitters from their gold and jewelled harness.

The coach door was locked behind the three. "And now we have a new prison," said Katrina, "but a comfortable one!" The yielding leather of the coach seats felt good against her almost naked body, bruised and abrased from the rough wooden floor of the slave cart. She jogged up and down, testing the soft cushions, and ran her fingers curiously over the raised, grotesque figures of the bright yellow tapestries.

I think," said Grog suddenly as the coach moved off, "that Prince Menshikov is likely to teach you a game or two, Miss Katrina."

Katrina blushed. The bear had crouched between the wide seats upon the swaying floor, with paws over its nose, troubled by the swaying motion of the coach. Katrina missed the bear's warmth. Grog leaned over and pulled a glossy ermine rug from the other seat, but as he put the fur over Katrina's shoulders, the bear reared up in sudden wrath. Its great paw, with claws that dangled like four-inch black scimitars, raked at the fur, missed Katrina's flesh by an inch as she shrunk away. "Quiet, bear," she commanded, trying to keep her voice calm. "It's only a bit of dead fur!"

When the bear had sniffed at the ripped ermine, it opened its damp jaws slowly and let the fur drop, then snuffled closer to Katrina, and dribbled upon her shoulder.

"There, now, he begs to be forgiven," said Katrina.

Grog, who had been badly frightened, grunted. "He begs to be shot," he said darkly.

The coach glided on, swaying up the trodden road from Pskov, where the tar barrels were guttering out in the early morning, and the slaves were being marched, shackled and shivering with cold, off to the various farms and boyars' estates of the vicinity. A few picked ones, purchased by Muscovite dealers, were being thrust into wooden carts for the long, cold journey to Moscow.

Grog stared back through the window for as long as he could. "Did you hear the bidding for them?" he said. "Ten women for four kopeks, and strong young Swedish soldiers for two kopeks each!"

Katrina shivered. "That's less than the price of lard candles in Marienburg!" she cautiously picked up the ermine rug and placed it over her shoulders again. The bear growled softly, but this time made no move.

"Life is cheap to the Russians," said Grog. "They say that when Tsar Peter was experimenting with his exploding firepots, he used to throw them among groups of slaves to see how many they would kill!"

Katrina's skin crawled under the warm fur. "The more I

hear of Tsar Peter, the greater my fear of him," she said. "He must be a terrible man!"

"Terrible?" said Grog. "From what they say, he's as tall as a forest tree, and thick as a siege gun! And strong—at a banquet once, they say Tsar Peter grabbed an armful of solid silver bowls and crushed them into a ball, as if they were napkins! When he went to Austria, they say he locked the door at one party he gave, kissed every man, unlaced every woman—and threw the Chancellor of Austria out of a window for being 'insultingly sober!' "

"This is the Tsar you want to sing for?" asked Katrina.

"Aye," said Grog, "for I am only a dwarf, as you know. But I have a giant's voice in my throat—the biggest in the world, and fit to be applauded by the greatest king!"

Katrina smiled softly, her mouth warm with friendliness for the crumpled little man in his soiled red velvet fineries, who sat beside her, his eyes so bright with dreams. "You have a giant's heart, too, dear Grog," she said. "A heart as big as any man I know."

But as the hours passed, and Grog slept, Katrina stared around the big, tapestry-hung coach, and at the particles of dust dancing in the sunlight from the thin windows, and she wept silently for the home that was destroyed, and the trees of her country that she would never see again.

Chapter Four

THE COACH STOPPED outside a low, rambling farmhouse, surrounded by a high wooden palisade, with musketeers on the gate. It was on rising ground overlooking the harbour of Nyenskans, recently captured by the Russians.

All around, the white stumps of chopped trees glistened. Menshikov's soldiers had been busy clearing the territory.

Pigs rested in the disturbed mud of the farmhouse. Dogs yapped at the coach horses, and were driven off by a man and woman who came from the house. The escorting soldiers, who looked like unearthly giants in their voluminous quilted coats, unlocked the coach doors and pulled out the three prisoners.

"Well," said the woman indignantly, "poor creatures!" She examined them in turn. Grog smiled up at her, and got an answering smile for his trouble. The bear was eyeing the dogs uneasily, and giving short coughing grunts, his claws widespread.

The woman from the house clicked her tongue at the sight of Katrina. "Look at her hair!" she exclaimed. "Who cut it off so badly? And she's hardly any clothes—why do you bring them here?"

"His Highness's orders," growled one of the soldiers. "Bought 'em at the sale, he did—or got 'em for nothing, as usual, I expect!" He chuckled, and exchanged winks with the woman's husband.

"Get those chains off them, Olaf," said the woman. "That bear doesn't look safe."

"He's all right," said Katrina quickly. "It's just that the dogs scare him."

The woman smiled. "All right, my dear, we won't harm your bear for you. But you don't want to spend all your life chained to him, do you?"

Olaf brought out a rusty anvil, and began to hammer at the chains. A young boy came from the house to watch. He was dressed all in black, and looked like a starved field crow. His pockets drooped under the weight of religious books, his black breeches were tucked untidily into black stockings, and his shoe buckles were twisted awry. His hair blew lankly around ears which were white and transparent as eggshells, and his face was pale as pearl, with dark hollows beneath each eye.

He peered shortsightedly, neck thrust forward.

"This, I presume, is more of my Royal Father's dastardly work," he said. "May the Saints frown upon his villainies!" His voice was thin and plaintive. He crossed himself and walked back towards the house, the book-crammed skirts of his long coat thwacking at his knees.

"Surely," said Grog to the woman, in whom he had recognized a potential friend, "that is not the Tsar's son?"

She nodded. "Yes, our little Prince Alexis, or 'Saint Alec,' as we call him. More made to be a monk than a monarch's son, he is!"

Katrina watched the boy wonderingly, her eyes puzzled. She pitied the stoop of the lad's shoulders, his bones protruding through the cloth of his coat. He did not look like any prince she had ever imagined.

"Why does he hate his father?" she asked.

"Ah, you may ask, my dear," said the woman, and said no more.

When the chain had been hammered and rasped from Katrina's neck, she felt surprised at the unaccustomed lightness and freedom. "It's like floating on air," she said and the woman Matilda gave her a motherly smile. "Run along into the kitchen, my dear, by the warm stove!"

The bear bellowed mournfully as Katrina went, and started after her. She had to wait, shivering in the cold air, until all the shackles were broken free, before she could seek the stove's warmth. And when the bear followed her into the kitchen, nobody dared to stop him.

With Katrina's help, the bear was tethered in a warm corner of the kitchen, that smelled of new baking and cooking meats. A great gleaming samovar bubbled and hissed upon the clean-scrubbed wooden table.

It was dark in the kitchen except for the firelight. The windows were covered with thick planks that had slits wide enough for the bulky muzzles of Russian muskets, and through which the pale daylight shafted.

"Where's Maria?" said the motherly Matilda. "She's never here when she's wanted."

"She'll be with the coach drivers," said Olaf. "I saw her wheedling them into the barn." He yawned and scratched himself. "I only hope she keeps off the fodder-straw," he said, "for she and the gate guard ruined four bales of it last week!"

"Shame on you!" said Matilda. "Go and fetch her—your own daughter!" She pushed him and Olaf went reluctantly, after stripping a handful of crackling from the spitted pig that roasted over the fire.

When the girl Maria sauntered insolently into the kitchen, she was still fastening the satin ribbons of her bodice, and wisps of straw clung in her rumpled dark hair. She was about the same age as Katrina, but bursting with plump white flesh that bulged and strained inside her dress.

"No use flirting with those chaps, Maria," said Matilda. "They all have fat wives and even fatter families."

"I don't care if they have ten wives," said Maria, and

wriggled her skirt into place. She stared at Katrina. "I see we have company!" She continued to stare, her plump hands on rounded hips.

"Go on off with you!" said Matilda sternly. "Get a dress for this poor child."

"Child?" Maria breathed scorn.

"She's a child compared to you, and your farmyard ways," said Matilda.

"One of my dresses?" demanded Maria sulkily.

"Yes, and hurry!"

Saying no more, Maria disappeared at a pace of insolent leisure, up the dark stone steps.

Matilda stooped to poke at the immense red fire until it crackled and showered a yellow hail of sparks. "Help me, child," she said to Katrina, and together they dragged a small bath in front of the fire and ladled steaming hot water into it.

Maria came back with a green dress that she flung ungraciously upon the table.

"It'll be funny watching you tuck her into that," she said, staring at Katrina's slenderness, outlined against the red fire.

"It's too small for me, or I wouldn't have let you put it on her, whatever you said." She grinned. "You could try padding it with a couple of armfuls of straw!" She gestured with her hands mockingly at her own ample bosom, and went off through the kitchen door back to the barn.

"Come on, child," said Matilda to Katrina. "Off with that skirt and let's see if we can get some dirt from you."

Katrina hesitated, for Olaf and Grog were still in the kitchen. Olaf was turning the spit, and picking bits of browned skin from the pig as it roasted. His eyes were upon Katrina, but quite disinterestedly.

"Unhealthy things, baths," he said, and then with no further concern in the affair, laboriously bent to adjust the spit handle.

Katrina shyly dropped the torn and filthy skirt from herself and stepped into the little bath. It came just to her hips, and the sting of the hot water made her wince. Matilda dipped a wet cloth into a big jar of fats and vegetable ash, and began to spread the creamy, scented lather over Katrina's short hair and mud-stained face. Katrina shut her eyes. She was comforted by the gentle lather and Matilda's motherly touch. Then she detected a whiff of tobacco smoke, and heard the jingle of spurred boots. She blinked her eyes wide, and saw Prince Menshikov, legs apart with his back to the fire, regarding her. He had taken off his jacket, and wore a high-necked silk shirt above his tight uniform breeches. His chest and shoulders were superb, and his brown, thickly curled hair showed only the faintest spattering of grey.

He was puffing at his pipe—the first Russian whom Katrina had ever seen smoking. "Why," he said interestedly, as he regarded her in the bath, "the child has a skin as pink and smooth as an English apple!"

Katrina lowered her gaze while he walked around her, and her eyes shone like great emeralds in the fire's glow. She concentrated on the now dirty water around her thighs. A blush reddened her face, redder than the fire's hot embers.

"But who put those whip marks on her?" he asked, running a finger over the raised sores. "Was it my soldiers? Or that lustful old goat, Sheremetiev?"

"It was my own people," said Katrina shyly. "Your Highness," she added.

Prince Menshikov laid his pipe carefully upon the table, and took the soapy, bubble-sudded cloth from Matilda.

Katrina smelt his tobacco above the odd perfume of the soap as he knelt on the floor and began to squeeze the water from the cloth, letting it cascade over Katrina's shoulders. The soapy water made a white path for its rivulets through the dirt.

He bathed her with surprising tenderness, easing away the caked mud from her shoulders and body to reveal the fair flesh beneath it.

"This gives me almost the same satisfaction as whittling the bark from a tree branch," he said. "The Tsar and I used to sit by the hour when we were boys, peeling sticks with our knives and dreaming of battles." His smile was fresh and pleasant, and he looked at Katrina with kindly eyes. "Up now," he said, "and into this good, warm towel."

He perched himself comfortably upon the edge of the kitchen table, swinging his long, polished boots, and he watched Katrina being helped by Matilda into the green frock, which was so much too large for her, even after Matilda had tied it at the waist with a black velvet girdle from her own tubby waist, that Katrina looked childlike and almost helplessly lost inside it. The frock fell from her shoulders at the smallest movement, and she had to gather the skirt around herself to walk in it.

"I think," said Prince Menshikov quietly, "that you had better come and grace my table when I dine tonight, little she-devil, and this monkey—" he picked Grog up playfully by his red velvet collar—"can come in and sing for us, eh?" Then, with typical, unaccountable Muscovite mischievousness, he dropped Grog into the bath.

"There now, Your Highness," said Matilda, without rancour, "look at the mess you've made on my floor!"

"He needed a bath I expect, as much as she did," said Menshikov, "but I'm damned if I'm going to play lady's maid to a dwarf." He put his arm around Katrina's slender waist, and bent her towards him, his face close to hers, his shrewd grey eyes smiling into her startled, slanted ones. "You, I think, can look after my personal laundry from now on," he said, "and make my bed for me."

Grog, little showman that he was, recovered from the shock of his plunge into hot, soapy water and, seated in the bath, began to roar out a boatsman's merry song.

Menshikov slowly released Katrina and listened with a smile on his face. When Grog had done, the Prince nodded. "Yes, dwarf," he said, "I think the Tsar is going to be amused by you."

The dining table that evening was set in one of the main rooms, before a roaring fire, with gleaming silver and glass, and cutlery that sparkled. Katrina, having tugged at her damp, short hair with a borrowed comb, and put her feet into a pair of the resentful Maria's shoes, which were much too big, entered timidly, uncertain of her new position.

Prince Menshikov was not there. But the Tsar's son, Prince Alexis, was hunched near to the fire upon a plain wooden stool, his lips stirring over a book. He did not look up as Katrina came in.

She coughed, and Alexis looked up sulkily. "So," he said, "you are one of my father's victims?"

"I suppose so," said Katrina, who did not quite know what to say.

"My father," said Prince Alexis, "is a villain. He is one of the damned of hell. The Evil One"—he crossed himself—"has stolen my father's soul. All this, my saintly mother has told me, from my cradle days." He blinked his crusted red eyes at her. "And this Menshikov," he said, "is one of his unhappy dupes, who had sold his soul, as my father did."

Katrina felt a cold wind of fear at the venom in the lad's thin voice.

"Is your mother still alive?" she asked. The boy nodded, and threw a quick glance around. "My saintly mother is kept prisoner under daily torment," he whispered. "Her sin was to love God and the Saints more than the Evil One. I pray for the day when my father shall imprison me, too, so that I also may hope for my crown of glory in paradise!" He crossed himself again, and leapt like a startled animal as Prince Menshikov came suddenly into the big room, filling it with his commanding presence.

"What!" said Menshikov. "Still bent over your books, my young friend?" His voice was not unkindly, but with a hint of mockery. "You will make your eyes sore. Come, let's have one jolly evening. This is surely not another saint's day? Be so good as to pour Katrina a glass of wine."

Prince Alexis stood as haughtily as his hunched young body would permit.

"This is a day of fasting and sorrow," he said shrilly, "and if in your ignorance, sir, you do not know which, then I shall not enlighten your heathenish darkness. But tonight food and wine shall not pass my lips." He bowed clumsily, picked up his heavy book, and was gone.

"The poor young gentleman," said Katrina. "Will he really fast tonight?" she had eaten hot soup, meat and bread in the kitchen, but was still hungry.

Prince Menshikov laughed. "Yes, he'll fast—until the servants are in bed. Then he'll scurry into the kitchen like a nasty little black cockroach, and stuff his mouth with all the food he can steal."

"But is it true what he said about his father—the Tsar?" asked Katrina.

Menshikov frowned. "In Russia, we do not question the Tsar," he said abruptly, and Katrina's stomach went cold with misgiving.

There was a brief, awkward silence broken by Olaf, who came staggering into the candlelit dining alcove with a steaming tureen of nettle, sorrel and cabbage soup, stiffened by red wine and meat juices. His wide thumb was firmly plunged in it.

"Careful, Your Highness," he gasped, as he banged the tureen down. "Nearly taken the skin off my hand!"

Prince Menshikov chuckled, and moved towards the polished refectory table, whilst Katrina stood, uncertain, her small nostrils twitching hungrily. He picked up one of the heavy dining chairs and placed it for her. Katrina caught a whiff of scented wine upon his breath, as he bowed, with a little, half-mocking smile. She seated herself shyly, but with a simple dignity that Prince Menshikov did not miss, and stared at the soup, and the accompanying dish of hot egg paté.

"Some wine?" said Menshikov. He spilled out a generous gobletful of sparkling hydromel wine that smelled of pine resin and honey, and tasted of flowers. Katrina's senses swam with its headiness as she sipped it. She hesitantly followed the example of the Prince, and smeared a heap of black, oily caviar onto hot buttered toast to munch while the soup was being removed and replaced by a silver dish of raw salmon, seasoned with oils, salts and vinegar.

Menshikov stuffed a large piece into his mouth. So did Katrina.

"Good, eh?" said the Prince, through crammed lips. Katrina nodded, her heart thudding with the excitement of being near to him. She felt his eyes dwelling amusedly upon her, and hitched up the green dress that would persist in falling below her shoulders.

Matilda came in with another dish. "Sterlet fish, Your Highness," she announced proudly, and Menshikov rubbed his hands. "Wonderful, wonderful!" he said. Katrina watched, her green eyes widening at the magical sight of the sterlet. She knew that each of these plump, rare and succulent fish was worth a peasant's yearly wages. Only the nobility could afford them.

Matilda had boiled the fish, and the water shone like liquid gold, sparkling in the candleshine. She placed the dish down and gave Katrina a kindly glance of encouragement.

Prince Menshikov slopped another great draught of fizzing wine into Katrina's goblet, and as she sipped it the intricate pattern around the wide bowl seemed slightly hazy now. She felt her shyness receding.

She laughed. "This fish tastes like clover grass," she said, and Prince Menshikov gave her a quick smile. "Ah—so you've found your tongue, eh?"

They ate then a heaped plateful of suckling pig in curdled cream, and Katrina, wiping the juice from her chin, hoped that Grog in the kitchen would be enjoying some of it, too.

"What did you say?" demanded Menshikov, and Katrina realized that she must have spoken her thoughts half aloud.

"I said—at least, I didn't say—I wondered, if Grog was having good food like this?"

"Grog—ah, the dwarf!" Prince Menshikov snapped his fingers, and a waiting manservant came out of the shadows. "Fetch up the dwarf from the kitchen—the singing dwarf." Menshikov nodded amiably at Katrina. "He shall sing for us, my little she-devil, though I must say you look interestingly angelic with your dress almost to your waist."

Katrina noticed that the frock had slipped again. She adjusted it upon her shoulders, and giggled, no longer with any feeling of embarrassment. She took another deep drink of the bright, resin-scented wine, and fondled her goblet as Olaf came in with a huge platter of roast kid and salt-cucumber dressing.

The Prince, his appetite blunted, began to draw Katrina out with shrewd, amused and friendly questions while they ate their kid and cucumber. The hot food, the perfumed wine, the roaring log fire, made Katrina's cheeks glow pink, and her eyes shone bright as jade against the candles. Grog came in, manfully drank his beaker of wine, winked at Katrina from one of his pouched eyes, and rubbed his fat little belly as a sign that he, too, had eaten well.

He sang them love songs, soul-stirring little melodies that made Katrina feel an almost overwhelming urge to cry, not in sorrow, but in a kind of sentimental happiness that was a new sensation to her. She did not know that she was nearly drunk.

Grog had obtained a balalaika, and he strummed the angular instrument delicately with his stubby fingers. Music was an art that flowed through Grog and overcame even the handicap of his stumpy hands. His songs, and the music, were a strangely disquieting mixture.

Katrina and Menshikov listened, nibbled apple bread and wild honeycombs, and shook their heads regretfully at the heaped plateful of hot, buttered blini pancakes that Matilda proffered as finale to the repast.

Grog finished a song, and while he refreshed himself from his refilled beaker of wine, Prince Menshikov nodded amiably at Katrina. "You eat well, girl," he said approvingly. "Almost like a man. I like to see that." He chuckled. "I'll wager that fat fool Sherémetiev didn't feed you."

Katrina shook her cropped, fair head. "Only black bread and water."

"No wonder you look like a hare that's run itself skinny. You should see how we eat in Moscow—this was just a tooth-filler," said the Prince, and lit his pipe with a contented belch.

When Grog had sung enough, Prince Menshikov fumbled at his pocket, and tossed him three or four gold coins. "Now, lad," he said, "fetch candles, and let us to our bed." He looked across at Katrina, who was flushed and drowsy with her good dinner.

"Come, my little she-devil," he said. "I shall not give you our Russian wish, that sleep shall come to you as soon as the candlelight goes, for tonight I do not expect that it will." He chuckled. "Indeed, I shall personally see to it that it does not!" He took her small hand and led her up the stairs behind Grog and the dancing shadows of the candelabra that the dwarf carried.

The rich wine covered Katrina's senses like a luxuriant cloak. She staggered slightly and Menshikov slipped his arm around her.

The bedroom was almost bare. It contained a bed, a dark oak dresser near the barricaded windows, and a table with dispatches spread upon it, a carafe of wine, and a tobacco box. Prince Menshikov's various resplendent uniforms hung upon nails around the untapestried wooden walls.

Grog jumped upon a stool to reach the twin candles that were placed in high brackets over the bed's two huge pillows. The candles had snuffers over them, worked by thin silver chains.

Menshikov drew the thick velvet curtains on three sides of the bed, unstrapped his glistening black boots and the ornately jewelled belt that held his dress dagger. He gently removed the shoes from Katrina's feet and took off the black velvet girdle from her waist. He had to stoop to the ground to reach the hem of her green gown, and as he drew it up beyond her white shoulders, Katrina's arms slipped limply from the over-large sleeves, and fell about Menshikov's neck.

He climbed into the big, yielding bed over her body and pulled her with him. Katrina's half-shut eyes shone green but unseeing in the candlelight. She gave a bewildered, lost little sigh at the cool touch of the silk coverlet.

Her mouth parted for his kiss. Menshikov turned and drew the fourth curtain, but one of Katrina's tiny, white feet was still visible, protruding beneath it.

Grog saw the muffled gleam of the two candles through the dark wine-red velvet curtains. He saw Katrina's slender naked foot arch and the toes clench and curl like fingers of a small fist. Grog rubbed his nose thoughtfully, and with a sigh that was partly contentment, and partly envy, he hopped off down the wide, curved stairway towards the warmth and companionship of the kitchen.

Katrina awoke late, and stretched contentedly in the warmth of the feather bed. She had never slept in a proper bed before. She felt at the feathers under the thin red leather mattress cover, and moulded them with her hands, tranquilly as a kitten pawing at its cushion. Inside the heavily curtained four-poster bed, the air was motionless and warm. Daylight filtered in, taking colour from the rich wine curtains, and filling the cavern of the bed with a rosy twilight.

Katrina remembered the adventures of the night as a dim unreality, misted by wine. She yawned and smiled. Love, if it were no more than this, did not seem to be much to make a fuss about. Yet it was pleasant, like wind in the forest when the sun was up, and sleepy contentment that came with hot food, or the ache in one's stomach after much laughter. It had been all these sensations intermingled, with—somehow—velvety wings of fear beating over it all, the delicious ecstasies that come with a dangerous pastime, like climbing high among slender treetops as they rocked in a boisterous wind.

Prince Menshikov had left the bed, and the deep hollow where he had lain was still warm. Katrina stretched her hand across to it and explored the place with a smile of half-tenderness curving her mouth.

The bedcurtains stirred and billowed. Somebody had opened the door. Katrina blinked awake, and tugged quickly at the silk coverlet to hide her naked breasts.

"Morning, little Katrina!" It was Prince Menshikov. He pulled back the bedcurtains and sat on the bed close to her. The mattress sagged to his weight. His tight breeches were moulded about his long thighs like a cream-coloured skin. Katrina felt pleasantly disturbed at his nearness. She noticed again how his hair, slightly wisped with grey, curled over the high collar of his uniform.

A great Cossack officer, almost inhumanly tall and sturdy, stamped into the room after Prince Menshikov. He had to stoop to let his wide bulk and tall hat through the door. His thick arms encircled a bundle of colourful materials. He wore baggy trousers of finest damask, tucked into red leather boots with silver filigree embroiderings and solid silver heels that jingled as he walked.

"See," said Menshikov. "I have a few little nonsenses for you." He indicated the Cossack with a smile. "Sten'ka and I rode out early this morning to the Cossack encampment and took our pick of the loot."

Katrina looked into the eyes of the Cossack, that peered through the downswept bush of his black brows, unblinking and inhuman as a hawk's, yet incongruously childlike in their clarity of health. His voice when he spoke seemed too rich and too thick, a kind of honeyed growl from the depths of his dark beard.

"Aye, some rich Swedish wench will never know what body her gowns finished upon!" He ran his tongue around his bristled lips, as though the words evoked disturbances within himself. His gaze never wavering from Katrina, he dropped the armload of garments on to the bed across her legs in a cascade of rich colours and perfumed, soft fur.

Katrina put out a hand to touch them, smiling with delight at the delicate textures that seemed to melt under her fingers.

"These—for me?" Her voice was small and overwhelmed.

"For nobody else!" Menshikov laughed. His swinging foot found the borrowed green dress that had fallen unwanted to the floor the previous night. He flicked it across the room to Grog the dwarf, who had followed them, grinning amiably, into the bedroom.

"Take that back to the kitchen wench, dwarf!"

Grog was enveloped in the green frock. He made a comic struggle of it, pretending to have difficulty in extricating himself. The Cossack watched stonily for a slow instant then threw back his great head and shook the room with his guffaws. Prince Menshikov chuckled softly, and Katrina's clear laughter joined in at the sight of the dwarf's shrewdly humorous antics.

Menshikov sorted among the fine garments on the bed and picked up a gown of ivory-hued Paduasoy silk, so delicate that it was almost gossamer. Its low neck and cuffs were edged with snowy ermine.

"For tonight," he said. "It will be almost as soft as your own skin, to sleep in."

"That—in bed!" Katrina faltered, amazed at the idea, and an excited smile lingered around her mouth. Never since she could remember had there been new clothes for her. She had gone rarely with her mother to the street stalls of Marienburg, to sort among heaps of musty and soiled clothes, and to barter copper coins for them, after an hour's weary chaffering.

"Up with you, and let's see if anything fits!" Prince Menshikov broke into her thoughts. He tossed down the thin silk gown and rummaged among the other garments. There must have been twenty or thirty of them.

Katrina did not move. She looked around the room, at Menshikov, Grog and the huge Cossack. Prince Menshikov saw the glance. "Oh, they'll not mind—they'll enjoy watching!" he said. "Big Sten'ka helped me get these things. We had to slap a few stubborn Cossack skulls to persuade 'em to part with their loot, believe me!"

Katrina slid her legs over the edge of the bed cautiously and reached for the nearest dress, but Menshikov picked her out from the coverlets. "Ah, why hide such beauty?" he laughed, and held her to him.

Her skin looked white against the vivid colours of his uniform. The bed had been warm, but now, as she sensed the cold buckles of his belt and sword trappings, she shivered, and Menshikov thrust one of the petticoats over her tousled head.

The first gown was of deep red velvet, and Katrina's mouth drooped with disappointment, for it seemed even bigger than the green frock she had borrowed from Maria the kitchen girl.

Prince Menshikov spun her round and looped the fastenings which pulled it tight from shoulders to waist, so tightly that her bosom arched almost out of the low neckline.

"Fetch that mirror, Sten'ka," roared Menshikov at the big Cossack. Whenever he gave an order to Sten'ka the Prince seemed to bellow at the top of his voice, as if he felt privately that his own authority was not enough without the added weight of a thunderclap. Sten'ka grunted and departed, to return with a heavy and ornately gilded mirror. As Katrina stood poised before it, the big Cossack dug into his tunic pocket, and passed a glitteringly jewelled necklace to Menshikov. "I was saving it for one of my own," he said in his growling voice. "But it seems not fitting for a man to watch a pretty neck go bare of a few paltry gems."

Menshikov took the necklace, that shone with priceless rubies and gold links. "If I know a Cossack, you have plenty more of those in your pocket," he laughed. But his lips were set a little sulkily as he pressed the clasp, and fitted the jewels upon Katrina's neck.

The Cossack grinned and made a sucking noise through his teeth, but Katrina could see only the reflection of herself, for the second time in her life, in a mirror. But now she was not dirty-faced and in soiled peasant skirt. She stood straight, slender and tall, her fair, shorn hair softening into waves, her long white neck proudly arched. The red jewels shimmered, and the red velvet gown rippled and whispered royally as she moved. She raised her arms, regarding the long sleeves that tapered down to her wrists, and was fascinated by the reflected echo of her own movements. She ran her fingers down the luxurious pile of the velvet, that lay tight across her body.

"The latest from Paris," said Prince Menshikov. "I don't suppose you know where Paris is, my child." His manner indicated that he didn't suppose Sten'ka knew where Paris was, either. Sten'ka grunted, and when, an instant later, Prince Menshikov roared the big Cossack officer had better get back to his men, Sten'ka went obediently enough, but his eyes lingered upon Katrina, and though they were merciless eyes there was nothing cold in their departing glance.

The rest of that day passed tranquilly for Katrina. She felt beautiful in her new dress that hugged her with incredible warmth and softness and seemed to make her taller. She had brushed her thick short hair until it shone in soft and feminine curls on the top of her head. After supper with Menshikov—a meal as succulent and massive as the previous night—they lay in the large bed with curtains enclosing them in a thick, warm darkness. Prince Menshikov had just snuffed the candles, and the acrid smell of the smouldering wick still lingered. A sudden blaze of light disturbed them, as a soldier crept into the bedchamber, his boots and equipment harness creaking awkwardly.

"You Highness!" he whispered, nervous of his task. He stood away from the bed. "Your Highness. . . ."

"What is it?" Menshikov's annoyed face peered through the curtains.

"I have messages, important messages from the Tsar, Your Highness."

Katrina was startled at the suddenness with which Menshikov jumped from the bed. His entire face and manner had changed.

Katrina could not hear what was said, but only the faint hiss of whispers. After a while came a sound she knew—the click of Menshikov's sword against its buckles.

The room was dark again as the door closed behind the Prince and the soldier. Menshikov had not spoken a word of farewell to her.

Katrina lay alone, and wakeful. The bed was warm around her, but her skin stirred with a strange chill. She wondered why she felt suddenly afraid.

Her fear was not explained by any sounds or voices. The house was silent, except for the occasional scurry of animals between the floorboards, and the continuous ticking of the ancient woodwork. In the darkness she crossed herself, and uttered a whispered prayer for herself.

She meant to stay awake until Prince Menshikov returned, but the wine and warm food made her drowsy. After a few confused thoughts, she was asleep.

Grog the dwarf listened from the small adjoining room, where the thirty dresses that Katrina had so recently acquired were hung from freshly made pegs along the walls. Grog had made his own bed in this closet upon a heap of cushions and discarded furs. He wanted to be near Katrina, and was prepared to take the risk of Prince Menshikov's possible wrath at finding him there.

When he heard Katrina's breathing become regular with sleep, Grog crept through the main bedroom and into the corridor. He, too, was perturbed at the Prince's sudden departure. He would not be able to sleep until he had solved this new problem. He prowled furtively, grotesque and tiny among the shadows of the corridor lanthorns, towards the kitchen, where he could hear voices. A soldier sat straddle-legged across a bench at the kitchen table when Grog opened the door. Foam flecks from a hard-ridden horse streaked the soldier's quilted scarlet tunic, and mud splashes mottled his face. He wore the uniform of a sergeant in the Tsar's Guard, and quaffed a tankard of steaming hot wine thirstily, one big hand wary upon a leather dispatch wallet.

"Have you heard the news?" Matilda greeted Grog, and nodded towards the soldier. "He brings dispatches from the Tsar for Prince Menshikov. A whole flotilla of Swedish war-ships is heading under full sail for Petersburg harbour, and the Tsar himself is riding here full speed to command the defenses!"

She lowered her voice confidentially, so that the soldier could not hear. "Dwarf," she said, "I fear for that poor child up-stairs. Tsar Peter is a terrible thunderstorm of a man—he takes his pleasures cruelly."

"But surely," said Grog uncertainly, "Katrina belongs to Prince Menshikov?"

Matilda sighed. "Prince Menshikov never knew his mother," she said. "He was a street urchin in Moscow. Yet if he found his mother tomorrow, he would roast her like a sausage on a skewer, and with no more compunction, did he think it would bring one smile to the Tsar's face. So if the Tsar wants Katrina," said Matilda, "he will take her. Poor child, for the Tsar has broken such pretty toys, and will break many more, I fear!"

Grog stared at her, his wrinkled eyes troubled. "When does the Tsar arrive?" he asked.

"Tomorrow," Matilda said. "Tomorrow."

Chapter Five

NEXT MORNING Katrina blinked awake to find the dwarf's comical face grinning at her amiably through the bed-curtains.

"I have brought you a bowl of hot buckwheat gruel," he sniffed greedily at the body-warmed air of the bed, and as Katrina ate from the bowl, Grog pulled himself up, curled at her feet, and waved his short, thick little limbs sensually.

"By the Scriptures," he said, "this is soft! I never had such a bed!" Katrina, busily eating, made a murmur of sympathy. "Man that I am," declared the little dwarf solemnly, "I'd almost allow to become a beautiful girl for the pleasures of such a bed!" He added: "I finished my sleep last night upon the kitchen floor. And the bear, you will be pleased to hear, still snores, still dribbles in his sleep!"

Katrina laughed. The discomforts of the slave cart that had brought them chained from Marienburg seemed far away. She scraped the dish. "I dreamed that I could hear cannons firing," she said, wiping her mouth upon the silk bedcover.

"Oh, by the True Fragments! I forget to tell you the news. Come to the window and you shall see such a sight!"

"You must turn away," said Katrina. The dwarf grinned and held his fingers before his eyes with mischievous chinks between, while Katrina slipped from her nightgown, wriggled into an icy cold dress of yellow French brocade and ran barefoot to the barricaded window. Grog dragged a stool for her to stand on, so she could see through the musket slits.

In the dancing sunshine upon the cold grey water of the Neva River, were three longboats, flying the blue and yellow flags of Sweden.

"But—they're our ships!" gasped Katrina. "Don't they know the Russian soldiers are here?"

"Aye," said Grog, "they know, all right. And they know the Russians have no ships at all to reach them. There are four Swedish vessels of war anchored to the river mouth. They sent three rowing parties past the shore batteries before daylight, to spy out the Russian defences here, and there they sit now, waiting for darkness to get back and report. Oh, my Household

Ikons, the Russians are hopping mad at it—your Prince Menshikov is like a man gone crazy!"

"Was it real gunfire I heard, then?" Katrina asked. Grog nodded.

"First daylight, the soldiers had a shot or two at 'em—but they're yards out of range. Oh, the great Tsar Peter was here himself—what a sight, Katrina—what a terrifying mountain of a man!"

Katrina had gone white. "He was here?" she whispered. "Here in this house?"

The dwarf nodded. "What a horrible thunderstorm of a fellow—I tell you. He's higher than—than this room!" He waved his arms in an agony of inability to show the size of the Tsar. "Dressed like a common sailor, with his face all twitched up and evil. It's no wonder your Prince Alexis is terrified!"

"Oh, the poor young Prince," said Katrina, able to spare a moment's sympathy for the boy whose fear of the Tsar was greater even than her own.

Grog laughed. "He sped out from the house with an armload of prayer books, the minute he heard the Tsar was on his way here. He's barricaded himself in the little shrine of St. Catherine, and won't come out!"

"Where is the Tsar now?" asked Katrina apprehensively.

"Gone with Prince Menshikov and some other officers to see what he can do about those Swedish boats," said Grog. "Though what they can do, I can't imagine."

There were footsteps on the creaking stairs, and a moment later Matilda pushed the bedroom door open with her comfortable buttocks. She came backwards into the room, her arms laden with clean covers for the bed. She stripped the mattress and began tossing it. Katrina moved to help her. As they worked together, Matilda said: "You must stay out of the Tsar's way, child. He has cruel moods and jests—especially with young girls. And today there's an evil temper in this house, for the Tsar's mad angry at those Swedish boats out there, right under his nose, and the Swedish warships outside the harbour."

"What might the Tsar do to me?" asked Katrina.

Matilda shook her greying head. "You just keep yourself out of the way until he's gone—and you, too, dwarf, is my advice," she said to Grog. "For the Tsar has his good moods, but today isn't one of 'em, you can take my word! He'll as soon fling you on the fire as listen to your singing, my little chap." She gathered up the discarded bedcovers, and paused at the door. "He robbed my little Maria of all sense of shame before she was twelve years old," she said, "and if you go in the kitchen, you'll see the results of another of the Tsar's jests." She blew her nose tearfully upon the bundle of bedclothing in her arms.

When Matilda had gone, there was a long silence. Grog and Katrina looked at each other in dismay.

"What has the Tsar done in the kitchen?" asked Katrina. Grog shrugged blankly. "I haven't been back there," he said, "since the Tsar and his soldiers came into it. But she's right that you must hide from him, Katrina. He's left the house now, it's true, but the kitchen is still filled with his men. And if you go down in that dress—"

"It's too tight," said Katrina uncomfortably. "What can I do? If I can't go into the kitchen, where can I go? I daren't stay up here, nor in the dining room, as they call it."

Grog blinked at her. Her fair, cropped hair shone in the slant of daylight from the window loopholes.

"Why not dress in some of Prince Alexis' clothes?" he said suddenly. "You'd pass as a boy in the gloom of the kitchen, if you kept your mouth shut and stayed in a dark corner."

The bedroom of Prince Alexis was like a monastic cell, its only furnishing a wooden trestle bed. An ikon with two guttering dried fish lights made the only splash of colour on the empty walls. Katrina crossed herself before it. Grog was rummaging in a cupboard amongst Alexis' meagre clothes and the tarnished uniforms he had never worn. One was a Dutch style sailor suit, its black shoulders green with age and disuse. It smelt dead and musty.

"Try this," said Grog, pulling it from the closet. "You can bet the Prince'll never miss this one. It's too much like his father's!"

"Watch the door, that nobody comes," said Katrina. She slipped from the yellow gown, and shivered into the knee-length, rough blue breeches, the shirt and long black jacket. "How do I look?" she asked Grog, for there was no mirror.

Grog came back from the door. "The breeches are too tight," he said critically. "They were made for the Prince's thin shanks.

And they're too slack around your waist, Katrina, you'll have to lap them over, and I'll find you a belt." He walked around her. "The jacket fits passably well," he said. "But the only footwear that seems to go with that lot are these tall boots—they look seamanlike."

Katrina struggled into the boots that, like the breeches, had been made for bony legs. They came well up to her thighs. Grog surveyed the final result.

"Doesn't look quite right," he said. "Sailors wear a short frock tunic, too. You'll have to keep your coat buttoned."

The kitchen was lit by blazing firelight, and two or three flaming lathes stuck into the walls. The air was thick with smoke and it was at first difficult to see across the room. The windows were still barricaded.

About two dozen of the Tsar's guard were crowded around the big table, scrambling each with a spoon for the best pieces from a huge, steaming trough of pork and partridges, chopped turnips and peas boiled in their shells. The men's eyes sparkled in the half darkness, and their unkempt black hair dangled into the trough. Two or three dogs growled under the table or yelped in sudden anguish when a heedless boot crushed their paws. In the rafters of the ceiling, a cockerel perched and crowed.

Olaf sat by the fire, his cheeks blazing red from heat. Sweat shone upon his nose. He had his rag-wrapped foot upon the neck of a live goose, and was methodically plucking it, as the creature squawked and stirred feebly. At the table the soldiers munched and cursed, the hot stew scalding the fingers that they plunged ceaselessly into the trough to assist their battling spoons.

Grog and Katrina crept into a shadowy corner, beyond the fiercest glare of the fire, and stared at the green tunics and busy red sleeves of the soldiers, whose crimson cloaks were flung back. Firelight gleamed upon their accoutrement buckles. Nobody paid heed to the torments of the goose, for it was a common enough Russian habit to pluck geese while they were still alive. Then Grog heard Katrina draw her breath sharply.

"Grog!" she said. "What happened to the bear?" She ran across the kitchen, towards where the bear lay in the corner, shapeless and without stirring. Its underjaw had been ripped away, and the bear was dead.

lieutenant. "Get on this ship—we're
"Ship!" echoed Van Zee contem
barge a ship!" But he and the oth
on board the almost flat-bottomed
with wood splinters. Half a dozen
oars to roughly made rowlock posts.
Van Zee still held Katrina by the e
"You can come and row betwee
said, "an' when we get back—if we
little talk, eh?" He hustled Katrina
prow of the barge.
"But I—I can't—" began Katr
unreal with fear.
The two sailors chuckled. "Ye
eyed man. "Then we'll have to teac
turns of a piece of thin, tarred ro
wrists to the oar shaft. "So ye won't
his slack mouth close to her cheek.
The barge swung out into the riv
downstream, with oars creaking lab
squatted silent and expressionless upo
muskets carefully held. The light was
faces were an invisible blur.
Katrina had to sway backwards a
sweep oar as it moved, and the two sa
close to hers on each side. They exch
cant remarks, enjoying the joke.
The twilight turned to darkness as
gainly craft crept, wallowing and c
shallows, bumping into little floes and
brushing against the river's frozen reed
Far down, towards the river's mout
ships were now discernible as blurred
shrilled faintly, signal cannon spoke in t
knew her countrymen were dipping
flags to the oncoming of night. She sh
out success to shrink away from the r
her over the toiling oar.
From barge to barge, quietly-spok
among the Russian officers, and soon
were disposed, half hidden among the

Katrina's quick dash to the bear had attracted Olaf's glance. He looked up from his writhing goose with a slow grin. He did not recognize Katrina.

"His Majesty done that, lad," he said. "Just after the news come of them Swede ships in the river. Old bear growls at the Tsar, and the Tsar shouts he won't take insolence from beasts as well as Swedes. An' he does the bear with his hands—just like that!"

Katrina stared with horror. She knelt beside the dead animal. "Oh, bear," she said, softly, "poor, poor bear!"

The door burst open. Two men, an officer and a corporal, hurried into the kitchen, bellowing and thwacking with their gloved fists at the soldiers around the table.

"Out of it, lads!" said the officer. "Get down to the river-bank—Sergeant Peter wants you!"

The soldiers dropped their food at once, and tugged their uniforms into tidiness as they hurried to follow the officer. "Sergeant Peter is the name the soldiers call the Tsar," whispered Grog. Katrina wasn't listening. "Grog," she said, "I'm afraid to stay in this house. This Tsar Peter is a devil!"

The officer saw them, now that the kitchen had emptied. "What, lad!" he shouted. "A sailor? Get down to the river—there's work for you!" He gave Katrina an amiable buffet upon the shoulder that sent her falling towards the door. The officer paused for a second glance at Grog, grinned, booted Katrina outside, and strode purposefully after his men. "Look after this sailor lad," he bellowed. "We can use him at the quay." The soldiers nodded, and thrust Katrina into their ranks. She gave an agonized backward glance, then was pushed roughly forward as the column marched off.

The day's brief light was already beginning to fade. Grog called after Katrina, but thought it best not to pursue her.

The tiny quayside was thronged with the Tsar's soldiers, all men of durable physique and wild, unkempt visages, but with a discipline that Katrina had not previously seen among the Russians. They stood watchful and alert, their faces turned towards a tall officer whom Katrina recognized with a quick excitement as Prince Menshikov.

"Men," shouted Menshikov, against the rising wind, "the Tsar wants you to take axes and chop our grain barges down

to the water line—quick as y
superstructures off 'em!"

The soldiers set to work on
barges in which the fodder anc
river. Many of the barges ha
into roughly shaped troop
musketeers, even with cuirassed

Axe blows rang upon the
splinters flew. The soldiers wo
grins upon their dirty, short-bea

Anything that "Sergeant Pe
right with the men of the Preobr

Two sailors, waiting their tu
craft ready, saw Katrina and la

"Come here, lad," said one w
origin. "You can handle a ba
took Katrina's ear between fing
her face. His scalp had been cl
greased pigtail that hung Tart
breath stank of fiery, ferment
jacket, lad," he growled, "and
a prize ship booty, or my name's

His mate crowded closer, a
Katrina's borrowed jacket. One
cheeks and forehead blue-ridge
some previous campaign.

"Silver buttons," he said, anc
A knife appeared suddenly in hi
old shipmates the loan of a few

While the sailor Van Zee he
his companion ran the sharp k
edges of her jacket, and collecte
his cupped hand.

Then Van Zee swung her rougl

"Now, my lad," he began, "y
your purse for ye, while ye len
jaws dropped as his glance fell u
that was disclosed as his rougl
jacket open. The two men exch
and Van Zee wiped his nose anc

"Hey, you seadogs!" piped

ambush, where the river narrowed. The men were silent, listening. The only noise now was the ceaseless gurgle of the dark water against their craft.

Van Zee and the one-eyed sailor were tense. Their bodies pressed close to Katrina, but although her wrists were tied helplessly to the oar, they did not now concern themselves with her. They, too, were listening.

The fur-hatted Cossacks, quick as animals, heard it first—the faraway, distant clue of noise, frail as the swirling mist around them, of the Swedish sailors rowing their three long-boats towards the parent warships.

The Russian musketeers fingered their gun primings stealthily. Katrina heard the brittle click of small hammers being pressed back. Soon she, too, could distinguish the singing voices of Swedish sailors, and the dip, slap of their oars in the black river water as they came nearer.

She wanted to shout and warn them, but fear choked her throat.

The first crash of musket fire from the dozen Russian barges came so suddenly that Katrina only realized she had jumped when the ropes tugged sharply at her wrists. She saw the Swedish craft clearly as the mist swirled low like chiffon in the wind, seeming to part in apprehension of the musket shots that screamed through it.

The Swedes, startled and many of them already injured, stumbled to their swivel guns, and swung bulky muzzles blindly towards the tall reeds. Their answering flashes came like sheet lightning. One of the barges in the reeds caught fire. The closely packed gunfire made a deafening, skull-beating din. The stench of scorched gun barrels was sickening. The one-eyed sailor next to Katrina grunted suddenly, with hands pressed to his stomach. He looked surprised as he drained white and crumpled over the oar, dead.

Two soldiers seized and heaved him into the river out of the way. Katrina saw him flop, spread-eagled, his clothes ballooning as he lay face downwards for an instant before sinking into the grey mud.

"Damn!" said Van Zee moodily. "He had all those silver buttons in his pockets, blast him!"

Many of the Russian soldiers now leapt from the barge into the shallows, and pushed it off the shoal, then scrambled back with thigh boots spurting water as the rough craft rocked its ungainly way towards the Swedish longboats. Katrina swayed helpless with a rhythmical oar.

The barge became one of half a dozen that now scraped against the hull of the nearest Swedish craft. The blazing wreck in the shallows lit the scene for Katrina. She saw, among the confusion of close-quarter fighting, one huge figure, roaring like a wild beast, a huge sword darting and flashing like the dance of icicles upon a shaken pine branch, in and out among his foes.

His face was splashed with blood, his thick-lipped mouth down-turned in a grin of concentration. His big sword plunged and hacked irresistibly. He was carving almost a one-man wake through the confusion of Swedish sailors.

Katrina, sick with horror, realized that this giant of destruction was the terrible Tsar Peter himself! Close beside him, urbane and unruffled, Prince Menshikov and Colonel Konigseck fought, their uniforms bright with blood streaks like the ribbons of decorations.

Some of the soldiers were grappling and dying in water up to their shoulders, churning the mud into a thick blood-salted surf around the barges.

Then, all at once, it was over. The Russian soldiers, eyes gleaming with that strange lust to destroy that is born partly of fear and partly of mania in the souls of men in battle, realized as they gazed around them that there was nobody left to kill. Slowly, and dazed, like men awakening from a dream, they dipped their knives in the water and wiped them free of blood, then clambered back into the barges. The shallows lay littered with dead and dying, with wounded who cried for aid and were left unheeded. The clumsy flotilla, putting triumphant prize crews aboard the Swedish boats, turned back towards the quay at Petersburg. Russia had won her first victory at sea!

When the soldiers had clambered boisterously ashore, yelling and thudding at each other with congratulatory blows of their hamlike fists, Van Zee snicked open his deckhand's knife and cut the sticky ropes that bound Katrina's wrists to the oar.

"Come," he said. His fingers, rough and warm as newly sawn wood, seized her wrist just around the roughened skin of the brand mark.

He twisted her arm painfully and lugged her along the uneven quay. Not until he had got away from the noisy troops who thronged the harbour-side and turned into the darkness behind a great wooden warehouse did Van Zee slacken his pace and his grip. Then, as his fingers stirred over the brand mark that had barely healed, his face became uneasy.

"What's this, eh?" He pulled her from the shadows to where a tar bracket spluttered, and peered at the red grooved imprint of the twin Satanic hooves upon Katrina's wrist.

"A witch! A witch! The devil-mark!" The sailor's voice strangled in his throat. He dropped Katrina's arm, gazed at her for one instant of paralyzed terror, then stumbled off up the path, his iron-shod shoes striking sparks from the stones.

"Witch . . . witch . . ." Katrina could hear his sobbing shouts, and knew that she must get clear of the quay before Van Zee spread his alarm. A witch impaling would make a magnificent finale to their victory for the Russian troops.

She hurried away along the only path she knew—the route the soldiers had taken from Prince Menshikov's house to the quayside. On each side of the road, dangerous swamps seethed in thaw, seeming to collect and boil the night mist until it swirled around her as she ran.

Musketeers stood at the palisade gates of Menshikov's house, their weapons propped against the wooden walls. They were in no mood to challenge anybody. They were drunk, their faces dewy with melancholy Russian tears. Victory had been won, but they had missed the sea battle and the glory. Nothing but vodka and weeping remained now to console them.

Inside the gates, Katrina hesitated. The house blazed with lights. The window barricades were down. The yard was full of horses and drunken grooms. Some of the house servants were building a bonfire. Katrina moved back into the shadows as she saw Prince Menshikov and Colonel Konigseck, with a group of other Russian officers, moving from the stables into the house.

Above them all, bloodstained and terrible, his face white with ecstasy and his eyes ablaze, was the Tsar himself, towering head and shoulders over even the lanky, stiff-necked Konigseck.

The booming, roaring laughter of the party and the Tsar's own terrible voice, made Katrina press her body against the dark sanctuary of the outhouse wall, until they had all entered the house.

Then she crept back to crouch and wait among the furthest outbuildings.

With Tsar Peter in the house, Katrina could not find courage to enter it. She shivered while the stars came out and a frosty moon scudded over wispy, trailing night clouds.

The crashing of glasses, occasional yelps of anguish at some rough horseplay, came to Katrina from the house, even above the noise of the servants in the stable yard, the crackle of the bonfire, the wail of the balalaikas. She listened but could not hear Grog's voice anywhere. With a shiver, she remembered Matilda's warning words to the dwarf: "Tsar Peter'd as soon fling you on the fire as listen to your singing, my little man!"

It was a chill night, and the mixture of the cold and the tight boots, made her legs tingle into numbness. She turned her gaze from the house's blazing windows, and observed a small, uncertain lantern light approaching from the gate path. It seemed to be bobbing along almost on the surface of the grass. Then she recognized the dumpy little man who carried it.

"Grog," she called, "Oh, Grog!"

"Katrina!" The dwarf's delighted basso voice boomed back at her. "I've searched everywhere for you, lass. I've been down to the quayside, and back. Everywhere. By all that's holy, Katrina, I'd swear you'd sunk into those hell-warmed bogs by the road!"

Katrina laughed, and caressed Grog's folded cheeks.

"Your fingers are ice cold, lass!" he said. "Why aren't you in the house, where it's warm, in that beautiful bed—" Then he realized, and his voice dropped to a whisper. "The Tsar—is he in the house?"

Katrina nodded. "I daren't go in, Grog—I daren't!"

"Pouf!" said Grog. "There's naught to fear!" But she knew that he, too, was afraid.

They stood together, with their flickering lanthorn and wondered what to do. "We can't sleep out here," said Grog, "but we might sneak into the stables, or—no, we'll go right into the house and find a bed there!"

"Where?" said Katrina fearfully. "Where?"

"Listen—in that room where your gowns were put to hang—not much bigger than a wardrobe. Prince Menshikov will never look for you there. And I'll admit to you," said Grog, "that I slept there myself last night, while you climbed into bed with your Prince!" He grinned slyly and Katrina blushed.

"Oh, Grog, you think we might sleep there safely?"

"By the Leaven Cakes, we might! Not stir from our hiding place until the Tsar has left tomorrow!"

The dwarf and the girl waited together, warming each other against the cold, until the stableyard fire had dwindled into embers and many of the torchlights in the big wooden farmhouse were extinguished. Then they crept into the kitchen, with Grog leading the way. Matilda and Olaf lay asleep together by the dying fire. Soldiers, drunkenly snoring, stretched upon the floor. The young girl Maria, her head flung back and mouth wide open, lay soundly asleep beneath a sprawled Guards Sergeant.

Rowdy music still sounded in the big hall, where torches flared and drunk-slurred voices were raised in bawling mirth. The Tsar and his friends had not yet tired.

Grog and Katrina crept up stairs that creaked and groaned betrayingly. Grog's lanthorn had gone out. He took a candle from the bedroom corridor and led Katrina into the little wardrobe room where his secret bed of cushions and furs lay undisturbed upon the floor, beneath the spread hems of the many coloured robes and gowns.

With a sigh of relief, Katrina sat upon the little bed and the dwarf pulled off her heavy, uncomfortable boots. "By St. Peter's beard," he said suddenly, "all the silver buttons are gone from your jacket! What happened? Did you breathe too hard?"

Katrina laughed softly. She felt comfortably conspiratorial with the dwarf, crouched together in the candlelight upon the floor of the tiny room.

"Two sailors stole them," she said. "But I'm tired of thinking about it. Please get me my—my nightgown from the Prince's bed." Her voice hesitated over the word. Nightgowns were enthralling new luxuries to Katrina. Grog hurried obediently through the adjoining door and found the wispy garment beneath a pillow of the big bed. Katrina struggled out of the mud-wet uniform and slipped thankfully into the silk gown. She padded on bare feet to wash herself in the Prince's bedroom, and combed her short, curly hair by candlelight in the big mirror that the Prince had given her that morning, which seemed so far distant now that it might have been a year ago in time. Grog settled down in a far corner, his jacket folded for a pillow.

Back in the hiding place, Katrina slid under the soft fur covering and stretched her aching body upon the cushions. They made a good bed, but already they seemed hard by contrast with the Prince's wonderful feather mattress.

Downstairs, in the main room, the ribaldry was beginning to die down. Tsar Peter had with his own hands flung a generous armful of logs onto the fire, and was kicking them into a fiery glow. His half dozen intimate friends were very drunk, but clinging doggedly to wakefulness.

They kept a wary eye upon the Tsar. One never knew what he might do next. But the Tsar, with a grunt of supreme contentment, had flung himself back into the depths of the great armchair and rested his large feet—still encased in sea-soaked boots—upon the ornate lions at the hearthside. The rich, beautifully worked leather of his boots was streaked white with salt, and their fur was spiked dark with bloodstains. He smoked his carved ivory pipe, which was almost twice as large as Prince Menshikov's. Its stem tugged his lip down and gave a sardonic twist to the smile upon his brutally handsome face.

Colonel Konigseck stood stiff and correct by the fire. He was full of wine, and heavy with sleep after the day's adventures. But Konigseck would yield to nothing. Whilst he was awake, he would stand, erect, uncompromising even at such a carouse, his uniform still buttoned as for parade. Menshikov lounged long-legged and in shirtsleeves across the table, a heavy drinking tankard canted in his jewelled fingers, telling a tale. The Tsar listened, his smile deepening.

Food remnants lay scattered upon the floor. Wine carafes had been smashed, goblets shattered against the wall, in triumphant toasts to victory. One of the Cossack chief officers sat blinking drunken beady eyes, white napkin clutched to a still trickling gash upon his cheek, torn in recent horseplay. Sten'ka the giant Cossack, almost the size of Peter himself, sprawled asleep, snoring unashamedly, careless of this affront to the presence of his lawful sovereign. Peter did not seem to notice.

Menshikov was chuckling: ". . . . and that old goat Sheremetiev, almost bowlegged from his amorous fatigues with his other Swedish wench, had, if you please, hacked off this Katrina's hair with a blow from his sword, then thrown her from his tent and ordered her to be shackled with this little singing dwarf, and the dancing bear..." He hesitated, his shrewd eyes twinkling.

"But I forgot," he smiled, "you met the bear this morning."

By the other side of the fire, Prince Fedor Romdanovsky spluttered with fawning mirth into his tankard. "Your Majesty must wrestle a bear when we get back to Moscow. It'd make good sport after dinner."

"I'll wrestle your head off your fat neck, Fedor," said Peter amiably, without removing his pipe, "if you interrupt Little Alec again. I want to hear about this shorn wench with the devil-brand, that Alec swears is the most beautiful girl in Russia." He took a deep swill of his spiced, hot wine, and spat a clove into the fire. "Blast it, Alec—if that's not treason, now I think on't! There's no wench in Russia can match my little Anna Mons—at dance, bed or banquet! What d'you say to that, eh?"

Konigseck's hairless eyelids dropped like a lizard's over his cold eyes. Romdanovsky took refuge quickly behind his tankard. Prince Menshikov became acutely aware of his perilous position. But he had handled such situations before. His voice stayed tranquil and amused.

"For a wager, it's unfair," he drawled. "No man knows about Anna in bed but you, Majesty. Who'd be the judge then, but you?"

Across the Tsar's sardonic mouth, a slow grin dawned, "The blazes with bed, then," he said. "A wager on sheer beauty, you slippery fox! You've seen my Anna, and you've seen your Katrina. Tell me, Alec, you damned, evasive merchant-tongued pie salesman—which is the more beautiful?"

Prince Romdanovsky hunched up his shoulders like a man expecting a fire-pot to explode. Konigseck ran a tongue over his tight, formal lips. But Menshikov yawned amiably. "Katrina's upstairs, Majesty," he said. "Why the devil don't you go and see for yourself?"

The boom of Peter's laughter shook the candles. He heaved his giant body from the chair and banged his empty two-quart silver tankard on the table with a crash like a fallen church bell. A sleepy soldier stumbled forward to fill it.

"I will indeed," said the Tsar. "I'll go and look at your little candidate. And if she isn't a match in beauty for my Anna, you shall embrace her on this very table under all our eyes, as forfeit for your damned insolence, eh?"

Prince Menshikov had the situation where he wanted it now. Win or lose, the wager would end in a jest. The calm smile never left his face as Tsar Peter staggered to the stairway and bellowed up it.

"Katrina! Katrina! Come down here, you little she-devil . . . you witch . . . you little spawn of hell. Come down here, I say—or must the Tsar himself come up and fetch you?"

Chapter Six

GROG BLEW OUT the candle. "We're safe here," he said reassuringly to Katrina.

"Will he—the Tsar—be gone tomorrow?" Her voice came hesitant, and Grog knew that she was still troubled by her fear of being under the same roof as Tsar Peter, who had been the fabulous bogeyman of all her childhood years.

"If he isn't," he said valiantly, "I shall hide you! I'll get food from the kitchen for you, and you shall stay up here until the Tsar has gone."

"Grog," whispered Katrina, "my father used to say Tsar Peter was ten feet tall, and ate babies for breakfast!" Her voice dwindled, then continued: "Well, I saw him today. He was a big man—the biggest I've ever seen, Grog. But he wasn't ten feet tall—or, at least, I don't think he was."

Grog chuckled, and his deep and musical voice rang in his deformed barrel chest like a cathedral organ.

"Sleep, little Katrina," he said. "I will sing you a lullaby." In the darkness, he sang softly:

My playmate was the silvery moon
He came to touch my pillow,
He brought me stars for necklaces

And kissed my brow as I lay dreaming,
kissed my brow as I lay dreaming. . . .

Katrina closed her eyes and when Grog finished his lullaby she was breathing on the brink of slumber.

Grog became silent and lay down upon his makeshift pillow. He could hear the rumble of voices through the floorboards. He listened idly for a while. Then he sat up in alarm.

"Katrina," he said urgently. "Katrina! Listen!"

Katrina blinked into startled wakefulness. "What, Grog—what is it?"

"Through the floor, Katrina, can you hear their voices? They're talking about you."

"Who—the Tsar?" Katrina was wide awake now.

"Sssh!" said Grog. "The dining room is just below us. I can hear their voices. I heard Tsar Peter say he was coming to fetch you—"

Katrina stared in terror, into the darkness. They both sat, fear-frozen, listening . . .

"Katrina! Katrina! Come down here, you little she-devil . . . you witch . . . you little spawn of hell. Come down here, I say . . . or must the Tsar himself come up and fetch you?"

There was no mistaking the commanding voice that boomed up the stairway, echoed against the walls, seeming almost to make the link flares dip and shudder along the empty corridors.

Katrina had jerked herself into a sitting posture, the skin of her scalp prickling as if a thousand needles had penetrated into her skull.

She began to whimper hopelessly. "What shall I do? What shall I do?"

Grog jumped to his feet. "Stay quiet!" he commanded. "I'll try to stop him!" Before Katrina could think what to say, Grog had groped his way out of the small clothes closet into Prince Menshikov's bedroom, that lay between Katrina and the stairway from which the Tsar had shouted.

He could hear heavy feet up the stair. The Tsar was shouting: ". . . and fetch her, then, confound it! Where is she, did y'say?"

"In my bed, I expect, Your Majesty." The calm amused answering voice was Prince Menshikov's.

"Holy Sepulchre!" prayed Grog fervently. He could see the

outline of Prince Menshikov's big bed dimly in the moonlight. Without any more time to think, he scrambled up onto the yielding mattress and pulled the counterpane over his head. He stretched his dumpy body, and lay with eyes shut, praying.

The room became brilliantly lit as the two men entered it, each holding a multiple candelabra aloft.

"Ah!" Peter saw the lumpy mound inside the bed, and stretched out his big hand to the coverlet.

"Come out of that, you little Swedish devil!" He wrenched the bedclothes back—then let out a bellow of laughter.

"By God, is this the girl who's prettier than Anna Mons?"

It was an amused face that the dwarf saw, laughing down at him in the candlelight. Grog was quick to respond to it. With his showman's instinct for humour, he blinked up at the Tsar, fluttering his pouchy eyelids in ridiculous mimicry of a bashful girl.

The chill of the stairway, after the roaring warmth of the fire in the room below, had sobered the Tsar and his eyes were alert as he watched the dwarf's antics. "This is a good fool, Little Alec," he said to Menshikov interestedly. "He's more than a freak—he's got wit inside him!"

"I can sing, too, Your—Your Majesty," gasped Grog, but fear and excitement had made his throat dry, and while he gulped to moisten it, the Tsar turned at a noise from the clothes chamber.

"The girl's in there!" he said to Menshikov, and strode across to the shut door.

Katrina had scrambled up in panic when she heard the Tsar's voice in the next room. It was not often she lost her head, and if she had stayed in her hiding place beneath the hanging gowns, she might have escaped being seen.

But deep terror moved Katrina. Her fear of the Tsar swelled inside her—a myriad remembered childish nightmares, horror tales underlined by the gunfire of the Marienburg siege—made her almost insane with fright. She pressed her body in the darkness against the furthest wall, and was standing rigid there when Tsar Peter thrust open the closet door.

Katrina's nightgown billowed with the sudden draught. She had to gather the frail, transparent folds around herself. The Tsar did not move, except to raise his candelabra and regard her with a quiet curiosity that brought a puzzled lift to Menshikov's eyebrows. This was unlike Peter, to have a terrified wench in front of him, and not make some violent, crude gesture to add to her terror. With a whimper, Katrina covered her face and turned to flatten herself against the wall.

Surprisingly gentle, Peter placed his great hand upon Katrina's shoulder and turned her to face him. Her eyes were level with his chest, fixed upon the rough blue jersey he wore.

"She's very young," he said. He put his finger under her chin, raising her head until she had to meet his gaze. She saw eyes so dark that they were almost black, a mouth curved with the arrogance of the absolute despot, but somehow softened by a glint of incongruously boyish humour. His chin was cleft deep, and his brows were savagely stern. But the expression in his eyes was quizzical, searching—almost fatherly.

"Hold still, child," he said. "I have to inspect you for a wager." He continued his scrutiny, saw the terror in her eyes turning slowly into puzzlement. He studied the beauty in her young face, framed in its unusual, short curled hair. Katrina's complexion was clear like pink shell pearl.

The Tsar nodded, and spoke over his shoulder to Menshikov, without taking his eyes from Katrina's.

"Little Alec, you might almost be right, by God!" he said. "We'll take this toy downstairs and examine it closer in the warmth."

He tucked Katrina under one big arm like a doll. She had to curl her fingers into the rough material of his jersey, to hold back from his encircling arm so that she could breathe. She threw a glance of appeal at Prince Menshikov, but his face was expressionless.

The six candles flared and spluttered in the heavy candelabra that the Tsar held aloft to light his way, as he carried Katrina along the corridor. He did not say anything to her, and only glanced down at her once, with a smile that she could not interpret. But pressed against the side of his huge chest, Katrina could feel a rumbling sensation. She realized the Tsar was chuckling to himself. They passed the door of Prince Alexis' bedroom, and Peter stopped. There were lights inside the young prince's room, and the gabbling chant of a prayer, in a boy's voice pitched to a high wail of terror, could be plainly heard. Katrina saw the Tsar's face broken. A deep, savage groove twitched like a bloodless sward cut down his left cheek—a nervous tic, that betrayed the stir of anger.

"Little Alec," he said curtly to Menshikov, "tonight we had a victory to celebrate. I did not see my son at table. Let him at least join us in a toast before we sleep." He raised his large boot and kicked the heavy door open. It had been locked, but the hasp and bolt fell away from the shattered fastening like wisps of hay as the door smashed open.

Katrina felt the terrible surge of strength in the body of the man who held her, as the kick was delivered. In the room, which she clearly remembered, young Prince Alexis knelt at his prayers on the bare floor. He looked up, his face grey with terror. His eyes seemed to sink even deeper into the muddiness of the flesh surrounding them, as he stared at his father.

Peter opened his mouth to speak, then swallowed. The boy, although staring wildly at him, had not discontinued his prayer. The chant went on.

For several moments the Tsar waited, his face twitching. Then he said: "Come down and drink a toast to our great victory today, my son." He tried to speak gently, but his voice was strained.

The young prince went on gabbling his prayer. His father drew a deep breath. He was holding Katrina so tautly now that she would have cried out, had she been able to find breath. But the Tsar did not heed her. "Stop!" he roared at his son, and Prince Alexis stopped with a convulsive shudder, like a man stabbed.

"Listen to me," said Peter, still striving to control his voice. "You must come downstairs. It shall not detain you long, but we have a final toast to drink before we sleep tonight—to Russia!"

Prince Alexis did not answer. He stayed on his knees, mute. "Come, lad," said Peter, with clumsy kindliness. "Get on your feet like a man. Here's a little playmate for you, a lass almost your own age. I'll give her to you, to teach you manliness. She's a Swede—and if she will drink a toast to Russia, then surely the Tsar's son will lead it? Come down, Alexis, and give us the patriotic toast!"

Prince Alexis rose slowly to his feet, and Katrina felt the Tsar draw a deep, exultant breath. But the boy had risen only to turn his back upon them and drop to his knees before the candlelit ikon on the further wall. An instant later, the oppressive nasal chant of his prayers rose again, and the Tsar turned abruptly from the room. But Katrina had seen his eyes. They were like the eyes of her own little brother Michael, when she had left him on the bridge. Katrina had glimpsed a wistful, and infinitely pitiful loneliness.

He did not speak to her or Prince Menshikov as he carried her down the stairs. But when he reached the dining room where his half dozen friends blinked interestedly at the sight of Katrina, hung over his arm like the doll in her thin silk nightgown, his manner changed again.

"Here!" he laughed. "The object of the dispute, my friends! Take a close look and decide—is she or is she not more lovely than my Anna? And shall Little Alec pay the forfeit?"

He set her down before the fire, in the middle of the group. The firelight made her garment transparent. She felt shy and uneasy. Yet she did not now feel afraid. This was anticlimax. She had not fear now of the great ogre who had stamped upstairs to seize her. With a flash of insight, Katrina had stumbled upon the truth, that there were two men—two souls, not one—within that fearsome, heavy-breathing frame. Never in all the years that were to follow, was Katrina ever to consider the Tsar except as two men—so different that they might have belonged to separate worlds—yet imprisoned, each within the other, inescapably like two enemies in a tiny boat upon some immeasurably lonely sea.

Now he was trying to make a bawdy jest of her before his drunken friends. But she remembered the eyes of the man who had turned away from the sight of his own son's skinny, denying back. And though a flush came to her cheeks as the eyes of the officers and princes dwelt upon her, her own gaze was clear and candid as she looked straight at Tsar Peter.

"Tell me about Anna Mons, Your Majesty," she said softly, and as her wide lips parted, they uncovered white perfect little teeth.

"Ugh!" said Prince Romdanovsky, "white teeth—horrible! Can't stand a wench who doesn't know enough to stain her teeth black, eh?"

Konigseck nodded curt agreement. But Peter sat down abruptly in his broad chair by the fire, and stared at Katrina, as she stood regarding him steadfastly from the middle of the hearth. He studied the delicate curves of her slender-waisted body. He missed Anna—the laughter with Anna, the nights with her, the companionship, and—somehow—the comfort.

"You want to know about Anna Mons?" he said gruffly. "Sit on my knee, child, and I'll tell you."

Katrina hesitated and looked towards Menshikov, who neither smiled nor frowned. Menshikov's face was a blandly handsome mask that told her nothing.

The others turned back to their tankards, smothering yawns. Obviously the jest was over. Peter reached out a long arm, and pulled Katrina down. She felt the heat of his body through her thin nightgown, and the iron firmness of his huge thighs beneath her own.

He gestured towards his big, replenished tankard. "Drink," he invited. She put her hands upon the wide handles, but could scarcely lift it. The Tsar, without a word, placed his hands over her small ones, and raised the vessel to her mouth, tilting it so the hot, spiced wine flowed into her throat.

She coughed at the strong, burning sweetness. It was fierily laced with vodka, and flowed hot through her. His hands still covering hers, Peter took the drink to his own lips, and sucked in a deep draught, almost draining it.

Everybody had become quiet. All the others, except Konigseck who still stood ramrod stiff, and Menshikov who had returned to his easy perch upon the table, were shifting deeper into their big chairs, and furtively shutting their eyes.

Katrina sat like a child upon the Tsar's knee, her hair fair against his dark jersey. She gazed at Peter's face, and her stomach stirred with an excitement at being so near to this man who had been the dread of her babyhood.

He felt her looking at him, and watched the dark sweep of her lashes over the curve of her cheeks. He yawned again. "Anna was just about your age, and I was a lad of sixteen, when I had her in the stables—where was it, Little Alec?"

"Preobrazhenskoe," said Menshikov immediately, and the Tsar nodded. He stretched his mouth in a deep prolonged yawn. "Sleepy," he said, simple as a child, and shut his eyes. His breathing became deeper.

"Thank God!" murmured Konigseck in a tight-lipped whisper, and stalked across to a couch by the wall, where his cloak was laid.

Katrina looked towards Prince Menshikov, who was still perched upon the table, swinging his long legs silently. The firelight shone upon his thick curls, and as his white-garbed thighs rocked rhythmically, Katrina felt a flutter of yearning for him. She smiled, her thoughts in her eyes. He answered her smile calmly, but did not speak.

The Tsar was sleeping soundly now, his face relaxed. He looked years younger. His deep chest rose and fell.

Katrina smiled again at Menshikov, trying to explain by glance and silent gesture that she was not upon the Tsar's knee by her own choice. "Your Highness," she whispered. Menshikov motioned her at once to silence, then toward the door. Katrina hesitated, unsure of what he meant.

"Get off to bed!" Menshikov whispered, and she sensed anger underneath the quiet words. She climbed carefully from Peter's legs, and went towards the door. When she reached it she paused and glanced back, hopeful that Menshikov might rise to follow her. He did get up, but not to go after Katrina. He went to kneel at the Tsar's feet, and to unfasten the Tsar's thick boots. He took his own fur-trimmed cloak from the table and laid it across the Tsar's shoulder that was furthest from the fire's warmth. His face held an expression of possessive tenderness as she looked down at the sleeping man.

Katrina went up the dark stairs with her mind confused. She did not feel afraid of the house now, and she climbed into the big bed leaving the curtains undrawn. The candles burned low as she lay awake listening and waiting for Prince Menshikov's footsteps upon the stairs. First one candle, then the second, flared brighter and fizzled out on its own liquid, leaving velvety blackness.

Now she could hear Grog snoring in the clothes closet. She could not sleep. Her thoughts stayed with the handsome Prince Menshikov who had been her lover, who had taught her love, and for whom she now waited hopefully. She remembered the expression that had been in his eyes as he laid his cloak upon the sleeping shoulders of his master.

And Katrina realized it was no use waiting for Prince Menshikov. He would not come to her. Prince Menshikov loved the Tsar!

She fell asleep alone, and gave herself to troubled dreams.

And though she was about early the next morning she did

not see him except in the distance, when the regiments of the Tsar marched away from Petersburg to a wail of bugles that thinned out, plaintive and threadbare, in the sleet-filled wind.

The soldiers faced into the wind, carrying the Holy Banners high before them, and the banners at first strained stiff as coloured metal, held taut by the wind, then flapped like big painted wings as the column turned away down the snow covered road towards Lake Ladoga.

The musicians had marched first, thumping their kettledrums with sticks gripped in red, swollen hands, and the fifes screamed shrilly among them. It was an idea the Tsar had borrowed from the British regiments he had seen on his visit to London. The red uniforms of his marching soldiers became harlequined with snow that quilted upon their chests and thighs and left their backs still bright scarlet.

Tsar Peter, with his three companions, Prince Menshikov, Prince Romdanovsky and Colonel Konigseck, rode just behind the musicians. Their horses danced uneasily in the whirling snowflakes and jewels winked upon their heavy bridles. The cloaks of the three courtiers were brilliant as parrots, but the Tsar's cloak was simple, thick and dark. He looked almost like some drab prisoner of his own armies as he rode, a head taller, among the bright uniforms of his aides.

Katrina stood with Grog and Matilda to watch the soldiers go. The wind whipped her cheeks to a pink flush, and snow clung white and thick along her eyelashes. The daylight was still early, glinting palely green behind the veil of scurrying flakes.

Katrina touched her lips where the Tsar had kissed her. She had been blowing the kitchen fire for Matilda, and was red and breathless from her effort when the Tsar had strode unceremoniously through the kitchen towards the stableyard.

Without a word, he had taken her by the shoulders and lifted her from her feet as though she were a tankard of ale.

Her mouth was startled, wide open, when he pressed his own thick and wilful lips onto hers. Katrina felt his bristled moustache, rough as gorse, and tasted the flavour of sweet wine with which he had swilled down his early breakfast. When he stopped kissing her, she had smiled up at him with understanding, almost with compassion. He nodded and passed on into the yard, and one might have supposed he was indifferent, but Katrina felt that somehow, in passing, the Tsar had warmed himself for an instant at her, as if at some comfortable hearth.

The sensation of the kiss had lingered, and she had stared after him, her eyes large and vague with a longing for something that she was only beginning to understand.

Grog slapped snow from his dumpy body, and stamped back into the kitchen, when the soldiers were out of sight. He flung out his arms delighted at the kitchen's emptiness.

"No dragoons, no soldiers, no bombardiers!" he laughed, and his rich, great voice made the cooking pans chime upon their metal hooks. "There'll be space by the fire for a couple of days."

"Only two days?" said Katrina. The dwarf tore a hunk of hot pastry from one of Matilda's cheese blini-cakes, and stuffed it into his mouth. "There's a garrison of only five hundred Swedes at Noteburg, half-starved and short of shot," he said. "That was just a mopping-up party, though you'd think from the size of it, the bugles and fuss, the Russians were off to conquer all Cathay! Aye, they'll be back in two or three days with fresh blood on their swords," he said, "and wanting wine, hot food—and wenches!"

In the corner of the kitchen, Maria giggled. Maria's eyes were sticky from slumber, her black hair tousled, and a red ridge lingered upon her beetroot-stained cheek, where the braid of a sleeping dragoon's coatsleeve had dented it.

Katrina regarded Matilda's wanton daughter thoughtfully, and amazed herself by saying suddenly: "Get out and wash, you slut!"

The words rapped out sharp and with authority, unlike Katrina's normal, husky quiet tones. It was so surprising, Grog blinked in wonder. But Maria rose without a word, and slouched out to the pump in the stableyard.

After a moment they heard the pump handle grinding, as Maria obediently sluiced herself in cold water. Grog swallowed his mouthful of cheese blini. "By the Martyrs," he grinned, "it seems to make a difference, in this house, which bed a girl sleeps in!"

Katrina busied herself at the stove to hide her own confusion. She realized that she had been unconsciously imitating the tones of Prince Menshikov's sharp commands to Sten'ka the

Cossack. It was the first time she had in her life given a direct order to another human being, and watched it obeyed.

It was afternoon of the fifth day when the Russians returned from the capture of Noteburg. Half starved Swedes, it seemed, fought even more stubbornly than full-fed ones. The victory had been dearly purchased.

Tsar Peter stormed into the farmhouse. His uniform was torn and streaked with hard patches as if smeared with dark brown clay. Menshikov, Romdanovsky, Sten'ka and the half dozen others of the Tsar's personal staff, were similarly bloodsplashed.

But Colonel Konigseck did not walk among them. Four soldiers carried his body in, on a litter made of poles and canvas.

Colonel Konigseck's handsome face stared out of the litter. It was waxy, blue-faced and almost transparent. As meat is frozen, so was the corpse of Konigseck, and the twitch of death, when it had come to him, had tugged down his mouth into an expression of unalterable disdain.

Death had taken Colonel Konigseck by surprise. But in the instant before eternity, his face had found time to show his utter disapproval of such an affront to dignity.

He lay there, thawing out on the kitchen hearthstones, his uniform crisp with frost. Dark, congealed blood marred his forehead.

"Candles, damn it!" roared Peter, and Olaf trotted clumsily in with a bunch of yellow candles. Katrina climbed quietly on to the top alcove of the fireplace, out of the way. Soldiers fetched in tankards, and straw-plaited wine-flagons. The officers drank and waited for Konigseck to thaw.

After a while, Prince Menshikov knelt by the litter and unbuttoned Konigseck's jacket. Tsar Peter sprawled tiredly against the big table that creaked under his bulk, and drummed nervously upon it with his fingers. This, and the fire's crackle, were the only sounds in the room.

Menshikov began to put the few belongings from the dead man's pocket onto the table. A gold snuffbox, an ugly jewel-studded watch, a few silver and leather coins.

"No signs of those artillery plans, Your Majesty," said Menshikov. "Only some personal letters." He pulled out a bulky wallet made of pig gut, but the water had soaked even into this, and the letters as he sorted through them, were sodden.

"Look in his back pocket, Alec," said the Tsar wearily. "Poor devil."

Menshikov lifted the dead man's uniform coat-tails. "Yes, here it is," he said with satisfaction, and pulled out the parchment battle plan.

"Blast it," said the Tsar. "In future the campaign maps stay at the command tent—and that's an order." His voice was flat, spiritless. The death of his friend had upset the Tsar more than it had troubled any of the others, for they suffered from Konigseck's arrogance. But to the Tsar, the pride of his courtier had not been offensive. He had seen the haughty Colonel's virtues, his manliness, his quick-witted courage, his coolness in trouble, his loyalty. He regarded the pathetic and sodden heap of belongings upon the table without at first really seeing them. Then, with an intake of breath like a man who had been unexpectedly hurt, the Tsar jumped to his feet, making the heavy table scrape back over the floorstones.

"Those letters—" he said, and picked up one, peering at the bold, smudged writing that covered the thin parchment. He stared closely, then moved to the fire and held the parchment to dry. His outstretched hand almost touched the cloth of Katrina's dress as she perched in the high alcove nook, but the Tsar ignored her utterly.

Katrina felt the atmosphere of the room change, as if the air had been pumped out, leaving it like a breathless void, waiting for storm. The soldiers who had carried the litter, stood stiffly to attention a few paces from it. Menshikov's grey eyes watched Peter like a cool hunter searching a thicket to see from where a wounded tiger might spring.

"Alec," said the Tsar, in a voice that was now small, plaintive and ridiculously childlike from such a giant of a man, "did you know?"

"Your Majesty?"

"These letters, Alec—these love letters—they're from Anna." His voice swelled. "Did you know, Alec? Love letters to Konigseck—from Anna—from my Anna Mons—to Konigseck?" His voice was a harsh scream, now. He brandished the parchment under Menshikov's face.

"No," said Menshikov, startled but sincere. "I only guessed an instant ago, when you took them to the fire." He took the dried out parchment from the Tsar, and began to read aloud:

". . . and so, my only true darling, my soul whispers its love to you betwixt the secret sheets of this letter—"

"Quiet!" Peter roared at him. He had covered his ears to shut out the sound. Menshikov went white, realizing his own danger. He had been reading on in thoughtless curiosity. He adroitly turned the Tsar's anger back to where it belonged. "That filthy dog, Konigseck," he said.

The Tsar stood up, and gazed around the kitchen. His own face was bloodless now. His cheek had begun to twitch, and this was not an occasional spasm of anger, but a relentless twitch that dragged his lips away from his teeth at one side. Across the Tsar's face were marching convulsions of a sick man. He strode to the litter.

"You traitorous Polish swine!" he said, and swayed. "Sneak my woman to bed, and still pose as my friend!" His leg trembled with its urge to kick at the silent man who had betrayed him. Part of the Tsar's own self tried to restrain this, but his foot swung out in exploding viciousness. The body of Konigseck rolled slowly, reluctantly, from the litter.

"Take him out—bind him to his horse—and beat it off towards Poland!" He turned away, trying hard to control his turbulent emotions. He went back to the fire, and rested his forehead on the wide shelf above it.

The soldiers began to lift the body back onto the litter. Menshikov stopped them with a gesture. "No," he said quietly. "Drag it."

Peter whirled round. "And get me the duty officer!" There was sweat all over his face and neck, in yellow beads like melting butter.

When the young officer came in, he saw the Tsar's distorted mouth, and shut his own lips with military precision upon the ejaculation that was about to leave them. As if to receive a medal he stood stiffly to attention, and waited.

"Captain Eckoff, leave for Moscow at once. See that Anna Mons is made prisoner to wait my return. Those are my orders and I shall hold your life responsible if they are not carried out!" He swallowed with difficulty.

"Sire!" The young captain saluted and turned on his jingling heels, his eyelids almost shut to mask their amazement. He threw a quick glance at Katrina, perched in the hearth alcove, her yellow brocade dress glittering in reflected firelight.

On various excuses, the staff officers slipped away, leaving only Menshikov with the Tsar, and in the far corner of the room, Sten'ka the Cossack, who stared over his tankard of vodka, only half comprehending the drama before him. Peter stood in torment, overwhelmed by his racing thoughts. His tight-screwed fists troubled with urgency to harm Anna Mons, to bruise her soft white body upon which he had lavished so much. The times he had planned and thought of making her Empress, and the confusion of times he had loved her . . . It was now all a discord in his brain. He felt his wrath dwindling into despair and weakness.

He turned after a while and looked again around the room. The body had gone from the floor. He walked unsteadily towards the table. A pulse was throbbing in his throat, just above the collarbone, as if it would explode, and the walls appeared to be stirring like curtains. The buffeting wind outside the wooden walls, and the drop of thaw, were magnified and distorted. The kitchen seemed to fill with black and silver bubbles, that floated and burst. He could see Menshikov and Katrina, who had jumped down anxiously from the hearth-nook. But they were like creatures viewed under water. He did not know that he uttered a shout that was half a scream. He did not know that he was falling.

He struck the floor heavily. His head banged upon the stones with a sound like that of a blow upon a wooden drum. The Tsar was unconscious, but he was not still. His eyes glared and rolled behind lids that never ceased to flutter. His limbs jerked and threshed. Katrina ran and knelt beside him. She pulled back her gown and tore a handful of cloth from an underskirt to bathe the Tsar's twitching face.

Olaf had come running in at the Tsar's scream. Sten'ka put down his tankard and came over slowly, his ape-like arms dangling.

"What is it, what is it?" gasped Olaf. The sight of the Tsar, twitching upon the stone floor, penetrated his obtuseness.

"Prepare a bed, quickly," commanded Menshikov, who was himself pale. "There in the alcove by the fire, away from these damned draughts."

Big Sten'ka helped Olaf drag in a mattress. The Tsar was lying still now, deeply unconscious. Using all their strength,

Sten'ka and Menshikov lifted his big, limp body onto the bed by the fire, and straightened his limbs.

Katrina had prepared a bowl of warm water, and had begun to kneel by the bed to continue bathing the Tsar's face when Menshikov laid his hand upon her.

Katrina stood uncertainly, and watched Prince Menshikov kneel beside the Tsar, to bathe his slack, white face with water. She saw the same strangely feminine tenderness return to Menshikov's expression as he became absorbed in his task.

Her torn underskirt hung raggedly below her gown. She caught Sten'ka's glance upon it, and after a moment of hesitation, Katrina left the kitchen and went slowly up the stairs to the Prince's bedroom to change her gown, to escape Sten'ka's eyes that followed her constantly, and to relieve herself from the atmosphere of tense drama that lay upon the kitchen.

She tugged the heavy brocade gown over her shoulders and unlaced the underskirt that she had ripped. Her shoes irked her, and she kicked them off. In merely a petticoat, a layer of white frills from her narrow waist to ankles, she poured cold water from the big silver jug into a washbowl and splashed her face, neck and bare shoulders.

She blinked up, refreshed, her fingers cool and wet upon her cheeks, and saw Big Sten'ka watching her silently. He leaned with his back against the shut door and watched her with his eyes bright, unblinking and inhuman as a bird's. He had removed his tall, conical fur hat and thrown it onto the bed. A few small pearls fell from it, and as Sten'ka came towards Katrina, his foot crunched the pearls unheedingly. His head looked flat without the fur cap, as if he had been cut off short. But he was still huge—almost as big as the Tsar himself.

As though she was conscious of taking part in a mad dream, Katrina continued to wash. The water was sparkling upon her shoulders, when Sten'ka surrounded her with his long, hard hands. Roughly, with lips curled back from his teeth like a beast about to bite, Sten'ka found her mouth. His teeth grated against hers, and pressed her head back. The words she was about to utter were smothered, and when she tried to wriggle away from him, he tightened his grip until her breath was choked inside her by a hot pain.

Her efforts to repulse his great body seemed futile as he backed her purposefully towards the bed. She felt the mattress against her thighs in the second before she fell back amongst the deep piled feathers.

There was a lot of animal in Sten'ka the Cossack. He was not a wicked man, for he did nothing that offended against his conscience. The trouble with Sten'ka was that very little in life did offend against his conscience, except physical cowardice.

He wished Katrina no harm. But he did wish to make love to her. There was not much room in his mind for more than one thought at a time, and this thought had, as it were, laid its hands upon Sten'ka's reins. He wished to make love to Katrina, and here was what seemed to him an excellent chance whilst everyone was preoccupied by the Tsar's collapse.

But the clear, animal happiness of subduing a half-naked and squirming female body beneath his own became displaced in Sten'ka's awareness by the sensation of another and less pleasurable touch.

Strong fingers had twined into his black hair, and Sten'ka felt his head being tugged back until his neck veins bulged like grapes.

"Drop it, Sten'ka," said Prince Menshikov as one might speak to a dog, and continued to force the big Cossack chieftain back by his hair until Sten'ka with a peevish snarl, wrenched himself free.

Katrina sat up from the bed, gasping. Her bare, wet shoulders were caked with a shimmering dark mud. "What's that on you?" demanded Menshikov. "Gunpowder?"

Sten'ka's eyes narrowed. He dropped his hand to his elaborately decorated Cossack bandoliers. Katrina's protesting fingers, beating and clawing at his chest, had torn his bandoliers, ripped the long, precious paper cartidges in them, and scattered black explosive upon herself as they had struggled.

"You little devil," said Sten'ka, his voice blurred with anger. He raised his fist. "You ruined my bullets."

"Get out, man! Get to your quarters!" The voice of Prince Menshikov was a whiplash of authority. It brought Sten'ka up short.

"Who are you to order me to quarters?" he growled, asking the question that had been gathering in his slow mind for a long time. "You command the garrison, not the Cossack cavalry."

"While the Tsar lies sick," said Menshikov, and his voice

thundered now, "I command the Grand Army. Get to your quarters!"

Prince Menshikov turned back to Katrina, and his voice became gentle. "Come," he said, "you can't be much hurt, for I followed on his heels upstairs. He had only one minute."

Katrina rubbed her bruised arms. "That can be a long time for a Cossack," she said. She looked up at Menshikov, glad of his gentle tone. "Thank you," she added, simply.

Prince Menshikov ignored this. "Get some clothes on quickly," he said. "I came up to fetch you. The Tsar has recovered his senses, thank God." He crossed himself piously. "He is awake. And," said Menshikov, "he is asking for you, child!"

"For me?" said Katrina, surprised.

"For you," repeated Menshikov a little sullenly. "The Tsar is undoubtedly feverish. Twice since he awoke, although it was I, his dearest friend, who knelt beside him to bathe his brow and wet his lips, he muttered: 'Katrina, come—I will tell you about my Anna.' Perhaps in his delirium he links you with his last happy thoughts of that betraying whore. But whatever the reason, he is the Tsar and you must go to him."

"You did not leave the Tsar unattended, I hope?" asked Katrina anxiously, and Menshikov permitted himself a tight smile.

"Damned if sometimes I don't think you might make a good friend to the Tsar—and me," he said. "But hurry into your gown. And do not worry, for Matilda and Romdanovsky are guarding him."

Menshikov followed Katrina's slender-waisted and graceful body down the winding stairway, and his grey eyes considered her shrewdly. She had no peasant heaviness. She was cool-headed and intelligent, although so very young. If she could survive the tempestuous seas that always surrounded the Tsar, her ship might well come home. A part of Menshikov was jealous now of Katrina. But the shrewder part of his brain dismissed this as stupid and unprofitable. Little Alec was too experienced a courtier to set himself the unrewarding and dangerous task of wading against the rising stream.

"One might do worse," he told himself, "than foster the chances of this young Katrina." After all, she owed him some gratitude for unshackling her from the bizarre discomforts of the Pskov slave cart. And he had been her lover.

Unaware that she had made a powerful ally in what was perhaps to be the hour of her greatest need, Katrina hurried anxiously down the stairs to attend the Tsar's summons. Menshikov, the one man who might have broken Katrina before her hopes were ever born, had in that moment upon the stairs made a decision that was to change the history of Russia and of the civilized world.

Katrina hurried into the kitchen. The Tsar's brief recovery had already lapsed into another quivering trance of epilepsy.

Prince Romdanovsky was watching in helpless awe. Peter lay rigid, with eyelids fluttering. His limbs jerked and a black trickle of blood issued from his lips. Katrina could hear the sound of the Tsar's teeth grinding together and it was like the scrunch of pebbles being walked on.

"Quick!" she said to Prince Romdanovsky. "We must open the Tsar's mouth—he's biting his tongue!"

Romdanovsky stared blankly. "Nobody must lay a finger upon the Tsar's face," he said.

"Why not?" demanded Katrina.

"Because he is the Tsar," he said stiffly. The Tsar had begun to utter deep groans inside his throat. He seemed to be choking.

"Rubbish!" said Katrina. She seized a wooden stirring spoon from the hearth, and forced it between the Tsar's clenched teeth. A spurt of blood splashed over the spoon as she managed to prise the jaws apart. Immediately, Tsar Peter's strong teeth clamped down upon the spoon handle and ceased to gnaw his own tongue.

Romdanovsky made a move to interfere. But Prince Menshikov halted him with a decisive gesture.

"Ah, that's better," said Matilda with relief. If her own courage had been less than Katrina's, her common sense was as great. "You're a good girl," she said. "I'll get fresh water to bathe His Majesty's face." She waddled off to the pump in the yard, and Katrina knelt on the big straw-packed mattress upon which the Tsar lay, and steadied the spoon between his teeth. When the fresh water came she bathed the Tsar's face. Soon he stopped twitching and lay tranquil, the skin around his eyes darkening into great black bruises.

Prince Menshikov had watched Katrina's ministrations with

an almost grudging smile, and when he saw the Tsar pass from epileptic frenzy into slumber, he gave a heartfelt sigh and lit his pipe. He took several puffs and seemed to making up his mind. Suddenly he said to Olaf and Matilda:

"Katrina will stay with the Tsar and be nursemaid to him, while Romdanovsky and I are away with the Army." Katrina did not look up from her task of cooling her patient's temples, and did not seem to hear, as Menshikov added firmly: "She is to be obeyed in everything."

Olaf nodded, and Matilda said eagerly, "Yes, yes—she has good sense." She did not appear surprised that the mastery of the house had thus passed in an instant from the hands of her husband and herself to a Swedish prisoner of war who had so recently been a slave in chains. Matilda and Olaf were used to taking orders.

"I shall send you a courier every three days," said Prince Menshikov. "You must give him news of the Tsar's condition, Katrina. And remember—I can be back here within twenty hours if need be."

Katrina nodded. Prince Romdanovsky said somewhat sulkily: "Surely, Alec you are not going to leave the Tsar with only a few kitchen servants?"

"We can't afford to waste a day hanging around here," said Menshikov. "While Charles of Sweden is busy in Poland with his Grand Army, we must take every inch of ground that we can around Petersburg. It is the Tsar's order."

Romdanovsky nodded, his chins multiplying like concertina folds as he did so. "Aye," he said, "that's true, but—"

"We march tomorrow," interrupted Menshikov firmly and finally. "The Tsar would have it that way."

Next morning, the soldiers unloaded several great boxes of provisions and medical supplies, and trundled off towards Dorpat, leaving only a company of the Royal Guards encamped around the farmhouse. Katrina did not go to the yard to watch them depart this time. Tsar Peter was flickeringly conscious now, but would not let her away from him. He seemed to capture strength from the nearness of her small, vital body.

Matilda brought hot broth, and Katrina sipped it gratefully. "Why did they not leave a doctor?" she asked.

"Prince Menshikov doesn't believe in 'em," said Matilda. "Not Russian doctors." She shrugged. "Some nonsense he and the Tsar picked up in England, when they visited that outlandish place. They will never let a Russian doctor drain the fever from their veins, though what harm it can do to draw a healing basinful of fevered blood from a sick man, I can't see."

"If you bleed too much, you die," said Katrina.

"I've seen folk die without loss of one drop of blood," said Matilda unanswerably, and stirred the broth pot to bring up its rich sediment.

Chapter Seven

IT WAS FOUR days later, when Captain Eckoff of the Tsar's Guard reached the gates of Moscow. Captain Eckoff had ridden almost without sleep through the entire chain of courier posts upon the three hundred and eighty mile journey between Petersburg and Moscow. His handsome young face was haggard in the grey dawn, as he swung from his sweat-streaked horse in the cobbled yards of the Streltsi Barracks and presented his demands to the elderly Colonel on duty, who listened incredulously.

"Arrest Anna Mons? Are you mad, Captain? Anna Mons is the Tsar's little bit of—er, hrrmph—? don't want to clap shackles on the future Empress of Russia, perhaps—eh?"

Captain Eckoff brushed a hand across his eyes, red-threaded for need of sleep. He was too tired to be polite. He said curtly: "Sir, I have orders to take the life of any who stand in my way—the Tsar's orders, sir!"

The Colonel blinked at the sight of Eckoff's travel-grimed fingers at his sword hilt. He tugged a watch from his uniform fob pocket, blinked at it, thrust it back, and blinked again at Eckoff. "Dashed early," he said, "Captain, the men won't have had breakfast yet. Hrrmph? You can surely wait until the dispatches are in?"

"No," said Eckoff bleakly. "I can't."

Anna Mons was awakened by a thunderous knocking upon the stout, iron-studded doors that led to her beautiful mansion in Moscow's fashionable German quarter from the street outside. Noise and thumping seemed to be coming from every corner of the house. She yawned and stretched herself resentfully. Somebody would suffer for this! She pulled the silk sheet over her ears and tried to recapture sleep.

Her pillow, embroidered with the impressive two-headed eagle of the Romanovs, was daubed with red and black stains that had rubbed from her face during the night.

The uproar seemed to girdle the entire house. Anna Mons swore, tugged viciously at the silken bell-rope, and even as her bedroom door began to open, she screamed:

"Tell those devils to stop that damned din!"

But the terrified little maid who scurried in came running straight on, unchecked. "A messenger from the Tsar, Madame," she said fearfully and did not add that the officer was demanding admittance, for she was too afraid of her mistress.

"The Tsar?" Anna's jewelled hands excitedly gripped the silk bedclothes. "Pass me my lace wrap." She sat up, forgetting her anger, and as she did so her thick black hair swept caressingly across her white, plump shoulders. She moved her head slowly, repeating the motion so that her hair stirred again like a ghostly hand across the nape of her neck, and at each turn of her head her body trembled to the voluptuous thrill of this sensation for as long as she dared dally with it.

Then she arose, wrapped the lace peignoir around her body and sat before her mirror and the pots, bottles, sprays and coloursticks arranged upon the glass dressing table. Her mouth was pouted almost like Peter's, and there were deeply etched horizontal lines under each of her luminously dark eyes that gave them a hint of wilfulness like his. The bone structure of her face was flawless. Her face was that of a woman who had imposed hauteur upon perfection.

The knocking and hammer thuds continued. "What is that?" demanded Anna sharply. Her maid licked frightened lips. "I—I don't know, Madame."

Anna dabbed perfume upon her ears, shoulders and wrists, and then was ready. "Where is the Tsar's messenger?" she asked, her eyes roguish.

"I—I don't know, Madame."

Anna struck her pettishly with the long-handled hairbrush, and went to find out for herself.

She found Captain Eckoff before the log fire in the great marble entrance hall. Captain Eckoff had washed the dust of travel from face and hands, but his Guards uniform was travel-stained, and his eyes were like twin red sores from sleeplessness.

Anna's brother Vilhelm, a pretty young man with wonderfully blonde hair, reclined upon a sofa munching scented nuts and staring with amused disdain at Captain Eckoff's crumpled breeches.

"Ah, Anna!" he said blithely, and his voice was light, shrill and emphatic. "This—this chap says the Tsar has ordered you to be kept prisoner here!" He nodded at Eckoff as he spoke, and his hair followed his movement like a sweeping curtain.

For an instant Anna frowned, creasing the paint upon her smooth forehead. Then she laughed, and it was a tinkly laugh, alive with studied music. This was obviously another of Peter's queer, crude, exciting jokes. He would have some idea of imprisoning, binding her—perhaps with silk, scented ribbons—to await his pleasure. He was undoubtedly, even now, riding hot for Moscow.

"Where is the Tsar?" she asked, shaping her warm mouth prettily.

"In Petersburg, Madame," answered Eckoff and something in his manner made Anna's skin tighten. A cold, bruised sensation seemed to spread through her stomach.

"This is—a joke, isn't it?" Her smile was an effort now. She glanced at her brother, but Vilhelm had glimpsed his own reflection in a distant crystal mirror, and was patting his hair absorbedly into yet more alluring contours.

"No, Madame," said Eckoff, swaying with weariness. "My orders are not a joke."

"But—when did the Tsar give these orders?"

"After Colonel Konigseck's death, Madame." And then Anna knew. She went closer to Captain Eckoff until her breasts brushed his tunic. "You couldn't keep me a prisoner." Her voice was passionless as an absentminded kiss, but her eyes sought his intensely. Captain Eckoff's youthfulness overcame his weariness. He blushed. "Please, Madame . . ." He backed away and she followed him slowly, stalked him with infinite care, until her body was once again touching him.

The hammering still continued and Anna knew now that it was the sound of soldiers putting barricades to ground-floor windows, hacking down garden statues and arbors to make clear vision for sentries who would guard her.

"Please," she coaxed. It was her turn to plead, and she did it with magnificent artistry. "Take your soldiers away, Captain. I know my darling Peter didn't mean what he said. He is sure to be angry if you take him seriously." She smiled, and it was like the sun breaking through storm clouds. "He'll be so angry if—if you frighten me like this."

But Eckoff was armoured by weariness. "Madame," he said heavily, "my orders are to keep you prisoner. You will not leave this palace."

She slapped him hard across his fatigued face. "Get out then, and play at watchdog from the other side of my door!"

"Yes, Ma'am." He went stiffly to the great door that was of solid silver, wrought into intricate Grecian style panels. Anna grabbed at a vase and hurled it after him. It missed widely, and shattered against the wall. Captain Eckoff, without loss of dignity, shut the heavy door behind himself.

"Anna," protested Vilhelm, "that was—"

"Oh, go to hell!" said Anna. Tear drops furrowed like blunt ploughshares down her make-up.

"A vase worth a thousand roubles," continued Vilhelm imperturbably. He groped beneath his frilled shirt with a carved gold louse comb. Sapphires twinkled along its handle.

Anna sat down heavily upon one of the deep couches, and stared around at the luxury she had gathered to herself. In this large hall, sumptuous extravagance was everywhere. At intervals around the great walls were pilasters of carven ebony, framing immense silver panels with Grecian carvings in bas-relief. A heavily-worked chandelier hung from the arched ceiling, and upon it swung hundreds of crimson, pear-shaped crystals. The ikon in the hallway was set with jewels that sent back fiery responses to the worshipful flame of a dozen tall white candles.

All this—to be sacrificed for the hours of satisfaction she had gained from coaxing passion out of the aloof, haughty Konigseck, the pleasure of watching straight-backed Konigseck babble with sex frenzy like any young Dragoon. . . . Anna knew now that she hated Konigseck who had been fool enough to cherish her wanton letters. Search her palace though he might, the Tsar would find no letters of Konigseck's, nor those of any of her lovers. Anna had always burned them all, at once, as soon as they had been read.

Her intelligent eyes narrowed. Her brother Vilhelm was

wandering away down the hall. She heard the shrill pitch of his voice in the distance, talking to the soldiers who were now his guards. Vilhelm was not such a fool as he looked. She knew this, full well.

"Anna, come quickly!" The wheezy voice belonged to her mother, who came shuffling over the thick carpets, her wrinkled old face querulous as a small monkey that had bitten something nasty. "Some fools are barring my windows. I shout at them to go away, and they grin at me like loons!"

Swiftly, bitterly and without mercy, Anna told her mother what had happened. Madame Mons worked the deep wrinkles in and out of her pursed lips as she listened. Your lecheries," she said. "I always told you—I told you."

Vilhelm came back, striding prettily on his toes. "My dear," he said gaily, "it's much worse than we thought. It isn't just poor old Konigseck, apparently."

"Slanikov, too?" asked Anna quickly. Her brother giggled. "No, dear, nor any more of your playmates, but the soldiers tell me about a new girl that Peter seems to be toying with—a Swedish witch." He waved his lissome hands. "But wondrous fair, they tell me, wondrous fair."

"Witch?" echoed Anna.

"Witch, indeed, my sister. A fair maiden who walked out of the ruins of Marienburg, and they say the Cossacks stood back to let her pass." He giggled again. "I can just imagine Cossacks doing that! But this does seem to make sense—they say she carries some kind of devil-brand, and has enchanted both the Tsar and Prince Menshikov. The dispatch couriers came in two hours ago, and they're full of the story!"

Madame Mons drew a deep, difficult breath. "Seek a devil to find a devil, Anna," she croaked, mouthing the ancient proverb. "Get Father D'Ameno, daughter. Only he can aid you against a witch."

Vilhelm hastily swallowed his half-chewed cachou, and coughed. "That black magician?" he said. He was impressed, despite his light manner. "But mother, he's dangerous—the wickedest priest in Russia—he actually does walk with Satan. He's a demon raiser—he struck the Count Kublenz blind!"

Anna had gone pale at the mention of Father D'Ameno's name. "Send for him," she said doggedly. "Tell that insolent

Captain Eckoff that my mother desires a priest. I will come to you when I am dressed."

Vilhelm shrugged with an attempt at flippancy, and departed to speak with the guards. Anna walked to her boudoir, quivering with excitement and dread at the prospect of meeting a man who walked with Satan. She chose a gown of black velvet, low across her shoulders, and fastened a thick cluster of pearls around her neck so tightly that they pitted her soft white skin. She covered her dimpled arms with jewel-encrusted bracelets that slid down to her wrists as she dropped her arms to her sides.

The jewel box was still heaped with precious adornments. Anna studied them with proud despair. "They're mine—they're mine," she said angrily, and carried the casket to her bed. She moved a small table from the wall, lifted the red silk panel from the wall decoration, and disclosed a space barely big enough to hide the jewel box.

She had made all tidy and was painting herself with elaborate, leisurely care when Vilhelm pranced into her room.

"Father D'Ameno is here, Anna," he said, and could not hide his own excitement. "My God, what a horrible man!" He crossed himself before he realized what he had done. "He looks like the walking plague!"

Anna smoothed her sheathlike gown as she rose. The twin creases beneath her eyes were set with determination. She clutched her brother's arm. "You really do believe in Father D'Ameno's spells, don't you?" she demanded, searching Vilhelm's face earnestly. "You do think he will damn this witch of Marienburg, don't you?"

Vilhelm wet his lips. "Now I've seen him," he said, "I'll believe anything."

Anna received the priest in her mother's private antechamber, that was suffocatingly draped by purple velvet curtains, and thick with incenses that rose from the several burners in the airless chamber, and curled hazily against the gold-leafed ceiling.

Father D'Ameno had been a monk in Spain, and had fled from the Inquisitors—who considered him with ample justfication to be a practising demonologist. He had found an uncertain refuge among the religious bigots of Moscow, where his survival was a daily miracle, probably based on no more than the fear in which he was regarded, for he had an astute knowledge of the Italian arts of herbal drugs and poisons, and was a successful practitioner of crude hypnotism. Also, it happened that he was possessed of some genuine instinct for clairvoyance, and had already made several remarkably accurate prophecies. But if he had any authority to call himself "Father," it was certainly not bestowed upon him by the Orthodox Church of Russia, although he had contrived to gain some ascendancy over a flagellant monastic brotherhood—the Sons of Melchizedeck—who lived in a shabby monastery in "the German quarter" of Moscow, near Anna Mons' private palace. The Sons of Melchizedeck sold spells and charms, and it was said in the German quarter that the revolting Black Mass of Manichee had been conducted with full rites more than once by the shabby Brotherhood, since they had accepted Father D'Ameno into their company.

For all these unsavory truths and for a thousand unfounded, hysterical legends, Father D'Ameno was feared, and he knew it. When Anna entered the chamber he regarded her silently from beneath his black latia cowl, which bore upon it an elaborate crimson crucifix that was so fantastically decorated and distorted as to have more the appearance of some demoniac Chinese dragon than a symbol of the Holy Church. His black monkish robe reached completely to the floor and made him look, as he stood there silently, like some unearthly dark fungus that was growing upon the purple carpet.

Anna winced at the sight of his eyes, for the eyes of Father D'Ameno were deformed. Some fault of muscle or nerve had caused each of his lower lids to droop so far down upon his cheeks that knots of red and blue veins were clearly visible, pulsing in the eyelids. The eyes themselves had the greenish yellow tinge of phosphorescent fish in those parts of them which should have been white, and the ring of colour in each iris was the brassy yellow of a hen's eye. Thick white lashes, dead as silken fringes, trimmed these monstrous optical glands.

A long white beard fell to his waist, yet was in no part of itself wider than the wet red underlip from which it hung.

"Please—sit down," said Anna, and passed a heavily jewelled hand across her face. She felt unaccountably dizzy.

"Thank you." The priest seated himself gravely and tucked his white rope of beard into his girdle. His eyes were upon

Anna's jewellery, and he moistened his already glistening mouth with a pointed, birdlike tongue, at what he saw.

"I had to bribe my way in here," he said significantly, and Anna began to feel more comfortable at this sign that Father D'Ameno was human.

"You shall be repaid," she said. "You shall be richly repaid, if you will serve me."

"A love philtre, perhaps?" said the priest. "Some magic potion wrested from demons and blessed by the Holy Church—very rare and costly—to restore the love of the Tsar to you?"

Anna hesitated. "Will it have power against witches?"

Father D'Ameno caressed his beard with long, shrivelled and black-taloned fingers, that looked strangely like a turkey's claws. "Witches?" he said, and with his other hand, made a swift sign that Anna guessed to be part of some magic ritual. He rolled his eyeballs upwards. "I shall consult," he said sepulchrally, "with those creatures of air and darkness, who have my soul in command." He mumbled a Latin chant, his fingers cupped as if waiting for rain. "I see a vision," he said suddenly. "I see a witch who rises from the flames of a ruined city, and walks into the heart of the Tsar." Father D'Ameno's news service was both speedy and excellent. But Anna was, for a moment, impressed. "Yes," she said eagerly, "yes?"

Father D'Ameno fluttered awake from his reverie. "The vision fades," he said. "I need some jewel, some valuable—a precious stone—to concentrate my thoughts upon." He blinked at Anna, and she watched the thick white fringe of upper eyelashes seem to flick into the tender flesh beneath themselves.

"The jewel," he said, "the ruby that hangs about your neck?"

Silently, Anna slipped from her neck the thin gold chain that held a pendant ruby worth hundreds of roubles, and passed it to the priest.

"Now," he commanded, "a candle."

Anna lit a tall white candle, and placed it on the polished table between them. Neither she nor the priest observed that her brother Vilhelm had appeared silently at the doorway of his mother's bedchamber. He stood partly concealed by the nearest curtain and toyed with his golden hair, a fixed smile upon his spoilt mouth.

Father D'Ameno had his back to Vilhelm. He was crouched forward, elbows firmly placed upon the table, swinging the ruby upon its chain to and fro in a rhythmical, pendulum motion. The red stone gleamed like a blob of molten fire in the reflected candle flame.

"Watch the ruby," droned the priest, "watch the ruby, my child, and concentrate ... concentrate ... until ... you ... seek to ... sleep ..." His voice was bleak, slow and measured, like the tick of a metronome.

Vilhelm watched his sister's mouth opening slowly in an expression of dulled bewilderment. "I feel dizzy," she said, in a small and faraway voice.

"Listen to me," said Father D'Ameno. "I see danger for you from this witch. You understand?"

Anna nodded heavily. "Danger from the witch," she repeated like a drugged child.

"I see only one way to safety," droned the priest. "You shall give all your jewels and gold into the pious care of the Sons of Melchizedeck ..."

"All my jewels," repeated Anna obediently. Then Father D'Ameno's commanding voice stopped suddenly with a dry little cluck of terror, for Vilhelm had moved soundlessly across the carpet and placed the wafer-thin blade of his jewelled dagger against Father D'Ameno's emaciated neck.

"Don't turn around priest," lisped Vilhelm, but his high voice did not for once mince nor slur his words.

Father D'Ameno sat stiff with apprehension. The ruby pendant dropped onto the table, and its small clatter awoke Anna from her hypnotized stupor.

At once she jumped up and shook her head to clear it. "He had cast a spell upon me," she whispered, in awe. "He had me in the grip of a spell."

Vilhelm giggled. "And now I have him in the grip of a spell, with my knife," he said. "Here, take it, my dear—take my dagger and cut his throat if you like. I positively couldn't endure to!" But he did not lift the blade from its pressure upon D'Ameno's throat, until Anna came and took the pretty, deadly little weapon into her own steady hands. Then she turned the point cruelly under Father D'Ameno's chin and he sat up in quick agony with a trickle of watery blood running freely down the grease of his white beard.

"Priest," she said coldly, "I did not summon you here to rob and spellbind me."

Father D'Ameno answered with difficulty, for knife point was cutting deeply into his chin.

"I will serve you," he quavered, "I swear by my Master that I will serve you. What is it you seek of me? I am an old old man. . . ." And Anna knew that she had won.

She did not remove the knife, and D'Ameno had to sit with his face stretched high to escape the blade, his wrinkled, sinewy neck stretched taut as a fiddle string.

"Your love philtres," demanded Anna mercilessly, "do they truly work, or are they hocus-pocus?"

D'Ameno uttered a thin, nasal wail. "They work, they work. . . ."

"Always?" insisted Anna, and D'Ameno rolled his repulsive eyes in pained fear. "Not—always," he gasped.

Anna smiled with grim satisfaction and withdrew the knife, but kept its delicate blue blade within a few inches of the priest's face. His eyes squinted horribly to watch it.

"Listen," she said, "by now all Moscow seems aware that the Tsar is enchanted by a witch from Marienburg. You knew this, didn't you?" D'Ameno swallowed painfully and nodded, his eyes fixed upon the knife.

"By the black arts," continued Anna, "this witch has disclosed to the Tsar my affair with Konigseck. I am now the Tsar's prisoner in my own palace, waiting death! And unless you have a better idea I shall tell the Tsar, when he reaches Moscow, that you, priest, were bribed by Konigseck to steal my virtue with your Satanic love philtres."

Her brother giggled in pleased astonishment. Anna ignored him.

"You and I shall burn together in Red Square, priest," she said formidably. "Unless you can summon magic to save us both. Now, what do you say?"

Father D'Ameno sat for several seconds like a man already dead. When he did speak, his voice shook. "I fear to die," he said. "I fear death, my child—be merciful. I have bartered my soul to hell, and I fear to die." Sweat oozed from his wrinkled old skin like thick gum from a gnarled branch.

"Is there magic that can save us?" demanded Anna calmly.

The old priest swallowed several times and tried to quell the trembling of his limbs.

"There is true magic," he said slowly, "there is Satanic magic, that comes to me sometimes. But where it leads and how it comes, I cannot always say." He blinked uncertainly at the big red ruby, that sparkled on the table, for though the jewel lay still, the candlelight stirred over it. D'Ameno reached out his thin fingers for the stone and began to spin it, to and fro.

"Do not watch the stone, Anna!" called Vilhelm, and Anna's knuckles tightened over the dagger handle. But D'Ameno said quietly: "Who watches the stone shall fall into a Satanic trance. This is all I know. If others watch, my will may command them. If I watch, my spirit is in some magic way released to wander abroad, and it is in such times that I have made true prophecies."

"Continue," said Anna. Her face was pale, but her eyes were hard with purposefulness. D'Ameno slowly, almost reluctantly, swung the shining stone, not now as a pendulum, but round in a circle, until its slender gold chain was knotted and writhen. The ruby gyrated before the naked flame of the candle, flashing and twirling. Father D'Ameno stared at the ruby . . .

Soon, his face went rigid. Froth gathered in the corners of his mouth and although his eyes continued to stare, they were unseeing. The black pupils were no longer narrowed by the candle's glare, but swelled wide in their unsightly veinous wells. He tried to speak but it was several moments before his voice came.

"I see an execution fire burning before the Kremlin," he said, and Anna shut her lips upon a painful breath. The priest's voice was blurred and dreamlike, yet somehow both Anna and Vilhelm sensed that this was no charlatanry. The priest's voice was emerging from his own throat but the brain that prompted the stumbling words seemed to be a long distance off, down some immeasurable corridor.

"The fire burns for a soldier," croaked the priest. "I do not see it burning for a woman." Anna released her pent breath.

"She who is called the Witch of Marienburg is not revealed to me," droned Father D'Ameno, "but I see a devil-mark that is born in fire . . . now I see her—ah!—" his breath caught noisily in his throat—"she triumphs until she comes to Moscow. I see the City of Golden Domes, and she lies white and still in the Kremlin gardens. . . ."

"And me?" demanded Anna harshly. "What happens to me?"

Her interruption seemed to disturb the priest, for it was several seconds before he spoke, but his voice was still like that of the walking dead. "Summer goes and winter goes, and you take your jewel casket from its hiding place behind the red silken wall near your bed, and you walk from your palace." The priest's voice began to grumble away into the throaty obscurity from which it had emerged.

"What of the Tsar?" said Anna sharply, but D'Ameno did not answer. His eyes were still glazed and he was deep in his trance. The red jewel hung now without motion, and the candle had burned down a full two fingers' width. "Answer me, answer me!" screamed Anna. "What of the Tsar?" Father D'Ameno gave a breathless little groan as he fell forward across the table. Blood spurted thinly from his neck. It was pale pink blood and it made a red mirror upon the polished table surface. In it, Anna saw the dagger's reflection, and the wafery blue blade of the dagger was pink, too, with the blood. She had struck at Father D'Ameno, forgetful of the knife still clutched in her fingers, and Father D'Ameno had slumped forward into the death that he so much feared.

"Well," said Vilhelm, examining his painted nails with elaborate care, "we may not have got out of him all there was, but we'll certainly get no more."

"Oh, shut up!" said Anna. Vilhelm, satisfied for a moment with his fingers, glanced up with a faint smile. "Summer goes and winter goes," he mocked, "and no harm comes to you! It sounds like wishful rubbish—all of it!"

Anna was very white. "Yet it was not rubbish," she said passionately. "Otherwise, how could he know about—"

"About what, pray?" asked Vilhelm.

"About my jewel box," said Anna quietly. "For I hid it before he came, and not even you knew of my hiding place."

There was a long silence. Vilhelm felt his fair skin prickling eerily.

Chapter Eight

KATRINA CARED FOR all the Tsar's needs. For days after his collapse he had no strength to stir. She sat with him through the brief daylight, and fed spoonfuls of broth, cream and eggs, to him. At night, she curled beside him, and slept lightly, ready to waken at each feverish toss or murmur.

The Tsar's sickness was more in his mind than his body. Often, and particularly if the fire leapt up at night to blaze and crackle, he would sweat with nightmares in his sleep and shout hoarsely. Then Katrina comforted him with her soft, husky voice, and raised his great, fierce head to suck water like a child, from a basin.

One night he awoke from the uneasy sleep of convalescence and sat straight up. "God," he said, "I have not known such nights since—" his voice quavered. "Light more candles, Katrina," he said, and stared about him apprehensively.

When Katrina had lit a great glitter of candles he became easier. She could see how tired and sunken his face had grown. "The soldiers came one night," he said, "and filled the Kremlin, carrying torches and swords. My half-sister Sophia—she was attempting a coup for the throne—I was a boy of about ten. The soldiers pulled my beloved old tutor from my arms—they tossed him over the balcony, and the Streltsi caught him on their spears..."

"Hush," said Katrina, "hush."

Peter shook his head. "It is in my brain," he said, "always in my brain. When the fire burns up, I can see it. The soldiers hunted my family through the Kremlin. I saw my uncles—everybody—I saw them dragged from hiding places—even from the churches. They spared my mother, the Tsarina—that was all!"

"They spared you, too," said Katrina softly. "They could not kill you, for it is God's will that you shall live to see your dreams come true."

"My dreams?" echoed Peter. "They are nightmare dreams, child. I had the falling sickness, then, after the massacre. My face twitched—tell me," he said with wild earnestness, "does it twitch now?"

Katrina gazed at him calmly in the candlelight. The Tsar's face was working horribly.

"It is no more than a little blink," she said steadily. "Just a wink, like a roguish fellow might give to a girl."

The Tsar was taken aback. But after a moment, his tense face softened and the twitch diminished. "All women are evil creatures," he said morosely. "My aunt Sophia, my wife Eudoxia, and most evil of all is Anna Mons!"

This was the first time that he had spoken of his wife to Katrina. She wanted to ask a hundred questions, but she did not.

"Your mother was not evil," she said, "and I do not think that I am evil, nor is Matilda. Women are like men—some good, some bad. I do not judge all men by Dakov who beat me, nor by Sheremetiev who hacked off my hair."

Peter said nothing, but stared into the fire for a long time, and if he saw visions there they did not seem to make him so much afraid. For after a while, when the candles had burned down, he said suddenly: "Fetch me wine, Katrina—and then, I think that I shall sleep."

There was better news to send to Prince Menshikov with the next courier who came. Weeks passed, and Tsar Peter found himself talking with surprising freedom to the fair-haired, green-eyed child, who with such quaint wisdom and simple humour could talk back to him, straight as a man might answer him, yet with a gentleness that he found comforting. It was good to find a girl who did not cower from him nor become tongue-tied in his presence.

Sometimes they would not talk, but just sit for hours at a time, he upon his bed by the fire, and she curled on the floor beside him, her head resting on the end of his pillow.

Soon he began to receive the couriers himself, and question them eagerly about the progress of the campaign, thirsting for the slightest detail.

"Alec must not take Narva," he said, "until I am well enough to be there." To the courier he said, "Tell Prince Menshikov and Marshal Sheremetiev that when they approach Narva's defences, they must halt and send a coach for me."

Katrina did not interrupt while the courier was receiving his orders, but when he had saluted and gone, she said: "Majesty, are you well enough to go to the war? You have not the strength to stir from your bed."

The Tsar considered her, with a faint flicker of amusement and affection in his darkly sunken eyes.

"Fetch me my jacket, little Kitty," he said feebly, and she brought him the dark, rough Dutch sailor coat he had worn when he fell ill. To Katrina it seemed big and heavy as a tarpaulin tent.

The Tsar groped with weak fingers through the pockets until he found a small black leather medallion-case. It held a heavy bronze medal, and Katrina picked the medal from its black velvet bed, curiously.

On the front of the medal was a picture of a man warming his hands at the muzzles of Swedish defence guns. The man's face was a cruel caricature of the Tsar.

"Is it supposed to be you?" asked Katrina, uncertain.

The Tsar nodded, and his face had begun to twitch again, very slightly. "It is," he said, "and on the other side, too."

On the reverse side the grotesquely caricatured Tsar was running, his ornate cap fallen from his head, and his sceptre dropped behind him.

"What does the writing say?" asked Katrina.

"This one says—" and the Tsar's finger shook as he pointed to the caricature warming itself at the guns—"it says 'Peter went out and wept bitterly.'" The Tsar was not bothering to read the inscriptions. He knew them by heart.

"The Swedes struck that medal to commemorate my defeat at Narva. See the date, 1700." Katrina could not read the date, but she nodded intelligently, pretending that she could. She remembered the rejoicings in Marienburg, more than three years ago, and how the Swedish dragoons had boasted about the Great Tsar's defeat at Narva. "Our lads couldn't get near enough to the Russians to kill them—for the Russians threw their muskets away and ran faster than we did," they had boasted. She did not mention this to Peter, but he could see that she knew.

"It will not be the same next time," he whispered grimly. He had exhausted himself.

"Oh, I'm glad!" Katrina had blurted the words before she realized what she had said, and the Tsar gave an amused little grimace. "And you a Swede?" he said. "You little traitor!" He laughed, almost for the first time since his collapse. "You love me, don't you?" he said, teasingly.

Katrina blushed, but met his dark, mocking eyes calmly. "Any woman loves a man whom she nurses, Your Majesty," she said. "And it is time for your broth."

She fed him spoonfuls, for his fingers could not yet hold a cup steadily. As she dabbed his chin, which was smooth where she had shaved him, the Tsar said "Little Katrina—Kitty—when I take Narva, you shall watch me. It will be a victory for me, I promise you." He took her hand, and it felt as it always did, like a tiny, warm animal as it nestled, trusting him. She had feared this big, terrible man when she did not know him, and now—after she had nursed him, tended his needs and soothed his nightmares—her feelings towards him had swung so much away from her first unreasoning fears, that she dealt with him boldly, pertly sometimes—taking risks that would have appalled such a practised courtier as Menshikov. Perhaps she did not fear Tsar Peter as much as would have been wise. But in the days of his slowly recovering strength, her innocent impudence seemed to delight him.

"Tomorrow," he said, "I shall get up and we shall look at the sea." It was late May, and the sun shone warmly.

"Tomorrow," said Katrina with smiling firmness, "Your Majesty may get up, but unless we can command the sea to visit the fields outside this house, Your Majesty will not see it, for a mile is too far to walk on your first day out of bed."

Matilda's eyes, as she listened, were wide with amazement. But the Tsar merely smiled. "A glimpse of the sea will do me more good than all your damned broth," he said comfortably.

Next day the Tsar walked falteringly out, and breathed the sweet air. Birds sang in the birch trees, and Katrina's lengthening hair stirred in a direct wind from the Baltic. "Smell it," said the Tsar, and sniffed pleasurably. "There it is—my window, my entrance to the Western world. Damn it," he growled rebelliously, "I must see it."

"So you can," said Katrina, "from this little hill behind the barns." She led him carefully up the gradual slope until a view of the Baltic stretched, grey and sparkling, before them in the distance.

"You see that island," said Peter. "I shall put a fortress there. And all this—" he gestured with his arms—"will be a great city. I shall build it with prisoners from the campaigns."

"Poor prisoners," said Katrina. The Tsar looked down at her. The curve of her mouth disturbed him. He bent and kissed her, with an almost thoughtful tenderness. Katrina stood on her toes and reached upwards to grasp his big shoulders for support. Though he had lost much weight, she was still like a doll in his arms.

"Being with you, little Kitty," he said, "seems to win me back to the days of my innocence, as if—as if I were the man I had dreamed of being, when I was a boy." He laughed, and his chest swelled to the fresh sea air. "It's good," he said, "clean—taste it!"

Next day the courier arrived, mud-splashed with a terse dispatch from Menshikov:

"Shall link with Sheremetiev's armies eight miles south of Narva tomorrow, to commence attack upon outer defences. Coach on its way."

By afternoon, the outriders clattered into the yard, followed by the glittering, breastplated officers of the Tsar's Guard, who escorted an ornately decorated black and gold coach, drawn by five horses with golden plumes. The imperial two-headed eagle of the House of Romanov was on the coach doors.

The Tsar limped out eagerly to inspect it; swung open the coach door before the attendant officer could reach it, and peered inside. Katrina, who followed him anxiously, heard his bellow of wrath:

"Blast that pie-boy—that Menshikov! Does he think a dead man is going to travel into battle!"

The inside of the great coach was sumptuously equipped with wine flagons in clips on the walls, link brackets for traveling lanthorns, even a small oil stove for making hot drinks. But there were no seats. The entire coach was taken up by a huge feather bed, deep as a snowdrift and fluffy as apple-blossom. To Katrina, it looked inviting.

The Tsar swung round upon the Guards Colonel in command of his waiting escort. "How long before the armies reach the outworks of Narva?" he demanded.

The Colonel considered. "Marshal Sheremetiev was repulsed yesterday evening, Sire," he said, "after the courier left with your dispatches. He had to pull his guns back half a mile from the outer defences, on the south and southwest approach. It may not be for a fortnight or more, now."

"Then I'll ride," said Peter sternly. "Saddle me a horse and leave this damned bed-on-wheels here at the farmhouse. We can take the journey slowly."

They moved off next dawn, the Tsar pale and uncomfortable in the saddle. Katrina ran to proffer him a pot of warmed wine and herbs before his journey. The Tsar drank it, and regarded her unsmilingly, but with a quizzical twist about his mouth. He put down his big hand and caressed her hair almost roughly. Then without looking towards her again, he set spurs into his horse's flanks, and the cavalcade clattered off in the sunlight. The big coach stood, clumsy and gleaming, in the courtyard.

"How far is Narva?" asked Katrina. Matilda, who had come from the house to stand beside her, said: "Nearly a hundred versts—about sixty miles, child. It will take them two or three days."

"He promised to take me with him," said Katrina, and her voice was tight in her throat. Matilda laid a comforting, plump hand upon her shoulder. "Ah, child, you should learn not to heed the promises of a great man. He'll say anything to suit his mood."

After the Tsar's departure, the couriers ceased to come every three days from the battlefront, and news drifted back slowly, with batches of prisoners and their escorts, to Petersburg. The army of the Tsar, it seemed, was still halted beyond Narva, struggling dourly to breach the outer defences.

It was a late evening of early August, and Katrina—who had slipped back into taking a share of the kitchen duties with Matilda—was cutting the meat for supper when a small group of horsemen came spurring up the road from the west. Katrina ran to the door.

She could see the Tsar among them as they swung into the courtyard. His face was tanned a deep brown, and his uniform splashed with the stains of the journey. He jumped from his horse before the beast had properly halted, and swung Katrina gaily from her feet.

"Sire," she said, when she had got her breath from his kiss, "your health has returned—you're nearly breaking my ribs."

The Tsar smiled. "I've missed your pretty impudence, little

Kitty," he said. "What's for supper? My men are hungry, and so am I. We're camped under the gates of Narva—and tomorrow we attack!"

"Then what are you doing here?" asked Katrina, wide-eyed.

"For you," said the Tsar. "I've come for you, little Kitty. I promised you should see the fall of Narva, and so you shall. Where's that coach—that damned bed-on-wheels, eh? We shall travel tonight in it."

"Tonight?" said Katrina faintly.

The Tsar boomed with laughter. "Aye, the biggest coach—the biggest bed—the biggest arms in all Russia to hold you tonight, little Kitty. We shall travel while we sleep, and sleep as we travel. What do you think of that?"

Katrina dropped her gaze and a blush spread suddenly outwards from the vivid red of her cheeks.

She was too excited to eat much supper that evening, too restless to sit contentedly at the long table. As the others ate plentifully of Matilda's good cooking and drank their fill for the long journey ahead of them, Katrina ran upstairs and looked amongst her dresses, nibbled at her lip thoughtfully, and wondered which of her gowns to choose for none of them seemed entirely suited to Army camp life as she had glimpsed it before.

The huge coach of the Tsar sped, jolting, over the road to Narva. Its five white horses were fanned out, pulling crazily as the driver's whip cracked among them. Alongside, a dozen tall young nobles of the Tsar's Guard bobbed at a pace between trot and canter over the broken, shadowy path, and the thin moonlight that shone upon their silver breastplates lit the coach's black bodywork in ghostly silver mimicry. Katrina was kneeling on the big silkspread bed of the coach to watch the soldiers riding near her. The semi-arctic summer night outside was spectrally blue.

"Blast these damned breeches!" Tsar Peter, struggling from his uniform in the cramped space between bed and coach door, lurched and sat heavily on the bed, that bounced and flung Katrina forward. The Tsar grinned, a bead of sweat upon his face. "Let's have that roof back," he said. His knees tunnelled deep hollows into the yielding mattress as he stretched up to release two silver bolts in the pink quilted roof, and heaved back a heavy flap that exposed half the coach to a sultry night sky. Katrina laughed up at the dim stars. "We travel so quickly," she said, "and they seem to stand still. They look as if they could melt down on us like thawing snowflakes."

The Tsar climbed under a thin silk cover that was fluffy with goose breast feathers. "Dwarf!" he shouted. "Where's that damned dwarf?"

Grog jumped down from his seat beside the driver, balanced himself upon the swaying coach roof, and blinked down into the moonlit interior.

"Yes, Majesty?"

"Sing, dwarf!" commanded the Tsar, and Grog's cheeks quivered with pleasure. He clung, grotesque and stumpy, to the seat rail and his deformed barrel chest swelled to a Livonian love song:

The white flowers in her hair had gone to sleep,
Her eyes like amber stars were deep
With dreams unharvested that shaded them
Was it the lovers' moon that faded them . . .

The young Hussars smiled up at him from their cantering horses and exchanged significant glances as they considered the drawn curtains of the jolting coach.

Katrina had returned to the kneeling posture by the window, holding the curtain for support. She looked down at the Tsar, and was suddenly afraid to exchange the sanctuary of shadow under the window, for the moonlit pillow by the Tsar's dark head. He watched her, and smiled. The dark curls of hair under his chest seemed like a deeper patch of the coach's shifting shadows.

Peter, without rising, reached across and fitted his big hands around Katrina's tiny, nipped waist. Black tree branches whisked overhead, shaking a dapple of shadow and silver across the Tsar's bare body, over which muscles writhed, as he lifted Katrina towards himself. The elements of storm were in the rocking coach, and the taste of blood ran stark across Katrina's tongue, as he crushed her mouth under his teeth. She gasped for breath, feeling helplessly frail beneath his strength. Her nails dug into Peter's hard brown shoulder, but the Tsar did not heed. The coach lurched and creaked, the cuirasses of the Hussars jingled like muffled silver bells, and the big wheels throbbed over the dark night road. But the Tsar heard none of these sounds, nor the deep, flawless voice of the dwarf above his head, singing of love into the fleeting night. He listened, as Katrina lay panting under his kiss, only to the half-suffocated, urgent little cries that came from her. The smell of clover and pines were tangled in her hair. The warm and misty night rushed past their windows and over their heads unheeded, as the watery stars wheeled slowly towards the dawn.

At Narva the Russians had built an encompassing wall to cut off the besieged city, which lay in a sharp bend of the River Narova. Their siege wall spanned the river from bank to bank. The Russians did not mean this time to be surprised from the rear. Behind the embattled wall lay the tents of the Tsar's Army. The first rows were the drab felt tents of Kalmuck Tartars, those squat and taciturn men with black stringy beards who watched from foreign-slanted eyes. Among their tents, prayer wheels hummed in hundreds of crude wooden pagodas that were painted and festooned with looted baubles of the long campaign.

The Cossack tents, on the river edges, were crude and gaudy. On such warm nights, the Cossacks chose the stars for roof, and their encampments were little more than twig bivouacs, upon which silks and pelts—worth a boyar's ransom—were negligently thrown. The tall Cossacks themselves, thin-hipped, arrogant horsemen, were up with the morning light; they wore jackets of scarlet, tightened by belts of gold cloth, and their damask trousers, baggy at the knees, were tucked into shining red or yellow boots, with jewelled and silver-studded heels. Their tall black lambswool hats gleamed with jewels. The Cossack was not born who could survive a battle without decorating his hat with a fortune in booty. They yelled and shouted in undisciplined high spirits as the Tsar's big coach trundled past.

The tents of the main Russian infantry, the steady and German-trained troops of the Tsar's personal regiments, were camped on the higher exposed ground among the gun emplacements.

They were almost beneath the shadow of Narva's thick grey walls. Their tents lay neat as planted turnip fields. Aloof from them, sheltered by a few bullet-torn trees, was the bannered Command Tent of Marshal Sheremetiev. When Katrina and the Tsar were dressed, their coach halted here, and Prince Menshikov came to greet them, with the Marshal waddling behind. Sheremetiev's eyes creased as he regarded Katrina. Before he could remember whether he recognized her, the Tsar smote him affectionately upon his lardy shoulder. "Let me jog your memory, Boru. You hacked off her hair at Marienburg! And now," said the Tsar, eyeing Sheremetiev's glistening bald skull, "she has my permission to hack yours off—if she can find any!" He bellowed in merriment, and as his Marshal grinned reluctantly, Peter grabbed a handful of his soft paunch and shook it until Sheremetiev grunted in genuine pain. "You live too soft, Boris! The only exercise you take is not enough. You should be forced to chase your women first!"

A blotched red spread over Sheremetiev's thick neck and across his hairless pate. He was glad when the Tsar turned from him to shout for the regimental tailor.

"Buzhenina! Buzhenina!" The call echoed through the camp from soldier to soldier.

Katrina glanced curiously at Sheremetiev, and for an instant his eye met her gaze. His lips were dry and quivering slightly, and she saw the faint scars her fingernails had made down his cheek. She knew that, although she was afraid of him, he was now much more afraid of her. The illustrious Marshal Sheremetiev was recognizable in that moment as a coward at least so far as such an awkward social occasion was concerned.

A small and bowlegged Kalmuck, breathless from his rush uphill, prostrated himself before the Tsar, who booted him good humouredly. The little Kalmuck looked as if somebody had swept up all the bits from a tailor shop floor and emptied them over him. His skin was dry, brown as an onion, and his face had the appearance of an amiable pig.

"Ha, there, my little pork-and-onions," said the Tsar. "Did you finish those Swedish uniforms I wanted?"

"Yes, yes, Sire—all fee-neesh!" The Kalmuck spoke jerkily in a high, chiming voice. "Bee-oo-tiful blue cloth—all fee-neesh!"

"Good," said Peter. "Judging from your own coat you couldn't sew a knot on a hangman's noose!"

The Kalmuck gave a wise Oriental smile. The superb uniforms of Prince Menshikov and Marshal Sheremetiev were testimonials of his skill.

"Now," said the Tsar, "I want a uniform for this girl—like an officer of the Muscovy Hussar."

The little Kalmuck looked at Katrina, considering her size and shape. If there were thoughts behind his wise, dim eyes, he did not show any outward clue to them as he passed his cord over her body, and deftly knotted measurements onto it.

"Yes, Sire. Tomorrow?"

"Tonight!" the Tsar shouted. "I don't want any damned Cossacks grabbing her, thinking she's a camp harlot." Menshikov gave a dry, amused cough, and Katrina was glad to follow the Tsar into the command tent, away from his eyes.

The tent was a wide, lofty dome of silk and canvas, stretched over a network of thin supports. It had ample room for the big couch covered with flowered silks, several chairs, footstools and map tables. Down one side was a narrow sideboard set with meats and flagons. A brazier burned in the centre of the tent, its smoke escaping through a circular hole in the roof. A copper samovar with golden ornamentations, steamed upon a gaudily painted stand near the brazier. Katrina saw the heavy bullion chest of Marshal Sheremetiev, and remembered her night's ordeal.

The Tsar was gazing around at the red damask drapings, the purple silks and green lace trimmings, his nose wrinkled in disgust.

"Is this where you sleep, Your Majesty?" asked Katrina.

"Alec and I share a skin tent down there," he said, gesturing briefly towards the crowded camp. "This scented stinking place is Sheremetiev's—and there's enough damned frippery wasted on it to pay the wages of a company of dragoons for a year!" He spat contemptuously into the brazier. "He sleeps here with his Swedish wench...." The Tsar remembered, and grinned mischievously. "What's her name, now?"

"Her name is Veda," said Katrina slowly. "She whipped me and had me branded."

"She did?" The Tsar was mildly interested. "Oh well, there's plenty of knouts and branding irons in camp, little Kitty, if you want an evening's sport." He laughed, but Katrina did not.

"Does she sleep here, too?" she asked quietly.

"Not tonight," said the Tsar. "I'm clearing Boris out for tonight, so you can have it. After tomorrow we'll sleep in Narva!"

By late afternoon the nimble fingers of the Kalmuck tailor and his assistants had completed Katrina's uniform. Without it, she had not dared to stray alone from the Command Tent, for fear of being flung to the ground by any passing soldier, like the hundreds of women camp followers who lived among the lines and were recognized as communal property, belonging to any man who chose to snatch a moment of life before the possible death of the morning.

Katrina laid the strawberry-red uniform jacket on the bed to admire its silver, corded froggings across the breast, and the silver chain mail epaulettes at the shoulders. She put on the long white overall breeches, each leg like a long, thick stocking. The finespun cloth moulded to her slender legs as if it were an added skin, and the jacket of Imperial Household colours, buttoned at her waist and bosom without an inch to spare. The chain links on her shoulders gave them a manliness that was belied by the slenderness of her neck and the soft fair curls above it. Silver spurs upon her black boot heels.

From the blunt, huddled towers of the besieged city of Narva, the sunset flag had been ceremoniously dipped and defiantly raised again, and the bugle notes of her homeland came faintly to Katrina as she watched the blue and gold emblem of Sweden rise and fall. The Russian campfires gleamed brightly now as the twilight that was all there would be of darkness, descended slowly. Lamps shaped like hanging baskets of wrought metal, perched on tall stems stuck into the earth, roared with new-kindled flames and dripped fiery flame-flakes onto the dust. The soldiers were grouped, sweating and unbuttoned, around the fires. Cossacks held quarters of fresh-killed lamb upon their cavalry swords to the flames, and toasted the flesh into edible succulence. Barrels of cherry vodka had been rolled from supply stores and gurgled ceaselessly until they were drained. Some men were already dancing the bizarre wild Cossack dances, dust rising like fine mist around their scarlet boots, while their comrades clapped and shouted.

Everybody rocked as they squatted and sang in chorus, including the Tsar himself. Katrina could hear the voice of Grog clear above the chorus. It was the raucous carousal song of the Don Cossacks:

Damn your mead and rot your ale!

Give me vodka, sweet cherry vodka!
Not from goblet, not from beaker—
But damned big swigs from a damned big pail. . . .

Katrina squatted beside the Tsar, and drank red vodka that flamed like sweet fire upon her tongue. A Cossack officer proffered a piece of roasted lamb upon the blade of a captured Turkish yatakhan sword, and Katrina took it, sinking her strong teeth into the tender, sizzling meat. The Tsar put his big arm across her shoulders, and Katrina felt a surge of wild, excited happiness.

He laughed down at her. "How d'you like being at war, little Hussar?" She threw back her head and laughed up at him, cheeks flushed with vodka. "Good," she said. "Good!" The campfire lit sparkles from the feverishly bright green of her eyes. Peter bent impetuously, and took her sweet, warm lips with a searching kiss. The soldiers around them paid no heed. Many were laughing and gasping upon the ground with their women. But other eyes watched Katrina and the Tsar. Veda, with Marshal Sheremetiev's fat, dimpled hand on her bare shoulder, was heeding nothing else as she stared across the fire's glow at Katrina. The hot flames danced, reflected in her white cheeks, but the pale blue of her eyes was cold as a Siberian wind.

The other watcher was Tsar Peter's son Alexis, who stood aloof, in the green uniform of Colonel in the fabulous Simonev Guard. It fitted Alexis' scrawny frame badly. He held a prayer book in his thin fingers, and he was not drinking. He glared from the shadows at Katrina, and his mouth stirred in prayer. "Saints in heaven," he prayed, "strike my father dead!"

Peter suddenly snatched up Katrina and strode to his tent, while she laughed and kicked in his arms, and another face turned jealous eyes to watch them go. Sten'ka the big Cossack chieftain considered Katrina's legs, wriggling in tight Hussar breeches, and passed his tongue across his bearded lips. As soon as the Tsar was safely out of earshot, Prince Alexis raised his voice into a querulous whine to be heard by whomever chose to listen, "My holy mother," he said, "suffers in torment tonight, whilst that witch, that branded daughter of Satan, revels with my accursed father. Has God no justice?"

Marshal Sheremetiev and some of the other officers nearby

affected not to hear. But Veda turned her gaze quickly towards Prince Alexis, and watched him thoughtfully as he walked away.

"Witch?" demanded Big Sten'ka drunkenly. "Is it true that she is a witch?" Prince Alexis did not pause to answer, but as soon as she could, Veda slipped from Sheremetiev's preoccupied embrace and approached Sten'ka, who blinked warily, recognizing the cloak she wore as Sheremetiev's.

"It is true," whispered Veda vindictively. "She has the witch's brand upon her body, and Satan who is on the side of the Swedes, has sent her to rob the Tsar of his senses!" She gave Sten'ka a long, significant glance from beneath lashes spiked with wax and charcoal. "I can school you against the witchcraft," she whispered, "if you will follow me discreetly."

Veda slipped away towards the shadows behind the tent lines of the Cossacks, and after a moment of hesitation in his slow brain, Big Sten'ka put down his leather drinking mug, and followed her. Marshal Sheremetiev continued to stare, unheeding, into the fire as his tongue struggled with a shred of meat that had wedged itself between his black teeth.

The torches in the command tent had spluttered low as Katrina slept. The misted night was on the brink of daylight, when she woke in sudden fear, to find rude hands arousing her. The Tsar had disappeared from his place beside her and now a dozen tall men filled the tent, grinning down at her, and she realized with shock that they were garbed in the blue uniform of Sweden.

Katrina sat up, wide-eyed, and snatching a torch from the bed-head link, was about to fling it among the close pressed, mocking faces, when she saw that Prince Menshikov was among them. She hesitated, uncertain if this was some nightmare, and Tsar Peter thrust the laughing men aside. He was exploding with mirth.

"See, little Kitty," he said, "there aren't enough Swedes to fight—so we make our own!"

Katrina, recognizing now the faces of a number of officers from the Tsar's Guard above the Swedish uniforms, hastily did up her rumpled red tunic.

"It's a ruse of the pie-man's," the Tsar explained, chuckling. "When we last tried to take Narva, the Swedes took us in the rear. This time we'll suffer the same—but it'll be our own lads disguised as Swedes!" He was delighted at the stratagem, and Prince Menshikov added modestly: "I think Narva will open her gates to these uniforms, Katrina."

Katrina blinked in sleepy bewilderment. The Tsar rumpled her curls with crude affection, then turned to join his officers, grouped around the map table. To the accompanying murmur of their voices, Katrina fell asleep again.

The siege guns began to roar with the first light of dawn, and the shattering salvo brought Katrina violently awake. Smoke drifted among the Narva battlements, and at one part by the west buttress visible damage was being done. A small area of the masonry had collapsed and seventy massed Russian siege guns were pouring eighteen-pound shot straight into this weak spot at the rate of dozens a minute.

All the officers, even the Tsar himself, were down with the batteries, darting busily from one gun to the next, for the Russian bombardier, left to his own devices, was a notoriously poor marksman. The ears of the gunners were trickling blood from the deafening and sustained concussion of their guns before the gap in Narva's defences was widened to the Tsar's satisfaction. He straightened himself and wiped his blackened face. "That'll do it, Alec," he said. "Give them the signal!"

A few moments later, from among the trees on the distant western bank of the Narova River, musket fire crackled like burning twigs, and soon Katrina saw a column of blue-clad Swedish cavalrymen fanned out under apparently murderous Russian infantry fire, galloping across the cleared four hundred yards to the sanctuary of Narva's walls. But the broken ground was making shooting difficult, and the galloping Swedes were almost within pistol shot from Narva when a nearby company of Russian infantry who had been crouched in a forward sap, surged out at them in a bayonet charge.

Blue uniforms mingled in a destructive whirl with the Russian strawberry-red of the Tsar's Guard. Sabres clashed and sparkled. Puffs of white smoke appeared suddenly, and men fell. The Swedish gunners on the walls held their fire for fear of endangering their comrades as the Swedish cavalry hacked its way towards the western gate, near the heavily damaged wall. The Russians fell around them. Strawberry uniforms sprawled on the brown earth, and as the survivors faltered, the men in

Swedish blue cheered—a thin cry torn into shreds by the wind —and ran or galloped towards the massive gates that were opening for them, as though a part of the impregnable wall itself were yawning to let them in. At once, the Russians who had lain for dead before the gates jumped to their feet and raced after them, as the picked men of the Tsar's Guard, who had been disguised in the Swedish cavalry uniforms, battled frantically to keep the huge gates open and the breeched wall clear of Narva defenders. With a great, throat-rending shout, the entire phalanx of Russian infantrymen poured forward like a tidal wave, and from the river flank on the west, the colourful Cossack squadrons thundered across. Dead became heaped like driftwood against the thick grey gates as they slowly yielded open to admit the yelling hordes of the Tsar.

Within three hours the Narva garrison had surrendered, and were now being methodically butchered. Tsar Peter, in shirt-sleeves, with naked sword in hand, leaned upon a balcony overlooking Narva's town square, and yawned in the hot sunlight.

It had been a busy morning. He had personally hacked down at least thirty Swedes, and was spattered with their blood. He had slapped the face of the fortress' gallant governor, Rudolf Horn, and was now occupying his private mansion.

Agony hung over Narva like a nightmare fog. Shouting, "*Netchai! Netchai!* Cut! Stab!" the impetuous Cossack cavalry were still clattering through the cobbled narrow streets, thirsting to destroy, and tossing flambeau torches into house windows. Other Cossacks were dismounted and smashing doors in quest of plunder and victims. The stolid Russian infantrymen had driven many hundreds of Narva's unarmed citizens into the churches and with no more emotion upon their faces than slight grins of satisfaction, were busily trundling barrels of pitch to burn them.

The slender, yellow-faced little Samoyede tribesmen, faces inscrutable as smooth pebbles, were aiming their short arrows at women on the roofs of buildings, who had dragged their infants through upstairs windows to escape rapacious Cossack hands. A wild troop of Don Cossacks, their horse-tail banner flying, swept across the square at full reckless gallop, and behind every horse trailed a young girl, roped by the ankles to

Cossack saddles, her garments dragged almost away. Many were already dead, but some still threshed and moaned. A knot of elderly men, like withered grey beanpods, hung from a thick marble balcony across the square. They were some of Narva's aldermen, and they jerked and strangled slowly. Even old men found it hard to die in the bright heat of midday.

The Tsar looked at Katrina, who was standing beside him. "Those Cossacks are wild devils, they always get a bit out of hand at moments like this. They owe to the Tsar only as much allegiance as they think fit."

"You mean," said Katrina slowly, for she was striving not to be sick, "that Your Majesty can't—stop—this dreadful—slaughter?"

"Dreadful?" echoed the Tsar. "But these have always been the spoils of victory." Then he said uncomfortably, "I suppose it's not very Western, is it, my little Kitty?"

Katrina swayed, and the Tsar had to prevent her from falling. "Please," she implored, "please—stop them. . . ."

The Cossacks were gathering in hundreds in the square now, laden with loot and victims. The uninjured were sorted out for the usual prolonged Cossack sport, which would end—as it had done at Marienburg—with the almost dead victims being pegged out as targets for the lances of galloping, drunken horsemen. All the Cossack chieftains were there, Big Sten'ka among them. Staff officer he might be, but Big Sten'ka had no time for duties today. His hair, damp beneath his heavy fur cap, clung to his brow in crinkly curls. His tunic was open and Swedish blood splashed his big chest. Even from the high balcony, the exultation of his face could be clearly seen, and he looked like a wild tiger.

"Yes," said the Tsar suddenly. "This is not what a monarch of the Western world would allow. You are right, my little Katrina."

He gathered his senior officers around him with a gesture, and hurried down the stairs of the Mansion House, into the crowded square.

Almost at the doorway, he came upon a group of red-coated Russian bombardiers, around a fair-haired Swedish lad. They had broken his back across a mounting post and were tormenting him unspeakably with their short, artillerymen's swords.

"Stop!" called the Tsar. They did not heed him. The square was like a prolonged explosion of discordant sound, and it was possible that they had not even heard him. He hacked down the nearest bombardier with his sword, and pulled at the shoulder of another. "Stop!" he commanded, panting with fury. The soldier met the Tsar's angered eye, and laughed foolishly. His muddy and bloodstained face held an expression of dazed, almost hypnotized, fatuity. He continued to probe at the dying lad with his sword, and it was only when the Tsar's blade penetrated his own body, that a glimmer of sanity returned to his brain as he bent forward and died.

Behind the Tsar came Prince Menshikov, with sword drawn, and Katrina followed among the half dozen staff officers. She did not want to go down into the horrors of the square, but she did not want to be left alone on a balcony overlooking them.

"Stop! Stop! Stop!" With each shouted command, the Tsar's big sword rose and fell. His staff officers followed him, helping to hack a way through their own troops to the centre of the square where the Cossack chieftains stood. Katrina was swept with them.

Gradually, the lust-crazed Cossacks became aware of the presence of their Tsar. Like a spreading pond ripple, an uneasy and watchful silence fell upon the square. The Tsar's head was tall above them. He lifted his sword. "This massacre must cease," he roared. "This blood upon my blade—see it—is Russian, not Swedish. My men shall not behave like Turks in a conquered city!"

Mazeppa, the Cossack leader—hetman of them all—regarded the Tsar through beady, expressionless eyes. He did not choose to make the first move. It was the slow thinking Sten'ka who spoke, almost as if the idea had been put into his brain by somebody else. He was remembering what he had learned the previous night among the tent shadows.

"Your Majesty has been bewitched!" He took two strides forward, until he was glaring down at Katrina. "This witch in the uniform of a Hussar!" he said contemptuously, and spat full in Katrina's face. "Our Tsar has become a woman, too," he roared, "in the uniform of a soldier!"

With a deep sob of pure wrath, Peter raised his sword. But Menshikov's hand checked the movement halfway. "Wait," said

Menshikov in an urgent whisper. "If you kill Sten'ka the whole lot of Cossacks may fall upon us!"

The Tsar looked around the angry countenances of the Cossacks, and heard a growl of rage swell, as the first rumbles of a snow avalanche might sound in the instant before it became disaster beyond halting. He, too, could think quickly, if not always coolly, in emergency. He slapped his blood-wet sword into its scabbard, and gazed around him for an instant like an angry, threatened hawk. A moment later he snatched a heavy whip from the belt of the nearest Cossack, and caught Sten'ka a blow across his upper arm that rang out like the sudden snap of a thick tree branch.

"Sten'ka, you pig," he shouted, "I am the Tsar, and I could kill you. But I will fight you as a man, as a soldier! I will fight you with whips—at your own Cossack game!" He turned to Mazeppa. "Get two whips, and match them for weight and length," he ordered harshly. "Then clear a duelling space in the square. Let us see if a Dnieper Cossack can flay with whip as well as his brother Don Cossacks, or if his strength lies only in his tongue!"

At once the massacre was forgotten. The Tsar, with a shrewdness worthy of Menshikov, had split the rebellious Cossacks, half of whom were the tall and aristocratic horsemen of the Dnieper, and the rest, including most of those in the square, belonged to the more wild tribesman of the Don.

Big Sten'ka rubbed his welted shoulder with an angry growl. His eyes were puzzled. "It is forbidden," he said slowly, "to raise a hand against the Tsar. This is a trap, to make me commit a hanging offence."

"You have already done that," declared the Tsar, "but I swear to you by the True Cross, that if you beat me in fair fight, no harm shall come to you."

At once, Sten'ka's face lit up. He was the only one among the thousands of hardened warriors who crowded Narva's bloodstained square, who could meet the Tsar's glance from level height. He lacked a little of Peter's broadness across back and shoulder, but his own chest was deeper and his arms equally thick. If anything, Tsar Peter was the more powerfully built of the two, but Sten'ka had the advantage of being nearly ten years younger. He measured the Tsar with a glance that he had never before dreamed of using—as an adversary.

And he nodded with a slow grin. "I am satisfied," he said. "I will tear the skin from your ribs, Your Majesty!"

There was a shout of laughter at this, and the Tsar smiled grimly. Menshikov had given whispered instructions, and an orderly slipped away. Soon, from an adjacent street, a column of hastily assembled infantrymen of the Tsar's Guard threaded in a single file through the jostling throng of Cossacks, Samoyedes and burly Russian peasant soldiers. Drummers beat a General Assembly, and other drummers slipped one by one from among the crowd, into their places, to take up the drum-roll. Some were dishevelled and some already drunk, but they drummed on, and gradually a square was formed, and the watching soldiers were pressed back to leave a sufficiently wide space for the duellists. Katrina stood by Prince Menshikov, her face pale with misery. If she had not beseeched the Tsar to halt the massacre, this would never have happened.

"Can't you stop them?" she whispered. Menshikov shrugged with a faint, half uneasy smile.

"It's too late to worry now," he said. "And the Tsar has fought whip duels before, in his boyhood. He knows what he is doing."

"But—mightn't he be killed?"

Prince Menshikov looked down at her and saw the searing anxiety in her eyes.

"Men have died in whip duels," he said, "particularly with these weighted Cossack whips. But these two are strong as bulls. I do not think the whips will kill them. I pray that it will not kill the Tsar!" And across Menshikov's sensitive face came the same expression of brooding, womanly tenderness which Katrina had seen before.

The Tsar had removed his shirt, and now took up the whip, carefully examined each thong, wrenching at the metal-shod tip to ensure its firmness, for his life might depend upon it. His cavalry breeches, buckled at the waist with a broad leather duelling belt to protect his kidneys, and his chest looked even more bulky and formidable than usual.

Sten'ka had stripped off his own blood-flecked blouse and stood in scarlet damask trousers. He, too, bent to study his whip, investigating each plaited knot for flaws. He bent the thongs in his fingers until the leather creaked. If a whip broke in the duellist's hand there would be no respite whilst a new one was fetched. It would mean merely that his opponent could at leisure flog him to death, unopposed.

The two combatants, although each stood well over six feet six inches tall, did not look abnormally large as they approached each other. It was the crowd of watching soldiery that seemed to be dwarfed. On the outside edges of the spectators, little Samoyedes and bowlegged Kalmucks dodged and bobbed to glimpse the spectacle, and seemed like toys in contrast with the two combatants. Prince Menshikov's glance fell upon Katrina's anxious face and he strove to find something to say that would give the appearance of being completely at ease, which he was assuredly not.

"There are very simple rules," he said, "in these Cossack whip duels. They grasp each other's left hand, and the loser is the first man who falls or releases his grip."

Katrina shivered. The drummer had been keeping up a significant mutter upon his kettledrum, and now—as Sten'ka and the Tsar strode towards each other—he crashed out a solitary drum note that made both men come to an abrupt halt. They looked at each other for an instant and Sten'ka grinned craftily, then each man grasped the other's left hand so purposefully that it seemed as if their intention was to dislocate the other's thumb.

Each tried at once to assert a mastery. Their arms and shoulder muscles knotted like twisted ropes with effort, and Katrina could see flesh stretched taut in a white band across each man's hand behind the knuckles.

In every other way, they stood like statues, not even looking at each other, but staring across the square in opposite directions with a gaze of utterly expressionless concentration. Both men were forcing all their bodies' great strengths down into that compact little battlefield of their clenched hands.

The drum beat once more—the first signal to strike. Katrina watched with hand pressed to her open mouth. She could see now why that grip was so important to the duellists, for in that split instant that the two heavy plaited whip thongs whirred through the air, the Tsar had managed to jerk Sten'ka forward and off balance for his strike, so that Sten'ka's metal-shod lash etched a red groove in the Tsar's big shoulders where the muscle was wadded inches thick, but the Tsar's own blow had fallen across the more vulnerable flesh just behind

Sten'ka's small ribs and over the exposed knobs of his lower spine. The metal tip had dug itself in like the peck of a vulture's beak, and Sten'ka was convulsed by a sensation that penetrated to his finger tips and down the calves of his legs, cutting his breath like the wrack of an acutely painful coughing paroxysm. Sten'ka uttered no sound, but at once began to sweat. There followed a few seconds pause, and again the silent, almost motionless struggle for hand mastery, until the next drum beat, when the two whips fell one after the other with dull slapping sounds as if they were blows from an open, gloved hand. This time the damage was not great, for each man had winced, in the only way that the game permitted, by jerking his opponent's hand upwards and inwards as the blow was delivered, so that the whipstroke was robbed of much of its force, and the deadly iron tip flicked harmlessly away.

The packed ranks of watching soldiers shrieked with disapproval, and when the next blows fell, each duellist was so determined not to flinch that both were knocked a half pace forward by the force of the stroke.

The soldiers, fickle as is any crowd, now roared raucous encouragement The Dnieper Cossacks yelled for Sten'ka: "*Netchai! Netchai!*" their familiar battle cry, "Cut, Cut!" The Russian infantrymen bellowed like a thousand bulls for their Tsar, and the Samoyedes wailed with shrill indetermination, catching the frenzy but without particular partisanship. The massed, colourful ranks of the Don Cossacks shouted in hilarious excitement for either man as their individual fancy chose, but to the careful ear of Prince Menshikov it seemed that most were calling encouragement to the Tsar, and he released his breath in a sigh of relief. If the Tsar put up a good show the brief revolt might well be over before it had begun.

And the Tsar was indeed putting up a good performance, for at the next exchange he received a quick whip stroke that gashed his upper arm as if with a blunted knife, but Sten'ka's body quivered like a bull attempting to rid itself of stinging flies, for the Tsar's answering blow shook him almost to his knees. Katrina's throat felt cramped and dry. The constriction of her tightly fitting Hussar's uniform, and the windless heat of the early afternoon sun, combined with her anxiety for the Tsar to make her reel, sick and dazed, against Menshikov's arm. The drum beats quickened and the blows came faster. After the first twenty slow strokes, giving the combatants opportunity to display their skill and hand wrestling, they were now entitled to a flurry of twenty quick strokes, almost at the speed of a heartbeat, to enable agility and sheer strength of arm to have its advantage.

In this quick exchange, the Tsar suffered, for Sten'ka had the responsive, hard muscles of a wild creature. Yet the Tsar walked into each blow, and drove Sten'ka gradually across the cleared space, until they were so near to Katrina that she could see the trickle of sweat upon the Tsar's thick eyebrows, and the haphazard pattern of injuries across Stenka's back.

Soon the period of slow blows came again, and the Tsar had managed to retain enough coolness and strength to wrest full weight of gain from them. Neither man had uttered a single sound, not even a gasp of discomfort, but Sten'ka had begun to chew at his underlip with an intensity that marked deep purple dents upon it. Each blow that fell came now across an existing pain, and to Sten'ka, as his head drooped further forward with each stroke exchanged, it seemed that all his life had been passed in a red agony of pain, that there had never been a time he could remember when pleasure and health had been more than a distant dream.

Anguish had become the only reality and the only believable eternity to Sten'ka. If the Tsar Peter's merciless hand-clasp had not been supporting him, he might have fallen. As it was, Sten'ka remained on his feet and continued to strike at each drum beat, but each blow that he received folded his wavering knees further, until he was visibly wilting and ready to collapse. His saturated trousers clung tight as wet gauze now to his legs. The Tsar's face had twisted into a hard smile. The jostling throng of soldiers who watched were yelling, shouting, and belabouring each other delightedly. This had been a duel to be long remembered, to be recounted to one's grandchildren, and worthy to win free vodka at taverns for many a year, in the telling of it.

Sten'ka had fallen. He lay prostrate, still clutching his useless whip. The drum beats stopped, but the Tsar continued to grip Sten'ka's hand and to strike, blow upon heavy blow, until Prince Menshikov stepped forward and grasped his arm. In the Tsar's eyes was that same expression of dazed hypnotized blankness that Katrina had seen in the soldiers' faces during the massacre. For a long moment the Tsar stood over his fallen opponent, and his chest heaved as he recovered his breath, whilst his wits came back to him and his delighted troops shouted. A staff officer dipped a cloth in cold water, and ran forward to lay it across the Tsar's shoulders. Its coolness brought the Tsar completely to awareness. He straightened himself and dropped the sopping red whip upon the ground.

Sten'ka lay on his back with eyes shut, and mouth sagged open. He was deeply unconscious, and from the snoring noises with which he breathed, it seemed that he had concussion. Some of the whip strokes must have damaged the base of his skull or his spine.

Mazeppa, the Cossack hetman, came forward grinning. It had been a splendid entertainment, and the crowning pleasure to the day's victory. Such things could bring simple happiness to a Cossack. Even the Dnieper Cossacks were grinning. They did not take the defeat of Sten'ka as a personal affront. Had he been victorious, Sten'ka would have been their champion, but in his defeat Sten'ka was an individual rebel. It was the way of the world, and particularly the world of a Cossack.

"What shall I do with him, Your Majesty?" asked Mazeppa, the grin still broad upon his shaven cheeks.

"Kill him," said Peter instantly. "If he had won, he should have lived, as I promised. But no defeated dog shall stay alive to boast of laying a whip across the shoulders of the Tsar!"

There was a great yell of delight from the Cossacks at this. If their joy had been huge before, it now overthrew all bounds. This was wit, indeed! They threw themselves upon the ground, and rolled in the hot brown dust, gasping with mirth.

Mazeppa, the hetman, not to be outdone, made his own jest. He strode to the still unconscious Sten'ka and laughed down at him.

"Always, he had a loud mouth," announced Mazeppa. "And in a moment he shall speak louder yet. Let him roar like a cannon!" He unscrewed his powderhorn, and poured a cascade of shimmering black gunpowder into Sten'ka's slack mouth, until it heaped up beyond his teeth and overflowed on to the earth in pyramids by his cheeks. A grinning Cossack handed his chief a lit linstock fuse, and Mazeppa touched off the gunpowder.

Katrina had turned away, shielding her eyes. She remembered

Sten'ka laughing by the kitchen fire, enjoying his pot of hot vodka, nodding his big head with slow pleasure to the lilt of Grog's love songs. She remembered Sten'ka's ruthless lips against her own. She hardly heard the dull little waft of gunpowder burst. The cheering flared up again, and as it wavered, it was interrupted by the sharp bark of commands from the Tsar's officers, beginning to get the men under control. The ranks broke up, sorted themselves out, and moved back to their various encampments in ragged but unwavering order. The brief rebellion was ended, and Sten'ka had paid the full, final price for it.

Chapter Nine

THE TSAR'S OFFICERS had prepared the Great Hall of Narva Mansion House for a victory banquet. Some, like Prince Menshikov, had changed into their brightest regimental tunics and sat at table like brilliant tropical birds, whilst others still proudly wore their battle-stained uniforms, and many had injuries nonchantly bandaged.

Katrina, still in her Hussar uniform, sat between Menshikov and Marshal Ogilvy, a small sandy-haired man, renegade from England, now resplendent in the silver-and-strawberry of the Russian Guards. Decorations and ribbons covered his thin chest, and he was regarding Katrina with curiosity, for this was Marshal Ogilvy's first meeting with the Tsar's new favourite.

Among the other officers sat the painted favourites from the camp women, their teeth like black pearls and cheeks beetroot-stained. They chattered and shrilled, shamelessly savoring the pleasures of orgy. Here and there, pale and red-eyed, was an occasional female survivor from the day's massacre. Nearly all these women had purple bruises upon their mouths, and torn gowns, and some were crying softly as their captors mauled and jested among them.

The Tsar himself, still wearing his rough cavalry breeches, straddled a carved stool in the middle of the assembly. With typical gauche modesty, the Tsar had left vacant the head of the table for whoever wished to occupy it, and Marshal Sheremetiev had promptly seated himself on the little dias, with his painted Veda, arrogant as an empress, beside him.

The Tsar wore no tunic. One of Prince Menshikov's precious Dutch linen shirts, soaked in medicated oils, had been smoothed like a plaster across the Tsar's whip-bruised shoulders, and knotted by its sleeves around his neck. The whip duel, it seemed, had caused little more damage to his sturdy physique than a fall among brambles might have done. The Tsar was enjoying himself, beaming with drunken bonhomie, roaring with aimless mirth. He interrupted the musicians, threw food at the dwarfs and freakish jesters who pranced in and out among the chairs and sometimes ran across the table itself, treading in the laden dishes. Occasionally a heavy silver goblet would be flung by some boisterous or exasperated guest at one of these prancing creatures, but rarely found its mark, for the whimsical little Kalmuck clowns had their wits very much about them on feast nights. When the goblets did strike a human target, it was usually another guest who howled with anguish and surprise. Katrina was protected from these missiles by Menshikov and Ogilvy, each of whom had stuck his jewel-hilted sword firmly into the table, so that the polished blades crossed in front of her face.

"Ogilvy," said the Tsar suddenly, with heavy and drunken solemnity, "our lads fought damn well today!" Marshal Ogilvy smirked with pride, and Sheremetiev, who had included himself in this praise, flushed like a pleased boy. "Damn well," repeated the Tsar, blinking bemusedly down the main table. "Everybody fought damn well . . ." He was interrupted by a roar of hilarious approval, and thumped on the table with his silver goblet until it was crumpled and flattened. "Your Majesty fought well, too," said Menshikov, who knew when to be bold. "As well with sword as whip!" There was another engulfing roar of applause, and by the time the Tsar had quelled it, his goblet had assumed the shape of a squashed silver mushroom.

"The thing is," persisted the Tsar thickly, "that *everybody* fought damn well—even my own son—I saw him—my son—saw him fight damn well didn't I?" He glared challengingly around the assembled company. "Didn't I?" he bellowed. There arose an immediate clamour of assurance that Prince Alexis had indeed fought well. It was true that the reluctant Alexis, grey with fear and clutching his prayer book more tightly than his sword, had taken part in the final cavalry charge upon Narva's stormed gates, but whether he had done more than simply retain his seat in his saddle, or if there was blood upon his sword, nobody really knew, though they felt they could guess. This did not hinder the courtiers from using their imaginations. And Katrina's green eyes became soft with a new pity, as she watched the Tsar inhale proudly the crude flattery of his son. It was, as usual, Prince Menshikov who made the biggest gesture. He unpinned from his own tunic the ribbon and star of the Order of St. George for valour in the field, and passed it with a smile to the Tsar, who snatched it with a drunken shout of satisfaction.

"Yes, Little Alec—my son shall be decorated for valour this very night—this very instant!" He blinked around. "Let Prince Alexis stand up and receive the Order of St. George!" There was an awkward silence. Prince Alexis was not at table. The Tsar, determined not to be robbed of his own good humour, forced himself to laugh. "That lad'll be at his endless prayers," he said. "Fetch him, somebody."

A young captain of the Simenov Guard—who realized through his haze of wine that if anybody was duty officer, it was he—hurried out to fetch Prince Alexis. It was a full half-hour before he returned, sober and white with embarrassment. He was alone.

Some instinct made the drunken Tsar restrain the great bellow of impatient wrath that he had been about to utter when he saw the officer returning without Prince Alexis. He beckoned the captain to him, and the message that he received was spoken in such faltering tones that Katrina, seated near, could hear it only with difficulty.

"Your Majesty—I found Prince Alexis on his knees in the chapel. His Highness says—I implore Your Majesty's pardon—he says that he prefers to share a cross of glory with his sainted mother, rather than to receive a cross of valour at—at . . ." The emissary's voice trembled.

"At what?" demanded Tsar Peter and the officer plunged on: "At—the bloodstained hands of his—his villainous father, he said, Sire!"

"You damnable fool!" Prince Menshikov had risen, and slapped the captain across the cheek with a stunning smack. Without a doubt, Prince Menshikov saved the officer's life, for in another instant the Tsar, whose big fingers were clenching convulsively, would have killed him.

The Tsar's face had begun to twitch sickeningly, exposing his back teeth in an inhuman, one-sided grimace. Katrina rose from her seat and hurried to him. For a moment it seemed that the Tsar might strike her, but he did not. He flung himself forward across the table, and buried his face in his great arms. The knotted muscles shook as he sobbed, and Katrina touched his neck softly. The banquet disbanded in a pell-mell of drunken, apprehensive confusion. Nobody wanted to be near the Tsar in one of his demoniac fits. Soon the great chamber was empty, except for a few sprawling drunkards, and Menshikov and Katrina, who stood behind the Tsar to comfort him.

Katrina twined her fingers into the Tsar's black hair and gently rubbed at his temples, soothing him with quiet words. Menshikov, watching her, marvelled privately at her composure and confidence. He had been the Tsar's companion since boyhood, yet he would have hesitated to touch him in such a moment. After a long while, the twitching diminished, and although the Tsar still sobbed, it was lessening into a quieter and easing grief.

Menshikov nodded then to Katrina and after hesitating for a moment, left the two of them alone. Katrina continued to caress the Tsar's head.

"Oh, my Peterkin," she whispered, and corrected herself in the next breath, "Your Majesty—what kind of a woman is she—who could so poison a son's mind against his own father?"

The Tsar's quiet sobbing stopped suddenly. There was a long pause. But when he raised his tear-crumpled face, the twist upon his lips that betokened illness had faded into little more than a rueful smile. He put one of his hands over Katrina's and said: "When we've finished here, Katrina—my little Katia—when we are returning to Moscow, in perhaps a few weeks, I'll take you to Susdal Nunnery, and you shall see for yourself what kind of woman she is!"

"Your wife?" said Katrina, and the Tsar let out his breath in a sigh.

"My wife," he said, "according to the Holy Church—but to nobody else!"

BOOK TWO

Chapter Ten

THEY STAYED for many weeks in Narva.

Katrina had her own small apartment in the spacious Mansion House, a bedroom, a sitting-room and an extra little room lavishly called the wardrobe room. During those weeks she never ceased to be excited by her surroundings; a hundred times a day she would finger the rich silks and elaborate brocades of the furnishings and the down-soft cushions of the enormous bed. The bed regally dominated the entire room with its elaborately carved ivory posts and curtains of pure black silk latticed with strips of gold. It was real gold. Peter, to tease her, pulled out one of the strips and melted it over the candle flame, and she cried out at the waste as it wept gold tears and mingled with the spent candlewax.

Katrina loved to pull the curtains around the bed and lie shrouded in the darkness, embraced by the deep feather mattress. She would watch the gold strands glinting in the candlelight. Sometimes, instead of delighting in it, it made her brood, for one small piece of it would have kept her mother and brother in luxury for more than a year, would have saved her mother from having to prostitute herself. The thought of the men, most of them repulsive men, who had come to the hut in Goreki Wood, made her shiver.

For always, even years later, when the luxury got too cloying she would think back to the poverty of her childhood, and become sickened by it.

She learned a lot of other things during those weeks at Narva. She learned to redden her lips, to wear jewels in her richly oiled curls, and to get used to the weight of priceless stones around her long slender neck. And bathe. The bath became something to be enjoyed, and cleanliness a delight which she had never before known. Her first bath had been at Petersburg helped by the handsome Menshikov; before that she had occasionally swum naked in the river, but only during the brief summers. Her family had never known or seen a bathtub.

Now, before she awakened, Grog and one of the maids would carry in jug after jug of hot water and fill the tub before the fire. It was a delicious sensual pleasure to slip into the hot perfumed water and have the log fire warm on her face and shoulders.

And so Katrina grew from the captured child into a woman, as much as her young and alert heart would ever allow. And through it all she learned to love the Tsar; to mother him in his sick self-doubting moods, and pity him in his raging tempers. Katrina in her peasant simplicity seemed able to give him something—something that none of his other numerous women had been able to give. Continually, she had to make herself remember that her lover was a king!

It seemed like a fairy tale she was dreaming which would all pass, and she would be back in the hut amongst the trees with Dakov increasingly tormenting her as she became more of a woman and less of a child.

They left the outskirts of Narva as the stars were beginning to grow yellow and huge above them. The bed-sleigh was warm and comfortable, curtained against the cold. The runners hissed and shirred beneath them, like sea waves on shingle, as they travelled swiftly over the hard packed snow.

As it grew darker grey wolves held shadowy, hopeful pace with the coach and its jingling cavalcade of silver breast-plated soldiers, headed by Prince Menshikov and Romdanovsky. Katrina knelt and watched the wolves through the tiny windows; they fascinated her and made her feel warm and contented in the safety of the great coach. Peter did not let her stay long at the window before he reached up and pulled her back into the big tumbled bed.

This time he was not gentle with her, but searched her out with an intense and questing passion that made her body quiver with muffled inarticulate cries.

They slept deeply till dawn when Peter, responding to daybreak, as always, like a seabird, sat up and thrust his huge legs into the narrow corridor between the bed and the coach door, groping for his deerskin boots. Katrina lay watching him as he dressed. There was wonder in her eyes and a grateful acceptance of the night's revelations.

When he was dressed he tugged the curtains aside. The coach had halted under the high grey walls of a convent, alongside its iron-studded gate.

"There's Susdal Convent, little Katia," he said, and Katrina struggled onto her knees and peered at the great bastioned walls from behind his shoulders.

"It looks more like a fortress than a Holy Place," she whispered, for there was such an air of slumber and silence upon the nunnery that it might have been a refuge of the dead.

The coach driver climbed laboriously down from his lofty perch. He had stuffed his quilted pelisse coat with straw to keep out the night's rushing wind, so that he walked only with difficulty. He stumped clumsily to the formidable gate and tugged at the rusted bell chain. Peter jumped from the coach, following close behind the driver with the officers of the Guard. They heard a distant clatter behind the walls and then a long silence.

Katrina hastened to dress and joined the group clustered against the staunch wood of the gate.

"What sort of a place is this, where nuns sleep until noon?" roared the Tsar in sudden wrath, and gave the bell chain a wrench that ripped it from its bracket in a shower of rust. Prince Menshikov grinned and stamped the stirrup-chill from his boots.

"And now, Sire," he said cheerfully, "if they didn't hear that ring, we'll need a siege gun to gain admittance."

But shuffling footsteps were approaching the gate, and after a fumbling delay, a small quizzing vent swung back. Two dim eyes, bleary with sleep, blinked out. "Who's there?" demanded a petulant voice.

"Open for the Tsar!" roared Menshikov, and the gate guardian jumped so violently that he banged his nose against the thick, metal-reinforced woodwork. It was a remarkable nose, for a segment of flesh had been neatly nicked from each nostril. "Did you see that, Sire?" said Menshikov. "A twice-convicted prisoner! What the devil is he doing here in Susdal?"

"An army deserter, too," said the Tsar, whose quick eyes had also seen the faded cross-shaped gunpowder tattoo upon the man's forehead. He thudded on the thick door with his fist.

"If you don't open this gate, my lad, you shall hang by your ribs from a meat hook!"

They heard the man gasp in fear, yet there was still a delay of several moments, and voices could be heard whispering furtively. Then, while the man with the nicked nose fumbled at the bar, other feet could be heard running away from the gate.

It needed another devastatingly authoritative bellow from Prince Menshikov before the gate's heavy iron locking bar was finally loosened. He and Prince Romdanovsky flung their shoulders to the gate and had swung it open whilst the bar was still only half removed.

They were in time to glimpse a gnarled little nun, like a black beetle scurrying into the main entrance of the nunnery.

"Come on," said the Tsar urgently, and they hurried towards the nunnery in such haste that Katrina had to raise the fur-trimmed hem of her gown to her knees to keep up with them.

They entered a refectory hall that stood dark and empty, with thin gleams of light slanting down through slit windows. Three heavy tables were set out with the remains of what must have been a rich repast. There were wine goblets half emptied from the previous night. The fireplace was grey with heaped ashes, now dead and cold. It had been a generous fire.

Romdanovsky's nostrils twitched. "Yes," said the Tsar, his eyes angry, "I smell it—tobacco!" He must also have detected some slight sound, for he dived towards a nearby door and wrenched it open. A young girl of about Katrina's age cowered in the shadows against the wall. She was garbed in the habit of a novice nun but her cheeks were red-stained, and over her shoulder she wore a bright green and crimson cloak. Her eyes were wide with terror.

The Tsar looked at the young nun bleakly. He took a step towards her, snatched the rich cloak from her shrinking shoulders, and held it out to Menshikov.

"Look at this, Alec!"

Prince Menshikov's eyes showed amazement, followed by suspicion. "The cloak of the First Regiment of the Streltsi Guard!"

"Those loyal officers," said Tsar Peter bitterly, "who massacred my family and tried to take my throne for Sophia when I was a child!" He turned on the nun. "Take me to Eudoxia!"

"But—but," stammered the girl, "the Tsarina will be at her prayers. Nobody—Your Majesty cannot disturb—"

At the word "Tsarina," which technically the ex-Queen was not, since she had undertaken holy vows, the Tsar's eyes narrowed. He grasped the young nun's wrist, wrenched it up behind her back until she was almost hoisted from her feet.

"Quickly," was all he said.

Prince Menshikov, with Katrina and the officers followed as the Tsar bustled the sobbing girl ahead of him, through a maze of corridors.

They came to a crimson-curtained door, set apart from the others, and the Tsar thrust her from him. A Guards lieutenant caught the girl adroitly, pressing his hand at once over her mouth. The warning shout that she had been about to utter was silenced. Menshikov gave the boy a quick nod of approval, and the Tsar flung the curtained door wide open.

Eudoxia was standing in the middle of a sumptuously furnished and wide-windowed room. She looked up in stark horror as she saw the Tsar. The back of her dress was unhooked, and her bodice drooped to disclose the beribboned top of elaborate, jewelled French pink corsets, over which a black wooden crucifix hung grotesquely. Katrina stared at her.

It was not until she found herself actually confronted by Tsar Peter's wife, that Katrina realized with what hidden anxiety she had been awaiting this moment. She had pictured the deposed Tsarina Eudoxia as tall, regal, haughty, and coldly beautiful. Somehow, one always thought of a Tsarina thus. To see a startled, guilty and almost middle-aged woman caught in the act of hastily exchanging her finery for the black garb of a nun, which lay in a heap at her feet, had an air of dreamlike unreality and relief to Katrina.

Eudoxia's hair was black, but with the lack-lustre black of herbal dyes. Her long aristocratic nose had thin, mobile nostrils of fanatic purposefulness. Some attempt had recently been made with only partial success to erase rouge from her thin cheeks. Eudoxia's lips were hungry and intense, and just now they were drawn back in a gasp of dismay to disclose teeth that had been cosmetically blackened with elaborate care, in the fashionable style of the beauties of the Russian Court, but not of nuns.

The little, beetle-like nun who had run from the outer gate

with warning of the Tsar's approach, shrank into a corner. The only other visible occupant of the room was the tall woman completely garbed with full propriety in the robes of a Sister of the Holy Order—Sister Kaptelina—who stood frozen in the act of assisting Eudoxia to change.

Eudoxia swallowed to control her terror, and bobbed in curtsy. "Your Majesty—I was just changing from my sombre garb as a Bride of Christ into a gown more suited to Your Majesty's—er, earthly fancies." Her glance considered Katrina quickly before returning to meet the Tsar's stare with deceptive frankness, now that she had mastered her first surprise.

But in her own nervous panic, Sister Kaptelina had not absorbed the point of this explanation, and continued frantically to unhook Eudoxia's elaborate stays, until the ex-Tsarina knocked her hands away with a disowning gesture, and herself stooped to pick up the nun's habit.

The Tsar's hand reached the garment first. It was, as he expected, cold from the cupboard, and the shoulders were green with the mould of long disuse. He dropped it to the floor at Eudoxia's satin-slippered feet, and stared around the room. There was another curtained door beyond, and as the Tsar took a step towards it, Eudoxia covered her mouth with a jewelled hand. This second room contained a wide bed, surrounded by a curtain shaped like a beehive to enclose the bed when required. A breakfast meal for two lay half consumed in silver dishes upon an ormolu table nearby.

The bed was rumpled and the Tsar pressed the yielding mattress thoughtfully. There were two pillows, each deeply dented. Peter regarded all this for a moment, then brought his big fist down on the frail table.

"Well," he said, his voice apparently calm, but the veins in his neck pulsing thickly, "where's the other—your bedmate—who doesn't seem to have finished breakfast, either?"

Eudoxia shut her thin mouth defiantly. The Tsar strode across the room to her, his fists knotted and raised to strike. Sister Kaptelina threw herself in front of the Tsar.

"It was I—I who shared the Tsarina's bed."

"The Tsarina, by God!" said Peter, and dropped his hands to his sides with a look full of significance. "Do you call her the Tsarina? Do you think of her, a consecrated nun, as the Tsarina still?"

Sister Katelina met his eyes with reckless antagonism. "All Russia thinks of her as the Tsarina, and the day will not be long—" She caught Eudoxia's agonized glance and broke off.

"Go on," said Peter, his deep voice deadly.

"Oh, God forgive me," said Sister Kaptelina, and would say no more.

Prince Menshikov suddenly bent and reached under the bed. With a swift pull he dragged out a man garbed in a martial blue uniform and wearing a beard square-cut in the shape of St. Peter of the Ikons.

"Ah," said Menshikov, "did we disturb your nap, Major Stephanov?"

The officer who now climbed to his feet was rumpled and slightly dusty. His uniform had been hastily buttoned, and the anticipation of death was in his eyes. But Major Fedor Stephanov, by Order of the Tsar Inspector of Convents and Monastic Fortresses, looked into the face of the Tsar with the resigned dignity of a gentleman who knew that courage was all he now had left of his life.

"I regret," he said calmly, "that your Majesty's sudden visit gave me no time to complete my toilet."

"And yet," said Prince Menshikov thoughtfully, "you will see, Your Majesty, that the Major wears his cloak. Whose cloak, then, did the little nun in the buttery have across her shoulders?"

"Search the place!" snapped Peter, and his Guards officers hastened to obey. But by now the convent had been brought to a state of alarm, and the Guards were impeded by dozens of nuns of all ages who thronged the narrow corridors. These were all driven into the refectory hall and kept under guard while Menshikov took soldiers through every room, cupboard and alcove.

The result was interesting, but disappointing. Five officers in the forbidden blue-and-scarlet of the disbanded Streltsi First Regiment were discovered, of whom four, warned by the hubbub, had found time to kill themselves, and the fifth was so badly wounded in a sword clash with an impetuous Guards lieutenant that he had to be carried, dying into the refectory hall.

"Obviously, Sire," said Menshikov, "this place has been a refuge for years of these damned renegade plotters!"

Prince Romdanovsky nodded agreement. "And as Chief of Police I can assure Your Majesty that a death warrant was long ago signed for each of these men."

The dying Streltsi officer lifted his head, and grated his teeth with pain before he spoke. "There are many more of us, Your Majesty," he said faintly, "who believe that Russia herself is under death sentence while you remain Tsar." Then he dropped his head and died.

One of the Tsar's officers hurried in, carrying an elaborate, gilt-framed portrait that had obviously been recently wrenched from the wall.

"We found this in the convent chapel, Your Majesty," he said. Tsar Peter, Romdanovsky and Menshikov crowded round the picture. Katrina came nearer to look at it. To her, the portrait seemed, at first, harmless. It showed Eudoxia and Prince Alexis—she in formal regalia of the Tsarina, and her son—Katrina gasped then, for she could see that Alexis was depicted with the sceptre, orb and royal crown of Tsar of All the Russias! Beneath the portrait was inscribed: *The Tsar and Tsarina—God's Will Be Done, Thy Kingdom Come!"*

Katrina, watching Tsar Peter's face, saw his mouth tighten. She waited for the hideous tic to attack his cheek, but it did not come. When he did speak, his voice was surprisingly calm. He turned to Romdanovsky, and said: "I think we'd better put a few questions to Major Stephanov. It would be instructive to know the names of the other gentlemen among my Court who wish to depose me."

"A pity," said Menshikov, "that we have got only Stephanov to work on. We might have got it out of any of these five,"—he indicated the five corpses—"but Stephanov will probably choose to die with his mouth shut."

"Sire," said Romdanovsky, his fat cheeks quivering hopefully, "leave him to me, Sire. He'll talk, I think. May I sharpen a five-foot stake, Your Majesty, and invite Major Stephanov to take a seat?"

The Tsar considered. "Ye-es," he said slowly, "it's worth trying, I suppose, though I'm inclined to agree with Little Alec here that Stephanov'll let it come out through the top of his head before he'll talk."

"Well, Your Majesty," said Romdanovsky, "we could take him to Moscow, where we've better facilities—?"

Menshikov shook his head decisively. "If we do that, Your Majesty, all the plotters will run for it. It's better to do it here if we can."

The Tsar nodded. "Yes, I think so. All right, Romdanovsky, try your stake. And I don't need to tell you to be careful. We don't want him dying too quickly. Put a fur coat on him if you're going to do it out there in the cold yard."

"Leave it to me, Your Majesty," said Romdanovsky confidently.

Katrina listened in silence, her eyes flitting from one speaker to the next. Surely they could not seriously be discussing such a subject as calmly as men might consider the merits of a horse? Yet she knew that they were. She wiped her sweating fingers upon her rich green dress, and swallowed painfully.

Soon afterwards came the thud, thud, as soldiers began to drive the carefully chosen stake into the winter-bound black earth of the convent courtyard.

By nightfall snow lay like thick cream upon the twisted, onion-shaped towers of Susdal Nunnery, while fresh snowflakes whirled into the bare courtyard, hissing against the circle of oil torches that lit the sharpened stake where Major Stephanov was dying in silent obstinacy. Chafing his own hands for warmth, Prince Fedor Romdanovsky watched. He had garbed the dying man carefully in rich furs against the night's bitterness, and frequently proffered French brandy to his torn, chewed mouth. But Major Stephanov had wisely, each time, spat the brandy away, not choosing to prolong his own agony by absorbing the strength of restoratives.

"Tell me, Stephanov," said Romdanovsky peevishly, "why must you choose to suffer like a dog? Just name one conspirator—just one, my friend—and I will end it mercifully for you—poof! All ended in an instant, my dear Stephanov. You will be dead, at peace, before that snowflake on your foolish beard can melt."

Major Stephanov did not answer, for by this time, despite all his agonizing attempts to remain utterly motionless, the stake had made its inexorable penetration so that merely to breathe was like gulping molten metal.

Exasperated, Prince Romdanovsky flung the contents of the brandy glass in Stephanov's face.

"Confound you, then," said Romdanovsky, "my supper grows cold, and there is a warm fire waiting for me. If you will not speak, will you at least have the grace to die?"

The tormented man's lips stirred, but it was not in the beginnings of confession. "Gladly," he whispered, "for I do not willingly keep you from your victuals, sir." And the effort of speaking even this pitiful, useless defiance almost brought to Major Stephanov the finish that he wished himself much more fervently than any of his enemies could. His head slumped forward, and he remained thus with eyes closed for a long time.

Romdanovsky turned at the soft crunch of footsteps. He saw Prince Menshikov, a hand cupped over his pipe to shield it from the snowflakes. "Get inside, Fedor," said Menshikov quietly. "I'll watch him for a while until you've had food."

Romdanovsky cast a wistful glance at the door, through which the inviting firelight could be seen. "Nay," he said reluctantly, "I dare not, Alec, until this traitorous fool has either spoken or shut his mouth for ever. The Tsar would kill me if I left without his orders."

"Indeed I would, Fedor," boomed the voice of the Tsar amiably from behind him, and Romdanovsky turned, startled. The Tsar had come upon them silently, masked by the veil of falling snow.

"But go inside and have your supper, lad," the Tsar continued. "You've stood here on continuous watch for nearly twelve hours, now. Alec and I will take over until dawn."

Romdanovsky wiped his snow-speckled face in a genuine weariness. "Pity this is not a task we can leave to the others. You never know which of them may not be in the damned conspiracy himself—or his father or brother. And it needs but—" he lowered his voice so that the man on the stake would not hear— "it needs but a push on Stephanov's shoulder now, and he is gone like a snuffed candle."

The Tsar nodded. "Go and get your supper, lad."

Chapter Eleven

KATRINA LOOKED UP sleepily as Prince Romdanovsky came stamping and shivering into the room where supper had been laid for the Tsar and his intimates. Grog the dwarf lay asleep in a corner, curled upon a fur rug with the Tsar's pet Samoyede dog beside him. Katrina had been dozing at her self-imposed task of keeping the log fire bright for the Tsar's return.

The Tsar's Chief of Police knocked the snow from his coat and unlaced it with numbed hands. Katrina poured him a goblet of hot spiced wine and Romdanovsky drank greedily. He blew out a long, contented breath, and held his cup for more wine. Katrina emptied the jug into it.

She glanced at him curiously as he sat down at the supper table. "It doesn't spoil your appetite, then, to put men to the torture?"

Prince Romdanovsky helped himself to a succulent slice of goose breast and stuffing. "I shouldn't ask silly questions if I were you, my child."

He had picked the goose clean, and was devouring a great hunk of cheese, when Katrina said suddenly:

"And did you get it?"

"Did I get what, girl?"

"Did you get what you wanted to know?"

Romdanovsky, having finished the cheese, searched for a few crumbs that had dropped among the folds of his expensive breeches. "I did not," he said. "He was a stubborn man."

"So what will you do now?"

"If you were my plaything, instead of the Tsar's," said Romdanovsky, contemplating the empty cheese dish regretfully, "I would find fascinating ways to stop your pretty little red tongue from going blab, blab with infernal questions when a man is striving to digest his supper."

In the nunnery courtyard the circle of oil torches burned more dimly as daylight came. The Tsar, at his vigil by the man upon the stake, yawned. He stooped and put his face within a few inches of the dying plotter. "Major Stephanov," he said loudly, "this is the Tsar speaking to you. Open your eyes man."

After a brief pause, Major Stephanov's eyelids, masked by snow, fluttered open.

"Name the others, Stephanov—quickly. Tell me their names and we can release you from this. We may even save your life, man!"

The bruised, death-blue lips of Major Stephanov twitched in the wraith of a smile. "Your Majesty—is liar—as well—as—devil." His head sagged forward into his last unconsciousness.

The Tsar exchanged a significant glance with Prince Menshikov. "And now what?"

Menshikov sucked with difficulty at his moist pipe. "Well, Sire, some of the nuns probably know something. They've concealed these people here. Couriers must have come and gone. Even if the nuns don't know much, the sight of them under question might loosen Eudoxia's tongue."

The Tsar's expression showed that he, too, had already considered this possibility. "All right, Alec," he said. "We'll force a drop of brandy into Stephanov, and if nothing comes of it we'll start after breakfast on the nuns."

"No use wasting good brandy," said Menshikov, and yawned. "He's quite dead, I'm afraid."

The noise that awoke Katrina might almost have been doves calling under the lee of the roof. But she knew instinctively that it was not. As she came wider awake she recognized the sound for what it was. It was the distant weeping of women.

Grog had awakened to it, and sat up from his nest of furs in front of the fire. Prince Romdanovsky, heavily asleep at the supper table, broke off his snores and opened his eyes.

"I thought I heard women crying," said Grog. He looked questioningly at Katrina and then at Romdanovsky, whose expression was stirring into awareness. "Apparently the Tsar and Alec had no more success with Stephanov than I did," he said. "They must be questioning the nuns. Is there any breakfast?"

Katrina became coldly awake. "The Tsar isn't—they're not mistreating the nuns?"

Romdanovsky massaged his fat cheeks sleepily. "Questioning them is the only logical thing to do. The place has been a beehive of conspiracy. Some of the nuns are bound to know a bit about it." He stretched stiffly, and plunged his fat fingers daintily into the congealed grease of last night's pork-and-carrot stew in quest of further edible fragments.

Katrina's voice sharpened. "But they can't hurt the nuns—they can't."

The Chief of Police sighed. "The Tsar is the Tsar, girl. He may do as he chooses."

"I won't let him!" Katrina ran to the door, and Grog, hastily buttoning his jacket, trotted after her down the cold corridor. Romdanovsky shrugged, and bent a thoughtful eye upon the gnawed skeleton of the goose.

Prince Menshikov stood in the doorway of the rectory hall. Behind him the sounds of weeping rose more loudly. As Katrina tried to push past him, he took her firmly by the arm.

"This is no place for you," he said calmly. "You'd only make a fool of yourself."

"But the nuns!" Katrina cried. "Is the Tsar—"

"They have sheltered the Tsar's enemies." Prince Menshikov spoke as if she were a child. "You see, little Katrina this is an affair of state. You can't stop the destinies of a nation because a few nuns plot against a throne. Besides, you have seen evidences here not only of treachery but of other corruption as well."

He noticed Grog, faltering in the shadows of the corridor. "Ah, Grog—take her away, dwarf. Let her go into the chapel if she wishes, and pray. But for her own sake she must not interfere here."

Grog and Katrina walked slowly into the chapel across the courtyard. Snow lay thick upon the golden domes. Inside, the chapel glittered with thousands of coloured stones set in ornate mosaic. Katrina crossed herself at each illuminated ikon, seeking to find solace. She and Grog approached as near as they dared to the high altar, and knelt to it hopefully. Nearby was a penitent's stool, its wood dented and gouged by the bodies of many generations of seekers after mercy, and after a while they went and sat upon this hard stool, close together.

They were still sitting there side by side when, some time later, Prince Menshikov found them.

"Ah, there, little Kitty," he said blithely. "You can come out now."

Katrina raised her tear-stained face. "Did you—find out what you wanted?" she asked.

"Enough, I think, Kitty. Enough to be going on with. Come now. The Tsar is pressing on for Moscow and we're to quarter tonight at the tavern beyond Susdal." He took her arms and said soberly: "Don't take these things too badly. What the Tsar does to his enemies is nothing to what they'd do to him if they got a chance."

Chapter Twelve

THE SILVER LAMPS gleamed invitingly in the big bed-coach, and soldiers were replenishing cupboards with food and wine for the journey, when Katrina and the Tsar went out to it. Grog had filled the coach stove with fresh wood and hot red embers, and was fanning them into a glow. The Tsar buffeted him amiably and sent him scrambling up like a monkey to the driver's seat. "You'd better sing like a lovebird tonight, my lad," boomed the Tsar boisterously, "for we're in the mood to listen!"

Yet it was with gentle, almost diffident affection that, when the red silk curtain had been drawn, he reached for Katrina and took her small ears between his fingers. Her mouth parted in surprise as the Tsar bestowed a restraining kiss upon her smooth forehead. The sleigh runners began to whirr, and the bells jingled upon the horse's trotting hooves.

"I was thinking," the Tsar said, "that when I have crushed this plot against my throne, I shall take a wife."

Katrina sat still, her heart beating until the pulses throbbed in her neck.

"Your Majesty?" she murmured huskily.

The Tsar continued: "Little Kitty, I'm not taking you to Moscow just to shut you in a perfumed bedroom." He tweaked her ears tenderly. "You are too rare to be a toy for a few nights and days. I can have a hundred women—a thousand—indeed I have had many a hundred, and never found one such as you." He smiled at her. "I shall put the seeds of sons in your little body," he said. "You must grow accustomed to life in a Tsar's palace, for one day your son will rule it."

Katrina stared at him, her eyes wide with wonder. Her lips moved, but she could think of nothing to say.

"Sons who will grow into strong men," said the Tsar fervently. "Not—not spoiled weaklings like Alexis—but all that is best of both of us. Strong Narishkin men—my sons and yours, who will rule Russia when I am dead, and bring her to greatness."

"Your Majesty . . ." said Katrina, again. She could think of nothing else to say, and her voice was a whisper in her throat. She felt the waft of heat from the now glowing stove and the stuffy atmosphere in the swaying coach seemed to blur her thoughts beyond comprehension. She passed a red tongue across lips suddenly dry. "Sons?" she echoed. And she looked so tiny, so bewildered, that the Tsar laughed as he pushed her gently down upon her back and put his great face close to her own.

"I will marry you," he said, as to a child in a game. "I shall make you the Tsarina of Russia!"

Katrina's arms went around his neck.

"Your sons—yes, give them to me," she said huskily. "Your Majesty—Peter—oh, yes . . ." The Tsar chuckled as he gently disengaged himself from her.

"Damn it, Kitty," he laughed, and straightened her rumpled skirt for her as a father might have done. "It's at least six hours to the next coach halt. Surely we've time to put our night clothes on?"

The last coach stage between Susdal and Moscow was marked by a crudely built wooden tavern with sharply sloped roof and one tiny upstairs window.

The Tsar, with Katrina and his officers, had breakfasted there on fish with garlic, hot chicken livers stewed in honey, and oatmeal pancakes. Between them they had drunk several jars of the Tsar's favourite morning drink of sweetened Dutch brandy. Now, sucking their teeth contentedly, the men lit tobacco pipes and strolled into the stableyard to inspect their horses. But when the Tsar came to his coach, the driver who should have been ready in his high seat, was crouched at the nearside sled runner shaking his head in vague, unseeing distress like a dog with a bone stuck in its throat.

"What the devil ails you, coachman?" demanded the Tsar.

"Toothache. Your Majesty," mumbled the man. Katrina was surprised at the concern and sympathy that spread immediately across the Tsar's face. He called worriedly to Prince Menshikov: "The coachman's got toothache! Get somebody to fill him up with vodka, Alec. And see if there's another man who can handle a five-horse team."

"I can drive your coach, Tsar," said a slow voice from the upstairs window of the inn.

Peter, looking up, saw an expressionless face framed by the window. The face had a bushy black spade beard that dangled over the window ledge like a spread rug.

"Damn your insolence wearing that beard—" the Tsar began, then suddenly grinned. "All right, lad, come down here, and you'll get five roubles to drive me to Moscow." To his own coachman, the Tsar said, "Don't worry, the vodka's coming."

Katrina put her hand upon the Tsar's arm. "Why are you going to give him vodka for toothache, Peter?"

He looked down at her in amazement at the ignorance implied by such a question. "Toothache can send a man mad," he said simply.

"Why don't you pull his tooth out?"

This seemed to bewilder the Tsar even more. "Kitty, you little simpleton, toothache is a disease in the jawbone, a sudden poison from eating bad honey or syrup usually. It would do no good to knock his tooth out."

"Look," said Katrina, and opened her mouth to display a small gap between her back teeth. "In Sweden when we have toothache we go to a dentist at the hiring fair or harvest fair, and he pulls out the tooth that hurts, and that stops the pain at once."

"The tooth?" echoed the Tsar. "It is the tooth itself that hurts, then—not the jawbone? Are you sure?" Enchanted at the possibilities of this new knowledge, he grabbed the coachman by the nose and underlip and wrenched his mouth open until the jaw cracked. "Show me," he said excitedly. "Which tooth, eh? Which tooth?"

Katrina peered inside the man's mouth, and tapped at several of his corroded teeth with the slender handle of her jewelled haircomb. When the coachman bellowed: aaawgggh—eek!" Katrina reported promptly, "That one!"

"By God," said the Tsar, who had been watching intently. "He did jump when you rapped that tooth, little Kitty, that's true. But how do you pull a tooth out?"

Prince Romdanovsky, who had spent a good part of the previous forty-eight hours unmovedly watching unspeakable torture, shuddered. "A tooth is bone in bone," he said sententiously, "and although by mishap one may lose a tooth, or an eye, it seems to me that to interfere deliberately would bleed the fellow to death, as frequently occurs when one cuts off a criminal's ear or nose." He shrugged. "I've seen it happen with just a thumb."

The Tsar looked expectantly at Katrina, who said, "Try it! Get him drunk and then try it—that's all I can say."

The Tsar needed no further urging. He was like a child with a new toy. Prince Menshikov, who had stood listening, grinned. "Now you've done it, Katrina," he said softly, "if this madcap trick works, the Tsar will have a new trade—Moscow's one and only dentist—to add to his woodcarving, boat building, masonry, blacksmith, and ship's gunnery certificate!"

"The Tsar does all those things?"

"And dozens more," chuckled Menshikov. "You've only to show him a new skill, and the Tsar will never rest until he has mastered it. He can make silver drinking cups, wooden candlesticks—even weave delicate lace for the cuffs of his jacket!"

But the Tsar, far from being flattered by this praise, was almost dancing with impatience. "Yes, yes," he said, silencing Menshikov with a wave of his hand. "Tell me, little Kitty, how is the tooth pulled out? Show me! Show me!"

Katrina hesitated, for to be truthful, she did not know. "They use a kind of—tool," she said vaguely. "It pulls the tooth like a nail from a plank."

The Tsar slapped her slender shoulder with such enthusiasm that she coughed. "Carpenters' tools! That's it!" He turned to Grog. "Fetch carpenters' tools—a long chisel, a mallet—"

"The tooth must come out whole," Katrina added hastily. "If you broke it off in the jaw, the pain would continue. It must be pulled up by the roots like a grass stalk."

". . . gouging tools!" the Tsar roared after the disappearing dwarf.

Meanwhile, a flagon of raw vodka had been carried from the inn and the unfortunate coachman's mouth was again wrenched enthusiastically open. "Here," said the Tsar, anxiously, "here, Alec—fill him up!"

By the time the dwarf had hastened back with an armful of carpentry tools, the vodka was taking control of the coachman's senses. He sat up, giggling feebly, with fur cap clutched, comforting his afflicted jaw.

Tsar Peter spread out the assorted crude implements. His hands lingered over them lovingly. "A bit of polishing and these would be a fine outfit, Katrina," he said, and his face shone with the enthusiasm of a schoolboy. Katrina could not help but wonder at the mixtures in him. She had seen those same hands clutching a sword in battle, a whip in brutal duelling—and known their gentle seekings as well as their fierce and utterly shameless insistence as the Tsar's moods of lovemaking changed quickly as clouds in the sky. Now, she saw the strong fingers for the first time as perhaps they really were intended to be—blunt, supple, and sensitive—a craftsman's hands, to which fate had given a sceptre but which had themselves never ceased to yearn for the humble tools of a workman.

"This one, I think," the Tsar was saying. He selected a long-handled tool used for gouging patterns in woodwork. The coachman, despite his potion of vodka, was now regarding the preparations with developing alarm.

"It's all in the leverage, I suppose," said the Tsar, ignoring the coachman's slurred protests that he would prefer to endure the toothache. "Open his mouth, Alec—wider—that's it, lad!"

To Katrina, watching, it was wonderful how dexterously the the Tsar removed the tooth. He had it out with one unerring twist of his powerful wrist, as if he had been removing teeth all his life. The coachman squawked and gulped.

"Damn the clumsy oaf," roared the Tsar. "He's swallowed the tooth, and I wanted to examine it. Make him cough it up, Alec!"

This was soon done, and the Tsar studied the retrieved molar. "Yes, Kitty," he said, "there's a hole runs through it, when you look carefully. That may have something to do with it . . ." He shrugged, as if realizing that there were some problems beyond even his alert intelligence. "You know what I'm going to do?" said the Tsar proudly, "I'm going to have this tooth mounted in gold—the first bit of dentistry in Russia!"

The shock of the extraction had for a few moments almost sobered the coachman, and now a delighted grin spread over his swollen face. "The pain," he reported, "it's gone!"

"Certainly it's gone!" said the Tsar sharply. "If it hadn't gone after I took all that trouble with you, my lad, I'd have made you sorry. Here, open your mouth again." He inspected the cavity. "Any more teeth aching?" he asked hopefully.

"Nunno, sir—your Majesty!"

"How about you, Romdanovsky? Any aching teeth?"

"Absolutely not one, Sire." The fat Chief of Police backed away with praiseworthy agility.

"Katrina? Alec? Any twinges?"

Laughing nervously, Katrina and Prince Menshikov protested their teeth were thoroughly healthy. The Tsar turned upon the officers of his Guard. "You—and you, lad—come here and let me see your teeth."

The officers approached and opened their mouths with reluctance. The Tsar probed and rapped at teeth with the stem of his pipe. "There's a bad one," he said with satisfaction. "You see, lad! It would have given you trouble when I was not around to fix it. I'll take it out for you now."

The young officer paled, but the Tsar did not appear to observe this. "Open your mouth wider," he commanded abruptly.

The tooth, being quite sound although discoloured, did not at first yield to the gouging tool, despite violent persuasion. The Tsar frowned. "Funny thing," he panted breathlessly, "why this one should be so difficult."

"Perhaps it's a good tooth, Your Majesty," grinned Menshikov.

"Nonsense, Alec. Certainly it's bad." The Tsar rubbed his chin. "It's a question of simple leverage, Alec. I'll tell you, I think I could get better results by using my sword point."

"Oh, my heavens!" Romdanovsky groaned, "Your Majesty is making my—"

"Teeth ache?" prompted the Tsar hopefully.

"Er—no, Your Majesty—not at all—never ached in my life—never!"

"Show me!" the Tsar commanded, and Prince Romdanovsky reluctantly opened his mouth.

"Why, there's one, Fedor—must come out at once." The Tsar drew his sword. He managed this extraction surprisingly neatly with the clumsy weapon, for the brown tooth flipped out smartly as a pip from a pomegranate, and Prince Romdanovsky had scarcely time to bellow a protest.

"I told you!" the Tsar said. "It's all in the leverage, Alec, you see. Now where's that dragoon got to . . ."

It was nearly noon before the Tsar was ready to continue towards Moscow. The big, black-bearded peasant had been fetched down from the upstairs window, and shoved up beside the driver. The Tsar grinned at Menshikov. "Imagine it, Alec —within twenty miles of Moscow, too!"

"Imagine what?" asked Katrina interestedly. But the Tsar merely winked and said: "Wait until we reach the gates of Moscow, little Kitty." Nor would he explain further.

The glittering cavalcade began to move off in the haze of noonday. Scarcely a man of the Tsar's Guard but now had a red-specked handkerchief pressed ruefully to his mouth. The Tsar contemplated them, delighted with his own skill. He rubbed his hands and beamed upon Katrina. "Look at them, Kitty," he purred. "Not a twinge of toothache among the lot of 'em now!"

"Nor many teeth, either," said Katrina, and suddenly began to laugh. The Tsar, after a half-frowning moment, laughed, too. And as the big coach-sleigh glided off with the still half-drunk driver cracking his whip madly, the Tsar held out his arms, and Katrina, shaking with helpless mirth, collapsed into his embrace. Kissing and laughing, they rolled together upon the bed, and the horrors of Susdal Convent were, for the moment, forgotten by both of them.

Chapter Thirteen

THE GREAT METROPOLIS of Moscow lay in the middle distance, down a sloping hill of snow-covered scrub wilderness that was empty, except for wolves' tracks, of any mark of life.

The Tsar stood upon the swaying coach-bed with the roof window folded back, and held Katrina up in his arms to obtain her first sight of Moscow. Wintry wind whirled into the coach and the silver bells of the five horses jingled as the great sleigh surged over Susdal Rise.

But it was not the icy wind that made Katrina gasp. Moscow lay before her glistening in the early afternoon like a thousand suns. There were, indeed, many more than a thousand brilliances. The golden beams that Katrina saw were reflections of sunlight upon the domes and spires of Moscow's churches, which made the blue skyline look as if it had been heaped with a mountainous, bursting basketful of gilded fruits. Domes shaped like smooth pears or dinted strawberries, like pumpkins, gourds, prickly pineapples were interlaced by blunt, knobbed towers in the fantastic shapes of golden cabbage stalks.

The roofs of more houses than Katrina had dreamed could exist, made an intricate carpet that, as the sleigh drew closer, broke into a pattern of twisting lanes around the square gardens and painted palaces of the boyar nobles. Looming above everything, dwarfing the huge, disorderly growth of this most densely populated city of the Orient, was the Kremlin, its gigantic white walls studded by bastions, turrets, observation towers; and gathering within its fabulous strength a nightmare bouquet of cathedral spires and domes, like a vase filled with poppies, tulips, puffballs, kingcups whose golden heads were festooned by glittering crescents, stars, discs and baubles.

"Look at it," grunted Tsar Peter. "Blasted town stuck in the middle of nowhere—miles from the sea, from Western civilization. Believe me, Kitty, before I die, I shall have shifted this whole damned lot to where ships can reach it!"

"I think," said Katrina, "that it is a beautiful city. And yet—I don't know why—I feel afraid of it."

The Tsar looked at her thoughtfully and became absorbed at the sight of her smooth, eager young face, the beguiling innocence of her wide green eyes, with the hint of wisdom, of the capacity to endure, in the almost Oriental upwards slant of the lids. Her mouth was that of a knowledgeable child, perky, generous and impulsive. He knew the taste of it, sweet as warm pastries; and the husky, hungry cries that his caresses could bring to her throat, so that he had sometimes listened almost in awe at the wonder and strangeness of her young voice calling out its urgent passion from beyond a dawn of sensation that was before words and speech. Her white teeth, free from any Oriental stains, fascinated him. So, too, her slender body was firm as a boy's and yet so softly vulnerable at breasts and swelling hips, and the poise, like a listening bird's, of her proud young head. His own arm was thicker than her waist. When she lay beneath his great, demanding bulk, she seemed helpless as a grasped thrush, utterly at the mercy of his strength. Yet the Tsar knew that there was a vital core of her he could never completely subdue, for this child held a pride within herself that was stronger than warriors and more alone than kings. What the Tsar did not know was that he was in love and that the virtues he saw in Katrina may, or they may not, have actually existed. Prince Menshikov had perhaps glimpsed something of a similar vision. But it was certain that Prince Romdanovsky had not seen anything like this in her, nor had Sheremetiev, though both these knew Katrina.

To men like Romdanovsky, as the Tsar was well aware, Katrina was no more than a girl, among the many thousands of plump, paint-daubed women of Moscow, who were in the Tsar's eyes soft and whitefleshed as creamy-headed cauliflowers, and available to feed any man's appetite with the bloodless indifference of vegetables.

In a long moment of searching contemplation, the Tsar realized that there might well be good reason for Katrina's apprehensions of his kingdom city. For her, Moscow would be filled with enemies and intriguers—men old enough to be her grandfather, who would greedily snatch any favour or advancement, even though the price of it might be Katrina's personal ruin, her despair and her death. Not, perhaps, such a man as Romdanovsky, who had the privilege of the Tsar's ear at any time. Nor Alec, of course. But there would be so many others: Tolstoy, Golitsin—hundreds of them. And there would be all the friends of Anna Mons. Indeed Anna herself would certainly by this time be brewing some wickedness against Katrina. Moscow would always be filled with enemies for a Tsar and for any whom he chose to honour as his favourite, especially when she was a woman from the Western world.

With quick, hungry affection, Tsar Peter reached for Katrina. "Yes, little Kitty," he said, "you'll have to be careful in Moscow. There are a lot of black hearts—cruel hearts—among those damned golden houses," he said. "You're little more than a baby, but I think you can look after yourself. I hope to God you can, for I will not be able to protect you all the time."

"What work does a Tsarina do?" asked Katrina diffidently, and the Tsar laughed.

"Whatever she does, there'll be somebody who thinks she does it wrong," he said. "See! We're just arriving at the gates of Moscow. Now I want you to see what happens at the gate to that peasant with the long black beard who sits on top of our coach."

The outer gates of Moscow were just big enough to let the wide coach through. When the guards recognized the Tsar's glittering bodyguard, they swung open the check bar without delay, and stood rigidly at the salute.

Tsar Peter thrust his head from the coach window. "What the blazes!" he bellowed. "Are you going to let this coach through with that fellow on top?"

The lieutenant of the Guard hurried forward in confusion. "Your Majesty, I—I thought—"

The Tsar roared at him. "You thought, did you? Confound it, lad, d'you want to spend the rest of your life as a baubled fool in my Court, clucking like a hen, perhaps, or grunting like a pig?"

"No, Sire!"

"Then get your duty done, lad. He's got a damn great beard, hasn't he? Get it hacked off him!"

At once, two lusty musketeers pulled down the rustic whom the Tsar had taken aboard at the last coach halt.

"Are you aware that your beard breaks the law?" demanded the officer formally.

"My—ah—beard?"

"Nobody may pass the gates of Moscow without having his beard trimmed," roared the young officer, acutely conscious of the Tsar's eye. "Nor may you enter the city in garments longer than the level of your knees!"

Tsar Peter turned back to Katrina as Prince Menshikov rode up beside the coach.

"Whatever's happening?" asked Katrina, puzzled. "What are they going to do to that poor fellow?"

"Cut his damned insolent whiskers off!" the Tsar explained. "It is my new law. How can my ambassadors be taken seriously in the courts of Europe, or my soldiers fight, if they insist upon big beards down to their bellies like their patron saints, and coats that sweep the ground?"

"The Tsar has ordered," said Menshikov, more patiently, "that every man in Russia shall cut his beard short, and wear Western style clothes. But it's a hard struggle, for when we hack off a fellow's great beard, he tucks the shorn hair inside his shirt to produce to St. Nicholas on Judgment Day!"

"My countrymen are fools," said the Tsar contemptuously. "They believe they will not be admitted to paradise without their beards." To the lieutenant of the Gate Guard, he roared: "Well, what do you wait for, man? Trim him, confound you!"

The shears crunched, and the struggling peasant went down on his knees in the snow, grovelling for the greasy matted tufts of his late beard.

Hung at the city gate on display was a typical European topcoat of the period, with embroidered cuffs and pleated skirt, such as any London shopkeeper might have worn. Above it was a three-cornered hat. The young officer, with his boot, drew the moaning peasant's attention to these objects.

"Take a good look," he ordered, "and tell your fellow rustics how the Tsar wishes them to dress. Now get going!" As the blubbering man passed the coach, Katrina could see that tears were trickling down his cheeks. The Tsar must have seen this, too, for he called: "Fellow!"

The peasant cringed, fearing some further indignity, but the Tsar flung him a generous bag of silver coins. "Take the next stage home," he said gruffly, "and don't worry, lad—you'll get into heaven, beard or not."

The peasant turned the purse in slow fingers, and gradually some of his woe faded. "I'll spend it on candles, to ask forgiveness of the Saints for my naked face," he said hopefully.

The Tsar shrugged. "Get on with you then, lad—if you haven't the sense to spend it on women and vodka . . ."

There was very little snow inside the city walls of Moscow, except on the roofs or piled against the houses themselves. Most of the rich boyars had their gardens scraped clear of it, and the narrow streets had been trodden dry, so that the sleigh now bumped its runners over hard earth, and the horses panted at this extra strain. Every street wafted a new stench. Garbage lay frozen in the road, and from each drinking house came the fruity odour of old woodwork that had been sodden by years of spilt spirits. The ordinary folk of Moscow, draped in tattered furs, thronged the narrow streets, their faces peering like those of highland cattle from beneath their shaggy hair.

A boyar's coach came arrogant and headlong down the crowded alley, with hundreds of tiny silver bells jingling on the horses' hooves and harness. The driver roared and slashed a pathway with his twenty-foot whip. But the passerby who reeled back with arms and cheeks laid open by the whip showed no signs of malice nor wrath, but merely of a childlike dismay, and the women shielded their infants' heads from the whip as passively as though in protection from an inevitable rainstorm.

"We're approaching the Street of the Barbers," said the Tsar suddenly. "You'd better shut that window, Kitty." And Katrina saw that ahead of them the roadway seemed to shimmer as if sprinkled by handfuls of powdered glass over a dark brown carpet.

Here, all down this street, men squatted having their hair or beards crudely trimmed. The clipped hair lay where it fell and the years, the centuries, had formed it into a solid springy turf that probably went several feet deep. The horses' hooves became muted as they passed onto this substance that looked like a Shetland tweed, of browns, blacks and greys. The hot sleigh runners swirled up the chopped stuff into a hairy cloud that stuck to the damp of the coach windows. Katrina felt an immediate itching at her ankles, for black lice were finding their way through the coach floorboards.

The Tsar, unmoved, stamped on such as he could see, and Katrina realized what it had been that shimmered in the frosty sunlight of the Street of Barbers.

"Shake 'em off," said the Tsar casually. "They soon die. The hair louse can't live on anything but human hair." He imparted this knowledge with an air of noticeable smugness, like a man making a classical quotation, and his next words revealed why. "I've studied lice under a microscope," he said with elaborate carelessness.

"A—what?"

"Microscope," said the Tsar. "Sort of a stick with glass in it. Makes 'em look big as beans. I saw it in Amsterdam," he said. "I'm the only man in Russia who's seen a microscope."

"Indeed?" said Katrina. "If it makes a louse bigger than it is, I don't see the good in it. I don't see how anything can make a louse bigger than it is."

"You don't know everything, you see!" said the Tsar, beaming with superior knowledge.

"Wasn't Prince Menshikov in Amsterdam with you, Your

Majesty?" asked Katrina in a tiny voice. "Didn't he see the microscope, too?"

"Well," said the Tsar sulkily, "I saw it first!"

They rode in silence for a while, Katrina with a mischievous smile around her mouth, and the Tsar carrying his chin high. But he could never sulk for long. As the coach turned into Red Square, he said: "It's going to be a fine night, Kitty. See how high the vultures are flying!"

Far up in the sharp blue sky, black vultures circled gracefully with spread wings. They did not flap, but slanted themselves into breathtaking curves and spins, enjoying the clear evening before dusk fall. Occasionally one or two would descend to perch upon the hundreds of rusted gibbet chains that hung outside the Kremlin walls, and blink disinterestedly at motionless bundles suspended from them.

The Kremlin vultures, shaggy birds with hooked, malevolent beaks jutting almost headlessly from their ruffled necks, were too bored to feed with any voracity. There was always a meal waiting for them.

In the Red Square were market stalls selling hot drinks and sweetmeats. Vendors hawked trays of honey cakes and meat pasties. The passersby munched and strolled. Nobody gave a second glance to the small group of women who squatted in the dirt, their scarved heads bent as they sang a tuneless dirge to the dead. This appeared to be for the benefit of a young woman, who, heavily chained and entirely naked, waited shivering, beside what seemed to be a freshly dug well.

"Whatever's happening there?" gasped Katrina. The Tsar glanced in the direction she indicated. "Killed her husband, probably," he said. "Sentenced to be buried alive up to her neck. It's the usual thing, you know."

"Then what happens?"

"The scavenger dogs, or starvation, or some such," said the Tsar vaguely, as the coach rocked into the Kremlin gates.

Katrina had never before seen a king's residence, and it seemed strange to her that the Kremlin should look exactly like an armed fort, beleaguered by the city it ruled. Grim soldiers manned the walls, and cannons stood ready with heavy stone balls pyramided beside their wheels. There were outer earthworks and inner defensive ramparts, tangled within which lay a confused huddle of churches and buildings of such ill-sorted sizes and architectural styles that they looked like a boxful of nursery toys. All windows were slotted and barred by forbidding iron gratings.

The Kremlin palace itself stood in the centre of this, and its appearance was that of a huge, vaulted puzzle box designed and daubed upon by feverish Easter Island savages.

All over the Kremlin palace, flunkeys, colourful as cockatoos leaned or sat, smoked, scratched themselves, spat, gambled, quarrelled and scrambled to attention at the approach of any official, but usually so tardily as to be almost invariably caught in their slovenliness and buffeted across the face.

The flunkeys had long since ceased even to blink at these blows, which throughout the day fell upon each of them, thick and inevitable as the dandruff upon their gaudy uniform shoulders.

Most of the Kremlin's rooms were small, dark-roofed and strung together by gloomy corridors, along which necessary lamps twinkled and smoked even at noonday. Every wall was luridly patchworked with red, yellow, purple—giving constantly the impression that a thumb was being poked in the eye of the beholder. Down these dark corridors shuffled an unceasing and apparently motiveless swarm of monks, soldiers, freaks, nuns, flunkeys and serving wenches, with occasionally a courier or merchant. They jostled and pushed, babbled, cursed, recited their beads or screamed with laughter. All were unwashed and many were drunk.

Such were the corridors of the Kremlin's outer rooms. Deeper inwards came a sudden widening, a great sweeping upwards of vaulted roofs in an architectural crescendo of magnificent splendour. Banquet halls, reception halls, throne rooms and audience chambers—with painted, glittering ceilings so lofty that in the gloom of the flickering lamps they seemed hardly visible at all and the walls might almost be arching up to the starry heavens. Among these sumptuous caverns, in the heart of the Kremlin's jostled confusion, the courtiers trod in velvet slippers, shushed and watchful. Nearly all wore suits of gold or silver cloth, crusted with jewels like rain-wet spiderwebs. They spoke in whispers, studying each other with careful eyes, and over all these great rooms hung a perfumed half-silence that held an unvoiced, perpetual threat.

"What d'you think of it?" Peter's voice echoed from the curved walls, and Katrina drew a deep breath.

"It's—it's like living in the cellars under some big, big church," she said. "And it smells queer. It has the odour of Pskov slavemarket."

The Tsar laughed. "Yes, all that," he said, "and it's a fortress and a prison, too. D'you think you'll ever get used to it?"

"I expect I shall," said Katrina with a sensible little smile, "when it stops giving me a headache."

"It'll never stop doing that," said the Tsar. "It's always given me a headache—ever since I was a lad!"

He gazed around him, seeing it all for the thousandth time, and added thoughtfully: "There's one thing, Kitty—and I hope the day never comes when you will have to remember this—but whoever controls the Kremlin, rules all Russia! Make no mistake. If I—if you were to find me dead in bed with a knife in my throat, Kitty, hold and defend the Kremlin—for our son." He smiled down at her. "Perhaps when I have moved the capital to Petersburg, we can afford to forget this place, for it is infested with our enemies. But until then we must never let it go. The rest of Russia stretches out like a great, headless giant. This—is the skull!"

"And what was that?" asked Katrina. A sharp cry, dying away into a sobbing wail, had come up from some hidden grating or from behind an obscure door. It was a cry of hopeless anguish, from some orgy, some brutality, betrayal or torture, that hung on the scented air momentarily and stirred its oppressiveness.

The Tsar listened. There was no repetition of the cry. His mouth moved a little strangely. "You'd get more than a headache if you tried to investigate every shriek you hear in the Kremlin," he said.

Chapter Fourteen

THE COURTIERS AND LADIES of the Russian Court, hardly any of whom had seen Katrina before, stared curiously as she entered the supper room. The Tsar, whether to spare her a social ordeal or because of the fatigues of the day's journey, had arranged for his evening meal to be served casually in a small chamber, and there were only a few of his special cronies and their ladies present, although—despite the informality of the occasion—everyone but the Tsar had taken pains to dress in elaborate French Court style.

The Tsar himself was sprawled at the table munching from a bowl of perfumed nuts and in obviously high spirits, when Katrina entered. He waved to her, checking with a gesture the movements of several of his officers who would have risen at her approach, and boomed amiably:

"Come, little Kitty, sit with me and try a handful of these!"

It was all easier than Katrina had anticipated. She sat down carefully, smoothing the stiff folds of her yellow and white gown, and with a laugh that made the jewels sparkle in her hair, held out her cupped hands for the scented cashews that the Tsar cascaded unceremoniously from his own big fist.

He was beaming, not merely at Katrina, but bestowing glances of pleasure whichever way his face turned. Something, it was very clear, had pleased the Tsar that afternoon, and Katrina—with her quick instinct for his moods—sensed that it was not only her own presence in the Kremlin that was causing such good humour.

The reason soon became apparent.

"You know, Alec," said the Tsar impulsively, "I think I'm beginning to understand my son Alexis better. He's growing up into quite a sensible fellow, I'm sure of it!"

Menshikov raised an eyebrow, carefully.

"I spoke to him this evening in my study," the Tsar continued. "He's convinced me that he knows nothing of his mother's—of Eudoxia's—conspiracy against me. He was most upset to hear of my discovery."

"Yes," murmured Romdanovsky, "he would be."

The Tsar ignored this remark. "He is absolutely sure that some of the Streltsi officers named as leaders of the conspiracy are loyal to me. It may not be as bad as we thought."

Prince Menshikov shrugged cautiously. He knew, as did Romdanovsky, from weary experience that the Tsar—shrewd and purposeful in all other ways—was almost childishly willing to believe any tale of penitence from his son Alexis.

"What exactly did he say, Your Majesty?"

The Tsar filled his mouth. "Well, for one thing he entirely

agrees with me about the need for teaching our people to dress like the other men and women of Europe. He agrees they cannot be taken seriously in foreign countries while they persist in wearing these absurd religious beards."

"He did?" said Menshikov quickly. "I would have thought that Prince Alexis, such a religious chap—"

"Well, he didn't," the Tsar interrupted. "He's gone off this evening with a picked group of Garrison officers, to patrol the city and instruct every citizen they see wearing a beard that it must be trimmed!"

Menshikov and Romdanovsky exchanged glances.

"Garrison officers, eh?" said Romdanovsky, and Menshikov said quietly: "What are you thinking, Fedor?"

"It seems strange that he should choose Garrison officers," said Romdanovsky. "They were never particularly loyal to Your Majesty. They're all former Streltsi—and Your Majesty never risks taking them on a campaign."

"Ah, but they are friends of my son's," said the Tsar. "If he sees things my way, so will they. Why," he began expansively, "this may be the beginning of a real end to all our troubles—"

He was interrupted by a messenger, carrying a hastily scrawled dispatch for Romdanovsky.

The Chief of Police, with a brief glance at the Tsar for permission, opened the dispatch at table and read it where he sat. The blood left his face, and when he raised his eyes, the Tsar said: "What is it, Fedor? What is it, man?"

Romdanovsky spoke with forced calmness. "Your Majesty," he said, "it seems that Prince Alexis and his friends misunderstood their instructions. At Vespers Mass this evening, Garrison soldiers burst into more than three hundred churches in the city, crying that it was the order of the Tsar. They wrenched out beards by main force—by the roots—from the faces of worshippers and holy priests of God. They fell upon the women and hacked off their garments to the waist—"

"Oh, my God," muttered Menshikov. The Tsar said nothing, but Katrina saw that his face had gone white and the deep twitch was beginning to stir his cheek.

Romdanovsky continued: "The soldiers drove the women from the churches and down the streets in their shame. And now, Your Majesty, there are riots beginning all over the outskirts of Moscow. The people are saying that the Tsar is dead, and that the Devil disguised as Peter has come to Moscow!"

The Tsar's heavy chair toppled with a crash as he rose to his feet. His teeth gleamed in a snarl of murderous rage.

"They shall hang," he said thickly. "They shall die—they shall all die. I will lay waste to Moscow—every man with a beard! Romdanovsky—I want a thousand rafts built with a gallows on each. By the time the ice breaks, the Volga shall be a floating forest of corpses. Corpses, d'you hear?" His great voice boomed, and broke. He fell forward onto the table, sobbing into his arms. "A river of bearded corpses," he repeated, shaken with grief but firm in terrible determination. "If my people will not let me help them to live, then I shall watch them die!"

Katrina tossed restlessly in her canopied bed.

The Tsar, refusing all offers of solace, had gone storming to his study after supper. Katrina, concerned for him in his sick wrath, waited until nearly midnight, but he did not come. In such a mood he was like a child alone with a grief, and yet there was also about him the menace of a wounded animal. As an ordinary man he would have been pitiable in his anguish and disappointment. But as a Tsar, with the power of life or death at whim, he was dangerous, too. Katrina found it difficult always to remember this.

The candles spluttered and flared. She picked an ermine rug from the bed, wrapped it around her shoulders and, hesitant upon velvet-slippered feet, went through the huge, carved adjoining doors to the Tsar's suite, to seek him.

Yellow light shone through the keyhole of his study door. Down the corridor, an impressive sentry leaned upon his halberd with eyes half shut, watching her. Katrina gingerly opened the Tsar's door, and a sudden cold wind whipped at her thin nightgown.

The Tsar was standing alone by the open window. He had torn away his cravat and stood barechested to the biting Russian midnight, as if trying to assuage a fever.

She glimpsed his face, and it was still obsessed with anger: the ridge upon his cheek lay black and deep. It was best, she decided, prompted partly by wisdom and not a little by sudden diffidence, to leave the Tsar until perhaps he had brooded himself into exhaustion and been comforted by sleep.

When she got back to her own bedroom, she smelt pipe tobacco as soon as she opened the door. Prince Menshikov was sitting on the edge of her bed, waiting for her. His lanky legs were crossed in his favourite lazy posture, but he was frowning.

"How is the Tsar?" he asked directly she came into the room.

Katrina closed the door. "No better." She shivered and hugged the ermine rug to her body. "He's got his window wide open, and the draught cuts worse than Dakov's whip." She shivered again, and Menshikov said gently: "Get into bed, Kitty. Your skin looks like a newly plucked fowl." He pulled the warm coverings aside for her, and Katrina crept in gratefully.

After a moment, she said: "Is it all right—you being here in my bedroom, Alec?" Menshikov made an impatient gesture. "I must talk with you, child. You and I are the Tsar's best friends. We must stop this intended massacre. If the Tsar persists in it, he may lose his throne."

Katrina's eyes widened. "It may come to that?"

Menshikov fumbled for his pipe. "It's the most dangerous thing that could happen," he said, "and so damnably clever—to spread a rumour that the Tsar is dead and the Devil, in disguise, has taken his place. The Tsar is sacred, but the Devil is certainly not!"

"What can we do?"

"We must try to make the Tsar change his mind," said Menshikov.

"Can Romdanovsky not postpone building the gallows for a few days until the Tsar has had time to get over it?" asked Katrina.

"Not Fedor," said Menshikov shortly. "You know him—an order is an order, if it costs him his own life or the Tsar his kingdom. But to hang every man with a beard—there will be revolt!"

"Could the Tsar not make them pay money for having beards," suggested Katrina diffidently, "and get money from them instead of hanging them?"

Menshikov's tired grey eyes gleamed. "A tax on beards," he said hopefully, "and keep on raising the tax—" His fingers shook as he held a bit of rush stem to Katrina's bedside candle, and lit his pipe. "Kitty, can you persuade him?"

Katrina nodded. "I will try—if the Tsar will listen to me," she said quietly.

"It's our only chance," Menshikov said. "Bless you, Kitty." He yawned, "I'm so damnably tired," he said, "yet tonight I can't sleep. Is there wine here?"

Katrina slid from the bed's warmth, and hurried on bare feet to the ornate cupboard. "I had wine and cherry vodka put here for the Tsar," she said. "He sometimes likes a drink if he wakes in the night."

She placed two carafes and two goblets on the bedside table, and scurried back into the bed in such breathless haste, shivering from the chill of the room, that Menshikov laughed in amusement. "You look such a wisp of a child to be discussing affairs of State," he said, his eyes lingering on her. He poured a generous helping of vodka, and gulped it down. Katrina took a fiery mouthful of hers, and whispered: "Put wine in it for me, please. Raw vodka makes my head swim."

Menshikov picked up the carafe, and as he poured the amber, syrupy wine, the smile came to his lips again. "Hydromel," he said softly. "It was this wine that made you tipsy on the first night we met, when I carried you to bed—"

"I'd never drunk wine before," said Katrina quickly.

"—and undressed you," said Menshikov. And Katrina became disturbingly aware of the light in his grey eyes watching her. He moistened his lips beneath the curling brown moustache.

She laughed, rather awkwardly, "Was I very drunk?"

"—and made love to you," continued Prince Menshikov, as though she had not spoken.

Katrina flushed. "That was a long time ago," she said hastily. "I've nearly forgotten it."

They stared into each other's faces in silence for a long while. The crinkles around Menshikov's eyes deepened. "I was the first man to possess you," he said, "and a woman never forgets her first lover, they say." Through the warm, yielding fur of the bed coverlet, Katrina felt the pressure of his hand upon the curve of her thigh. She stirred, disturbed. "Alec, I belong to the Tsar. He's going to marry me—" Her voice was husky and dry.

"I know," Menshikov took her chin in his fingers, and turned up her face. "I found you and I gave you to the Tsar—for I too, belong to him, with all my heart, as you know."

"Then we mustn't—"

"But I have never forgotten you, little Kitty," he whispered. "You were so tiny—so little more than a baby—yet you quivered and clung to me, and called out in that faraway, dim little voice, like a waterfowl calling across a fen—and you were hungry for me—oh, yes, you were—for you wouldn't let me go, I remember . . ." He put his face near to hers. "And I remember that the taste of your mouth was sweet, like a calf's breath, sweet and milky—"

Suddenly, his body was pressing her into the yielding feather bed, and her small cry of surprised protest was smothered. She could not escape from him. He held her trapped inside the bedcovering like a mouse under a pocket handkerchief. His big limbs spread to hold her and after a while Katrina's struggle faded and her last protest as he whisked the ermine rug away from between them was a shuddering sigh. . . .

It was perhaps an hour afterwards that the door of Katrina's bedchamber was suddenly flung open. The Tsar stood there, huge in his heavy silk nightshirt, holding a candle aloft. He peered into the room and dimly saw the shrouded, canopied bed.

"Kitty!" he called harshly. "Are you awake?"

Katrina fluttered into sudden, heart-thudding wakefulness, and scrambled up from the bed, just as the Tsar's candleflame arched, writhed and extinguished itself against the cross draught between room and corridor.

Prince Menshikov, beside her, stiffened in apprehensive awareness. "Yes, Sire—yes," she said quickly. "What is it?"

"Come," the Tsar said harshly. "I cannot sleep alone. The room is filled with shadows—I see faces in them. Come, Kitty—I want you!"

She ran to him, barefooted.

"Oh, Your Majesty," she said, "how you startled me!"

"Did I?" He spoke absently, feeling his own lonely terrors too vividly to detect the fear in Katrina's voice. His big arm encircled her.

"Come," he said, "come to my bed and drive away my shadows, child, for you are the only one who can do so, I fear."

The Tsar's bedchamber was ablaze with candlelight, and a great fire, recently lit, roared in the hearth. "I stood by the open window, brooding," he said, "and chilled myself." He put down his candlestick and put his hands upon her slender hips, "Why, Kitty," he said, "you've been crying. Your face is smudged with tears."

She swallowed. "Oh, Peter!" Her arms reached up to his shoulders to try and embrace him. "Oh, Peter, I do love you—with all my heart. I belong to you, don't I?"

For an instant the angry crease in his cheek disappeared in the beginnings of a smile. Yet there was still a hard light of remembered hurt in his eyes, and she knew that the Tsar had not yet forgotten his son's perfidy, as he replied: "Belong to me, Kitty? If you don't know now, child, you shall be certain of it by daylight. For I need you, I need you, d'you hear?" He spoke the last few words through clenched teeth, and Katrina gasped, the breath driven from her body, as he picked her up between his two powerful hands and pressed her backwards upon the massive study table. Parchments and documents rustled beneath her shoulders, and she felt the icy chill of a big silver inkstand against her neck.

The Tsar bent over her, holding her easily as though she were a kitten, while he twined his fingers into the folds of her silken nightgown, and tore it away. His heavy embrace upon the hard, unyielding surface, made Katrina gasp with sharp discomfort: "You're—hurting me—" The Tsar laughed almost cruelly, then more amusedly, as comfort came to his tormented, urgent loneliness from her helpless subjugation. He picked her up and carried her to the thick, hot rugs by the fire.

"Now," he said breathlessly, "sing to me, Kitty. Make your wild music in your throat—your little jungle cries—"

And he laughed exultantly as she obeyed him, driven by a pressure of need behind her own conscious inhibiting.

When his lovemaking was done, he took her to the big bed, and they lay together watching the fire shadows dip and twirl upon the arched walls.

Katrina begun to talk to him of the plan that she and Menshikov had discussed. She did not mention Menshikov.

The Tsar listened, half impatiently at first, then with increasing attentiveness.

"And so," Katrina said finally, "Your Majesty will know your enemies by their beards, and at the same time raise revenue from them!"

He laughed, hugging her to him. "Kitty," he said, "little one, sometimes I think you are shrewder even than Menshikov!"

"Two heads are sometimes better than one, Your Majesty," she said demurely.

The Tsar had not drawn his bedcurtains, and the first glint of daylight awakened him abruptly, as it always did. He never failed to arouse to dawn as if a bugle had sounded in his bedroom.

But Katrina slept on, undisturbed, beside him. As the Tsar watched her the thought came to him as it so often did in these grey hours when he was first awake—a sense of marvelling at the fresh, new innocence of her, so calmly and trustfully asleep, her smooth, small face almost saintlike in its absence of any expression except that of contentment. Her cheeks were pink, and there was no mar of resin under the long fringes of her eyelashes. Katrina in sleep gave an air of wholesomeness, warm and fragrant as a loaf from the oven.

He touched her carefully, with a quiet smile. Katrina asleep did not care that it was a king's hand upon her body. She turned with voluptuous unconcern away from him, seeking deeper sleep among the warm, yielding feathers.

He kissed her temple, and drew a delicate line with his finger from her white shoulder, along arm and sensitive forearm, to the tracing of thin blue veins at her wrist.

This half roused her, as he knew it would. In the beginnings of wakefulness her falling sleep had been disturbed by a fleeting dream of what Prince Menshikov had done to her, and it was in troubled conscience that she turned, still asleep, towards Peter and huskily repeated the last words she had spoken before Menshikov had pressed both speech and resistance from her.

"I belong to the Tsar," she sighed. Peter, listening, smiled and fortunately did not understand, except that what he heard was sweet to his ears.

It was to the sensation of his breath in her hair that Katrina fully awoke, and when she saw who it was that held her, relief made her eyes fill immediately with tears. "Oh, Peter," she moaned, and clung to him. . . .

The first morning back in the Kremlin was always a busy time for the Tsar. Petitions lay heaped upon the desks of his various chancellors and secretaries, awaiting his delayed authority. And on this morning, no sooner had the Tsar pulled at his bedside bellrope for tea, than a watchful chamberlain passed a signal to the outer room, and instantly the Tsar's bedchamber became invaded by an eager crowd of courtiers, messengers and petitioners.

Katrina, who was sitting up in bed hopefully awaiting her tea, gasped at the sight of them, and slid beneath the coverings again.

For half an hour the Tsar lolled by her side in the big bed, rapping out orders, listening to hasty messages from breathless couriers, cracking the heavy seals of dispatches, whilst a chamberlain served hot perfumed tea from a bright copper samovar. After he had handed a brimming Dutch teacup to the Tsar, he came on silently to Katrina's side of the bed, and with Oriental face devoid of any spark of expression, performed a similar service for her. Katrina sat up diffidently, covering herself with the sable rugs. She felt many eyes watching her, and was uncomfortably aware of her own urgent need for a comb, and a touch of rouge upon her smudged lips. But there did not seem to be any hint of criticism in the faces that regarded her with unwinking frankness.

After a while, the Tsar, too impatient to be at grips with the day to spend a moment longer in bed, jumped up unceremoniously and—unclothed as he was—strode across to his wardrobe chamber, where hot water, his valets, barber and duty chamberlain awaited him.

The petitioners and courtiers streamed in pursuit of him like hens after a feed bucket, and when the last had gone, Katrina scrambled from bed and ran for her own chambers.

Grog was waiting for her. His face broke into a great smile of welcome.

"By the Saints, Katrina!" he boomed. "You must be hungry!" He had the stove roaring hot, and on it glistened an array of bright cooking pots. There were fresh oven cakes, dishes of scalding soups and stews, trays of sizzling, fresh-griddled sweetmeat cakes.

"See!" He lifted a silver dish cover. "Calf brains and hares' kidneys stewed with milk and ginger! Delicious! Will you try some?"

Katrina crammed warm white bread into her mouth and nodded eagerly. The dwarf ladled out a generous bowlful and gave her a silver spoon.

"A crowd of hefty, black-teeth bouncing wenches came storming in here just after daylight," reported Grog, "demanding to play serving wench to you, Katrinushka! Dressed in fripperies and jewels, all mincing and flopsy—there was not a decent lass among the lot of them. I sent them all packing off, squealing like mice. 'When my mistress wants her bedchamber packed with painted bawds at this hour of the morning,' I said, 'she'll ask for them!' "

Katrina smothered a giggle. "Those were probably the daughters of half the noblemen of Muscovy," she laughed, "come to pay me their respects as ladies-in-waiting."

After a moment's consideration of this, Grog dismissed the affair with a shrug of his misshapen shoulders. "Then they'll be back again tomorrow," he said philosophically.

When Katrina had refreshed herself in a steam bath, she dabbed her slender body with scented powders and delicately coloured oils from the dozens of bottles with which her chambers were filled—relics of luxury loving Anna Mons. She put on a hoop-skirted day gown of rose taffeta trimmed with black sable, and was fastening a tiny rose diamond stud to the black velvet ribbon around her throat when Prince Menshikov came in, unannounced.

Katrina looked up at him, her eyes wide and vulnerable, but her mouth set in a small, firm line. Menshikov was too charged with good news to observe the danger signal of her lips.

"Bless you, little Kitty," he said fervently. "The Tsar gave orders this morning to abandon the mass hangings, and simply to put a tax on beards! Kitty, you're a marvel!"

"I am glad," she said coolly, "that you are able to be so happy this morning."

He said quickly: "The Tsar—he didn't suspect us last night?"

"Would we be here this morning if he had?" she answered, and Menshikov smiled wryly. "I see what you mean." He saw now the hauteur of her young face, and could not forbear teasing her. "Perhaps it's not so bad as that, Kitty. The Tsar and I've shared other women, you know."

She felt a flush of blazing indignation burn her face. "I'm not to be shared, d'you understand that?"

"You could tell the Tsar I took you by force," he said quietly. "The blame would then be mine."

She met his eyes for as long as she could, then dropped hers in confusion. "I shall not tell him," she whispered. "You know I could not. But it must never happen again."

There was an awkward pause. Prince Menshikov was still standing near to her, disturbingly.

The long-handled silver hairbrush slipped from her distracted fingers on to the white rug, and he bent to pick it up. As he gave her the hairbrush without a word, their fingers touched, and impulsively Katrina closed her hand around his.

"Alec," she said softly, "we both love him—and he needs us both. It mustn't happen again. Never!"

Menshikov straightened himself and his lips brushed her forehead lightly and elusively. It was not a kiss. It was hardly even a touch.

"I came to take you to the Audience Hall," he said. "The Tsar is receiving foreign ambassadors, and he sent me to fetch you. He needs you, Kitty, it seems."

She looked up at him quickly, and met his smiling eyes. "He needs you, Kitty," he repeated, and the smile reached his lips. "He needs us both—and it shall not happen again."

Chapter Fifteen

THE ROYAL AUDIENCE CHAMBER lay along one of the Kremlin's widest and most magnificent corridors, which had formidable stone pillars every few yards. The ceilings were arched ever higher, until by contrast, one seemed to be shrinking in size as one came nearer to the Tsar's imminent presence.

This sensation was enhanced by the officers of the Tsar's bodyguard, who stood at intervals down the corridor, their strawberry-red jackets of velvet edged with black sable fur, and their caps bright with pearls and precious jewels. Each pair of Guardsmen stood taller than the last two, adding to the impression of growing height, until those who guarded with crossed gold and silver halberds the entrance to the Audience Chamber itself, were giants of fully seven feet tall.

At the approach of Prince Menshikov and Katrina, each guard stiffened to attention with a clash of weapons and armour, raising his halberd for them to pass under into the throne room. And although the corridor had been illuminated at each pillar by clusters of candelabra, lit even in the daytime, it seemed to Katrina as she stepped into the vast Audience Chamber, that she had stepped from a dark tree grove into a great sunlit clearing, whose ceiling was the bright sky itself. Two hundred brilliant crystal chandeliers sparkled from roof and walls.

Along raised and tapestry-covered seats down each side of the great chamber, sat—in utter and paralyzing silence—at least two hundred boyar noblemen, dressed in suits of gold, silver and bright velvet, that twinkled with myriads of jewels. Their seats were upon long platforms, four steps high, so that their silent faces gazed down upon all who entered, in a terrifying avenue of eyes.

Prince Menshikov, accustomed to this, walked calmly enough with head held high, but Katrina felt herself shrinking. She had to fight herself, not to stumble. And as she saw the throne itself at the far end of the breathtaking chamber, her throat tightened in awe, for the throne seemed to be built of pure sparkling gold, set so massively upon seven ascending steps, like a pyramid, that it entirely dominated even the vastness of the audience chamber.

Just beneath the throne stood four of the tallest nobles in the kingdom, dressed entirely in white ermine with great chains of gold hung upon their breasts. Even their knee boots were of white ermine, and their caps were glazed with pearls. Each of these terrifyingly statuesque figures held a gigantic silver battle-axe across his shoulder, and from time to time would turn his head slowly upwards to gaze at the face of the Tsar who sat upon his throne, as if inviting all beholders to marvel at his majesty and splendour.

The sight of the Tsar himself was so frightening and strange that Katrina felt her eyes swim with tears of dismay. He did not seem to be any man she had ever known. He was a stranger who sat huge and giantlike upon his glittering pyramid of a throne, and his gold crown—itself shaped like a pyramid, alive with jewels and surmounted by a high golden cross—altered the shape of his face to make it almost unrecognizable to her.

He sat holding his royal sceptre, and bending slightly forward to listen to the voice of a foreign ambassador who, with one knee upon a purple cushion at the approach to the throne steps, was delivering some kind of formal speech in a foreign tongue, his voice dissipated into the vaguest shreds of sound by the vastness of the chamber.

"Kitty!" The Tsar had caught sight of her. With no further regard for the ambassador who was addressing him, he stood up. "Kitty!" he boomed again. As he rose, all other persons in the chamber at once came instantly to their feet. It sounded like the rushing of a great wind through forest trees.

"Come and sit up here, child," called the Tsar, and made an inviting gesture to the wide throne seat beside him.

Katrina's throat was dry. Uncertainly she lifted her gown, steadying it from bobbing indecorously upon its hoops, and ascended the seven throne steps with as much dignity as she could. As she reached him, the Tsar sat down, pulling his vestments aside to make room for her. When she had seated herself, there came a great subsiding rustle, as everyone else who was privileged to sit in the presence of the seated Tsar, now did so.

The foreign ambassador, apparently quite inured to such events, restored one velvet-clad knee to the cushion, and continued his peroration, which the Tsar now entirely ignored.

"By God, Kitty," he demanded in a penetrating whisper, "where'd you disappear to this morning? Did you get any breakfast?"

"Ye-es, thank you," said Katrina, and felt her face flush hot at the sound of her own voice in the echoing golden canopy of the throne. Below her, on every side, a blurred sea of stern faces seemed to be turned up towards her, staring, staring. . . .

"Villainous-looking lot, aren't they?" the Tsar said complacently, and seemed to be about to cross his legs, but checked himself in time. "It's all right," he added, catching sight of Katrina's shocked face, "they can only hear you if you shout down the steps. It's something in the acoustics of the place—carries your voice up, somehow, to the ceiling."

Katrina absorbed this interesting fact, her eye following the concavities of the arched, vaulted roof. Slowly, as she began to feel more accustomed to her exalted seat, she fingered the golden ornamentations of the throne itself.

"Is this all real gold?" she asked, awed.

The Tsar chuckled. "Not it," he said. "It'd bend like wax if it were! This is gold on silver—just a sham, like all the rest of this jiggery-pokery! Don't worry, little Kitty"—he patted her knee encouragingly—"just lift up your chin and glare right back of them. They must get used to seeing you up here—their future Tsarina."

Katrina raised her chin obediently, and beneath the constellation of crystal chandeliers, her fair hair shimmered and her eyes glowed softly, until the green of them became almost gold in the yellow reflection of the throne.

Below, the dry voice of the foreign ambassador droned incomprehensibly on....

The banquet that evening was painstakingly formal, and went with a sumptuous stateliness that made the Tsar frequently gulp down his yawns like pills, with mouthfuls of wine. There were many foreign diplomats present from the courts of Europe, and the situation in the war against Sweden was too delicate for the Tsar to risk his usual boisterous horseplay. In theory, he was on his dignity, but he sat and squirmed in his gilt chair exactly, Katrina decided, like a restless small boy at a grown-up party.

Shortly before midnight, the Tsar made his official exit from the state drawing rooms, and went to his small private study overlooking Red Square. After him trooped the privileged little group of cronies whose company he craved. Katrina was with them.

No sooner had the padded door shut behind them, than the Tsar ripped off his starched linen cravat with a bellow of laughing relief, and struggled from his heavy, cloth-of-gold tunic in such haste that he broke several of its fastening hooks. He tossed the costly garment to Romdanovsky. "Here, Fedor," he said, "you play at being Tsar. I've had enough for tonight!"

It was apparent that the fat Chief of Police had often been called upon to play this masquerade before, for he donned the jewelled uniform without hesitation, and for a while the two big men played a solemn game of buffoonery with each other that won shrieks of delight from their friends.

Then the Tsar, laughing and entirely restored to a mood of bantering good humour, threw himself into a deep chair and took Katrina on to his knee.

Prince Menshikov had removed his own jacket, and perched on the edge of the table in his favourite lazy gesture, sucking a long Dutch pipe. Sandy-haired Marshal Ogilvy had taken a big chair opposite the Tsar. He had drunk a great deal at the banquet, but his incongruously childlike blue Scots eyes were still brightly watchful.

The Tsar beamed upon them all equally—at his naval strategist, Francois de Villebois, a deep-chested former French smuggler; at the plump, chuckling Polish Jew, Solly Shapirov, who could match wits on any topic with any of them—except perhaps Count Andrew Tolstoy, chief of the Tsar's chancellors, who sat in a corner by the fire, polishing his monacle with the neat, nervous air of a grey squirrel nibbling an acorn.

The sight of Count Tolstoy reminded the Tsar of the unfinished business of the day. He said good-temperedly: "Have you made arrangements for my wedding at the Cathedral of the Annunciation, Andrew?"

The remark was addressed to Count Tolstoy, but everybody in the room seemed to hear it. Talk and laughter stopped. Suddenly, there was a silence. It fell like a night frost. The smile dropped from Shapirov's creased, good-humoured face. De Villebois stiffened his broad shoulders like a man about to attack an enemy. Even Menshikov checked, for a moment, the placid rhythmical swing of his booted leg.

The Tsar blinked into the tense silence. "Well?" he demanded thickly, his impatience mounting. "What's the matter with you all?"

Each looked at the other, silently imploring somebody else to speak first. It was Count Andrew Tolstoy who, putting the monocle to his eye and grasping it firmly by a practised twitch of his cheek muscle, said: "Your Majesty, such a wedding would be most unwise."

Katrina felt the Tsar's great muscles harden like rocks beneath her. His glance went angrily around the room. "Alec—Fedor—Shapi—is he drunk? The joking is over—"

Prince Menshikov said quietly: "Your Majesty must try to

be patient. Such a marriage might cost you your throne!"

Seeing Katrina's startled face, he added gently: "I'm sorry, little Kitty—but the good of Russia must come first."

"Damn it!" bellowed the Tsar, and stood up, dropping Katrina from his lap like a forgotten kitten. "Damn it, what are you trying to tell me?"

"We must face facts," said Count Tolstoy doggedly. "If your Majesty marries Katrina, the Church will make trouble."

Tsar Peter thrust back his heavy chair with a growl. "Let them make trouble. They never do anything else."

Prince Menshikov reached out his hand to Katrina and said gently: "You see, Kitty, a Royal marriage at the Cathedral of the Annunciation would last four or five days. Every other church in Moscow would be expected to hold services, too. Just now, at this ticklish moment, it would be a fine chance for the Tsar's enemies to get into their pulpits and remind the people that the Tsar's first wife is still alive, a prisoner in Susdal Nunnery."

"And it's not only the Church," said Romdanovsky, rubbing his fat cheeks embarrassedly. "The Tsar would have to order the usual amnesties and release thousands of political prisoners, at just the wrong moment."

"To spread the rumour that the Tsar was killed in battle, and the Devil has come in his disguise to Moscow," lisped Solly Shapirov, with a sad look at Katrina. "You aren't marrying just a man, my dear—you're marrying a political situation too!"

"Aye, an' ye're a foreigner to these Russian folk," said Marshal Ogilvy in his careful, drunken Scottish voice. "Ye mustn't forget ye're a foreigner."

All these remarks were addressed to Katrina but she knew that they were intended by his friends for the ears of the Tsar. And the Tsar, who had stormed from his chair in fury, gradually relaxed as he listened and the wisdom of the advice sank into his brain. He turned to Count Tolstoy, who sat without speaking, lips primly pursed.

"All right, Andrew," he said heavily. "You sit looking as if you have acid in your mouth. Has it sharpened your wits?"

"Your Majesty?" Count Tolstoy calmly fixed his monocle into his eye.

"What must we do, man?"

His Chief Chancellor spread thin hands resignedly. "Postpone the wedding, Your Majesty, until the Swedish war is finished."

Katrina's colour left her cheeks, and the Tsar snorted: "Oh, for God's sake! The war may go on for years—and I want sons. I can't wait forever. Can't you think of something, any of you?"

It may have been that Count Tolstoy had already thought of "something," for his bland smile did not even flicker as he said quietly: "If Your Majesty would consent not to be wed in a church—"

"But—how is that possible?" gasped Katrina. "Surely one must be married in church?"

Count Tolstoy cleared his throat with a lawyer-like cough, dry and parchmented. "The Tsar of Russia may wed by declaration if His Majesty so wishes. The statute declares that the Tsar may proclaim his marriage in a public place, and if there is no dissenting voice—"

"There's bound to be a dissenting voice," growled the Tsar, and was turning away impatiently when Tolstoy said: "That window opens on to Execution Square and that is a public place."

The Tsar raised puzzled black eyebrows, but Menshikov, perceiving the plan, said delightedly: "You mean the Tsar should announce his marriage now?"

"Why not?" Count Tolstoy stirred his thin shoulders. "If any citizen is in Execution Square at this hour—past midnight—he need only raise his voice in protest, if he objects."

The Tsar was grinning broadly now. "Is it legal?" he demanded. "Is it a real marriage by Russian law?" And when Tolstoy nodded, the Tsar smacked his scholarly shoulder with an affectionate blow that made the Chief Chancellor gasp. "Andrew, you're a wizard! More wine, everybody! My little Kitty, you shall be married tonight. I shall proclaim our marriage through this window, and my officers of State here will witness it. You will go to bed tonight the Tsarina of Russia! How d'you like that?"

Katrina looked up at him. "If that is the way you wish it, Sire," she said softly, and it was then that he saw the tears in her eyes.

"You wanted the rites of the church, didn't you?" he said compassionately. "But this will make you my lawful wife, I promise you. And in a few months, when things have settled down, we can be married in the Cathedral of the Annunciation and every bell in Russia shall peal for you!"

The Tsar wrenched open the casement window and beckoned her to come and stand beside him on the snow-covered silent balcony. "See," he said, and his voice was unusually gentle, "see out there—all the white roofs of Moscow, Kitty! There never was a bigger cathedral than this—and all the stars in heaven to be your priests and witness my vows."

From a smooth-tongued lover like Menshikov such a speech might have seemed trite. But hearing it spoken so quietly by the big, simple-hearted man at her side, Katrina was deeply touched; and when he looked down at her with such a pleading earnestness, she had to smile. "Yes, Your Majesty," she said, "I think it will do."

They went back into the room, snowflakes gathered thick upon their shoulders, and the Tsar's friends looked up expectantly from their drinking cups.

"Was there anybody who objected?" smiled Menshikov.

"No voice that I heard," said the Tsar solemnly, and Katrina joined in the shout of laughter.

Chapter Sixteen

IT WAS A DESTROYING WINTER in Russia that year, and the invading armies of Charles of Sweden had been appalled by it. They had expected snow and even bitter cold, but never such a winter as this!

Birds had toppled frozen from the trees, and men upon the steppes had died as they merely breathed the icy wind. It had come like an answer to the fervent prayers that rose from Moscow's two thousand church domes and cathedral spires.

Marshal Sheremetiev had burnt every Russian forest and twig, destroyed every Russian village and hut that lay upon the path of the Swedish advance. He had withdrawn before them and let the Swedes exhaust themselves in starvation and the bitter cold.

When eventually the thaw came, Marshal Sheremetiev sent out a cautious exploratory patrol. They found the remnant of the once proud Swedish Army huddled in an encampment that was ringed with its own corpses.

"—and now, Your Majesty," came the urgent dispatch from Sheremetiev to the Tsar, "is the time to attack!" It was a method of warfare that never failed the Russians.

Tsar Peter had not himself wasted the opportunities of winter. He had melted many of the church bells into metal for cannons, and wrung his kingdom for extra soldiers. Even the company of Simenov Guards who had been assigned the task of guarding the mansion of Anna Mons were withdrawn. "I cannot waste good fighting men to play watchdogs to old, dead lusts," he had said.

Anna, watching from behind the barred windows of her prison, saw the soldiers march away through her gates, and drew a deep breath of triumph.

"You see!" she said to her brother, and her voice was shrill with vehemence, "the prophecy of Father D'Ameno begins to come true!" Her brother Vilhelm, peering over her shoulder, recited sibilantly, "... summer and winter goes, and you shall walk free from your prison ..."

"I knew this would happen," said Anna. "The Tsar cannot live without me. He is weary of that Witch of Marienburg. Her spells have failed her." She spat with careful superstition. "It will only be a question of time now before the Tsar comes back to me, only a question of time!"

Vilhelm shuddered delicately. "Must you keep using that dreadful word 'time'?" he lisped. "After months of being cooped up in this place I've developed quite an aversion to time!" He patted his shoulder-length yellow hair with painted fingers, and regarded himself in the mirror that hung upon the peeling wall.

"I've not grown any younger, either," he murmured, "and I must say that you haven't, my dearest!"

Anna struck him venomously with the cutting edge of her fan, and blood trickled down his pale cheek. "All this hellish waiting, day after day for the executioner to come and take me to burn in Red Square—three years of waiting whilst that Witch of Marienburg dug herself into the heart of the Tsar with her black magic—and you dare talk to me of lost youth!"

They glared at each other. Both had changed considerably from the smooth, confident and exquisite courtiers they had once been. Both, in their hearts, knew it. Except for a few sulky servants, and the blank-faced men of the Tsar's Guard who kept them imprisoned, they had seen only each other, and that sight had long since thoroughly palled. Three years of expecting death had brought bitterness to Anna's once almost flawless face. The tiny wrinkles under her eyes were now deeply etched and fanatical. Her once eagerly pouting mouth was undeniably sulky now.

The one thing that had sustained them—the prophecy of Father D'Ameno—had lost much of its comfort after Katrina arrived in Moscow, and months had gone by, and still she did not lie "white and still in the Kremlin garden." Neither Anna nor Vilhelm would lately admit how much they had clung to the hope of the prophecy. And now, here it was under their eyes at last beginning to come true!

The river ice was melted, and the earth had begun to show black patches through the snow. The Tsar's armies stood ready to advance and drive the Swedish invaders out of Russia.

"Will you march tomorrow?" Katrina asked. It was a dark, blustery night, and the Kremlin draughts tore at the candle flames. The Tsar sat hunched by his study fire, sucking morosely at his pipe.

"I'd have gone four days ago, damn it," he said, "if I could have found that blasted son of mine." For days the Tsar's messengers had vainly searched Moscow for the young Prince Alexis who was to have ridden with his father upon this campaign, and who had—typically—at the last moment gone into hiding. Everybody in Moscow knew Prince Alexis was a coward.

Katrina passed her hand soothingly over the cords on Peter's massive neck, and sat beside him on the wide arm of his favourite chair. She wanted to make him smile. She could have struck Alexis for the disappointment he brought to the Tsar.

"Take me, instead," she coaxed, trying to make her voice sound gay. "Take your little Hussar. Teach me all you would have taught Alexis."

The Tsar stared down the white stem of his Dutch clay pipe. "That wouldn't be taking my son," he grunted. Katrina smiled and nibbled a sweetmeat of preserved orange peel.

"In a way it might be taking your son," she said calmly.

For a long instant the Tsar sat, not realizing the significance of what Katrina had said. Then he sat up suddenly, spilling her box of honeyed peel in a shower down her dress. His pipe fell and broke, but he did not heed these things. Prince Menshikov, who had been studying campaign maps at the Tsar's desk, looked up quickly, and fixed Katrina with a shrewd stare from his penetrating grey eyes. The Tsar pulled her urgently on to his knee. His face, a moment before sagging in gloom, now shone with eager pride. "Is this true, Kitty? You must know for sure—Alec, fetch one of those blasted physicians—this is something they have knowledge about."

"They'll all be in bed," said Menshikov blandly, "and anyway, you don't need a doctor. Kitty knows."

"God damn it!" The Tsar threw back his head in a roar of exasperation. "Get me a doctor, confound you—get one out of bed!" As Menshikov rose with a smile, and went towards the door, the Tsar called: "If this child should resemble you, you pie-man, I'll have your—"

Menshikov grinned back from the doorway. "Pity," he said, "but it would be a miracle if it could, by this time . . ." He shut the door quickly and the Tsar's goblet smashed against it.

Peter picked up Katrina, held her exultantly aloft, then gingerly put her down again. She laughed up at him. "So may I come with you?" She wanted with all her heart to accompany him on this campaign. He shook his head. "No, Kitty, this time you remain here."

Her voice dropped with disappointment. "Having a baby isn't so difficult," she said rather sulkily. "It will be summer before he comes."

"You'll stay here," said the Tsar firmly. "I'll be back before the summer." He bent and kissed her. "God bless you, little Kitushka," he said fervently, "you must take care of my son."

"Supposing it's a girl," Katrina asked demurely. The Tsar looked genuinely surprised.

"Nonsense," he said, in his most authoritative voice, "of course he will be a boy!"

"Anathema! Anathema!" The chant of execration surged up from the crowd in the Kremlin's Execution Square like bubbles of steam exploding upon a seething cauldron. A circle of black-garbed priests chanted around the execution fire. Mazeppa the Cossack leader had turned traitor at Baturin, and was being excommunicated by the Holy Church. The Tsar's executioner, dressed in blood-red blouse, was preparing an effigy for his roaring, purposeful blaze. Katrina watched from the Kremlin balcony. The gardens were warm with summer sunshine, and a strong scent of roses came up to her, polluted by acrid wafts of dark smoke from the pyre that, cheated of Mazeppa's actual body (for that wily Cossack was far away), was licking its flames towards the reviled dummy.

"And when Mazeppa dies," said Grog, watching the ceremony in the square with fascinated eyes, "he will have no soul. An excommunicated man is doomed to flit forever in the shape of a vampire."

"Oh, Grog," protested Katrina with a shiver.

Her child stirred inside her, and she pressed her hand upon it, seeking the thrilling contact. It had been a lonely spring without either the Tsar or Menshikov, and without all the gay entourage. Katrina had made no real friends among the ladies-in-waiting who served her. They were all white-fleshed, soft indoor women, who ate greedily as caterpillars, and seldom spoke. They showed neither curiosity nor envy, and responded to conversation with only bleating, breathless little giggles. The few remaining men were either priests, elderly guards, or clerkly court officials who busied themselves with their documents when Katrina approached, and only looked up slyly after her when she had passed.

She was glad of the companionship of her stirring, unborn child. A son he had to be, she reminded herself, and smiled tenderly. A son, because the Tsar had insisted that it must be so. . . . Her reverie was broken by the rising wail of the repetitious chant: "Anathema, Anathema! . . ."

"Grog!" she said, "I don't know how you can stay watching all that! I'm going for a walk in the garden until it's over. Are you coming?" Grog nodded absently, hardly hearing what she said, for the climax of the excommunication ritual was about to begin. Each black-clad priest had snuffed his candle; the books of damnation were being thumbed, and the bell had begun to toll the soul of Mazeppa into hell.

Vilhelm Mons, standing with his sister Anna upon the edge of the crowd in Execution Square, had not once taken his glance from Katrina, as she stood upon the balcony with her dwarf. Anna, hungry for crowds and excitement after her long months of confinement under guard, had not yet noticed her rival and Vilhelm did not draw her attention to Katrina. He felt a stir of interest at the sight of the girl who had captured the Tsar's favour.

"There's something damned attractive," he muttered, "almost boyish—"

Anna, said, without turning her head, "What are you mumbling?" Dressed in her elaborate best, faded and slightly out of the height of fashion though it now was, Anna felt happy. She had painted her face with a careful white mask of rice paste and put two circles of red rouge upon it for rosy cheeks. Scraped of all this, Anna's face, structurally perfect, might still have looked only slightly less than beautiful, but in the strong sunshine she appeared bizarre.

"I was looking at the Witch of Marienburg," said Vilhelm clearly, and knowing how much it would annoy his sister, he added: "She has been standing on that balcony up there, but she's just disappeared."

With an angry little hiss, Anna turned to glare at the empty balcony. "Vilhelm, you fool! You knew I wanted to see her!" She stared hungrily along the terraces of the Kremlin balconies for a glimpse of her rival, and after a while was rewarded by the sight of Katrina descending the private stairway that led towards the garden.

"That's done it," said Vilhelm with a malicious grin. "She's going into the gardens, and they're forbidden to us commoners."

To Anna this was a bitter reminder that the Kremlin gardens were no longer her personal playground, as they once had been. "All the same," she said, "I'm going!" She grabbed her brother's sleeve viciously, taking care to ensnare a painful fold of flesh, and drew him out of earshot of the crowd.

"Don't you remember, you fool?" she demanded. "Don't you remember the prophecy?" And Vilhelm's jaw slackened. "Oh, lord, yes," he said, awed. "In the Kremlin gardens, of course—and the execution fire!"

"Give me your knife," said Anna, "and wait for me in the coach." Without a word, Vilhelm unbuckled his dainty jewelled dress-dagger from its velvet sash, and gave it to her . . .

Katrina walked, cool and pleased with herself, under the summer trees. The Tsar, over-anxious for the safety of his unborn son, would have gone into a rage had he watched Katrina jump lightly on to a fallen log, and then over it, stooping quickly to examine flowers, or to pick up some stranded beetle. Katrina did not feel her expectant motherhood a burden. Her lively young body, slender though it was, had a peasant woman's strength. She swung along through the arbor, indulging the harmless conceit of all shapely young women in perfect health who are within a month of becoming mothers—that her condition was hardly visible to an ordinary beholder.

"I'm sure I could wear my best tight-waisted evening gowns tonight if I wanted to," she told herself, "and there'd be hardly any difference!"

The child kicked and Katrina smiled at its lustiness. "Kick, then," she said softly, "kick and grow strong, little prince!"

Katrina's favourite walk led through a sunken green dell among the rustling silver birch trees and flowering shrubs. It was so far from the Kremlin's public courtyard that Vilhelm Mons, watching from the window of his coach, could glimpse Katrina's white dress only occasionally.

He could not see his sister Anna at all. If she was still following Katrina—and Vilhelm was coward enough to half hope that she was not—she was doing it very astutely. But, then, Anna knew these gardens as well as she knew her own, and had probably gone by way of the orchard wall to surprise Katrina where there would be no observers. Vilhelm Mons mopped the sweat of anxiety from his cold, white and carefully manicured hands.

Katrina did not expect to find anybody at all along the pathway, for this part of the garden was particularly reserved for the Tsar and his intimate friends. It was an unpleasant shock to discover Prince Alexis sitting hunched in the path, his thin legs spread spiderishly. Prince Alexis was perhaps the last person that Katrina wanted to see upon such a pleasant summer day. Also, it was obvious that the Prince was painfully drunk.

"Why, Alexis," said Katrina resignedly, "what are you doing here?" It was always a struggle for Katrina to like the young Prince Alexis, but he was the Tsar's son and therefore—as she had often had to remind herself—there was a part of Peter's blood in him, and for the sake of this Katrina always made a deliberate effort to include Prince Alexis in her affections.

The Prince muttered drunkenly to himself. His lips drooped, grey and moist as slugs, with their burden of wine. He did not lift his head when Katrina spoke to him.

"Come," she said, "let me help you up, Alexis." And as he still did not answer, she persisted: "Alexis! Surely you know me!"

He looked up at her then, blinked and wiped his wet mouth upon his sleeve. "Know you?" he echoed thickly, "ev-body knows you—the Whore of Marienburg—" He struggled to his feet. His face lurched near to her, with a sour-sweet waft of wine, and his bony fingers began to paw at the front of her dress.

Katrina knocked his hands away calmly. He didn't anger her any more. He was barely a year younger than she was, but to Katrina he still seemed a sly, cowardly child, a living weapon of revenge upon Peter by the deposed Tsarina Eudoxia, even from her shut nunnery cell. As long as Prince Alexis lived, he would be a blow in the face of the Tsar's pride. Katrina knew that it was too late to do anything to mend it. Yet she could not forbear from saying all those same useless, hopeful things to Alexis that one always said to him, and which never made one whit of difference.

"Oh, why do you sneak off and get drunk like this every day?" she said. "And why didn't you go with your father to the wars? Why won't you try to be a man, Alexis? The Tsar loves you—think how many times he's forgiven you—again and again!"

Prince Alexis scowled darkly and unsteadily. He flopped his hand before his face to indicate that he did not wish to hear more. Katrina persisted: "Only this morning, I had fresh dispatches of your father's latest success against the Swedes. He's coming home, Alexis, to both of us. You've been drunk every day since he left, nearly six months ago. Please, won't you pull yourself together, for your father?"

Anger almost sobered Alexis. "Too bad he wasn't killed. Why didn't he get killed in his cursed war—and let Russia live again—back to her glorious past . . ." He sat down suddenly upon the ground. "I feel ill," he said, and buried his face in shaking hands.

"Oh, be ill, then!" said Katrina. "Perhaps you'll feel better afterwards," she added with all that was left of her patience.

She turned away and took a few running steps to try and recapture her previous mood of gaiety. This sudden movement surprised Anna Mons, who was waiting silently around the bend of the thickly foliaged path. Anna had not expected, any more than had Katrina, to find Prince Alexis in that part of the garden.

Anna and Katrina came face to face, and Katrina halted abruptly. The sight of Anna Mons, standing straight in the middle of the scented green path, and staring at her with such silent malice, sent a tingling shock through her. Anna was taller, nearly ten years older, and by that much advanced in poise; and in the merciless sunlight her red and white painted face looked unreal as a tiger lily.

As she stared, Katrina took control of herself, her own natural courage sending her chin high.

"Who are you?" she challenged, and knew the answer to her own question before she asked it.

Anna took the few strides that fetched her up to where Katrina stood. Anna's eyes shone with hate. "So this is the little lovebird," she drawled, "all cosy in its nest!" Her own plans, her painstaking following of Katrina into the privacy of the garden, whatever scheme she had decided upon when she took the dagger from Vilhelm—had all vanished now. Here was her rival, and it was not in Anna's nature to withhold from screaming abuse at her. "D'you know who I am?" she demanded, her voice already rising harshly.

Katrina said simply, "No." But she was so certain in her mind who it was, that she began to turn away even as she spoke the single brief denial. A fear had come upon Katrina of a kind she had never before experienced. It was a fear not for herself but for the safety of the child within her.

Anna moved to block Katrina's path. "Well, I'll tell you. I'm the one who should be here—not you—you little Swedish slut!" Her glance fixed upon the significant shape of Katrina's waist. "You get out, d'you hear? Get out!" she screamed. "The Tsar is mine—Peter was always mine! Get out—get out!"

"I'm married to the Tsar," said Katrina as steadily as she could. She tried to make her voice dominant, but against the tense rage of this taller, older woman, she wavered.

This remark, however, angered Anna beyond sanity. She put heavily jewelled hands upon Katrina's shoulders, and swung her around. And in that moment Katrina saw the wafer-blue blade of the jewelled knife, just one fraction darker than the summer sky against which it hung poised. She had barely time to twist herself away from the direct line of the stroke, and she fell to the ground with the blue blade deflected to its haft in her back, along the shoulder bone. It was not a fatal blow, although enough to wrench the knife from Anna's grasp.

Breathless, shocked by the sharp, broken-glass pain of the knife, Katrina lay for a moment inert. Then Anna kicked at her, purposely aiming the pointed toe of her shoe at Katrina's stomach. The shock of this made Katrina's face empty instantly of all blood and colour, and her head lolled like a broken thing. Anna, now certain her rival was dead, left Katrina sprawled upon the path and ran along the green arbor towards her coach.

Prince Alexis, a few yards away, had paused in his spasmodic discomforts at the sound of women's voices raised. But when, after Katrina's brief scream, there was silence, he wiped his mouth uncertainly upon his black sleeve and faltered towards the Kremlin without a backward glance. He was rid of the burden of his wine and this was a signal to Alexis to go in quest of more. He was in a mood to care little about anything else.

Vilhelm Mons lay stretched languidly across the cushions of his coach as he waited for Anna. He was taking almost comical precautions to seem completely at his ease and unafraid. He had tended his hair and nails, and was now primping the silver lace of his jacket cuffs, with a frowning perseverance as if it were a duty that had to be accomplished cost what it might in personal effort and sacrifice. When Anna scrambled into the coach, panting and shaken, her thick make-up cracking as the sweat of panic gathered beneath it, Vilhelm straightened himself elaborately.

"Ha!" he said, and touched his fingers to an artificial yawn. "Done it?" Anna nodded, her own throat too dry for speech. She made a fluttering gesture with her hand to indicate that the coachman should be ordered to drive away. Vilhelm nodded, and as he reached up with his gold-knobbed fop's cane to tap a signal to the coachman, he lisped: "Good for you! And where is my dagger?"

It was obvious from Anna's face that she had not got it. Vilhelm froze in mid-gesture, his cane halfway to the coach roof. "You don't mean to say you left it?" he shrieked, all pretence at calmness vanished. "My knife? But the Tsar knows it! His tutor gave it to me!"

"Oh, my God," said Anna, her voice quavering.

Vilhelm wrenched open the coach door and, with one wild glance around to make sure that no palace officials or guards might be alert to observe him, ran towards the garden arbor in the distance where he had last glimpsed Katrina's white dress among the trees.

The sudden stench of soured wine upon the grass where Prince Alexis had been sick brought Vilhelm up abruptly, with his heart and pulses fluttering, at the same time that he caught sight of Katrina lying on the path just ahead. She was alive, there was no doubt of it. As he watched she moved slightly, and he saw the handle of his knife glint as it began to slip from the shallow wound.

Vilhelm's fingers went distractedly to his hair, and his eyes searched the nearby bushes. The vomited wine puzzled him. There must have been somebody else here! He saw his knife fall to the reddened grass as Katrina tried to sit up. Anna had made a fine mess of this!

It was Vilhelm's chance to finish the job properly that his sister had begun, and he would have been quite safe to do so, for Prince Alexis was staggering across the flower beds towards the Kremlin without thought or care as to what had happened to Katrina.

But Vilhelm hesitated. He was the type of self-absorbed man who could have performed deeds of reckless heroism before admiring eyes. But, alone in the garden with his problem, Vilhelm faltered. In his own way, he was fond of his sister. But he was much more profoundly fond of himself.

"Oh, damn Anna!" he said hoarsely, and stumbled forward towards Katrina.

"Your Majesty," he said as he knelt beside her. "Your Majesty—oh, dear God—are you hurt?"

It was in the trembling, aching arms of Vilhelm Mons that Katrina was carried towards the shelter of the Kremlin, where she was laid in her own bed, convulsed with premature labour pains.

Chapter Seventeen

TWO MOUNTED COURIERS passed each other upon the dusty, wheel-rutted track beyond Kalouga on the Moscow road that evening. One was Major Ekhov of the Tsar's personal staff, spurring towards the Kremlin with news of the latest Russian victory and orders to prepare the city for a triumphal return of the victorious Grand Army.

The second courier, bent low over the horse's neck, was in too grim a hurry even to rein up and pause for a comradely word with Ekhov as they drew level upon the winding road; for the dispatch bag thumping at his knee bore the seal of Prince Romdanovsky, Chief of the Tsar's Police, and he was carrying southwards to the Tsar the news of what had happened to Katrina. "Let the Tsar but arrive too late," Romdanovsky had said to his courier in the flat, calm voice of disaster, "and I shall crack your spine for a start, my lad, before I begin to ask about the reasons for delay."

The Tsar had left the field and the spoils in charge of Sheremetiev and was riding towards Moscow at the head of the Grand Army, when the courier reached him, grey with dust and babbling with fatigue. Tsar Peter split the red and yellow seal with his thumb, and absorbed Romdanovsky's scrawled message. His expression scarcely changed. It was in almost a normal voice that he said to Marshal Ogilvy: "Take charge here. There's been an accident. I shall ride on to the Kremlin."

"Is it Katrina?" asked Prince Menshikov, with quick intuition. And lively-witted Shapirov slipped from his own saddle, saying: "Take my mount, Your Majesty. He's carried less weight than yours, and stands as tall."

The Tsar nodded: "Thanks, Solly." He turned to De Villebois and rapped: "Francois, follow me with a troop of cavalry. I shall ride hard—let as many keep up with me as can." He jerked his head to Prince Menshikov. "Come with me, Little Alec." And in the use of the affectionate diminutive, his voice faltered for the first time. Prince Menshikov swung his horse out of the slow moving column without a word, and the two galloped towards Moscow, with De Villebois and sixty cuirassiers of the Simenov Guard stringing out behind.

Throughout the seventy miles the Tsar hardly spoke. They changed horses twice at post-houses, and within two hours beyond midnight, his escort's hooves were drumming on the wooden paving slats of Moscow streets.

A covey of ladies-in-waiting scrambled twittering to their feet as the Tsar strode into Katrina's candlelit bedchamber. Four court physicians leapt anxiously from their chairs, their eyes seeking the Tsar's as if to plead: "You see—I am here—correctly on vigil!" The Tsar thrust through them without a glance.

Romdanovsky sat by Katrina's bed. The Tsar thrust him unceremoniously aside and looked down at his young wife's face. Her eyes remained shut, the lids bruised and dark. He gently touched her hand and Katrina's unconscious fingers closed around his trustingly.

"Well?" demanded the Tsar, and Romdanovsky said flatly: "This popinjay Mons brought her in from the garden. He swears it was his sister who stabbed her, and I believe him." The Police Chief's thick eyelids drooped. "She seems to have kicked her, too," he added significantly. "I put a guard on her house, to await your instructions."

"Anna?" said the Tsar, for the dispatch had not told him this. He and Romdanovsky looked at each other.

"D'you want Anna, Sire?" asked Romdanovsky quietly, and the Tsar's voice was expressionless as he replied: "Yes, Fedor, I want Anna. I want her brought here in chains—naked—and tonight!"

Anna Mons had not slept. She had paced all night through the curtained salons of her house, her eyes lit with nervous wakefulness.

Her servants leaned against the silver-panelled walls and dozed as best they could, with half an eye warily upon her. Every candle blazed in the gigantic crystal chandelier that dominated the entrance hall of her mansion, and it was within an hour of dawn. Anna had waited vainly all night for news of her brother. She had no hope now that he would return to the house. He must have been arrested.

Coach wheels came grinding up her driveway, and no coach bells tinkled. There was only one coach in Moscow like that—and it belonged to the Chief of the Tsar's Police. Anna sat rigidly upright upon one of the black velvet sofas beneath the chandelier, and sipped French brandy with painted lips that she strove to restrain from trembling.

Romdanovsky waddled in, and Anna steadied herself with a deep, desperate breath.

"Good evening, Fedor," she greeted him calmly. "If you are seeking my brother Vilhelm, I am afraid that he is not here."

Romdanovsky nodded, and gestured to the three men who had come in with him that they should remain on guard by the door. They were all thick-limbed and swarthy, with greased black hair hung like ram's wool down to their muscular shoulders. They wore the mustard-yellow tunics of the Tsar's police, and black baggy breeches tucked into Cossack style boots.

Two of the men carried between them a large and ungainly leather bag, which they lowered carefully to the floor. Anna stared for a moment at this, then turned her carefully rouged face towards Prince Romdanovsky again, with flattering attentiveness.

"You keep late hours," said Romdanovsky with the glint of an admiring smile. As Anna sat thus, with her white satin gown clinging to the curves of her body, Romdanovsky found her undeniably attractive. Anna was his type. He had always privately envied the Tsar his possession of Anna Mons. She had a generous physique, a sumptuousness of appeal that, Romdanovsky felt, Katrina somehow lacked.

Anna did not look as if she could run or ride a horse or wear a Hussar's uniform or laugh blithely. Anna belonged indoors, by candlelight, set to music and wine, with white satins and black velvets, as she was now, seated under her chandeliers in an atmosphere so dense with perfume that one had almost to brush it aside like a bead curtain. Prince Romdanovsky considered all this as he stood regarding her, and Anna—being the woman she was—read his thoughts. Hope began to rise inside her. He seated himself without invitation upon one of the black velvet couches opposite Anna.

"Why should I be looking for your brother?" he asked blandly. And now his fat face had become as expressionless as a big round butterball.

She said tersely: "Really, Fedor, I'm not a fool." Romdanovsky inclined his head in silent agreement at this. Anna Mons was not a fool, he knew.

She went on quickly. "Vilhelm has not been home all day. By nightfall you put guards on my house. They do not come in, but they watch. And my servants bring me tales of—" despite herself, Anna had to swallow before she could say the word—"of the Tsarina Katrina, assassinated in the Kremlin gardens . . ."

"So?" said Romdanovsky patiently.

"Well—" Anna tensed herself for the betrayal, "I—I shouldn't say this, but—"

Romdanovsky prompted her: "You think your brother Vilhelm did it?"

"I know Vilhelm did it!" said Anna, then put her hands to her mouth in dramatic dismay. "Oh, what have I said?"

"Mmm?" The Chief of Police seemed to be only half listening. His glance was wandering in frank admiration from Anna's jet black, elaborate coiffure down to her gold-threaded satin slippers.

"Oh, Fedor," said Anna, and pressed her hands to her soft bosom, "I deserved my own imprisonment. I knew I'd done wrong. But Vilhelm—it embittered him so—he hated the Witch—the Tsarina Katrina," she corrected herself hastily.

"Go on," said Romdanovsky, and settled his ample haunches more comfortably upon the sofa.

"Yesterday morning as we were driving from the Kremlin Square, we glimpsed the Tsarina walking alone in the gardens. It was the first time Vilhelm or I had ever seen her, and—" Anna's voice broke, "Vilhelm suddenly clutched at his dagger and rushed from the coach, across the garden . . ."

"Why didn't you give the alarm?" asked Romdanovsky, and Anna's dark eyes were round jet jewels of appealing innocence as she answered: "But Fedor—I didn't know he was going to kill the poor Tsarina, did I?" She crossed herself piously with fluttering white hands.

"I suppose not," said Romdanovsky. He reached forward and helped himself to a glass of Anna's brandy. "You'll be glad to hear," he said sipping slowly, "the Tsarina wasn't killed. It was only a slight wound, a puncture of the shoulder." His thick-lidded eyes, apparently almost on the brink of slumber, missed nothing of Anna's expression as he added untruthfully:

"The Tsarina is sitting up in bed at this moment, asking about you."

"Oh, my God!" said Anna bleakly, and her face betrayed her as surely as any written confession. "Fedor," she babbled, "Fedor—be merciful. Give me an hour to escape—we were almost lovers once . . ."

"Were we?" said Romdanovsky, interestedly.

"I'll give you anything—anything," gasped Anna. "My jewels —myself—"

Romdanovsky stirred his portly bulk upon the black velvet sofa, and made a gesture towards the three men who stood patiently by the door. Two of them stooped to pick up the bulging leather bag. As they moved toward Anna, muffled clinks came from it. Anna eyed it apprehensively, her hands clenched.

"Shackles," explained Romdanovsky blandly. "A gift of solid iron jewels from the Tsar's Police." His fat cheeks creased into an almost affectionate smile, like that of a middle-aged uncle to a favourite young niece. "My official orders are to load your every limb with chains, my dear, and by the time that's done—" he dabbed at his brandy-moist lips with a large handkerchief—"it wouldn't matter much whether you'd be willing to give me your body or not, Anna. For it will hardly be yours to withhold any more, will it?"

Tsar Peter sat by Katrina's bed, and with a careful forefinger stroked her hot forehead. He did this task with all the gentle clumsiness of a man attempting to smooth out a crumpled foil of old leaf. His wrath was a swelling lump inside him, waiting an opportunity to burst out. But he sat still, controlling himself, for Katrina was awake. She had been in labour for hours. And now she lay in a little armistice between pains, her slanted eyelids tightly shut above a heavy fringe of lashes that weeping had stalagmited into black spikes. The short, puffed sleeves of her nightgown made her arms seem unbearably frail. An almost oven-like warmth rose from the bed, but there was no flush upon Katrina's cheeks. A new pain approached, and she began to turn her head from side to side. The Tsar cradled her in his arms, and Katrina's hands curled in a tight possessive grip upon his jacket.

"It's all right," she whispered. "It's just—what anybody has to—put up with, when they have a baby." And as the pain tugged at her, her slender shoulders convulsed to it, so that the bandaged knife wound bled afresh.

The Tsar did not look up when Prince Romdanovsky tiptoed in, his fat legs grotesque in their cautious movement. "I've got Anna Mons in the coach outside, Your Majesty," he whispered. "Is it in this room you want her?"

The Tsar drew a deep breath. He carefully uncurled Katrina's relaxing fingers from his coat, and laid her carefully back upon the pillows. The pain was beginning to ebb for a while. "No," said the Tsar, "bring her into the next room, Fedor. I'll be out in a few minutes."

Prince Romdanovsky was a man capable of the most appalling cruelties, yet he was not by instinct cruel. Tortures and death had for so long been a daily part of his duties that they did not give him an instant's qualm. But he did not seek to inflict pain for its own sake, and as he had watched Anna Mons dragging her shackled limbs in slow humiliation up the Kremlin stairway, he had signalled to the yellow-smocked assistants that they should help her with her fetters. It had taken him long enough, he told himself, to get her this far. One should risk no further delay.

In her own home, Anna had screamed and struggled until she was exhausted, while her clothes were removed and thick, roughly cast gyves riveted to her limbs. She had scratched and bitten. Anna was not the type to suffer in martyred silence, nor did Prince Romdanovsky, for his part, see any good reason why she should.

So now the party shuffled slowly towards the Tsarina's bedchamber, with the three uncouth attendants gathered around Anna Mons like diabolical train bearers, carrying the weight of the huge, brutal links in their hands. And even thus, it was all she could do to walk.

The chains were a standard police set, as laid down for a felon. Thick circlets of iron clamped her ankles and neck, each being joined by heavy chains to the others. Her arms were fettered at the wrists to grievously weighted links that were in turn welded to ankles and neck-collar. The whole felon's outfit must have weighed at least as much as did Anna Mons' pale soft body. Dignified movement was impossible, and

Anna quivered with angry humiliation rather than fear, for she was beyond terror.

The boudoir antechamber was empty when they arrived. The doors that led to the bedroom itself were shut. Anna stared around the poignantly familiar room. She had herself chosen the white and gold French brocade curtains, and there was a window cushion upon which she had sewn a floral pattern that was still unfinished.

From behind the doors came a faint murmur of voices. Once, there was a muffled sob of pain, and she knew this to be Katrina's voice.

As soon as they had brought her into the middle of the room, Anna's three jailers unceremoniously dropped their handfuls of heavy chain links and stepped back from her. Anna caught sight of her reflection in one of the room's panelled mirrors.

In that moment, Anna Mons became glad of the ugly fetters that festooned her body. It was three years since she had last confronted the Tsar, and at that time the Tsar had loved her with all his heart. Anna could not believe that this was now unalterably changed. Some spary of ardour must still, she felt sure, have remained alive. Anna had no doubts of her own allure. And now, standing thus pitifully shackled, she hoped that the sight might move the Tsar to mercy as nothing else could. Should she kneel to him submissively, Anna wondered, or draw herself up with shackled arms outstretched in appeal? Romdanovsky, watching her with a smile, knew full well what Anna intended. It was not his duty to interfere, either way. If the Tsar should be stirred to clemency, Romdanovsky would not blame him. If not, then Romdanovsky was just as prepared to dispose of Anna Mons in whatever manner the Tsar might indicate.

But as the doorknob turned, and a chamberlain flung the door open for the Tsar to pass, the chief of Romdanovsky's jailers, with not an instant's thought about it, gave Anna Mons a professional shove that sent her sprawling across the floor with a clatter as loud and violent as if a bucket of nuts and bolts had been emptied over it.

That then was the Tsar's first sight of his sweetheart—neither standing nor kneeling in supplication for his mercy, but down on hands and knees, with her naked body arched, and snarling like a vixen. Tsar Peter looked down almost unbelievingly at

Anna's frenzied face, at her distorted black hair that he had never known except perfectly coiffured, at her thickly painted cheeks gridironed with creases, her smudged mouth an almost geometric square of passionate rage.

The Tsar's eyes dwelt upon these, and if there had remained one private pang of nostalgia for Anna Mons, it did not live beyond that moment.

Perhaps it was a greater mercy than Anna knew. If the Tsar, searching his heart, had found any lingering fondness for Anna's bold charms, he would have slain her as a personal sacrifice to his young wife who was bearing a son for him through such danger and pain, in the adjoining room. But when the Tsar looked down at Anna, he knew that it no longer mattered to him now whether she was alive or dead.

Yet justice had to be done. He turned to Romdanovsky, "If my son dies," he said, for he could not think of the unborn child in any other way, "this woman shall die." His eyes wandered blankly around Katrina's pretty drawing room. If Anna could see traces of herself in it, the Tsar obviously could not. "Keep her here," he said abruptly. "I shall leave the bedroom door ajar, and she can lie there and listen. Each time Kitty groans, she can hear it, as I shall have to do."

Anna had recovered herself, and was holding out her arms to him as best she could. "Peter—remember our nights together . . ." She had hoped to find magical honeyed words that would win him back to her, and this was all that came.

The Tsar, ignoring her, said: "I don't want Kitty disturbed by any noise. If this woman makes any disturbance, Fedor, have one of your fellows put his boot in her mouth."

Romdanovsky nodded placidly, and the Tsar moved back towards the bedroom. He seemed to be speaking almost to himself, as he added: "If my son dies, or is born deformed, this woman shall be hung alive by the ribs on a hook from her own chandelier."

Four hours later the child was born; a tiny creature that glistened moistly in the light of candles and fire. The Tsar took it reverently into his great, warm hands—a wrinkled red goblin, as if it had shared the agonies and effort of birth.

"Will he live?" the Tsar whispered to the physician, and Katrina, lying back upon her pillows, smiled, for it was the first time she had ever heard the Tsar whisper.

"Yes, Your Majesty," said the chief physician, "I am certain of it."

"But he's so damnably pink and wrinkled," protested the Tsar.

"So were you, Your Majesty," said a white-haired old midwife, reaching out her capable hands to take the child from him. "I remember well," she chuckled, as she covered the baby in warm shawls, "for I was there!"

And then the Tsar's strong laugh boomed out. "Kitty," he said, and kissed her damp forehead. "Kitty, this is a splendid day for Russia!"

When, after the first excitement had subsided, Romdanovsky came into the bedroom to seek instructions for the disposal of Anna Mons, the Tsar did not at first seem to know what his Chief of Police was talking about.

"Oh," he said vaguely, "Make out a banishment order, I suppose—anywhere you like out of Russia—and I'll sign it tomorrow. For her brother, too."

"The chains, Your Majesty?" asked Romdanovsky patiently, "Shall I release her from them now?"

"Eh?" said the Tsar. "Chains? Oh, yes, anything you like, Fedor. But don't start any damned hammering near here."

"No, Your Majesty," said Romdanovsky, and his butterball face was expressionless as he added: "I will take her to my quarters, and knock the shackles off her there . . ."

Chapter Eighteen

KATRINA GRASPED the tall bedpost with both hands and expelled her breath obediently.

"Oo—ug!" she gasped. "Vanity—is it worth the tr-ouble?"

Grog the dwarf, with one foot perilously balanced upon a gilt and satin chair, and his sturdy knee thrust into Katrina's back, continued to tug relentlessly upon the lacing ribbons at her waist.

"Stop prattling," he commanded, "and breathe out a bit more!" In afterthought he added absently, "Your Majesty." And as Katrina forced out her ultimate reservoir of breath the dwarf hauled the ribbon to its final anchoring loop over the eyelet hole, and knotted it triumphantly so that it could not yield by a fraction.

He jumped down from the chair, satisfaction crinkling his cheeks. "There," he boomed, "exactly the same measurement as before you had your baby."

Katrina spanned her waist experimentally. "The only difference," she laughed, "is that I used to be able to breathe before!" Her cheeks were flushed and her eyes bright as she twirled in front of the great mirror to admire her new dress. It was made in the fashion of a Friesian peasant girl's, and had been fetched from Paris by special courier with a dozen hampers of the latest perfumes and fashions, all the way across Europe for her.

"Look at it!" invited Katrina, laughing to her ladies-in-waiting. "When I was a peasant girl, I would have fainted at the sight of such splendour."

Katrina's ladies-in-waiting, were flitting about her suite, or perched upon cushions as they toyed with picture books and sewing needles, worked at elaborately carved spinning boards, else busied themselves with primping irons, teasing bunches of stiff frills into Katrina's petticoats. They came now at her call and gathered near by, cooing soft as ringdoves in admiration at her dress.

Katrina was happier these days with her ladies-in-waiting. She had managed to select a dozen young girls her own age from among the available daughters of the Muscovite nobility, and from as far as Kazan Kalgua and Archangel. They were mischievous, merry creatures and Grog had promptly appointed himself supervisor of the Tsarina's young ladies. Now, each day, as he waddled among them beaming with grotesque good humour, their delighted laughter pursued him like silver bell chimes.

"Madame," one of them called to Katrina from the far doorway, "your baby is awake!" Then, appalled at her own daring, she hid her blushing young face behind a mother-of-pearl fan, and giggled helplessly as Katrina ran past her into the adjoining nursery.

The baby was staring up from the silken frills of his golden beehive cot. The early morning sun caught Katrina's bright gown, and its shimmer made the child's face crinkle into a toothless smile. Little Peter the Second, Prince of Russia, and son of a Swedish servant girl, smiled and kicked his dimpled legs in joy.

"See!" laughed Katrina. "He knows me!" She crooned endearments into the cot that was embossed with images of Virgin and Saints, and surmounted by the fierce Romanov two-headed eagle, emblem of the Royal House of Russia. Her joy at having given the Tsar a son had not diminished with the weeks. Both she and the Tsar Peter were entirely certain that the little face in the cot was a perfect image of the Tsar's own.

"Little Petrushkin, little Petrushkin," said Katrina softly. And her son gurgled back at her. At two months old, his eyes were still the azure blue of far horizons, reflecting, she thought, the distance he had travelled from another world.

Grog came and stood beside her, breaking into her reverie. "The Tsar is awaiting you, for breakfast," he said. "And I fear he has had bad news. Turkey has declared war . . ."

The news that Turkey had declared war upon him did not blunt Tsar Peter's appetite for breakfast. He poured himself a large glass of Dutch schnapps and kummel.

"Clears the tongue splendidly," he announced, draining it at a gulp, then reached for his customary dish of six eggs and fresh salad to "promote the juices" as he waited for his breakfast.

Katrina ventured a wary sip of the strong liqueur and—as always—choked upon its sweet fire. The Tsar passed her a silver bowl of rich, yellow-curded mare's milk. "Here," he smiled, "wash the taste away."

She drank gratefully, and then took a modest helping of three eggs and salad on to her own plate, to sustain herself until breakfast came.

One by one the Tsar's chiefs of military staff came hurrying in, summoned urgently by messengers.

Prince Menshikov, whose suite of palace rooms was next to the Tsar's own, arrived first, adjusting his corded gold aiguillettes. He sniffed hungrily. The Tsar pushed a chair forward with his foot, and Menshikov sat upon it, reaching without need of further invitation for one of the brown-roasted young pullets that had just been fetched in.

Shapirov, with tunic buttoned awry, saluted and mournfully accepted a glass of watered brandy and a slice of apple bread. "My insides," he sighed, "are killing me." De Villebois, lean and clear-eyed, straddled a stool and hacked himself a magnificent portion of loin of veal, trussed with bacon that still sizzled.

Field Marshal Ogilvy went straight to the brandy, and on his heels came Prince Romdanovsky. "I was just starting breakfast when your summons came, Your Majesty," he said plaintively. "I had to abandon the juiciest pink ribs of lamb in all Moscow."

"Juicier and pinker than that?" The Tsar, mouth full indicated with his knife a silver platter on the long sideboard, and Romdanovsky's eyes shone. "No argument," he beamed, and promptly settled himself beside it.

As they fed, and sipped aromatic French brandy, dark as syrup, Tsar Peter grunted: "What are we going to do about these damn Turks?"

Katrina smiled. Affairs of state and councils of war sounded so tremendously impressive. And here was what it almost always came to in reality at the Court of Russia—six untidy men with their mouths full! Yet she realized that beneath those six hastily combed heads lay some of the shrewdest brains in all Europe.

"Can they be made to invade?" asked Shapirov, hopeful of being able to employ yet again the favourite Russian strategy of enticing an enemy to invade and letting him perish among the wintry wastelands. But Prince Menshikov shook his head emphatically.

"The Turks are too smart to invade," he said. "They'll just starve our forts at Azov and shut us out from the Crimea." He looked at Ogilvy for confirmation and received a nod.

"It will mean a long campaign then?" sighed Romdanovsky. But the Tsar was more cheerful. "Perhaps not so long, Fedor. The army's ready, thank God. If we can provision quickly, we might push the Turks right out of the Balkans. Call it a holy war against the Moslems and the Church will probably pay for it."

Menshikov and Shapirov exchanged smiles. Trust the Tsar to think up some way of getting his wars paid for by somebody else!

"We beat the Turks before," the Tsar reminded them, "when we'd hardly got an army at all."

"Hay, straw—hay, straw," chanted Menshikov softly, and both men exploded with reminiscent laughter.

Katrina, who usually knew better than to interrupt a war council, could not resist this.

"What does that mean, about hay and straw?"

The Tsar did not seem displeased to tell her. "Our first army was a rabble of serfs and farm yokels, Kitty. They didn't know left from right, so Alec made them all fix straw to one leg and hay to the other. We taught them to march by shouting 'hay—straw!' And the first guns most of them had ever handled were ones they picked up from dead Turks."

"And yet you won?" asked Katrina proudly. The Tsar inclined his head. "Yes, we won," he said, with a smile, "and we shall win again."

Katrina was quick to take advantage of his good humour.

"Please let me come with you this time," she urged. "I hate it so much, waiting for you."

The Tsar considered this, frowning. The truth was that he would very much have liked to take Katrina. "Wars are never child's play," he said.

Solly Shapirov put in: "Your Majesty, it would be a good way to get the blessing of the Holy Church upon your marriage. When you both return victorious from a Holy Crusade, the Patriarch could hardly withhold his blessing."

The Tsar's face lit into a smile. "By Anthony, you shall come with us, Kitty! There should be little actual danger, God knows—we shall drive the Turks before us like chaff!"

Chapter Nineteen

WHEN THE RUSSIAN Grand Army trooped out of Moscow a few weeks later, it looked more like a carnival parade than the formidable war machine it undoubtedly was.

Katrina rode alongside the Tsar dressed in her Hussar's strawberry-red tunic and white doeskin breeches, sitting her horse astride like a boy, and the sight of her straddled limbs made the Moscow churchmen blench as they assembled at Spasky Gate to bless the departing crusaders.

Behind Katrina came her twelve ladies-in-waiting, frolicking upon their jewelled ponies. They wore velvet hunting costumes of green and brown, or of Ryazan scarlet. A few had daringly flattered their mistress by imitating her, and were perched astride on borrowed cavalry saddles, with velvet skirts hitched up to dimpled knees. It was the first time in history that ladies of the Russian Court had accompanied the Grand Army to war, and the tall officers of the Sovereign's Guard could scarcely keep their eyes from straying towards the rustling, perfumed little cavalcade.

Grog carefully straddled a child's pony, not much bigger than a large dog. He bestrode it importantly, with a great cavalry sabre buckled to his belt. He was the self-appointed leader of a company of court fools and freaks who shrieked and cavorted around him.

But the impassive squadrons of cavalry, the closely packed regiments of infantry—veterans of the long, bloody Swedish campaigns—marched with firm purposefulness. The Tsar had been correct, that their morale was high. They strode steadily, grinning and singing, munching sweetmeats that women in the crowd tossed to them, but with step unbroken and weapons devastatingly bright.

In the rear of all, stretching for fully a mile, trundled the supply carts, their axles creaking and sagging under heaped loads of meat casks, wine barrels, camp furniture and war munitions, surrounded by swarms of painted, chattering women camp followers who clung to the rocking carts and flaunted themselves upon the munition limbers.

At the head of the supplies, rode Prince Alexis. This had been a triumph for Alexis. It seemed as if he had at last become the kind of son the Tsar hoped for. He had said: "I can't accompany you against the Turks, sir—for as you know I must go to Germany to my bride-to-be. But if you like, I will arrange for the army's supplies."

Katrina had never seen the Tsar more happy. "Kitty," he said gleefully, "I think the boy's going to be all right. Marriage will make a man of him—you'll see!"

Yet when the merchants Alexis had traded with presented their bills, Prince Menshikov was shocked. "My God!" he said in dismay. "Didn't you bargain with any of them, Alexis? Did you agree to the first price they asked?"

Prince Alexis did not deign to reply. The Tsar clapped his son upon his thin, aloof shoulder. "Never mind, my boy. Let's be thankful the Church is paying for most of it!"

Prince Alexis rode now in a courier's coach at the head of his baggage column. He disliked the discomforts of the saddle. At Smolensk, Prince Alexis and his personal escort turned off towards Dresden, where the pretty blonde German Princess Charlotte of Brunswick waited to greet for the first time the husband who had been chosen for her.

The Tsar's armies marched off towards their own grimmer assignment.

The Tsar watched his son's coach out of sight. He turned to Katrina and Menshikov. "I'll bet he wishes he was coming with us," he said. "And by the Holy Ikons, we'll be shooting with his bullets!" His face shone with pride. Katrina and Menshikov exchanged glances. Without fully understanding why, they both felt deeply sorry for the Tsar.

Up in the west, Sheremetiev, with twenty-two picked regiments had already made contact with the Turks. But the Tsar's army came up slowly, reserving its strength. Not until they reached Yasay, within a few miles of the Turkish front line, did the Tsar order his troops to deploy for battle and unload the supplies.

He was in the command tent with his staff officers, studying maps, when Baron Shapirov came in, his face woeful.

"Your Majesty," he interrupted urgently, "the meat—it's all bad!"

"Oh, my lord," breathed Menshikov.

"Fifteen thousand barrels of meat," the little Jew continued despairingly, "all packed without salt—in this hot weather!" He shrugged, his shoulders eloquent. "It's just fifteen thousand barrels of maggots we've fetched from Moscow!"

"If there's any justice, somebody should be flogged for that," growled De Villebois bluntly. The Tsar's nostrils went white, and Menshikov put in quickly: "We should see if there's anything wrong with the other supplies, Your Majesty."

The Tsar nodded. "Open everything," he said harshly. "Every barrel, every sack."

Soon the reports came back. "The flour is mildewed—must have been rotten before we left. . . ."

"The cannon balls are wrong size for the guns . . ."

This was the most disastrous news of all.

"How the blazes could that happen?" demanded the Tsar

and De Villebois told him. "They're ships' munitions, Your Majesty—seventy thousand rounds of battering shot. Useless for our cannon. His Highness must have got them cheap, at a junk dealer's."

The Tsar sat down, and for a long while was silent, his face curtained in his big hands.

Nobody spoke. De Villebois shrugged and lit a roll of leaf tobacco with an affectation of nonchalance that he did not feel. Menshikov fingered the campaign maps.

Suddenly he said: "There's a big Turkish supply dump at Braila."

"How far?" snapped Ogilvy.

"About a hundred miles from us. Less than that from Sheremetiev."

The Tsar raised his head. His face was haggard, but his voice was a hard growl. "De Villebois, ride to Sheremetiev. I want him to divert his whole army and take that supply dump at Braila. I want it all—the lot, you understand?"

De Villebois nodded. "If it costs every man," the Tsar repeated, "I want those supplies!"

When the Tsar had left, his aides exchanged glances. "Thirty-eight thousand men," Ogilvy moaned, "to be risked for the folly of one lovesick young puppy!"

Romdanovsky laughed shortly. "Lovesick? Don't you believe it. Alexis must have made a fortune out of that deal!"

The Tsar walked towards his own tent, his unlit meerschaum pipe canted savagely. Katrina ran after him and slipped her hand into the bend of his arm. He did not look down at her, nor did she say anything to him at all. They walked in silence up the black valley, through the bivouac lines, towards their own tent that stood slightly apart in the shelter of a tree copse.

The trees, that had been standing all evening in breathless hush, now began to rustle, murmurously, and a great wind came rushing down the valley, rumpling the spiky grass and blotting out the stars.

The Tsar stopped outside the tent, and stared up the long, cragged ravine of the Pruth River valley. As he continued to stare towards the dark hills, Katrina saw the wet sparkle of teardrops along the fringes of his eyelids.

She squeezed his arm, and waited, in what was almost a panic of love and anxious pity for him.

The first warm, big raindrops had begun to explode upon the tent's stretched silk before he spoke. Then, it was merely to tighten his hand upon hers and say in almost a normal voice: "Better get inside, Kitty."

If the Tsar had raved at his son's perfidy, if he had ranted and sworn, she would have been glad, but he did not. Almost, she would have welcomed the deep, sick twitching of his cheek muscles, that had always before come to him in his hours of darkest grief. But nothing stirred upon the Tsar's set face. Not even his lips trembled.

He went to bed with her, quietly as a child might have done, and held her fair head to his shoulder, comforting himself without word or murmur, holding her silently.

Two of her ladies-in-waiting, whose duty it was that night to be in the tent to serve her, were already asleep upon their down-feather cot behind a velvet curtain. Katrina heard them awaken to the storm, and their soft young voices begin to murmur. The Tsar must have heard them, too, and ordinarily he would have roared some shameless, jesting advice as to how they might be quieted that would have sent the girls into giggling silence. But tonight he said nothing. Katrina listened to his slow-thudding heart, and to the quick raindrops, until her eyes prickled from forcing them into wakefulness.

Yet she was almost asleep when De Villebois stumbled out of the stormlashed night into the firelit shadows of the Tsar's tent. He entered with such dramatic suddenness that the young guard's surprised sword point flickered up before he recognized him.

De Villebois swept the weapon aside and lurched towards the bed.

"What the devil—" Tsar Peter sat up. His bedside scabbard swished as his great sword glittered into his hand. He was halfway out of bed when he recognized De Villebois. "I thought all Frenchmen had good manners—" he was beginning, when De Villebois breathlessly interrupted:

"Your Majesty—the Turks have crossed the Pruth under cover of the storm. We are completely surrounded!"

The Tsar was fully out of bed now. He stood naked and terrifying in the dim lantern light. He sniffed the brandy-sweetness of De Villebois' breath.

"Francois," he said suspiciously, "how drunk are you?"

De Villebois swayed. "Drunk enough, Your Majesty," he admitted. "But this is true." And then the Tsar saw the fresh blood on De Villebois' sleeve, and grey spatters of powder streaks across his tunic.

"By a mercy," panted De Villebois, "I met Colonel Ekhov riding in from Sheremetiev with dispatches—apparently they'd spotted something going on. I sent him back with your orders. Then on my way back here, about three miles beyond Colonel Janus' outposts, I spotted the Turks coming through." He grinned ruefully. "They spotted me, too—but the storm helped me."

"And Janus?" asked the Tsar quickly.

"Stood to his guns, of course, Your Majesty. But with no shot for them except what's in the gunlockers."

The Tsar said nothing more, but walked to the lantern on the table and turned it up to a bright glare.

"Here's a map, Francois. Mark where the Turks are, and send it to the command tent. Then get some sleep, for you'll need it by morning."

He put on tunic and trousers, hesitated at the bed and gave Katrina a vague, preoccupied smile. A moment later he was gone, and Katrina heard the bugle calling his staff officers. She lay sleepily wondering if she should get up and dress. But the Tsar had told De Villebois to sleep, so there must be time yet. Curiously, Katrina discovered that she was not afraid. She turned her face into the silk pillow and almost at once was asleep.

De Villebois had finished his hasty work upon the map, and dispatched it with the tent guard. He picked up the Tsar's brandy carafe and helped himself generously.

The stuffy atmosphere of the tent made his head throb. The veins of his neck and wrists pulsed like wounds with the heat of the brandy.

He blinked towards the bed where Katrina lay. It seemed blurred, as if water was running over it. De Villebois felt his throat to be in flames. He slopped out another glassful of the Tsar's brandy and gulped it. The tent now had a wraithlike, misty texture to De Villebois as he staggered across to the large bed. He saw it only as a bed. He had forgotten, or no longer cared, that it belonged to the Tsar, or that Katrina was in it. The soft mattress yielded to his body as he sat unsteadily upon it and fumbled to unbutton his tunic.

He became aware then that something had stirred and sighed near to him and that there was a gentle perfume, like flowers in a warm garden. De Villebois squinted his red-veined eyes into focus as best he could, and for an instant saw Katrina's hair spreading golden over the white silk pillow, her cheeks vividly red and her childlike mouth pouting in slumber. She breathed leisurely, trustfully asleep.

It was more than the vision of the instant that now plagued De Villebois' drunken senses. For months he had lived close to Katrina. He had been vividly aware of the significance of her delicately arched nostrils, and the lively, generous spread of her mouth. With true Gallic insight, he had interpreted the lilt of her body's movements. Her eyes, so green and childlike, fascinated him.

Now, through his red flame of brandy, De Villebois was hardly aware that his hands had reached out to tug away the silk sheet that was covering her. He grasped Katrina's shoulders and fell unsteadily upon her as he tried to cover her lips with his. He had probably meant no more than to salute her with a gallant's kiss, but when he felt her struggling beneath him, De Villebois lost the last shreds of his senses in the warm urgency of such a conflict.

Katrina struggled into wakefulness with a sensation of being suffocated. De Villebois' teeth bruised her lips. She gasped out a scream, and her two ladies-in-waiting ran terrified to her bedside.

They fluttered helplessly while De Villebois with drunken strength entangled Katrina's struggling hands in the silken sheet. And as she sobbed for breath, he thrust a handful of the cloth into her mouth to silence her.

At the screams of the ladies-in-waiting, the fever suddenly went from De Villebois. Then with a groan of self-condemnation, he gathered himself up and staggered to the nearest chair, where he sat with head in hands, gasping dry-throated apologies.

Katrina, crimson with humiliation and distress, gathered the bedsheet around herself.

"The Tsar will kill you for this, De Villebois," she cried. "He will kill you!"

The Tsar came striding to the tent, summoned by the alarm, but his expression was still blank and dazed.

De Villebois stood to attention before him, sick drunkenness and sicker shame making a paradox of his handsome face.

"Francois," said the Tsar dully, "you are a drunken fool."

Katrina panted breathlessly: "Are you going to kill him?"

The Tsar looked at her, his black eyes dead and lusterless. "Kitty," he said, "by tomorrow we shall all be dead—unless you escape with your life into a Turkish brothel. I cannot kill the men who will rape you then, Kitty. I shall have to watch, probably, for our friends the Turks are humorists in these matters." He sighed heavily, and his face was like a dead man's face.

A chill crept over Katrina, and even De Villebois seemed to feel dismay for the Tsar's attitude of fatalistic, stunned hopelessness.

"Surely, Your Majesty—" he began, then gave a shrug echoing the Tsar's fatalism, for he, too, could now hear the guns.

"They're on the hill overlooking the valley," he said, as if that explained everything. The Tsar nodded. Katrina said urgently: "What does that mean?"

The Tsar took a heavy breath. "It means," he said, "that Colonel Janus' men are being killed in hundreds, and by evening the camp will be encircled with Turkish cannon." For the first time, the hint of a smile came wearily to his face. "We have less chance than a mouse in a jar. If we can hold out more than two days, it will be a miracle."

"What are you going to do?" pleaded Katrina.

"Do?" The Tsar shrugged. "What is there to do, except to pray that we may not be taken alive?"

He sat down at the table and began laboriously scratching out a dispatch to Moscow. *Gentlemen, by the time you read this. . . .*

"Am I free to go, Sire?" De Villebois asked, still slightly puzzled.

The Tsar looked up. "For the moment, yes," he said absently, and added: "Try to get yourself usefully killed, Francois. It will be neater."

De Villebois bowed and looked straight at Katrina, his face wooden. "I will do my best, Sire," he said stiffly. "Her Majesty's honour requires that I should do so." He clicked his heels and was gone.

Katrina sat upon her rumpled bed, rubbing her bruised shoulders. "You haven't even asked if I was hurt!"

"Are you?" asked the Tsar, without lifting his head.

"Oh! You—you—" She ran angrily behind the curtain, and began to dress with furious, fumbling haste.

By the time she finished, the Tsar had gone from the tent and the sun was beginning to climb into full daylight.

Chapter Twenty

IN A NARROW GULLY behind one of the nearest Russian gun batteries, Katrina found Prince Menshikov, working bared to the waist, with about a hundred soldiers, apparently digging large rocks from the black soil.

When he saw Katrina he straightened and smiled.

"What are you doing, Alec?"

"Digging up stones," he answered laconically, "for the guns. They'll not carry far and they'll rip the guns to pieces, I know. But we can use them for a couple of salvoes when the Turks have begun to overrun us. It should get quite a few of the devils before they get us. It's the best we can do."

Once more Katrina found herself confronted by this almost terrifying Russian national characteristic, a stolid and almost Oriental acceptance of death being very near.

"Is that really the best we can do?" she demanded. "Just shoot a few stones at them, like children, before they kill us all?"

Menshikov grimaced, and Katrina laid her hand upon his bare arm in quick apology. "No, Alec, I didn't mean it that way. At least, it's more than the Tsar is doing," she said bitterly. "He isn't even with his men, just sulking in his tent, writing dispatches to Moscow to tell them we'll all be killed."

"The stones were his idea," said Menshikov simply. "And anyway," he demanded, genuinely puzzled, "what else do you expect him to do? There'll be time enough tomorrow for waving swords and being heroic. Somebody's got to write dispatches."

"Yes, I know, but—" she found it difficult to explain her

fears, even to Menshikov. "He has no time, no word for me. And if we are all to die—"

Menshikov picked up his tunic. "Come," he said calmly, "let us walk a little way." He led her out of the gully. "Look!" He indicated where the harmless-seeming smoke of the Turkish cannon was becoming visible now as the sun climbed the valley. It looked like no more than tiny white puff-balls, apparently having no relation at all to the thunder that rumbled across the far ridge of the Carpathian foothills.

"The best the Tsar can hope for you, Kitty," Menshikov said quietly, "is for one of those cannon shot to kill you, quick and clean, before the Turkish soldiers start running in among us."

"But surely he could—" She broke off helplessly.

"You mean you want to die with his arms around you, don't you?" he said. She nodded, her throat cramped by tears that would not come. "Perhaps the Tsar loves you more than you think," he said huskily. "And his soldiers love you too. They call you 'Little Mother' among themselves. Did you know that?" Katrina shook her head mutely.

Menshikov's eyes went to the open throat of her white silk Cossack blouse. He said suddenly: "Bury that brooch, Kitty. You don't want the Turks to get it—not with the Tsar's picture on it."

The brooch hung from a thin chain around Katrina's neck. It was a locket brooch with a miniature in oils, painted in Amsterdam, of Tsar Peter's face. It was set with thirty blue-white diamonds, each as big as a fruit berry.

Katrina turned it in her hand, so that it sparkled like a palmful of liquid fire. "What a fool I was," she said quietly but without rancour. "I brought all my jewels with me. So did all my ladies, poor things."

Menshikov was incredulous. "The Romanov rubies—the star sapphires—the Golitsin diamond—all of them?"

"Nearly all," said Katrina. She was beginning now to feel the same fatalistic calm that she had recognized in Peter's face. The disaster was too big. "A king's ransom in jewels," she went on, spinning the brooch upon its chain until the diamonds sparkled into a globule of blazing light. "A king's ransom—Alec!" Suddenly she clutched Menshikov's arm, but his own quick brain had already raced away with the idea as soon as it was born. "Yes!" he exploded. "That old fox Baltagi Mohamet is probably the likeliest man in all Turkey to accept a rich bribe. Come!"

He hurried her toward the Tsar's tent. "It's an idea and it might work! The Turks can't yet know we have no ammunition and our food is all rotten. They don't know we can't possibly hold out until Sheremetiev cuts a way through to us." They were almost running now. "Get all your jewels together," he said, "and those of your ladies, too. Pick out some French silks and Dutch laces as well. Bless you, little Kitty, little darling! We might see Moscow again yet!"

"And Peterushkin," said Katrina, her voice breaking.

One of Katrina's ladies-in-waiting, skirts held high, was running and stumbling down the slope of the hillside toward them. "Madame," she sobbed, "oh, Madame—His Majesty—he's having a convulsion—I think he's dying."

They found Tsar Peter twitching like a newly killed hare upon the floor of his tent, his face like wax.

The convulsions must have seized him as he was working upon his dispatches, for documents and courier satchels littered the ground alongside his body. Prince Menshikov quickly gathered up the papers, and stamped out the oily flame of a fallen candle. Katrina was already on her knees beside the Tsar, forcing a fold of cloth between his grinding teeth, lest he bite his tongue. He was deeply unconscious.

Another Turkish salvo screamed destructively down into the tent-thronged valley. "We must get him away from here," said Menshikov, and did not wait for Katrina's reply, but snatched up a rug and spread it beside the Tsar's body. The two guards helped him hoist the Tsar on to the rug, their hands trembling at thus touching the royal flesh.

Katrina ran to her jewel box and scooped out its glittering contents, cramming the two pockets of her Hussar breeches and emptying the rest of the jewellery inside her silk shirt. She shivered at the chill touch of priceless diamonds, rubies and thick collars of pearls that lay against her flesh like cold river pebbles. She flung a cloak across her shoulders and ran after Menshikov, who had gathered more helpers. They were stumbling down the hillside now towards the safer haven of the command tent, with the Tsar carried among them upon the thick rug.

The senior staff officers at the command tent crowded around their unconscious Tsar. "Is he wounded?" asked Baron Shapirov anxiously.

"Just a convulsion," she said, forcing her voice to calmness.

They made Peter comfortable upon a palliasse by the stove, and Katrina emptied her jewels on to the map table. Soon each of her twelve ladies-in-waiting had followed their Tsarina's example offering their own jewellery. There were heavily gold-linked torques of rubies, carcanets of diamonds, emeralds, sapphires, pearl brooches like bunches of white grapes.

"We're lucky it's Baltagi Mohamet," said Ogilvy, screwing up his shrewd blue eyes. "Yon heathen would sell his own fingers for the value of the rings on them! Aye, it's worth trying, Alec." He added with a wry chuckle: "God bless the ladies, for being such little fools as to bring their jewellery on a war campaign!"

"I suppose," Shapirov sighed resignedly, "that as I speak the best Turkic, I shall have to do the bargaining with the heathens?"

"You will," said Ogilvy firmly, "and as I have never yet tasted Turkish brandy, I shall have to go with you!"

They smiled at each other slowly. The Turks had paraded poor Count Tolstoy, the Tsar's official ambassador in Constantinople, naked through the streets and flung him chained into a dungeon, before they even decided to declare war. What they might do to a couple of emissaries suing for armistice, was not comforting.

Not until Katrina laid herself down upon the palliasse with her face almost touching the Tsar's, and her arms cradling him as best she could, did he cease to twitch and shudder. For a long time then he slept, seeming to thirst for unconsciousness, drawing it into himself with huge gasping breaths while the sweat ran from him. Katrina lay with thrills of cramp stabbing her arms, and watched the sky darken. The culverin salvoes seemed to have diminished, but all afternoon until long after twilight the valley echoed to musketry, like the rasping of staccato insects. Then thin bugle calls echoed from hill to hill along the valley peaks, and all at once there was utter silence.

Katrina must have dozed, for the silence woke her and she saw through the tent flap that it was dark outside, a night sky that was alive with blue Carpathian stars.

"Have a glass of wine," said Menshikov quietly, at her side. She looked up dazedly. Except for a couple of Denschik orderlies, she and Menshikov were alone in the command tent with the unconscious Tsar. Menshikov met her unspoken question with a smile. "They're all in their tents," he said, "praying and waiting for news. The firing has stopped, and that's a good sign. It means that at least the Turks have received our emissaries."

"Poor Solly," said Katrina softly. "He was so frightened."

"But he went," said Menshikov simply, and leaned forward to regard the sleeping Tsar. "I think there's a little colour coming back into his face," he said. "He should be better by morning thanks to your nursing."

"Let us pray God that he is," Katrina whispered. "Where's De Villebois?" she asked suddenly.

"De Villebois took a hundred volunteers early this morning," said Menshikov, "and started up the hill to try and knock out the nearest Turkish battery. I think he got it, too, for it was silent about four hours before the others."

"Poor De Villebois," said Katrina. "If he'd only waited—I would have forgiven him."

"Perhaps he didn't find it so easy to forgive himself," said Menshikov. He saw that Katrina's lips were trembling, and put his arm around her shoulders. "Never mind," he said. "It was done—and it's over now. Come have a drink of wine and some food. It will be daylight soon."

The Tsar roused into sudden wakefulness with sunlight blazing down upon the stretched silk of the command tent. He had heard the unmistakable half-tone wail of Turkish bugles. He staggered from the palliasse to the tent doorway, sword in hand, and saw a long column of ox-drawn Turkish provision carts lumbering into his camp. Around them shrieked a medley of Turkey's savagest warriors; Janissaries in glittering chain mail shirts with green and yellow cloaks, upon heavily armoured horses; Delhi warriors in tiger and panther pelts, Dervishes with their self-torturing hair smocks, who waved scimitars and yelled *"Hawa! Hawa!"* as they caught sight of the flags of the Russian command tent.

Katrina hurried to the Tsar's side. "It's all right, my dear," she said to him, as if he were some great, distraught child. "See—the white flag. And listen—the valley is silent, no more gunfire. It's all over now." Prince Menshikov came to take the

Tsar's other arm and led him back to a chair, explaining to him what had happened. A few moments afterwards, Baron Shapirov came in, beaming.

"His Mighty Eminence the Grand Vizier of Turkey presents his compliments and respects to Your Majesty," he said formally, "and begs favour to present his emissary the Bashaw Hassan who brings a wagon train of provisions, and a request."

"Request for what, damn it?" growled the Tsar, still considerably bewildered. His throat was dry and saltless, his lips swollen blue. In his prolonged sweating, he had lost a great deal of strength.

Shapirov hesitated, and grinned. "Apparently, the Bashaw's instructions are to present himself personally to the Tsarina Katrina, and to request the honour of kissing her Tsarish Majesty's hand. It seems the Grand Vizier thinks the Tsarina is a very remarkable woman."

The Tsar's mouth twitched. "So do I, damn it," he said. "So do I!"

It was later in the afternoon that the Turks carried De Villeboise back to the Russian camp. They conveyed him in a ceremonial palanquin, borne by six huge Jainissart soldiers. With them, upon a caparisoned pony, came a Turkish staff officer of equivalent rank and station to De Villebois, as his escort.

"His High and Mighty Eminence the Grand Vizier Baltagi Mohamet sends greetings," he said in carefully rehearsed Russian, then relapsed into a splutter of Turkic.

"What does he say?" demanded the Tsar. Baron Shapirov translated. "He says the Grand Vizier is proud to make peace with an army that has such soldiers. Apparently De Villebois did a lot of damage up in those hills before they managed to quiet him."

The palanquin curtains fluttered feebly. De Villebois peered out with dazed eyes. He had four musket wounds and half a dozen scimitar cuts. His head was bandaged and the unshaven face beneath it was so translucent from loss of blood that one could see the hair roots.

"My apologies, Your Majesty," he whispered with a flicker of bravado. "I did my best to get killed, but it seems I am a blundering fool . . ."

Katrina's thoat tightened. The Tsar was watching her. "What

now?" he said quietly. "He's a very sick man. A bullet through his skull would be more merciful than death by the knout."

"No—please—" she begged, "don't kill him." The Tsar's face gave no hint of emotion, neither of pleasure nor disappointment. He turned to De Villebois, who had always been one of his favourites.

"All right, Francois," he said gruffly. "The Tsarina awards you your life. It's the only damned medal you'll get on this campaign, my lad!"

The Tsar would not consent to any punishment of Prince Alexis, though his son's blunder had nearly cost the lives of the entire Russian army.

"Let me investigate, Your Majesty," pleaded Romdanovsky. "I will sit some of those plump Moscow merchants upon cosy hot braziers. We shall soon learn if Prince Alexis knew those stores were rotten when he loaded them and if he took bribes."

The Tsar shook his head stubbornly. "No, Fedor." And his Chief of Police became silent, as he understood. Tsar Peter was not in any private doubt about his son's perfidy. He simply did not wish to have it proved to him.

That night, alone in their tent, the Tsar said suddenly: "Kitty, we shall not go with the others to Moscow, just yet. You and I will ride straight to Dresden."

"To see Alexis?" she asked quickly.

He grunted affirmation. "I can't forever be giving him second chances," he said. "This time he must wed his German princess and begin to act like a civilized European—or he goes straight into a monastery, and I shall pass the succession to—" he hesitated, as if it took him all his strength to say the words—"to Petrushkin."

"To our son?" said Katrina, amazed.

"Why not?" demanded the Tsar. "Sometimes I wonder if Petrushkin is not more lawful firstborn than Alexis is."

Katrina was genuinely shocked. "But the royal succession is sacred. God chooses it."

The Tsar wrinkled his brow as if bewilderment had come upon him like a pain, and came to place his great head upon Katrina's lap. "I know, Kitty, I know," he said, for he too had his deep-rooted beliefs about the sacredness of the royal succession. "What shall I do, Kitty? Petrushkin is our son, born in love. And poor Alexis was brought up to hate me! Which is God's will, Kitty. What must I choose?"

Katrina stroked his tousled black hair. "I don't know," she said sensibly, "but I am sure that if God wants a thing, He will have it so, whatever we try to do. So, come to sleep, my dear, and we will talk about it again, tomorrow."

The Tsar sat up abruptly. "If Alexis is rude to you in the Dresden Court," he said, his jaws working, "I'll—by heaven, I'll—"

"Hush, dear, hush," Katrina soothed him. "There must be no risk of that, so I shall wait at Thorne, and you shall go to Dresden alone. This must be settled between you and Alexis. I don't think I ought to be near."

The Tsar lay back, considering this. "That may be best," he agreed reluctantly. He must have exhausted himself, for he was soon asleep. But for a long time Katrina lay awake, her heart beating as if with fever. One word from her uttered at the right moment—and her own son could become the heir of all Russia. Yet Katrina also knew that she could never bring herself to say that word, and to take such advantage of the love with which Tsar Peter had trusted her.

Chapter Twenty-One

THE SIGHT OF PRINCESS CHARLOTTE, the new wife of Prince Alexis, was a surprise to Katrina. She had expected the well nourished sturdiness, the ample-bosomed motherly strength of the German women she had met in Moscow, who had all the bulk and vigour of the Russian women with an added self-assurance. Such a girl might have done some good with Alexis. But Charlotte was such a frail flower of a child, with a delicate look about the way she carried her head on her slender neck.

Behind Charlotte came Alexis, his face fixed in its usual expression of sardonic aloofness. Marriage had not made him look happier nor better groomed. Katrina sighed and extended her hand to the girl, whose blue eyes were staring at her candidly.

"Welcome, my dear Charlotte. I hope you will be very happy with us."

"Thank you, Your Majesty—" the girl stammered. Her hand lay cool and unresisting as a lily in Katrina's warm-hearted grasp. Charlotte continued to stare at the most notorious queen in Europe. "How beautiful you are!" she said suddenly, and the blood spread beneath her transparent skin in a tremendous blush that covered her neck, ears and bosom.

Katrina's mouth twitched. "You are very pretty too, my dear. Alexis is a lucky boy."

There was an awkward pause. Alexis looked as if he would have loved to snub Katrina. But his father was present and he had not the courage.

"Perhaps I am," he said noncommittally and, with a brief bow to his father, turned away.

After the wedding at Dresden the Tsar had fetched the bride and groom to Thorne where Katrina had awaited them. It was his intention that the party make another twenty miles towards Petersburg before darkness, and Katrina had already loaded her possessions into the big coach.

"Why not let the two young people stay here in Thorne for a few days?" she suggested as she saw the weary droop of Charlotte's shoulders. "I think they will need a few days to get to know each other. They could follow us to Petersburg later. We could send the bedcoach back for them."

Tsar Peter considered this. It had one obvious advantage. Riding in the bedcoach with Katrina he could travel straight through the night.

A slow smile came to Alexis' face and he put in quickly: "Sir, if we may—I mean, I am sure the Princess Charlotte would like to rest."

Charlotte's face immediately radiated happiness. Alexis did love her and want to be alone with her, and Thorne—although foreign soil to her—was a great deal nearer home than Petersburg.

"Please," she begged breathlessly. "May we, Your Majesty?"

The Tsar's expression melted at once into a gratified beam. He slapped Alexis' thin shoulder. The boy was going to make a go of it, after all.

"A few days alone together, eh?" he boomed. "Certainly, my boy. Nothing would please me more than for you two to be happy. But mind you—" he took Alexis by the elbow and drew him solemnly aside. "She's a very shy gentle little thing," he murmured. "Damned if I've ever seen such a little dreamer! You'll have to be very careful, lad—and patient. You understand what I mean, don't you?"

"Yes, father," said Alexis meekly, his face utterly without expression. "I understand."

The huge coach clattered along the flat west bank of the Neva, its five sleepy horses sweating in the dawn chill. Peter pushed back the observation panel in the coach roof so that he and Katrina could stand upon the yielding bed to gaze at their new city. Katrina had last seen the place as a sparse encampment of huts and skin tents upon the Neva's swampy estuary. Swedish prisoners of war had been busy then, under the whips of their Russian conquerors, knocking thick logs into the churned mud to get a foundation firm enough for building.

Now, only a handful of years later, here was Petersburg—a great and glittering city!

Church towers, domes and gilded minarets shone here and there, as in Moscow. But most of the buildings were tall and stately houses, built of stone or brick, with steep Dutch styled roofs, and painted in various washes of yellowish orange with pilasters and relief decorations picked out in piercing white. It was like a city of almond-iced creamcakes, set among wide, tree-lined roads.

Peter held Katrina steady as she gazed in amazement. His own face was lit by pride, relaxed and grinning.

"Wait until you see the summer palace," he said.

"And will Petrushkin really be there waiting for us?" demanded Katrina eagerly.

He laughed and hugged her bare bed-warmed shoulders. "Do you think he'll know you after all these months?"

"He's hardly old enough to know anybody," said Katrina sensibly.

The coach halted outside a plain two-storied building of brick and yellow-painted stone, with a steeply slanted roof of Dutch red tiles, and large ground floor windows. It was beautiful, yet in a way entirely unlike anything Katrina had ever seen. It was not Russian in style, nor Swedish. It did not resemble any of the houses in the Moscow German quarter which reflected most of the English and French fashions of architecture.

It had a simplicity and an air of peaceful correctness. "An Italian built it for me," Peter explained briefly, and Katrina nodded without speaking. She did not care who built it. The little palace was perfect.

The Royal Guard turned out in a hasty clash and scramble. Yawning servants in the pearly dawn light hurried to their duties, tugging braided tunics into place as they ran.

"Quickly, Peter—where is the nursery?" asked Katrina.

"A moment, a moment," he laughed. "I haven't yet got my boots on."

"I must go," she said, and ran from the coach into the graceful, parqueted hallway of the palace. "My baby?" she demanded, and a startled flunkey pointed speechlessly up the wide stairway. Katrina gathered her skirts and took the ascent without pause.

In the neat, windowed upstairs corridor, she stopped suddenly. A grotesque little figure was hobbling to meet her, with white linen baby cap, ruched by coloured ribbons, pulled down over its misshapen head. The distorted barrel-shaped body was dressed in frilled baby smock that almost reached the floor, and a satin sash was wound around its waist.

"Mama!" it squeaked, and Katrina recognized the solid music in even such a distorted yelp.

"Grog, you fool!" she said, with sudden tears making her green eyes shine. She had sent the dwarf on from Thorne, being hungry to make some contact with her baby son.

"He's in here," said Grog, reaching for her hand. His quick sensitivity had recognized the urgency of Katrina's need to see her child. This was no time for buffoonery that would ordinarily have made her laugh.

Petrushkin came running from an inner room, stumbling upon legs that did not seem to belong to him. But they were straight legs, and sturdy. He was a dark-skinned toddler with black hair in profuse curls. Huge, solemn dark eyes dominated his face. He halted suddenly as he saw Katrina and regarded her in blank wonder.

She ached to sweep him up into her arms, but wisely offered him her hand instead. "Hello, Petrushkin," she said softly.

He took her hand gravely and after a moment's hesitation gabbled something in the mysterious private language of childhood. Katrina could not understand but she nodded, matching her absurd solemnity, and then smiled. He stared for a moment without response. Katrina continued to smile down at him, and his face remained rebuffingly indifferent.

Then, as her lips began to ache and her eyes to prick with tears, Petrushkin suddenly answered her smile with all the full-hearted generosity of childhood. His dark-skinned little face broke into sunshine and when Katrina, with a sigh, bent and picked him up in her arms, he did not resist but let her kiss him, and patted appreciatively her cheeks and shining fair hair.

The Tsar seemed glad to be in Petersburg. He thrilled at the new buildings that were ever increasing. His own apartments overlooked the sea. He loved the constant movement and smell of it outside his wide windows. For hours he would watch it, sitting in his armchair and leaning forward against the window ledge, his chin on his arms, the wind churning his black hair into a knotted mass and lashing colour into his face. Gradually the war-worn look began to slip away with the passing of tranquil days among his beloved ships and with few worries beyond the occasional routines of State. There was peace now and he was able to be calm.

He spent his days rejoicing in his escape from the old capital, from the close-knit, puritanical and stifling atmosphere of Moscow—from the airless Byzantine tangle of her buildings. Now, he felt he could breathe and expand. Close to the West, he felt part of it, part of the spacious European way of life he had so long admired and was never to forget. Miles behind him were the clothes, customs and religion of the Russia of his forefathers.

All of his Court followed him to Petersburg. Many of them came reluctantly for they could not conceive of wanting to set up home hundreds of miles to the west of Moscow, alongside a bleak sea. They had heard stories of the thirty thousand prisoners who had died in the swamps while laying the foundations for Petersburg. They never tired of saying that it was built on the bones of dead men and cursed by ghosts.

They disliked the style of their new houses. They missed the ornamental stoves and the cramped overheated rooms. The weather gave no comfort, for it greeted them with mists and chill, howling winds.

Peter kept himself aloof from these creatures of his old Court, with their nagging and gossiping. He spent his evenings before the fire in the inn of the Four Frigates with Menshikov, Romdanovsky and his other close friends listening to the music of his German orchestra. Or he spent them drinking with Menshikov in his new home on the east bank of the Neva, which almost rivalled the Royal Palace in size and certainly outdid it in lavish furnishings.

The weeks passed and now word came from Prince Alexis at Thorne. The Tsar waited patiently for a month before even sending a courier. He received a polite evasive message from Alexis several weeks later, saying that he and Princess Charlotte had left Thorne and were staying at the house of Nicolai Bolovdin for the winter.

"Who the blazes is Bolovdin and where the devil does he live?" demanded the Tsar when he had frowned a few moments over this surprising missive.

Romdanovsky blinked. "Near Susdal, Your Majesty. He's—" He checked himself.

"He's what?"

The Chief of Police shifted with embarrassment. "I was only going to say, Your Majesty, that Bolovdin is one of the merchants who supplied those shoddy provisions for the Turkish campaign, and nearly cost us all our lives."

"And Susdal, Sire," said Menshikov thoughtfully, "is still a hotbed of plotters."

There was an awkward silence until Katrina broke it. "I am worried about little Princess Charlotte," she said.

"Nonsense," answered the Tsar curtly. He rubbed at his skull behind the ear, where deep-rooted pain was lately seeming to come with more persistence each day, and his temper was not good. "None of you will give the boy a chance," he growled. "Here, Fedor—you have to go to Moscow in a week or two. Call at this place near Susdal and tell Alexis I want him to bring Charlotte here. Tell the young devil a honeymoon can't last all winter and there's work to be done."

Romdanovsky nodded. "And if he doesn't choose to come?" he said hesitantly.

The Tsar swore impatiently. "Of course he'll come. Tell him it's my order!"

But when Romdanovsky reached Susdal, Prince Alexis had fled to Italy, and Romdanovsky had to devote several careful hours to applying red-hot wires to the merchant Bolovdin's nostrils and armpits before he could discover a clue where Princess Charlotte was.

It was another week before he found her, chained by both wrists to a damp wall in the cellars of the Monastery of the Brotherhood of Melchizedeck, in Moscow's foreign quarter, sobbing and coughing and almost three months pregnant.

Tenderly, patient as a lardy old brood sow, the Chief of Police nursed her to Petersburg in the Tsar's own bedcoach, stroking her damp, pale hair, wiping the red flecks from her lips each time she racked her pitiful body with coughs.

Princess Charlotte was put to bed in Petersburg Palace, and half a dozen doctors fetched. Katrina stayed beside her all night, and the Tsar came next morning. He was unshaven and grey with wrath.

"Look at this!" cried Katrina. She lifted back the bed covering, and even the Tsar, hardened in a lifetime of wars and torture chambers, choked at what he saw.

From shoulders to ankles, the once smooth body of the young Princess Charlotte was ridged, welted and mottled. Her toe joints were abcessed where torture screws had been applied. Her eyes burned bright with fever, and her cheeks held the significant flame-heat of the coughing sickness that now constantly shook her.

"But why—?" cried the Tsar in utter bewilderment, and Romdanovsky told him.

"The plot was simple enough, Your Majesty. Prince Alexis and his churchly friends had made a fortune from the sale of rotten supplies to our armies." Tsar Peter winced at this but said nothing, and Romdanovsky went on bluntly. "With this, they schemed to bribe the Kremlin Guards while Your Majesty was here in Petersburg. Then the church would declare that it was against the law of God to move the capital city of Russia from Moscow to Petersburg. Alexis was to ascend the throne in the Kremlin, and Your Majesty was to be declared an outlaw."

"It was a madman's plot," said Menshikov. "But so mad it might have worked."

"Perhaps it was mad," said Romdanovsky, "and perhaps not. But they made a mistake. The church dignitaries insisted that Alexis' German wife should publicly avow she had changed her religion and—" Romdanovsky spread his plump hands with a shrug—"on this comparatively insignificant detail, they wasted vital weeks. For it seems that the Princess Charlotte persistently refused, despite all their persuasions."

"Poor, poor little creature," said Katrina and suddenly found herself crying.

The Tsar's frown abruptly darkened. He rubbed at the ache behind his ear, and the deep cleft of his old sickness tugged at his cheek.

"Fedor," he roared, "I want Alexis. I want him here—in Petersburg."

"Your Majesty," said Menshikov carefully, "if your son is in Italy, this will be a ticklish diplomatic job. Don't you think Count Tolstoy—"

"I don't give a damn! Send Tolstoy then." The Tsar stood for a moment, his teeth bared by the distorting spasm of his cheek, and glowered at them all. His knuckles were kneading savagely into the aching spot of his skull, and in that moment he looked a very sick man.

"Peter—" gasped Katrina. But he turned from her and without a further word, strode from the room.

In the months of diplomacy and intrigue that followed, while Count Tolstoy was trying to lure Alexis back into Russia, Princess Charlotte's cough grew worse. Katrina spent many hours with her, stroking her white, transparent hand. They sent for books of German fairytales, which the Princess had loved. But she would not look at them nor listen to the stories.

"I just want to die," she whispered. "I want to die before his baby is born. I hate it—hate it being a part of me. If it is born alive, I will find some way to kill it." The effort of speaking made her cough.

"Hush, dear, hush," said Katrina softly. "Don't talk now." But Charlotte needed to talk.

"The very first night," she whispered, "they came and beat me. They made me lie on the floor and they beat me until I fainted. There was a redheaded servant girl called Affronsinia. She was the only woman they would let near me—she used to laugh, too, when he—hurt me . . ."

"And where is she now?" Katrina asked, and all the pity she felt was in her voice.

"I don't know," Charlotte whispered. "But I know she wen

with him." She began to shake in another long agony of blood-flecked coughing.

On October 25, Princess Charlotte's child was born. It was an early birth and mercifully so, for she was rapidly dying.

The wind and tiny fluffs of snow sneaked in through the niches in the windows. The doctors and Katrina waited patiently through the night while the boy was born. He was a pale, sickly baby, who was to survive to become a pale, sickly king—Peter the Second of Russia.

Charlotte refused to feed her child or take him into her arms, and herself died within a few days.

Chapter Twenty-Two

KATRINA FELT a disturbing sense of shock and loss. Her own bright vitality and practical nature was completely different from that of the ethereal little German princess, yet they had discovered themselves to be natural friends in the waiting days before Charlotte's death. Tsar Peter had recently seemed to be withdrawing into himself, troubled by head pains that gave him sleepless nights, and working himself mercilessly as though he were attempting to fulfil ten emperors' destinies in the space of one foreshortened lifetime.

With Katrina patiently beside him, he was in his study among his chiefs of staff, sipping hot brandy to quell his headaches and pouring over architects' plans for docks, schools, libraries and fortresses of the rapidly developing Petersburg, when news reached them a few months later that Count Tolstoy had returned from Italy and was now coming to Petersburg as fast as horses could bring him.

"Has he got my son with him?" demanded the Tsar. He sat with both great fists clenched, his dark eyes burning through their red-rimmed weariness.

"Yes, Majesty. Also the redhaired wench, the servant named Affronsinia."

The Tsar considered this while the messenger waited.

"Get two dungeons prepared in the harbour fortress," he ordered. Katrina blenched, but did not speak.

"Your Majesty," broke in Prince Menshikov quickly, "surely this needs careful thought. What is it you propose to do to the Crown Prince?"

The Tsar thrust back his chair and stood up to his full, immense height.

"Do? What am I going to do?" His voice was strained and sickness stirred across his face. "I'll tell you what I'm going to do," he said harshly, and turned to the terrified messenger. "Have a knout put upon the wall of my son's cell. I'm going to give him the thrashing he should have had long ago. A soldier's thrashing, do you all understand?" There was foam upon the Tsar's lips, and he swayed as he spoke.

"Sire," said Menshikov, "you're not well. We've borne patiently with the Prince for half a lifetime. Let us consider this again by daylight when Your Majesty has rested."

"Aye, patiently for half a lifetime," said Peter. His hands groped behind him for the support of his chair arms. "While Russia and the men of Russia have bled and waited, too. We have waited too long, Little Alex. I shall thrash him," he went on. "A soldier's thrashing, Alec. No more—but by God, no less. We've seen it perform wonders upon some kinds of fellows—uncertain fellows we've both known who heard the first voice of manhood from the tongue of a knout across their shoulders, and learned to straighten them thereafter, as a man should."

"Yes," agreed Menshikov doubtfully. "We've seen many men thrashed, and some who took it like men, and others who were flogged like spinning tops into damnation."

Peter made a gesture to silence him. "It's my only chance," he said. "It's all there is left me to do. There's so little time."

For a long while nobody spoke. Most of them waited with downcast eyes for somebody else to break the pall of silence. But Katrina, although she did not speak, fixed her eyes upon the Tsar, and felt her eyelids pricking with a blend of love and pity and sadness for him.

That night the Tsar asked Katrina to pray for him. "Little Kitty," he said huskily, touching her cheek, "say a word to Him for me, and tell Him that I am tired. Ask Him to stay with me through this night. Tell Him that tonight this tired old king is like a child who needs his father."

"Oh, Peter," said Katrina, her throat aching. "Shall we pray together? God will perhaps hear our two voices if we pray together."

Peter began to kneel, then straightened himself and walked to the window. "You pray, Kitty," he said. His mouth twitched into half a smile. "For I am sure He hears small voices better than great roaring ones, and I'm damned if I haven't forgotten how to whisper."

She looked up and laughed quickly at this slight sign of relief from his desperate pressure. Their eyes met and caressed each other for an instant, then he turned away to the window. And Katrina prayed for him.

Next morning he went off to the Peter and Paul Fortress by the river. He had slept badly, and so had she, knowing the purpose of his morning errand.

Katrina went to the nursery, sorrowing for the Tsar. She had seen him do many bloody and violent things without a qualm; but this was too near his heart.

Baby Peter was lying in his cot kicking at the silken sheets, with the sunlight of the strengthening day making live gold of his Germanic yellow hair. Katrina found it hard to believe that any part of this innocent child could belong to Alexis.

Petrushkin, already awake, came and greeted her with solemn satisfaction. He was growing taller, and his black unruly curls looked darker than ever.

"Look, Petrushkin," she said as they both looked down into the baby's cot. "He's smiling. See, he is smiling at you." Petrushkin stretched up onto his toes to behold this important matter. He was grasping a scarlet and green soldier, and dangled it commandingly in front of the baby. "Soldier," he said. "See—soldier!"

The baby held out small pink fingers toward the flash of colour, but Petrushkin did not surrender the precious toy. "No, he's mine," he said with amiable finality. "And anyway you're not old enough to know he's a soldier. You think he's only a doll."

"The Tsar has gone to the fortress, I see," said Grog's deep voice behind them.

Katrina turned quickly. "What have you heard, Grog? Has he—do you think he will punish him too severely? Alexis' shoulders are so thin—" She shivered.

"I hope he'll get all he deserves," said Grog bluntly. "If he were my son, which God forbid, I'd—"

"Where is my father?" Petrushkin demanded. He had sensed some drama in the brief conversation. "What is he doing? Tell me!"

"It's nothing, darling," said Katrina quickly. "Stand beside Petrushkin, Grog, and let us see who is the taller." This was a game they played constantly, and Petrushkin stretched himself up eagerly whilst Grog sank his neck as far into his shoulders as he could without attracting the child's observant notice.

"Only the width of my hand between you," said Katrina gaily. "Only four fingers to go, Petrushkin. Soon I'll not be able to tell you apart." Her lips twitched. "Except for the hair," she said, looking from Petrushkin's profuse curls to the polished pate of Grog's almost hairless head. "Remember, my dear friend, how much hair you had when first I met you? Red, it was, too, red as a log fire."

Grog touched the weathered skin on top of his head, puzzled by her remark for an instant before he remembered Madame Gluck's red wig. "Red hair," he said. "Aye, that was the day. A handsome fellow I was!" There was no bitterness in the irony of his deep voice. His eyes twinkled. "When we first met," he echoed, "that was indeed a day!"

"Day? What day? Tell me!" Petrushkin demanded. Katrina picked him up and held him lovingly. "Yes, darling, that is a fairytale I'll tell you one of these days."

From the window she could see the harbour fortress with the cold grey sea of the Baltic behind it.

It was so far into the evening when the Tsar came back to the Palace that the night guards were on duty, and the two small princes were long since asleep in their separate nurseries.

Katrina had dismissed her ladies, for the lateness of the Tsar's return troubled her. She knew that he would want to come straight back to seek comfort from her after he had thrashed Alexis, and in moments of private crisis such as this, the prattling of her young ladies disturbed Katrina's forthright brain.

She lay now in her deep armchair, with eyes half closed. The logs on the fire were red and flameless; most of the candles had flickered down to puddles, but she did not touch the hanging bell-sash that would have summoned a servant to replenish them. She felt Peter would be glad of the half light.

He came and stood beside her chair without speaking. She could not properly see his face in the gloom, and the thick beaverskin jacket he wore made him seem fantastically larger even than the Peter she knew.

She greeted him softly, whispering because there seemed so much silence in the big room. The Tsar did not reply, but walked over to the fire and kicked the red logs into a sparkle of flame. And then Katrina could see that he was ashen pale.

"Kitty," he demanded suddenly, "do you think that God meant Petrushkin to succeed me? Our son, Kitty?"

Katrina said carefully, "Who knows God's purposes?"

But the Tsar was unable to let the question rest. "Kitty," he said, "Petrushkin is all that is best of both of us. He will be strong as I have been, kindly as you are. Already he is brave. And he will grow to manhood in love, not hatred as Alexis did." He came over to her chair and knelt upon the footstool beside it, gripping her wrists earnestly. "Kitty, have you no ambitions? Aren't you human? Do you not want your own son to be Tsar of Russia some day?"

Katrina stirred unhappily. "Oh, Peter, I want what is right. What do you plan to do? If you send Alexis as a prisoner to some monastery, the plots will still continue. If you banish him, there will be those who seek always to bring him back. You cannot stop these plots by putting Petrushkin on the throne—not while Alexis is still alive."

He did not answer. She eased her hand from his grip and touched his face, and felt tears under her fingers.

"What is it?" she said quietly. "What is it, Peter?"

He buried his face in the silk of her gown. "Alexis is dead," he said, his voice muffled.

"Oh, God, no!" Katrina spoke with appalled accusation in her voice. "No—you didn't—"

"Kitty, I didn't kill him. One stroke of the knout—that was all. It barely marked him. I swear before Heaven, my little Kitty, he died of terror. I wasn't to know that would happen—Kitty—" He wrung at her hands pleadingly, his great throat shaken by sobs.

She believed him. It seemed to pass from his hands into hers, the sensation of belief in him. "Who knows about this?" she said, and her voice was completely calm. She noticed the gray in Peter's hair and thought detachedly that it seemed to have increased noticeably during the past few days.

"Nobody knows," he said, gathering calmness into himself from her demeanour. "I ordered that nobody was to enter his cell. He is—just lying there." She felt his breath warmly upon her thighs through the silk of her garments. Stroking her fingers gently through the curls on his neck, she felt how much thinner his great frame had become.

Like a slowly withering tree, she thought, like some great tree whose strength had sheltered her and all his people, and now the tree was failing, and all the multitude of leaves that hung from it and drew their strength and sustenance from its proud strength, must fall, too.

He let her help him into the bedroom, and she stayed with him until he was asleep. Then with a fur-lined cloak around herself, she went out, along the echoing night corridors of the Palace, and into the starlit courtyard, thinking of what Peter had said about Petrushkin's succession to the throne. It seemed difficult beyond human reason to think that Petrushkin, slumbering so placidly now in his cot, could grow up to become Emperor of all the Russias, and that there would be a day when Peter was dead.

"God, please spare him a little longer," she breathed. "Give me a little more time, so that I may grow the strength to carry on without him." The night sky seemed very close as she looked upwards with her prayer, and she could see the soft brilliance of stars through the dark tree branches in the courtyard.

A cold wind was blowing. The furred hood slipped from her head and she did not restore it, but shook out her hair so that it flowed free over her shoulders. It was a strange sensation to her, to be walking alone. An unusual freedom. The guards stiffened in salute as she passed, staring woodenly beyond her as though she did not exist except as a disembodied command to bring up their halberds or muskets rigidly.

Soldiers, soldiers. A kingdom is held upon the gun-muzzles of a king's soldiers, she thought wryly. And how long would it be before the peasants who now screamed their loyalty to her in every public square would come looting and pillaging through the Palace corridors like wolves, were it not for the soldiers who guarded her?

She walked down the secluded path that led round the acute bend of the Neva estuary, to Prince Menshikov's house, and was relieved to see the downstairs rooms still blazing with light. She looked in at each window as she passed, and found herself smiling at the glimpses of Menshikov's rich furnishings, for it amused her each time she visited his house to see how much more lavish it was than the Tsar's own Palace. And she remembered Peter's comment upon him once . . . "Little Alec—a splendid lieutenant, but I doubt if he could stand power."

Yes, she could see now what Peter meant. Whilst one could draw Menshikov's strength upwards, towards a leader whom he loved—she trembled a little—then Menshikov was strength indeed. But place him on the utmost pinnacle, and his love of pomp, of flattery and intrigue, would crumble him and all of Russia with him. It was strange what wisdom was beginning to come to her, now that she was beginning to learn to look at men as Peter saw them—not as individual, not as friend, foe or lover, but as a separately coloured thread in the complex tapestry of power.

Prince Menshikov sat comfortably in his study with Romdanovsky. The two men were smoking and had large tankards beside them. She watched for an instant through the window before she tapped upon the pane. They turned, startled, and Menshikov jumped from his chair when he saw Katrina smiling in at him from the darkness. He opened the glass door, took her arm gently and helped her across the tall step. She let her cloak slip from her shoulders, and Menshikov whirled it gallantly away as he settled her in the chair he had just vacated.

"Did you know that Alexis is dead?" She put the question bluntly and could see the surprise upon both their faces. It was genuine enough. Obviously they had not known. And the last crumb of doubt was dissolved inside Katrina. She told them what the Tsar had told her, explained to them until the shock and the disbelief faded from their eyes and she could see that they accepted the truth.

Romdanovsky grunted, his chin buried deeply inside his collar. "The Tsar should have told us. We could have had the body in the Cathedral by now. It's got to go there, of course. Unmarked, you say? Good. We'll have the Patriarch of the Church himself among those who anoint it—let him see with his own eyes."

Menshikov had perched himself upon the table edge and was swinging his long legs, studying the glint of diamonds on his velvet slippers. "So this is the end of Alexis and all his schemes," he said. "Life will be too easy, eh, Fedor?"

"The succession will not be easy," said Katrina quietly. "The Tsar named Petrushkin tonight as his heir."

"Your son!" Menshikov took a moment to absorb this, and then threw back his handsome head with a shout of delight. "A sturdy little Prince as heir to Russia. My God, that's worth—" He came over to Katrina, took her hand and kissed it gently. "That's worth a man's while to die for," he said. "Kitty, aren't you proud? I'd expected Siberia at best when the Tsar—"

"When the Tsar dies," Katrina finished his uncompleted sentence for him. Her voice was steady. "One should not think such thoughts, Alec. He is sick, it is true. But he had been sick before, and recovered his strength. He is young enough yet, and strong enough yet, and I pray with all my heart that God will spare him to me for a while longer."

"I know." Menshikov patted her hand. "I know, my dear. One has such thoughts. They come and they go. When one stands so close to the throne—"

"There'll be trouble with Eudoxia's family," said Romdanovsky moodily.

"Damn the Lopukhins!" Menshikov roared. "We've got a healthy prince—Katrina's own child. It's a new lease of life for us all! And," he added in a quieter tone, "It's Heaven's own mercy for Russia." He saw Katrina droop suddenly in the lulling warmth of the fire, and said: "Come, I'll take you back. You should not have come all this way alone. Ah, but you don't need me to tell you that. Leave things to Fedor and me. We'll have it arranged by morning."

"Aye," said Romdanovsky, "if the Tsar wakes, tell him he can rely upon us to have all arranged. Everything will be all right."

Katrina gave them both a grateful smile. "Thank you. Thanks to both of you. I know that you will do what is best. You always do. You are his good friends, and mine. And you are good friends of Petrushkin's, I know. Russia has need of friends like you." And that was the first time she had ever spoken of Petrushkin in the convention of heir to the throne. She felt warm and exalted.

For several weeks thereafter the Tsar had a mood of being drawn near to Menshikov and Count Tolstoy, and the three were closeted constantly together over state affairs, planning and toiling.

One night Peter came from his study to where Katrina was dozing lightly and half expectantly, awaiting him. A cockerel crowed prematurely into the breaking darkness.

"Damn Menshikov," said the Tsar, "and damn Tolstoy. If I were to turn my back for an instant they would be at each other's throats." Katrina was wide awake now. It was so unusual for the Tsar to speak of Menshikov by anything but his affectionate diminutive of "Little Alec," that she sensed something was amiss.

"What is it, Peter? What's gone wrong?"

The Tsar passed his hand uncertainly across his strained eyes. "Somebody's got to learn to take over," he said. "Somebody's got to learn to balance all this, guide the reins for Petrushkin until he finds his feet, when I'm finished."

He sat on the bed with the lurching heaviness of a man wearied beyond his strength, and fumbled with his boots.

"Let me," said Katrina. She was out of bed quickly and kneeling at her husband's feet unlacing the reluctant thongs, her hair flecked by the light of the solitary bedside candle.

The Tsar reached out and touched her hair. She looked up at him with a smile. "Kitty," he said, "my good little friend. The soldiers called you 'Little Mother,' didn't they—at the Pruth, remember?"

She nodded. "Yes," she said, "I remember. They called me 'Little Mother.' They still do, I think. But why—what is it, Peter?"

"All right," he said. "It's all right. It was nothing. I'm just tired, and my tongue was wandering."

But the next day when he awoke and went to his council chamber, he took Katrina with him. "Spend a little more time with me, Kitty," he said. "I know Petrushkin needs you, but I need you too. I draw strength from you."

And so it was for all the months of that late summer and autumn, that whenever the Tsar held council, or spread his maps or discussed his new reforms, it had to be that Katrina was by his side, listening and absorbing. All the years they had been together she had watched Peter conduct his matters of state and government. From the instant he awakened to find his bed surrounded by petitioners, secretaries, importuners and emissaries, into the late night sessions at which his own personal clique were his only companions, she had nearly always been at his side. Her reunion with her baby son had for a while altered this. But it was obvious now that Peter needed her again in his closest councils, with some feverish urgency that he had not yet managed to bring himself to explain. His eyes had grown daily more sunken, his shoulders more wasted. He was still immense, with the bulk and strength of two normal sturdy men. But Katrina realized one night with a sick shock, as he leaned over her to quench the bedside candle, that for the first time since she had known him, she could see a profound hollow beneath his collarbone, and glimpse the cording of sinews where always before had been stirring, hard depths of muscle.

The storm that came before evening was severe and filled with electrical disturbances. Thunder rolled over the empty grey flats of the Neva estuary, and blue storm-balls flickered like fireflies among the signalling masts of the river fortress.

At first it seemed that, with the heavy deluge of warm rain, the worst of the storm might have passed. But the atmosphere continued to be hot and ominous.

Shortly after midnight there came distant rumblings of another artillery of thunder. Katrina, sitting on her dressing stool, stopped brushing her hair to listen. She looked towards the bed to see if it had wakened Peter, but he slept, sprawled untidily over the cream silk sheets where he had thrown himself, exhausted, half an hour before. Many weeks had gone by since the death of Alexis, the hot summer had almost passed, and Peter had learned to sleep again.

The death of Alexis had been accepted with surprising calmness by the State. The soldiery had never liked the skinny Prince, and had been frankly delighted at his death, nor had they troubled themselves concerning the circumstances. The highest dignitaries of the Church had been given every opportunity to satisfy themselves that the death was not murderous, nor—by the standards of the time—due to any untoward violence. Any father could be forgiven one blow at his son.

The enemies of the Tsar, of course, did their best to spread the rumour that Peter had killed his son, but this was little worse than anything they would ordinarily have said against the Tsar. They had even called him the Anti-Christ, and he had survived that, too.

All the old difficulties were beginning to seem far away to Katrina. She was still deeply concerned by Peter's health, but lately this had appeared to be improving. He had recovered some of his old vitality, and even found time to play with Petrushkin. He delighted in the sturdy manliness and frankness of the child, and had journeyed over to the old Palace in Moscow to unearth from long-forgotten closets his own toy soldiers and cannons that he had so much adored in his childhood. He had even repainted them himself, working earnestly upon them as he did upon every task he undertook, with frowning concentration and skilled fingers. He and his son played with the soldiers upon the sun-warmed tiles of the nursery floor.

Now, as Katrina sat tending her hair, the six candles on each side of her mirror fluttered to a sudden draught that had found access through the shuttered windows. She laid her elbows upon the cold white surface of the dressing table and stared candidly at her reflection. Undeniably she was older, but still young enough, she decided, and made an approving and impudent face at herself in the mirror.

She went on bare feet to the nursery with a cloak over her nightgown. The two guards at this door stood respectfully back to let her pass. All was quiet. Little Petrushkin was asleep in his elaborate gold and copper cot, guarded by the metal figures of saints with wings spread over his sleeping head. The door to the nurse's room was ajar and Katrina knew that she would be sleeping lightly, listening for the slightest murmur from the prince. For a long while Katrina stood and watched her sleeping son before she gently touched his dark head with her lips and tucked the silken sheet close around his neck.

The air in the nursery was oppressive in spite of the fact that the window had been fastened wide open. Katrina smiled as she saw it. The nurse was German. No Russian would have opened a window with the storm so close.

Katrina turned her glance upwards to the ikon that shone from the bedroom wall over the cot, with a cluster of white candles blazing to illuminate it. She remembered the paltry dried fish strips that her mother had set spluttering into meagre flame before the hut's faded ikon, to try to quench with hopeful light the feared darkness of her necessary sins. "Sins of the body but for which her children might have starved for bread," said Katrina, and did not realize that she was speaking aloud until she felt a sentry's curious gaze upon her. "I was thinking of my mother," Katrina said simply and without shame.

After a while Katrina returned to her own bed. The storm was sweeping nearer, prodding sudden snake-tongues of brilliant lightning towards the uneven Petersburg rooftops. The processional music of the thunder grew in volume.

Katrina dozed and planned for the morning, which would be fine and clear after the storm. She would be up early and out in the gardens with Petrushkin, watching the workmen toil on the fountains and figures which were to line an elaborate avenue down to the sea.

It was just approaching dawn when the biggest lightning flash came. Katrina was awakened by it. It lit up the night outside and seemed suddenly to penetrate into the room. The explosion of thunder that came instantaneously made her ears sing.

The scream which followed it, tore through the adjoining rooms. Katrina sat upright, knowing something was wrong, but not yet comprehending what it was. The lightning came again and she saw herself reflected in the mirrors across the room.

"Peter!" She shook him into alertness. "The lightning—it struck the Palace!"

The Tsar sat up beside Katrina. "Yes, something is burning," he said, his voice bewildered with sleep. "Must have struck the roof rafters."

Katrina was already out of bed. "Petrushkin will have been frightened. I must go to him."

The Tsar started to follow her, then halted decisively. "The servants are already too afraid of thunder. We must not look as if we are frightened by it. I'll follow you in a few minutes."

She walked as calmly as she could towards the nursery.

The corridors were in a whirl of nervous excitement. Servan maids shrilled and scurried. The guards were standing at thei correct duty posts, but several were crossing themselves an muttering prayers. As Katrina reached the closed door of th nursery, a long wail sounded from the room. It was not th cry of a child but of a woman in terror, and through the pani and fear of it, Katrina recognized the German nurse's voice.

It was from behind the nursery door that the stench of burning came so powerfully that it caught at Katrina's throat. Her hands quivered as she turned the latch.

The room was dark by contrast with the well lit corridor. The nurse's watchlight had been extinguished and Katrina could see her only dimly as a white heap upon the floor. The nursery reeked of a bitter, metallic odour that was thick in the air, and Katrina could see that the window hung torn from its fastenings, like a broken wing.

"Lights!" she called huskily. "Lights!" After a moment, a guard came, holding a candelabra snatched for a corridor table.

As the room became alive to the yellow glare, she saw her baby son.

He lay on a mattress that was now no more than a heap of congealed soot. The burnished copper angels were melted away as if they had been figures of wax. The tongue of forked lightning had flickered upon the little cot and transformed it into crumpled wreckage, and the child was dead.

It may have been a moment, or an hour, before Tsar Peter came and stood at her side. He pulled her up from the floor and held her close to him. The child was so obviously dead. Neither of them made a move to touch him.

"Oh, Peter," she said, and somehow she could not cry, nor make her voice convey her grief. "He's dead, Peter. What shall we do?"

Peter's dark eyes were rigid with awe as he stared through the broken window at the storm-swept night. But his voice came flatly as if in everyday speech: "It is the curse of God upon us. He is punishing me for my sins."

Peter touched the melted and misshapen wing of the angel that had been sculptured to guard his son, and whose spread metal plumage had attracted the thunderbolt. The metal was still hot. He let it blister his finger without feeling any sensation of pain.

Chapter Twenty-Three

THE TEDIOUS and elaborate funeral rites for the baby Prince Petrushkin, with all the wearisome formalities of the medieval Orthodox Church of Russia, dragged out the next several days in a merciful half-oblivion of incense-stifled dirges and exhausting prostrations upon the bare floor of the new Cathedral of Petersburg, which was soon so thick with the reek of innumerable censers that each wrought pillar of the Tserkvi was scarcely visible from its neighbour.

The Tsar and Katrina, quivering with strain beneath the fantastic weight of their formal mourning robes, pursued the ritual disinterestedly. Katrina derived little comfort from it, for her the future seemed to stretch endlessly without the joy of possessing Petrushkin. Katrina sorrowed for her son as a woman and mother, and might have believed that no sorrow could go deeper than her own.

But Peter was suffering a torment that it was beyond even Katrina's sympathetic understanding to comprehend fully. More than missing a beloved young son who had brought him genuine happiness, Peter was also missing an heir.

To the Tsar Peter, the destructive message of the thunderbolt from heaven was not only one of doom to Petrushkin but also to all his own life and works.

It seemed as if the sky of God had opened to condemn him for the evil of his modern reforms, and that the sword of the Angel of Death had cut off Tsar Peter from any hopes that his Westernized notions could survive beyond a mere handful of years. There was nobody now upon whom the Tsar could build any hope for a continuance of all his endeavours to keep his people from returning to the Eastern habits and dark, superstitious prejudices from which he had begun to uplift them. With his own death, it seemed sure now that the jungle of intolerance and ritual would immediately overgrow all he had ever done or tried to do.

The enemies of the Tsar were already saying even as the funeral ceremony continued, that God had spoken personally to declare him wrong.

His successor must logically be the baby Grand Duke Peter

son of Alexis. The Tsar could scarcely have announced any other successor, now Petrushkin was dead, without ripping his Empire down the middle in immediate civil war. Yet it was also to be expected that as soon as the Tsar died, the powerful faction of his enemies, led by the Lopukhins, would claim the Grand Duke Peter in the name of his only remaining direct relation in blood—his grandmother Eudoxia. Peter was bitterly aware what would then happen. Eudoxia would be sure to make it a matter of fanatic duty to raze everything Tsar Peter had ever erected, and to put to sword or flame every human being whom he had ever smiled with favour.

Katrina could see that he was in the last throes of severe exhaustion. Without consulting him, she sent an urgent message to the officiating Patriarch, asking that the rituals be curtailed for the sake of the Tsar's failing health.

This was the first hint to the Patriarch that his old enemy the Tsar was no longer robust. He was immediately spurred by such encouraging news into frenzies of further ceremonial. It was Tsar Peter himself who finally called a halt to it all, by quitting the Cathedral and refusing to return to it.

"God and all the Saints have turned from me," he said shakily. "What good are my prayers for my dead son? God has turned His back upon me, and I shall turn my back upon God."

It was the remark of a sick man, but it made Katrina blench. "You must rest," she said sagely, "and you must not say such things. You will feel better when you have had a rest."

"Damn a rest!" the Tsar barked. "Get me brandy!"

The smell of spiced brandy came so strongly from the gardens of Petersburg Palace that crowds had gathered in the streets outside to sniff appreciatively at it.

Some bold young fellows had scrambled up onto the Palace wall, risking a ball from the sentries' muskets, to peer down among the shrubbery of the garden. They were now yelling excited comments upon what they saw to the lake of avid peasant faces that grinned up as they listened.

The interminable funeral arrangements had dampened the entire city. The peasants were childishly eager now for some kind of spectacular relief. And Tsar Peter must have felt the same, it seemed, for he was having a party. That was, so far, all that the crowd knew.

They had watched the boyars, nobles and court favourites arriving all through the afternoon at the Palace.

Now that the Palace gates were shut and locked, grinning guards confided to the hilarious mob outside that the Tsar's orders to the gatekeepers were: "Let no sober man or woman leave the Palace."

Oh, he was a joker, this Tsar Peter! The soldiers of the guard adored him and the peasantry revelled in his rough pranks. One had to go up considerably in the hierarchy to find the Tsar's enemies.

And now the torches were being lit in the gardens' scented twilight and the party had begun. Every court favourite, every notorious libertine in Petersburg, was stalking the grounds, dressed in some comical costume. Each was followed by six tall Grenadiers carrying among them a large silver bowl of strongly spiced brandy.

Their orders from the Tsar, which had been uproariously received, were that they were to move among the crowds of guests, seize each person that the favourite cared to indicate, whether man or woman, boyar or general, and pour brandy down the victim's throat.

The Tsar himself, dressed in the costume that always comforted him most, that of a Flemish workman with rough blouse and blue sailcloth trousers, was busily doing the same, roaring with overloud laughter, his eyes diamond-bright with fever.

Katrina, pale with concern for him, her smile forced, moved among the guests. If the Tsar in his sick despair felt that he wanted a carousal and there was no apparent way to prevent him, then Katrina decided sensibly that the only place for her was in the thick of it with him. He had eaten no solid food, she knew, for days.

The music, feasting and incredibly rough horseplay that were the only standards of amusement and relaxation which the Russian Court had ever known, and to which the French and British plenipotentiaries had always found it difficult to accustom themselves, were at a crescendo. Many of the feebler participants had already begun to succumb, and buckets of cold water were being flung over them with ribald yells.

A wisp of frosty moon gleamed high in the night's darkness. Clouds were gathering and the torches flared more brightly among the bare-branched trees of the garden. Katrina saw that the Tsar had stripped open his blouse to the waist. He had drunk tremendously, inhumanly, yet somehow his fever had kept him almost steady. But as she watched she saw him lurch suddenly and clutch at his body below his heart.

"Peter," said Katrina urgently, "Peter, please let me take you inside." He stood swaying for a moment, then disengaged her hand, quite gently. "No, I shall stay here," he said thickly, "I shall be all right . . ."

Menshikov worked his way to her side and said: "Kitty, for pity's sake get him to bed. He's ill."

"Oh, Alec, I know," Katrina said tensely. "What can we do? Will you go home, and I'll tell him you've gone? It might sober him, if he think's you've gone."

He nodded earnestly. She watched him go through the gardens towards the main gate and after a moment caught the flash of burnished metal as the tall gates swung back for him.

She found the Tsar in the centre of a throng. He had a drum slung around his neck and was beating it with savage skill, as though to drive his own nightmare thoughts away from himself by a persistent clamour of it.

She could see that the blue veins above his left ear were bunched and throbbing. He was obviously gripped by one of his severest headaches. And something of his mirthless intentness was communicating itself to those around him, even through the cloud of brandy and vodka that obscured their brains.

Katrina ran to him and pressed herself against him. She could feel his body burning with fever. "Peter," she implored, "Peter, please stop it!"

He looked down at her with bewildered, unfocussed eyes. "Kitty," he mumbled vaguely, "have some brandy."

Tears filled her wide eyes, and the Tsar saw them. He frowned. "What's wrong?" he demanded, his arm encircling her. "What's wrong?"

"Alec's gone," she said simply. "He's gone home." The Tsar's face darkened. He thrust the drum away, breaking the thick leather strap with a jerk of his hand.

"Gone, has he?" He glared wildly among those nearest to him, and his big fists clenched.

Katrina saw that several of the Tsar's most loyal favourites were staring at him in puzzlement and the beginnings of apprehension. Her eyes implored them silently. "Can't you see? He's ill—help him—help him . . ."

De Villebois sensed the beseeching urgency of her glance and stepped forward. Prince Romdanovsky started to heave his bulky body closer through the throng.

But it was Count Tolstoy who claimed the Tsar's attention. The cool grey eyes of Tolstoy were the only fully alert ones among all those who surrounded the Tsar. There was no brandy flush in Tolstoy's face, and how he had managed to achieve this personal miracle was a tribute to his wit.

"Sire," he called, "why do we not punish our poor, deluded friend Menshikov? Ban him from every tavern in Petersburg! Let's take pots of beer to his house and sit around his bed and drink until we drive him mad with thirst! We shall have him back as a penitent before daybreak."

There was a roar of laughter from those listening, and the Tsar's mouth twitched reluctantly. It was a crude joke, but the court of the Tsar liked crude jokes. "Come," shouted De Villebois, "who will volunteer to sail across the Neva tonight as missionaries of Bacchus and fight for poor Alec's thirsty soul against the horrors of staying sober?"

Grins broke out. In a moment the tension that had been developing in the garden vanished. The Tsar was almost swept along in the press of his friends, towards where his royal barge was dipping in the swift tide. The crowd swarmed around and behind them. Freaks and dwarfs jigged. Musicians blew wildly upon their instruments.

Count Tolstoy spoke in Katrina's ear. "We must begin to disperse the party when we get to Alec's house," he said. "I think the Tsar is really too ill to go with this." She nodded gratefully and pressed his arm.

The more privileged of the roisterers crowded upon the shallow, broad-bottomed craft. There had been rain in the hills beyond Petersburg, and the river was running swift and grey, bringing down twigs and tree branches.

Romdanovsky viewed the gurgling water apprehensively. "Will it be safe, Sire?" he ventured.

"Who cares?" the Tsar roared. His oarsmen had despaired of handling their oars amidships and had gone to the stern with two long propelling sweeps.

The craft began to move out, and as it did so Katrina saw

Grog on the quayside. Grog had been determined to go in the barge, but had not been able to force a way through the drunken, disordered throng. He stood now upon the brink of the quay, his eyes forlorn as a deerhound's, considering the distance of several feet between barge and shore.

"Grog!" Katrina called, and waved to him consolingly. Grog saw her and misunderstood the gesture. He tried to jump. It would have been no distance for him once, but the years had slowed him, and he fell headlong into the swirling grey river.

Grog's incongruously deep, musical voice brayed out in a choked cry of despair and Katrina caught a glimpse of his terrified face as the dark tide engulfed him.

The Tsar straightened up. The dwarf's shout and Katrina's cry had penetrated the sick fever of his brain. He shouldered a path in brutal haste to the side of the barge. His tremendous voice bellowed down the river above the yells and clamour from the barge to shore.

Distantly, the Tsar's shouts were answered by a voice fully as deep but broken by despairing, drowning coughs.

The Tsar plunged into the running river and the darkness, and was swept insantly out of sight.

The dwarf was dead when Tsar Peter brought him ashore to the quay. His humped little body was slack with death, and his mouth spilled dark river water upon the wooden plankings.

The drunken laughter and yells of the crowd upon barge and quayside had faltered into an uneasy silence. Some of the courtiers gathered around the Tsar now, and Romdanovsky silently put a cloak upon his shoulders.

Peter sat upon a warp post for a moment, shivering. Then he stood up with a petulant shrug. "I'm all right," he said and seemed to speaking to himself.

Romdanovsky was not in time to catch the Tsar's great body as it lurched forward and fell, with a thin cream of white foam upon the mouth, and eyes rolled backwards. He was still unconscious when he was laid upon his bed.

Katrina had summoned Menshikov by urgent messenger to return to the Palace. He came presently and told her quietly, "I have sent for the priests." His eyes were grave. "You must change your dress," he said, and Katrina observed for the first time that her gown was saturated.

She went obediently, and when she came back she wore the old dark green dress that had always been Peter's favourite from among the hundreds that now crowded her wardrobe chamber.

The Tsar was still in a coma, his breathing fierce and dry, his face clenched in a rigid spasm, and his staring eyes bloodshot. He seemed to be looking straight at Katrina, but it was apparent that he could not see her.

For three days Katrina stayed by the Tsar's bed. She tended him with her own hands, as she had always done, and occasionally the Tsar seemed to swim upwards from the darkness of his oblivion. His lips would move and his eyes rove bleakly around the large, gloomy chamber, as if in search for something he could not find.

The Patriarch had come hurrying from the Cathedral. A special chapel was built in the room alongside where Peter lay dying, and all night and day Katrina could hear the mumbling monotones of the chanting priests.

She knew that the Tsar was going to die. There was no doubt of it this time. The great Tsar of all the Russias was about to give his life for the sake of poor, crumpled little Grog. It would have been the dwarf to whom Katrina would have turned seeking comfort in her grief for the dying Peter. And now, he was dead, the valiant little one, and the great one was dying, too.

And Katrina knew that she would soon be alone. Not merely as a human being is alone, but in that greater loneliness which only the widows of great men can know, the loneliness of the wives of dead kings.

But she did not begin to weep until she saw the Tsar's limbs uncovered for full anointment with the Blessed Oil. When the priests had laid him bare, and she saw how thin his mighty frame had become in so few days, the tears came scalding into her eyes and she could no longer withhold them.

The slow moving, dark-garbed priests were never still from their ritual movements and chantings, and Katrina feared they would serve only to exhaust the Tsar further, and to rob him of any small chance he could have of falling into a slumber from which he might derive some flicker of strength.

"Leave him," she had commanded firmly. "He has been anointed enough and shriven enough." And she dismissed all the high church dignitaries from the room, herself closing the door upon the last of them.

It was then that she slept, and was startled into heartpounding wakefulness by a movement on the bed itself.

Peter was awake. She heard the rustling of his hand along the bedcover. His eyes were open, and she could see that there was recognition in them. She kissed his damp forehead.

"Kitty," he said, and his speech was no more than a sibilant breath. "Thank you for being here.... Oh, God.... Pray for me, Kitty . . . don't let . . . Eudoxia . . . destroy . . . everything . . ."

"I promise you she shall destroy nothing." She touched his lips with her fingers as if to seal inside the tiny spark of strength that had come so unexpectedly. "You've worked too hard. God understands. He will be watching. He will give me strength to see your work finished" The words were choking her "I will protect all your dreams for Russia," she said, and saw the tension ebb from his face. "Bless you," he said, and did not speak again.

She had sat back upon her cushion and was drowsing again when, with a quick, jerky movement, the Tsar sat up, scattering the bedclothes. With an unexpected strength he swung his legs over the side of the bed. His eyes were staring past her. She put her hands upon his shoulders and at her touch he began to fight towards the void that waited for him behind her, that neither his eyes nor hers could see.

"Kitty," he whispered urgently, "she mustn't—" and then fell back upon the bed, his head lolling limply.

His eyes were staring, and she watched them for a long while to see if they blinked, but they did not. Her fingers trembled as she gently closed them.

As she stepped back from performing this task the bedside became at once surrounded by doctors, priests and courtiers, who had come silently to swarm around the dead man's bed, summoned by the vigilant sentry at the doorway who had seen her gesture.

Menshikov shouldered his way into the room. He looked at the bed and crossed himself fervently, and grief was like a cold serpent inside him. But what he had come to do was for the sake of the dead man he had loved, at least as much as for himself. And it was this knowledge that gave him strength to continue with his purpose, nor let himself be halted by a sensation of loss that was like the moment before the oblivion that followed a severe wound.

He took Katrina by the elbow. "Quickly," he said, "you must come with me at once." She was herself too numb and dazed to resist.

They were at her own bedroom, and Menshikov flung open the door. She had not entered this room for three days, and the delicate fragrance of her own perfume came refreshingly to her nostrils after the reeking incense of the death chamber.

"Sit here!" commanded Menshikov, and pressed her down upon the quilted satin stool of her toilet table.

He hurried into her wardbrobe chamber and came out with a heavy travelling robe. "No time for anything else," he said. "We can get clothes elsewhere. Come, Kitty, we must hurry if we are to save ourselves."

"What do you mean, Alec?" She passed a tired hand across her eyes. "I want to go back to him . . ."

Menshikov steadied his own impatience with a deep breath. "Kitty," he said, "any moment now the Tsar's death will be announced. And last night in late session the Council of Ministers decided that the rightful heir to the throne of Russia was the Grand Duke Peter—Alexis' son. Eudoxia and the Lopukhins are to be the Regency Council. Eudoxia, Kitty! The Patriarch has already sent a coach to Susdal Nunnery to fetch her. As soon as she gets here, that means instant death—or worse—for you, and me, and for all Peter's friends. We must get away at once."

"And then?" said Katrina soberly.

"Saving our lives is the first thing," said Menshikov. "Alive, we can plot and counterplot. But dead, we are useless. Let us but save our lives, and we will still stand some chance."

"A chance?" echoed Katrina bitterly. "Is that all we have left now—a chance?" She glimpsed her face in her dressing mirror and saw how pale it was. "Alec," she said, "I know you are a brave man. God knows I have never doubted it. But are we to run and save our skins and watch all Peter's work—all he lived and toiled and dreamed for—snatched away from him? Would you have it all destroyed by Eudoxia's people?"

Menshikov said harshly: "What else is there, Kitty? What else?"

She said: "Alec—if you want to get me suitable garb from my wardrobe, then fetch me that white Hussar jacket I wore in the Turkish campaign." She picked her jewelled comb up and pulled the disorder of her hair.

"But what—Katrina, what can you do?"

"I'm not sure what I can do," she said, "except that I can't run away." She raised her head proudly. "I won't run, Alec—not even to fight another day. I am going to try and keep the throne for the memory of—of Peter." She laid red rouge upon her lips and shaped it into her cheeks until they glowed with pink warmth. "You and I, Alec, my dear friend—we know what Peter would have had us do. I am going to stay. Will you stay with me?"

The door opened. Romdanovsky peered in. "Ready?" he said anxiously. "There's not an instant to lose. General Repnin has ordered a general muster of the Hussars, the Palace Guard and the Simenov Guard. The square will be filled in a few minutes. We'll not be able to get through."

"We don't want to get through," said Katrina firmly. "We're not going."

Menshikov was already placing the heavy, gold-braided white Hussar tunic over Katrina's chilled shoulders. Romdanovsky's eyes widened in comprehension. "Is that the game, then?" he said uncertainly.

"Will the soldiers listen to me?" Katrina asked. "Will they, Fedor?"

Menshikov said: "They'll hardly listen to anybody. They've had no pay since Petrushkin died." Katrina winced, but her voice remained steady. "Tell General Repnin that the pay of all the Guards is to be doubled, and that they will be paid tonight."

"By whose orders?"

"Tell him," said Katrina quietly, with Menshikov's hand still lingering upon her shoulders, "that it was done by order of the Tsarina."

"Fedor," said Menshikov, and Katrina felt the exultation tingling through his fingers, "not by order of the Tsarina. Tell him it is by decree of Her Imperial Majesty Catherine the First of All the Russias—and tell him he may sound the palace guns in the royal salute. And see that a pistol is directed at his belly if he hesitates for an instant."

Romdanovsky's throat worked uncomfortably. His gaze settled for a long moment upon Katrina with a penetrating stare. "Then get ready to make an appearance on the balcony, for God's sake, where the troops can see you."

Katrina nodded, not trusting herself now to speak. Her heart was thundering right up to her throat, and she wondered if Menshikov could feel it. Menshikov said: "Give me a few minutes to rally our friends, Kitty. They're all standing by ready to flee, to cut our way to the boats if need be. I've got to tell them."

"Also," said Katrina chokingly, "when I show myself on the balcony, you stand behind me with your pistol. If they don't acclaim me, Alec—you must shoot me. It might save your own life. Even if I fail, we mustn't give up."

Menshikov gave her a long look, almost as Romdanovsky had done, and she knew that both these friends of Peter's were weighing up the cold chances with all the valour and unfaltering loyalty that was the nature of both of them. Menshikov's stare ended in a smile. "Kitty," he said, "win or lose, I'm damned if I'm going to be the one to shoot you. Let Romdanovsky do it, if somebody must. But come, we must hurry—there is much to do!"

Marshal Ogilvy and Count Tolstoy were waiting in the Tsar's council chamber, the windows of which commanded the balcony that overlooked the Palace yard.

Ogilvy was grinning. "Listen to that!" he said. From the packed parade ground below the balcony came a swell of excited, ragged cheering. It had not the orderliness of an acclamation, but was a shout from the throats of three thousand men who had simultaneously found themselves in good humour.

"We've just told them the news," said Ogilvy, "that the Empress Catherine has ordered their pay doubled."

His glance sought Katrina's face as he spoke. She stood pale and uncertain, but her head was still proud with new authority, and something made the grin fade from Ogilvy's jubilant face.

"With—er—your Imperial Majesty's permission," he added uncomfortably to Katrina. She gave him a sad smile and walked past him towards the window.

Marshal Ogilvy jumped to open the tall glass doors, and with the wintry air came a crash of cheering that filled the council chamber and made Katrina halt as if she had been struck in the face.

Menshikov said urgently: "Kitty, for God's sake—for all our sakes—"

She drew a deep breath, and shut her eyes for an instant. Menshikov's hand went to steady her, but she gently disengaged his grasp.

"No, Alec, not for our sakes—but for Peter's sake." Her voice was hardly more than a whisper, but for a moment there was a look almost of Peter's own wild strength in her green eyes that were shadowed from so many unsleeping hours and so much recent weeping.

She stepped out onto the balcony. She gripped the cold balcony stonework and stared straight ahead of her. She did not see the soldier-crowded Palace yard at all, nor the glint of a triple-thousand silver cuirasses, the flash of drawn swords raised in salute.

And the cheering broke over her like the dark river water that flowed over Grog and Tsar Peter, like the pain that had surged and roared in her ears as unconsciousness drowned her once, long ago—or was it only a moment ago—as the ugly brown whip of Dakov the bailiff had eaten into her shoulders when she was a servant girl in the Gluck's household . . . like the surge of birth pangs . . . like the wail of one's baby crying in the night breaking through one's dreams.

"Mother!" the soldiers were calling, "Mother—our little Mother!"

"Little Mother! Little Mother!" The fierce enthusiasm of the old soldiering nickname was Coronation enough. When she turned away from the balcony at last she was still not crying, although her throat ached with lonely, remembering tears.

Her supporters followed her back into the council chamber, and stared at her and at each other, and for a long moment nobody spoke. It had been a gamble. Eudoxia, the rightful claimant, against a little Livonian servant wench. Eudoxia, the wife whom the Church upheld, against Katrina, whom Peter had loved, and whom the soldiers had loved, too.

"Well," said Tolstoy, and the slightly cynical smile still lingered on his mouth. "It only remains now to arrest a few of the Council of Ministers—" his voice was dry—"those who did not appear to have the best interests of Your Imperial Majesty at heart during the debate last night." His eyes twinkled. "With Your Majesty's permission, of course," he said. Menshikov frowned at the mockery in Tolstoy's voice. But Katrina knew that Tolstoy would always jibe, would always mock, yet would serve her with his life if need be. Her voice was entirely calm and sure as she replied: "I will receive all my loyal Ministers immediately, Count Tolstoy, and I—"

"And we—" prompted Menshikov, with a faint grin now showing for the first time upon his weary face.

"And we will receive the officers of our loyal regiments at the same time as I—as we—"

Tolstoy's smile was genuine now. He took her slender hand and slipped the Imperial ring upon her finger. It was so large that she had to shut her fist upon it. One by one, each of the men bowed and kissed the ring.

"I understand, Your Majesty," he said, "and may I say that it was a very good idea!"

Tolstoy and Ogilvy went to attend to the lesser details of the coup that was now all but over. There was no doubt now, that they had won. Eudoxia would never reign over Russia. And Tsar Peter's dreams could go on, though he was dead.

Menshikov was looking at her. "Peter would be proud of you," he said huskily.

"I shall always be proud of him," she answered. And it was then that the withheld tears all seemed to come at once, so that her throat filled and her eyes brimmed with a scalding flow of lonely misery.

She lifted her face to him as he stroked her hair. "Alec," she said in a choked voice, "do you see any gray hairs?"

He laughed and took her tear-wet face gently between his hands. "None," he lied tenderly, "none at all, my dear!"